The Opportunity

AN AGE-GAP ROMANCE

THE SECRETS SERIES
BOOK THREE

T.M. RICHARDSON

Content Note

Hello Lovers

This is an age-gap, FFM, mono/poly romance. Well, what does that mean or include? That means one person in the relationship is polyamorous, the other is not. It's not cheating, however. *Let's be very clear.*

For more information, visit this helpful website: https://joeborders.com/ mono-poly-relationships/

This is not a trigger warning, simply a preamble.

Trigger Warnings: *homophobia, biphobia, racism, sexism, church/religious hurt, cuckold fantasies, voyeurism, squirting, consumption of bodily fluids, premature pregnancy, mention of domestic violence, therapy sessions, edging, use of BDSM apparatuses.*

This was a tough book to write. No worries! *There is always a happy ending.*

I hope the semi-slow burn is satisfying. As always, take care of yourself as you read.

Love,

TM

"An honest answer is like a kiss on the lips."

—(Proverbs 24:26)

Hey Black Woman,

It is never too late to be free.

Never.

The Opportunity

Pronunciation Key

Alisa- (Ah-Lee-Sah)
Tatum- (Tay-Tum)
Zaire- (Zaa·eer)
DigiCo- (Didg- E- Coh)
Flournoy- (Floor-noy)
Devi – (Deh-Vee)

<u>Brand Names</u>
Cohiba Behika- (ko-ee-ba, Be-ee-ke)
Fleur de Sel- (flur- dee- sale)
Casamigos (Cah-Sah-Me-Goes)
La Fete Du Cotes Rose' (Lah- Fett- Do-Coat)
Louboutin- (Loo-Booh-Ton)
Brahmin- (Bra-Men)

Prologue

SUMMER 1989, WAYCROSS

"Paul Dee!!! Paul Dee!!

Paul Robeson Davis looked up from the hood of the Buick Skylark he was working on to see his wife Grace dragging their daughter Nadine by her curly, sandy brown ponytail across the yard. A dust of red clay trailed behind them like a devilish tornado. He wiped the sweat from his eyes and turned down his radio that was blasting Public Enemy's *Fight the Power*. He let out a sigh. *What had the girl done now?*

When they got closer, Paul Dee's heart nearly broke at the sight of his oldest daughter locked in a battle with his wife. Tears streamed down Nadine's face, her hazel eyes red and puffy. She tried to squirm away, but Grace held on to her ponytail even tighter. She dare not wince or even scream, otherwise her mother would slap her again.

Paul put down his wrench and wiped his hands on his Dickie coveralls. "Grace, let the girl go, now. Whatever she did, it can't be that bad."

"Oh, you say that now!" declared Grace, her burgundy-red Jheri curl swinging. "You ain't heard what she did yet! She embarrassed our good name!"

"Embarrassed, how?" asked Paul. He turned to his daughter. "Deanie, what you do, girl?"

"Daddy, we were just playing house!" Nadine said, declaring her innocence. "I swear it."

Grace turned to her daughter, fuming. "Oh, really? You call what you was doing with Mae Alston's daughter, playing house?"

"Gracie," Paul chuckled. "All this over playing house? Ain't you overreacting just a bit?"

"It ain't funny, Paul Dee!," screeched Grace. "And it wasn't as innocent as you think it was!"

Frustrated, Paul folded his arms across his broad chest. "What was it like then?"

Grace gave Nadine a scorching look before continuing. "Well, I went to pick her up from the Scouts meeting and we couldn't find nary one of them. We was calling out for them for a good five minutes. Finally, me and Mae went out back behind the house to the little clearing near the creek. We caught Deanie and Allison kissing like grown ass folks in the woods, rolling around in the damn dirt. They was kissing on each other like a bunch of filthy dykes! I'm telling you, Paul Dee, it wasn't normal! It wasn't what kids their age do!"

Paul sighed. "But they still kids, Grace. They don't really know what they doing."

"You ain't seen it, Paul. Them girls' skirts was hitched up around they waist, panties all exposed! Uniforms full of grass and dirt. I am telling you, it was disgusting!"

Grace turned to Nadine, who was looking down at her filthy Brownie uniform and her red clay streaked Keds. "What you got to say for yourself, Nadine Paulette? Lord Jesus! They probably gonna kick you outta Girl Scouts now!"

Tears welled up in Nadine's eyes again. She could only whisper her response. "We was just playing, Mama, that's all."

Grace folded her arms and shook her head. "You need to talk to her, Paul Dee. 'Cause I ain't raising no nasty bulldagger. This is a Christian household! Nadine needs to act like she was raised right. I serve on the Usher board with Mae! And you know she's gonna tell everybody!"

Paul leaned against the car, studying the vexed expression on his wife. "Grace, you go on in the house, now. PJ said he had some summer camp permission slips that needed signing anyway. Imma go 'head and talk to Deanie."

"Fine," Grace huffed. "You give her a good talking to, Paul Dee. Cause if you don't, I might kill her."

Nadine watched as her mother made her way up the steps. The slamming the rickety screen door made her nearly jump out of her skin.

"Come over here, Deanie," said her father in a soft voice. "Help me work on this car."

"Ok, Daddy." Nadine wiped her runny nose with the back of her hand and walked toward her Daddy, head still slightly bowed.

"Hand me them big pliers, there, Deanie."

Nadine rifled through the toolbox until she found the pliers, handing them to her father. She sat on the step stool near the tool box, watching him work. They said nothing to each other for several minutes, the sound of metal scraping metal filling the void.

"Your Mama is real upset, sugar." Paul as he stared straight ahead at the engine.

"Am I in trouble?"

Paul shook his head. "No, sugar. You ain't in no real trouble." He stuck the pliers in the back pocket of his coveralls and stooped down to be eye-level with Nadine. "But you and Allison can't be kissing like that in the woods no more. Or ever."

"Why?" asked Nadine. "She's my friend. And I like her."

"You can like her, Nadine. But you ain't gotta kiss her. At least not like you'd kiss a boy."

Nadine frowned. "Kiss a boy? Eww. I don't want a kiss boy. I don't like boys."

She thought boys were probably the most vile creatures on earth. They farted, ate boogers, scratched their butts, and smelled musty like a bag of Vidalia onions. Well, not *all* of them. Teddy Johnson always saved the pink Starbursts for her, sliding them in her hand in Sunday school. Coincidentally, he always smelled good. He also didn't dare eat a booger or scratch his butt. He was the exception.

Paul chuckled softly. "You say that now, Deanie, but you ain't but nine years old, sugar. You don't know what you like and don't like. You'll grow out of that."

Nadine looked up into her father's similar hazel eyes. "I like Allison, Daddy. She's… *nice*. I kissed her *because* I like her." She'd seen her father kiss her mother a million times like that. Isn't that what you did when you liked someone that way?

Paul sighed, grabbing his daughter's tiny hands with his oil-stained ones. "Nadine. The natural order of the world is that a man and a woman be together. To love each other. Like how me and your mama are. Don't you want to get married someday? Have a husband and a family? Wear a pretty wedding dress and let me give you away in a church?"

Nadine furrowed her tiny brow, her bang sticking to her sweaty forehead. She didn't know why her daddy was asking her any of this. She was only nine. "I don't know."

"It's alright," laughed Paul. "That ain't a question you gotta answer now. But in time, you'll realize that girls are supposed to like and kiss *boys*, not girls. Girls and boys are to be together that way. Not two girls, understand? And you can love your friends who are girls, baby, but just… not like *that*? Just be normal, alright? Understand?"

Normal? Nadine didn't really understand what that meant, but she nodded her head anyway. "Okay, Daddy."

He leaned over, kissing his cherub-faced daughter on the cheek. "Good. Now, go in and apologize to your mama. Then call Mrs. Alston and apologize to her. Tell her it won't happen again." He paused, carefully choosing his next words. "And maybe you and Allison need to take a break from each other. Go play with Alisa and Tatum next door instead, ok?"

But she didn't want that. She played with Alisa and Tatum all the time. She didn't want to play with them the way she did Allison. Allison tasted like watermelon Bubblicious and hot dill pickles. She felt soft and round, with mahogany skin as smooth as silk, and smelled like baby powder. She was *her* special friend, no one else's.

But Nadine didn't tell her father any of that. Instead, she nodded obediently and replied, "Yes, sir."

"Go on, now." Paul patted his daughter's head and resumed his work on his car. Nadine got up from the stoop, making her way to the house.

"And Deanie," Paul called out from under the hood, stopping Nadine near the steps.

"Yes, sir?"

"You're still a good girl, baby. You just made a mistake is all. God forgives sin, sugar."

Nadine chewed her lip, mulling over his choice of words.

Mistake

Good

Sin

Was she a sinner? Pastor Josephs said that sinners go to hell. Was she going to *hell* over a kiss? Was kissing Allison a sin? Was she still a good girl if she had sinned? Was she a good girl if it was a mistake?

Nadine stared down at her dirty Brownie vest and shook with anger. She ripped it off, buttons flying to the ground, and threw it in the trash.

CHAPTER 1
Memories

"Nadine, did you hear what I just asked?"

Nadine turned her attention away from the fruity scented candle, back to her therapist. "Sorry, what did you say?"

"I asked if you've been journaling like I suggested," said Dr. Flournoy.

Nadine huffed. "Sometimes. Well, rarely if I am being honest. I'm too busy."

"I see." Dr. Flournoy gave her a slight smile as she looked at Nadine, puzzled. "Where did you go, Nadine? What memory came up for you?"

Nadine smoothed out her skirt, shaking her head. "Nowhere special."

"I don't believe that," challenged Dr. Flournoy. "I've learned over these past couple of years that when you get quiet, you're trapped somewhere. Usually in a memory."

Nadine finally answered.. "Just thinking about...Bubblicious."

"The gum?"

"Yeah," Nadine pointed behind the therapist. "Your candle kind of smells like it. My friend chewed it all the time."

"Which friend?"

"Allison."

"Ah," a look of realization appeared on Dr. Flournoy's face. "Allison? Is this the same girl…"

"Yes." Nadine interrupted, not wanting to rehash it. "She's married now. Three kids. High school principal. Gorgeous family. At least, from what I can tell on Facebook. I am not stalking her or anything. I just got curious. Found her after our last session. She won't accept my friend request, though. I didn't expect her to. We stopped talking to each other by the time we reached middle school."

Dr. Flournoy nodded. "Given how the friendship ended, maybe reconnecting with you is painful for her. Ever thought about that?"

"Or maybe," Nadine countered. "She wants to pretend like she doesn't remember me or anything. It's fine. No big deal. I've moved on, too. It was just a silly childhood friendship."

"Have you?"

Nadine frowned. "Have I what?"

"Moved on?"

"Of course I have."

Nadine watched as Dr. Flournoy silently made a few notes on her tablet. She hated when she did that because she always felt as if she'd said something wrong. But the long pause in conversation did give Nadine an opportunity to look at her therapist's legs. Rina Flournoy had *amazing* legs. She had to work out or run a lot, Nadine presumed. She shook her head. *Stop it, Deanie. You are here to get help, not stare at people.*

Dr. Flournoy tapped her pencil. "I wouldn't call what you felt for Allison a silly childhood friendship. You know, this is the third time you've brought up Allison in session. I wonder if the dissolution of your friendship with Allison made an impact on you more significant than maybe you realized?"

"I don't know. Maybe." Nadine wrung her hands together. They felt hot and sticky. Had she really mentioned Allison that many times in therapy? That was utterly ridiculous.

Dr. Flournoy leaned forward. "Nadine, I think that early memory with Allison reminded you that the nature of friendship can be tenuous. And friendships are important to you. You also mentioned feeling disconnected from Alisa and Tatum. Could it be that you feel their friendships are dissolving as well?"

Nadine's eyes began to water. "What does any of this have anything to do with my friendship with Alisa and Tatum? They've always been there for me."

"Yes, but you're feeling disconnected from your friends and their new lives. Lives that are far different from your own."

"I am happy for my friends!" objected Nadine. "I mean, I didn't understand at first but they're happy. As long as they're happy, I'm alright with it."

"Yes, but when we got to the root of it, you realized how their choices initially made you a little uncomfortable due to your faith and upbringing."

Nadine's throat felt dry. She could admit she initially came across a little sanctimonious when it came to Tatum and Alisa's decision to both enter into polyamorous relationships. She tended to be that way sometimes. She meant no harm. In her mind, she was doing it out of love. *Just like her mother.. fuck...*

"I think there may be something else going on here. I know you initially came here to talk about postpartum depression, career, and marriage. How you're struggling to balance it all. How you feel you're not connecting with your husband anymore. And those things are still important... but I'm noticing a common theme here. I'm noticing that some of your issues are connected. I think it's worth exploring if you're willing to go deeper with me."

"Dr. Flournoy, " Nadine rolled her eyes. "There is nothing deeper. I'm just a stressed, overworked, Black woman who is rambling and being charged an astronomical amount of money by the hour to vent to you. So what a candle triggers a stupid memory about a girl I kissed. It's not important."

"Nadine. Don't downplay your feelings. Triggers happen for a reason." Dr. Flournoy stared at her with kind eyes. "You look tense. Breathe, Nadine. Please."

Nadine closed her eyes, letting out a breath. She was spiraling, and she knew it. When she opened them, Dr. Flournoy was staring at her with a smile. Nadine gave a tight smile in return.

"Better?"

"Yeah, Doc. But, look, I'm not trying to talk about something I've tried to forget for thirty years. Digging up the past is just going to cause unnecessary heartache."

"Or it could set you free."

Nadine furrowed her brows, turning the word *"free'* around in her mind over and over. Free? What does that even mean for someone like her?

Dr. Flournoy, sensing Nadine's confusion, explained. "Free meaning not binding yourself to this idea of who you should be. That starts with facing your past. As a young person, repressing a troubling event can be helpful, protective even. However, as an adult, repression no longer serves us and only keeps us living in the past. Dealing with those difficult memories... your repressed feelings... will allow you to truly move on. And yes, going there can be emotional, possibly traumatic but maybe in our next session..."

"Shit!" Nadine looked at her watch. "I have a meeting and it's going to take me a half hour to make it back to the office."

Nadine wasn't exactly lying. She always had a meeting scheduled after therapy, and that was on purpose. She kept this therapy session strictly to one hour. No more. No less. Mentally, she couldn't handle more.

"Ok, Nadine." Dr. Flournoy put her tablet down, standing to walk Nadine to the door. She put a gentle hand on her shoulder. "But we can't avoid talking about it forever. I won't push, but... when you're ready, I'll be here to help you work through it. Okay?"

Nadine nodded as she gripped the straps of her purse. "Ok. See you next week."

CHAPTER 2
Same Day, Same Shit

Nadine exhaled another deep breath as she leaned back against the plush leather of her car seat. She'd been sitting in her Mercedes for nearly forty-five minutes in the driveway of her West Midtown mansion, staring at the door of her six-car garage bay. The air conditioning in her car was getting stale and despite having it on full blast, her thighs were sticking to the leather seats.

Nadine's job as CEO of PharmaDigital, the world's largest online pharmacy, had her running on fumes. She was busy from the time she arrived at work at 7 a.m. until she left for the day, which was usually at 6 p.m. most nights, if she was lucky. Then, she'd have to contend with the snarling Atlanta traffic to get to her home. In actuality, she didn't get home until almost 7 p.m.

Home.

The word should evoke a sense of comfort and warmth. For Nadine, home just meant clocking in for her unpaid jobs of wife and mother. Sure, she had a nanny, chef and housekeeper helping her with much of her daily tasks. But it was her job to manage the home, including setting the schedules, menus, and making sure that everyone knew their task. Being Eddie Moody, former all-star NBA player turned Division-1 coach's wife, meant endless fundraisers, non-profit events and galas. There were countless hours in heels and makeup. She had to look and be perfect at all times.

But the most taxing part of being Eddie's wife was that she had to somehow muster the energy to climb on top of her husband's 6'5" frame and fuck him. Every minute that ticked by as she rode his dick was time lost. She'd much rather be catching up on valuable sleep. With how infrequent they had sex, Nadine was sure that Eddie probably felt the same.

Her life was exhausting. Relatively fulfilling, mostly angst inducing, but fucking *exhausting*. And it was an endless cycle that she repeated every damn day.

It used to not be like this… life used to be… I used to be… fun.

Sighing, Nadine hit her garage door opener and pulled her car into her designated area. She opened the door from the garage to her mudroom, kicking off her heels and putting her Brahmin bag on the hanger. Rounding the corner toward the playroom, she found her nanny, Glinda, picking up toys from the floor. Nadine shook her head, looking at the mess strewn about. EJ was a mini-tornado. Tonight, she was surprised that the amount of toys that Glinda was putting away seemed minimal.

Glinda paused her tidying and gave Nadine her usual warm smile. "Good evening, Mrs. Moody. How was your day?"

"It was ok. Busy as usual. How was EJ? No trouble, I hope."

"Of course not! My sweet boy was good. School drop off and pick up went fine. He wanted to play a little before bed, so I let him. He's just a rambunctious boy. Had to get some energy out. Oh, by the way, there are some handouts from the school on the counter. Pre-K kids are doing a play next month. I think it's about Red Riding Hood. EJ is so excited. He's going to be The Wolf. He couldn't stop talking about it. He hopes you'll be there."

Nadine's heart twisted in her chest with crushing guilt. She didn't even have to look at her calendar to guess that she probably already had a meeting scheduled that day. She'd missed so much of EJ's life since returning to work after a two-year long maternity leave. Although, if she was being honest, she was still working a little here and there, putting out fires, while on leave. But once her leave was over, Nadine threw herself back into her role at PharmaDigital, trying to prove that she could be a superwoman and have it all. She wanted to shut down the folks who were whispering that she didn't need to work there because she had a "rich" husband. She wanted to stand on her own two feet again as Nadine Davis-Moody, badass CEO, not just Eddie Moody's wife. She wanted to be taken seriously.

But at what cost?

Nadine blinked back tears before she answered. "I'll definitely check my schedule and try my best to make it. Maybe Alex will have a break in classes, and she can go. If that doesn't work out, maybe you can get plenty of video for me and Eddie at the very least."

Glinda scratched her graying temple. "Well, that's the thing, Mrs. Moody. I don't know if I'll be able to make it."

"Why?"

Glinda, with a worried look etched across her face, sat on the couch. "I think you need to sit, Mrs. Moody." She gently pat the space on the sofa next to her.

This had to be bad. Glinda's tone had never been this way with her. She'd been a wonderful nanny, being in EJ's life since he was born, like a pseudo-grandmother.

Nadine lowered herself slowly, bracing herself for the worst. "What is it, Glinda?"

Glinda looked down at her clasped hands. "It's my sister, Gloria. She had a mild stroke a few weeks ago." Tears filled Glinda's eyes and Nadine reached out for her hands, clasping them tightly. "You know we're very close. She lost her husband years ago, so she's all alone and needs help as she rehabs. I need to head down to Florida to take care of her. Until she gets back on her feet. So, this is going to be my last week. For good."

For good? The words were soul crushing to Nadine. Glinda had been such a constant in her life since having EJ. She'd be entirely lost without her.

"Oh Glinda, I am so sorry. I totally understand. I am here for you. Whatever you need. So if it's money or anything, let me know." Nadine meant every word of that. Glinda was part of her family. She hated to be without Glinda, but family came first.

Glinda let out a shaky breath. "Thank you, Mrs. Moody. So much. I am not going to leave you all high and dry. The agency will have my replacement here in about a week. That'll give Gloria's son enough time to make sure things are in order before I get there, and he heads back to Manila. He's in the Navy. My nephew is sweet but a little scatterbrained so…"

"It's fine, Glinda. If you need to go down earlier, trust me, I can manage for a few days. Maybe I'll take off or something." Nadine had so much vacation time accumulated it was ridiculous. As CEO, it was virtually unlimited, but she rarely took it because she worked herself like a dog.

"No, Mrs. Moody. Let me take care of it. I sprung this on you last minute. I'll make sure my replacement has good notes and is prepared for everything. I'm on top of it and the agency will make sure my replacement will be, too."

"Are you sure?"

Glinda pat Nadine's hand. "I'm positive. Now, let me finish putting away these toys before I head out for the night. Chef Kim made you and Mr. Moody's favorite. I can heat it up for you."

"That's ok. I'll try and wait for Eddie to get here so we can eat together." Nadine didn't know why she told that lie. Eddie, with his new job, was coming home late every night. He claimed he was looking at scouting videos with the coaching staff, but Nadine wasn't sure she believed that. Something felt off. It had been for months, if she was being honest. Yet, trying to get anything out of him was like trying to break into a maximum-security vault. Damn near impossible. Maybe tonight would be different.

After checking on a sleeping EJ, Nadine found herself eating alone in the dining room and checking her work email on her phone. *Again.* She tried not to bring work home, but that seemed damn near impossible. The negotiations for their partnership with DigiCo, an online superstore, were on the line. It was a make or break deal that Pharma-Digital couldn't lose.

She placed the last mouthwatering piece of Steak Diane in her mouth. She tried FaceTiming her oldest daughter, Alex, but once again didn't get an answer. *Typical.* Alex didn't have time for her these days now that she was in college. They used to be so close. She wasn't sure when the rift between them started or when it became a deep chasm, but it hurt, nonetheless. As she picked up her glass of merlot, Nadine heard the alert for the garage. She looked at her watch and shook her head. It was almost 10 p.m.

Nadine heard Eddie's heavy footsteps lumbering toward the dining room. Upon entering, he kissed her on the cheek, smelling like sweat and cologne. The action was robotic at this point. She didn't even bother to look up.

"Sorry I'm late, babe. I was…"

"Looking at scouting videos," Nadine interrupted. "I know."

Eddie sighed, rubbing hand across his low waves. "I'm sorry, Deanie. I know you're disappointed and so am I. Every day, I say I am going to be home in time to read EJ a bedtime story. And shit just comes up. With signing day coming, I have a lot on the line here."

Nadine looked up from her cell phone, giving him a weak smile. "I get it. I missed bedtime too. I know this is your first year coaching on the collegiate level. There's a lot of pressure."

Eddie pulled his chair closer and pulled Nadine onto his lap, the action lowering her defenses. She instantly melted into his embrace. "You're under pressure too, baby. I see the hours you've been putting in, especially with that deal on the line. I know all of our hard work won't be in vain."

"You sure about that? I feel like we're failing our family. Failing each other. We work so much that we're missing out on things with EJ all the time. And don't get me started on Alex. Unless it's an issue with the credit card, we don't hear from her."

"Baby, Alex is fine. Just being a typical college kid. Don't you follow her Instagram? TikTok? She posts like every day."

"I think she blocked me."

"Damn," Eddie chuckled. "That's Alexandria for you. Don't take it personal."

Nadine ran a hand over her husband's low beard. "What about us, Ed? I feel like it's not just the scouting videos and coming in late. That feels like an excuse. I feel like you're so distant. Be real with me? You're blocking me, too?"

"I…" Eddie's impossibly long lashes fluttered. He inhaled slowly before answering. "It's…nothing."

Nadine furrowed her brows. She could tell he was holding back. "Are you sure? Eddie, whatever it is, you can tell me."

Nadine watched the Adam's apple in Eddie's throat bob a few times before he spoke. "How was therapy, Deanie? You did go today, right?"

Nadine blinked. "It was fine." He was clearly changing the subject, but she didn't feel like getting into that with him. She never said more than that. She wasn't ready to talk about it, not even after years of sessions. Besides, what she said to her therapist was personal.

"That's it? Just fine? Your answer is always that it's fine."

Nadine said nothing. Eventually, he lifted Nadine off his lap and back onto her chair. "Yeah. Imma just head to bed, Deanie. Don't stay up too late." Eddie leaned down to kiss Nadine on her temple and walked down their impossibly long hallway, then up the stairs toward their bedroom.

This was how it had been every night, it seemed. Expecting a different result was pointless. *What is it that they say about insanity?*

Nadine poured another glass of merlot, downing it.

💋

NADINE FELT THE SPACE NEXT TO HER IN THE BED, FINDING IT COLD AND empty. Squinting, she looked at the time on her phone. It was nearing 2 am and Eddie wasn't in bed. Nadine was worried and slightly annoyed. *I bet he is watching those damn scouting videos instead of sleeping.* She slid her feet into her slippers and padded down the hallway.

She looked in the upstairs theater room and didn't find him there. *Maybe EJ had a nightmare?* Eddie was always better at soothing EJ after a nightmare. He had the magic touch. Nadine moved down the hall to EJ's room, only to find her son hanging halfway off the bed, still clinging to his stuffed Bluey plushy. After maneuvering EJ back into bed, Nadine went downstairs. There was a sliver of light coming from Eddie's office. If he was still up watching scouting videos, Nadine wouldn't be surprised.

Nadine peeked through the door, then froze as the light illuminated from the computer made everything clear.

There, with his hands in his boxers, was Eddie jerking his dick frantically.

What the fuck?

Nadine's eyes tried to make out what was on the screen. In the dark, her eyes finally focused on the flickering images. A man was tied to a chair, intricate red ropes tied in knots, as he watched his wife get fucked in the ass. His dick was weeping, pre-cum pooling on the floor in front of the couple. Eddie's face was a mix of agony and pleasure, his eye glued on the scene before him.

"Sit there and watch, nigga. Watch me fuck your wife, bitch!"

Nadine's eyes widened. *What the actual fuck?* Her hand flew to her mouth in disbelief. Sure, Eddie jerked off. What man didn't! She'd been a fool not to know that. *But to this kinda shit?* As soon as the man fucking the wife came in her ass, Eddie also exploded all over his boxers and into his hand.

Slowly, Nadine tip-toed back upstairs to her bedroom and got back into bed. She stared up at the ceiling, trying to scrub the image of her husband jacking off to *that filth* out of her brain. She tried to calm her nerves, to make her hands stop shaking. Nadine jerked open her nightstand, found her bottle of Ambient and swallowed one without water.

When she heard Eddie coming back into the room, she covered her head with the duvet and pretended to be asleep. The weight of the bed shifted as Eddie leaned over and kissed her exposed shoulder. Nadine didn't move. She couldn't even take an exhalation of breath.

"Sleep tight, babe," he whispered sweetly. Nadine rolled her eyes. *As if he hadn't been downstairs jerking off to some weird shit.*

When she knew he was fast asleep, Nadine grabbed her phone and texted Alisa and Tatum in their group chat. She was sure they were asleep, but they'd see it tomorrow.

> Nadine: Emergency lunch tomorrow. I'll text you details.

Eventually, the sleeping pill kicked in and Nadine fell asleep.

CHAPTER 3

Trippin'

At a small table in the back of the Cuthberts on Peachtree, Tatum and Alisa sat in silence as they watched Nadine down her second margarita in less than ten minutes. She'd insisted that they meet her, declaring it was an emergency. But she hadn't said a word, just drank.

Alisa sighed, rubbing her very pregnant belly. "Nadine, can you please tell us why you summoned us here? You know I had to damn near sneak out the house to get past Christophe and Kadeem. They are like paranoid prison wardens. They have me on house arrest until the babies come. I had to slip my driver $100 to keep quiet."

"Yeah," chimed Tatum. "I had to reschedule a department meeting for this. As the new chair of the English department, I can't afford to be away from campus right now. What's up with all the secrecy?"

Nadine downed the last of her margarita. "I'm sorry. It's just..." She burst out into tears, which was out of character for Nadine. She was always so stoic. So put together.

Tatum and Alisa looked at each other stunned. Slightly embarrassed, Nadine wiped her tears with the black cloth napkin and collected herself.

"I think Eddie is unhappy. Maybe he wants to leave me."

"Oh girl," sighed Alisa. "Where is this coming from? You know Eddie worships the ground you walk on."

Nadine pointed her finger. "I have proof…I think."

"Proof?" Tatum rolled her eyes. "Ok, Deanie. What does that even mean? What kind of proof?"

"Well, he's been acting really strange. I mean, Eddie has always had his ways, but he's turned it up a notch."

"Turned up a notch, how?" asked Alisa. Her stomach was so big she could barely lean forward.

Nadine sniffed, dabbing her red cheeks with the napkin. "We used to communicate, and now he's giving me short answers all the time. He's coming home later and later, blaming it on work."

"This is his first year as a head coach. Give him grace," Tatum gently suggested. Alisa nodded, agreeing.

"It isn't just work. It's much worse."

Alisa frowned. "How is it worse?"

Nadine leaned closer across the table. "He is watching very different porn. I caught him red handed. Well, not really handed. His hand down in his pants, jerking off to it."

"How different? Like pregnant grandmas? Or Brazilian little people?" asked Alisa.

"Is that really a thing?" asked Tatum, an amused smirk on her face.

"Probably. Anything is possible in the porn world." Alisa shrugged.

"No!" whisper-screeched Nadine. "Not that. Now it's a lot of… threesomes. Very *specific* kinds of threesomes."

"Specific how? I wish your ass would get to the point!" Alisa was frustrated and hangry. The twins were doing a number on her and she regretted leaving the house without a snack.

"Fine! It's threesomes with the husband watching his wife get fucked by other people. Men, Women. You name it. Video after video of the same scenario."

Nadine had woken up an hour early to do a thorough search of Eddie's porn history. Shocked wasn't even the word she could use to describe the things she saw. Husbands getting peed on, jerked off on, whipped. All while tied up. All while watching their spouse or partners get fucked out of their minds.

There was a beat of silence before Tatum and Alisa looked at each other and burst out laughing. Nadine couldn't believe her two best friends were laughing at her plight. She was pissed. Her life was literally blowing up and they thought it was hilarious.

"Nadine, I know damn well you didn't call a meeting because Eddie has been looking at threesome porn," laughed Tatum.

"Of course, you'd laugh, Miss Taking-Three-Dicks-At-A-Time, but Eddie isn't like that. Why would he wanna watch someone fuck his wife? He's never mentioned anything like that to me before. I thought we shared everything. There are no secrets between us."

"First off, Imma let that slick comment slide." Tatum signaled the waiter so she could order something stronger than the sweet tea that she was drinking. She was going to need it. "Secondly, what's wrong with his porn preferences? Many men have unusual fantasies. That's normal. Besides, Deanie, it isn't like you're the most open-minded person when it comes to sex."

Nadine chewed her lip. "While that may be true, he still could talk to me. This isn't normal for Eddie! Maybe he's trying to say something. Maybe I'm not enough. Maybe I'm…"

"Or maybe," Alisa interrupted. "The man is bored, Nadine. Maybe he's embarrassed to share it with you because you may shame him."

Nadine blinked. "I wouldn't shame him!"

Alisa raised an accusatory brow. "You sure about that? Because you damn sure shamed me and Tate and our situations."

Maybe I am kind of shaming him, actually. Dr. Flournoy would definitely say I am shaming him. Nadine folded her arms across her chest defensively. "Well, excuse me if some of us aren't willing to get cum shot up in us every-which-way."

Tatum choked on her Cosmo. Alisa looked as if she was ready to box Nadine upside the head, pregnant or not. When she felt backed into a corner, Nadine reverted to being snide. She regretted saying that the second it came out her mouth.

"That felt like judgment, hoe." Alisa fumed as she tapped her fingers on the table.

Tatum agreed. "That was hurtful Nadine."

"I'm sorry but…"

"Ain't no sorry," Alisa interrupted. "Don't be mad because our sex lives are jumping and yours is on life support."

"Is it really jumping if you don't know which one of your husbands is the father of your kids? Stirring up sperm like cake batter."

"Nadine!" Tatum hissed, slapping her head in frustration.

Nadine bit her lip. She just couldn't turn off being a bitch sometimes. *God, she really was turning into her mother.*

Alisa's eye was twitching. Tatum shook her head, rubbing Alisa's back. "Don't get worked up, Alisa, the babies…"

Alisa had had enough. "Nadine, I'll knock your ass between this booth and the wall. Pregnant or not. Keep on fucking with me!"

Tatum looked around the restaurant, hoping no one had heard them. "Lower your voices, you two!"

Alisa threw her hands up. "See what I mean? Judgmental. When is the last time you even fucked Eddie without counting the number of pumps? No wonder Eddie is looking at hella porn with your stale pussy ass."

"Stale pussy?" Nadine was turning every shade of red. "Really, Alisa…"

Alisa was on a roll. "You act like you're so damn perfect. Always have. I *know* you've got secrets too, Deanie. You just pretend like you don't because you got your perfect image to uphold!"

"I don't have any secrets!" Nadine swallowed that whole lie, as it stuck like a rock in her throat.

"Okay! Okay!" Tatum interrupted, trying to cool down the situation. "Let's not go there, y'all." She turned to Nadine. "Babe, why don't you just talk to Eddie? Be honest. Ask him what he wants to explore and maybe the two of you can come up with a reasonable compromise. Maybe it'll reenergize things."

Nadine shook her head. "I cannot compromise getting fucked by someone else while my husband watches. Especially another man!"

"What do you mean by *especially* another man?" asked Tatum.

Nadine shrugged, quickly dismissing her answer. "I don't know why I said that. You know what I mean."

"Scared you'll enjoy it?" Alisa raised a brow, a smirk firmly on her lips. "C'mon Deanie. Join me and Tatum on the dark side. Clearly, Eddie wants you to."

"Ugh, you're the fucking worst."

"And you need to learn how to be bad. Always been a good girl with a stick up your ass!"

Some good girl I am, thought Nadine.

Nadine chuckled nervously, hoping that her best friends could see that she was just wound up. Even though beating her ass still wasn't totally off the table for Alisa. She could see it in her eyes.

Nadine fiddled with her napkin. "It's just...y'all know how much I compromised in my first marriage. Andrew put me through hell. And I said I'd never change who I was just to please a man. Period."

Hell was an understatement of the bullshit that Alex's father, Andrew, put her through. She thought meeting him her senior year at Spelman was a godsend. Finally, she could squash all memories of any desire she may have had for anything other than "normalcy." Nadine had changed herself inside and out for him. She picked an MBA program that she was just lukewarm on because Andrew got into his dream residency program. They joined a church that Nadine hated. Andrew had resented her first corporate job, begging her to quit as soon as she got pregnant. To be honest, the pregnancy was a mystery. She'd never missed taking her birth control. Nadine was pretty sure Drew had switched out her pills for placebos.

Even though she was on the fast track to the C-suite, Nadine kept the baby to save her marriage. Her mother, with her traditional Christian upbringing, convinced her that the pregnancy was a sign that she needed to listen to her husband as the head of the home and focus on being a good wife and mother. Despite never desiring to be a stay-at-home mom, Nadine convinced herself that maybe it was for the best, pouring everything into her marriage and motherhood. She figured if she gave her all, then Andrew would too. If she gave it her all, she could be the wife and mother her parents wanted her to be. What Andrew wanted her to be.

Andrew cheated on Nadine every chance he got. A successful surgeon, Andrew had banged every doctor, nurse, and physician's assistant he could. When Nadine was brave enough to confront him, he took no accountability. She sought counsel in her pastors, who told her to just try harder to please her husband. Despite doing any and everything he wanted sexually, Andrew's insatiable need for pussy was never satisfied. He wouldn't stop with his wayward dick. He declared he was her husband; he was the head of the house, and he could do as he pleased. When she begged him to stop, he put his hands on her like a coward. It took only him putting his hands on her once for Nadine to take baby Alex and leave. She was unemployed, homeless, and a single mother. She had to start over, living with Tatum and Franklin for a brief time until she got on her feet. They didn't ask for a thing in return. She told herself that the next man she met, she'd never compromise. Ever.

When Nadine met Eddie, she thought she'd hit the jackpot. Despite being a successful athlete, Eddie was kind, generous and attentive. He had no obvious red flags and for a professional athlete; he was rather dull. He was frugal, yet didn't mind spending money where it counted. He preferred staying home over the glitz and glamour of exclusive events. Most of all, Eddie wasn't out chasing pussy, even though women threw it at him all the time. He only had eyes for Nadine. He fell in love with Nadine quickly and loved Alex like she was his own daughter. He was the only daddy she'd known since she was six. He didn't rush marriage, waiting three years to walk down the aisle. He was her world, and she thought that he was hers.

When it came to sex, Eddie didn't push her. After Andrew, she wasn't interested much, and Eddie understood. It wasn't fireworks all the time, but it was satisfying for the most part. Satisfying was better than terrible in Nadine's eyes.

Maybe Eddie wasn't really satisfied at all. Maybe all men were the same.

Tatum reached out for Nadine's hand, taking her out of her thoughts. Reluctantly, she eased her palm between Tatum's. "Nadine, Eddie is not Drew. Not even close."

Alisa added her hand to the pile. "Drew was a piece of shit in every sense of the word. Go talk to Eddie instead of making assumptions about what's going on. Besides, all change isn't bad."

Nadine nodded, sniffing back tears. "You're right. I'll talk to Ed. I promise. Maybe I'm just stressed, you know? Maybe we both are. So much is going on. Alex acts like she can't talk to me anymore since she's in college. EJ is getting big. Work is getting so stressful and time consuming that I'm missing out on EJ's milestones. Now, Eddie seems distant." She squeezed Alisa's hand. "I am sorry for what I said, Lis.

You have two great fathers for the babies who love you. That's all that matters."

Alisa tossed her blond-streaked weave over her shoulder. "It's ok. I know you're just upset, even though I know it's over nothing. I'll forgive you. *Eventually.*" She gave a small smile. "Go talk to Eddie, Nadine before you call another meeting of the minds."

"You're right." Nadine looked at the menu. "Maybe I'm tripping. Let's just order some food."

"Good, because I am starving," Alisa grumbled. "And you're paying Nadine. That's the least you can do since you dragged us here. And you insulted my baby daddies!"

"Actually, she should pay for lunches for the next six months!" declared Tatum.

"That's fair," Nadine laughed. "I'll pay. Only because I am not trying to starve my nieces…or should I say nephews?"

Alisa said nothing as she stared down at the menu. She had been so tight-lipped about the genders of the babies, making it damn near impossible for Tatum and Nadine to plan a shower.

"You still aren't telling us the sex of the babies, are you?" Tatum teased.

"Nope. And honestly, it doesn't even matter. I just want healthy babies. It's a wonder that this even happened. I can't believe after all those rounds of IVF, we have our little miracles." Alisa's eyes were brimming with tears.

Tatum squeezed Alisa's shoulder in a side hug. "I can't wait to see their faces. They are going to be beautiful."

"Of course they will be! They got two fine ass daddies and a fine ass mama. They hit the genetic jackpot."

Nadine rolled her eyes. "Hopefully, they'll inherit some humility from somewhere."

"Why should they be humble?" Alisa countered. "They will be rich, Black and fabulous. Speaking of which, Tatum, what's up with you and your trio of fabulous men? You hadn't given us the rundown in a minute. Everything all good?"

Tatum peeked over the menu. "We're fine."

"That's it?" asked Nadine. Tatum had been suspiciously quiet about anything going on with her fellas for weeks. That was so unlike her. She hoped everything was alright.

"Yeah. Nothing much. You know, same ol' stuff."

"And what does that mean?"

"Deanie," Tatum let out an exasperated sigh. "Let's just eat so I can get back to work."

"But Tate…"

"Deanie, let it go, girl."

Alisa and Nadine looked at each other with suspicion, but they knew not to push Tatum, otherwise she'd clam up and not say a word. She'd let them know what the issue was when she was ready.

Nadine gave Tatum a slight smile. "Ok Tate. I'll let it go."

"Now that that's settled," Alisa clapped her hands. "Let's talk about more of Eddie's porn habits. Is he into threesome with pegging? Oh! Would he be into you wearing a strap? Because I can give you some tips like…"

Nadine held up her hand. "Alisa! Imma need you to shut up right goddamn now."

"I'm just trying to help you out," mumbled Alisa as she stared at the menu.

"You got one more thing to say before I renege on planning your baby shower."

"Oh, about that," Alisa hesitated. "Kadeem and Christophe don't want you all to do a thing. They're hiring a planner. Someone who did one of the Atlanta housewives' wedding or something."

"Well, we still can decorate the nursery," suggested Nadine.

Alisa waved her hand. "Oh girl! Don't get me talking about the nursery. They hired an interior designer for that too."

"Wow, they are some true Daddy-Zillas." Tatum chuckled.

"I told you. They are obsessed. But I don't blame them. I'm a little obsessed, too." Alisa rubbed her belly lovingly. Tatum and Nadine smiled. Seeing Alisa glowing and radiant as a mom warmed their hearts. Especially because she had been ambivalent toward having kids, given her own relationship with her parents. Love had a way of changing a person.

"A little obsession isn't bad, right?" asked Nadine. "It just means they really care about you. Shoot, I wish Eddie felt that kind of obsession." *Shoot, I wished I felt that kind of obsession, she thought.*

"Be careful what you wish for," Tatum warned, playfully nudging Nadine.

Nadine shuddered. Tatum's harmless words shouldn't have felt ominous, but they did. She didn't know why.

"You ok, Nadine?" Alisa looked at her, worried.

Nadine shook her head, focusing on the menu instead. "I'm fine. Let's just eat."

CHAPTER 4
Rinse and Repeat

Despite getting home about thirty minutes later than normal, Nadine was able to get home in time to read EJ his bedtime story, eat dinner, and pamper herself with a hot bath. She sat in the great room, soft music playing through the Sonos and candles lit, wearing her finest silk backless Natori nightgown. Nadine waited patiently, sipping on a gin and tonic for Eddie to come home. It was forty-five minutes past the time he normally got there. She tried to shake off a yawn that was coming down. She had a plan and dammit, she was going to execute it. Sleep be damned.

The alert for the garage door chimed as Nadine fluffed her hair, pushed her titties up, and crossed her legs, showing as much thigh as possible as she waited on her husband.

"Deanie, where you at, babe?" Eddie called out.

"In here. In the great room."

Nadine watched as Eddie rounded the corner. He paused, looking around the room, confused.

"What's this all about?" Eddie looked at his watch. "Shit, I know it's not our anniversary. It isn't, right?"

"No babe," Nadine chuckled, patting the empty space next to her. "Come here."

Eddie put down his LV messenger bag and came over to the

massive couch where Nadine sat. After letting him kiss her forehead, she eased closer to him, running a hand over his smooth, ebony waves. She loved waves. The way they felt under her fingers always turned her on.

"EJ go down easy?" asked Eddie. "How many stories did you have to read tonight?"

"Just two stories. Thankfully."

"So," Eddie looked around the room. "What's all this for?"

"I just wanted to do something special for you. I missed you, that's all."

Eddie gave a slight smile. "I've missed you too, boo." He put the edge of her nightgown between his fingers. "You look good. Is this new?"

"I've had it a while."

"Well, it's nice. Blue is definitely your color"

"Now, do you want to take it off me?" Nadine smiled seductively as her other hand found its way to Eddie's crotch. No use in beating around the bush. He wasn't hard, but she could definitely get him there. She hoped.

"Uhm," Eddie stilled, his body going rigid. "Deanie, as much as I'd love to take this off you, I'm kinda beat. I was going to head downstairs to the man cave, watch a little more scouting footage, and smoke a cigar before bed to decompress. If that's cool with you."

"No, it's not cool with me!" Nadine rolled her eyes. "Eddie, I am trying to fuck you. Can't you see that?"

"I can see that," he responded flatly.

"But you'd rather go smoke a cigar?"

"I mean, you can join me, I guess." He shrugged.

"Wow! Seriously, Eddie!" Nadine was flabbergasted. Here she was, oiled up, dressed in silk, smelling good with a wet pussy, courtesy of a lube suppository she had inserted half an hour ago. She was desperate to connect with her husband. Instead, he wanted to smoke a Cohiba Behike.

"Babe, c'mon. Let's not do this."

Nadine stood and began pacing the floor. "We haven't had sex in six months, Eddie. Six months! I know we are busy, but what's the deal? Do you not want me anymore?"

"I'm just tired, that's all." His eyes didn't meet hers at all.

"Eddie, stop lying. Be honest for fucking once."

"Fine, you want me to be honest? Why does it matter if we haven't had sex in six months? I don't want to have sex. And it's clear neither do you."

"No, it's not!" huffed Nadine.

"Deanie, c'mon now. You know it's true. Why have sex? What's the point? Because when we do have sex, it's not like you're enthusiastic about it."

Nadine's eyes widened. "What are you talking about?"

Eddie leaned back on the sofa. "Be real, Nadine. You treat sex like it's a task to check off. A fucking chore. My dick is on your checklist like one of your board meetings. I bet it says, "Give Eddie a couple of twirls on his dick, five to be precise, and that'll shut him up."

"Wha…no, I don't!" Nadine scoffed, a little resentful that he was calling her on her shit.

"Yes, you do. And it's the same thing over and over. It's not exciting anymore. Honestly, it's never been exciting, and I get why. But damn, it's been years of the same shit, Deanie."

"Oh, so let me guess. You want me to tie you up and you watch me fuck someone else to get you off?"

Eddie blinked. "What are you talking about?"

"Don't play dumb with me. I saw you! In your office. Jerking off and watching cuckold threesomes. That's all that's in your damn search history!" This wasn't how Nadine wanted to talk to Eddie about the porn. She was hoping she could fuck him out his misery before she brought it up. But rage had other plans.

A vein pulsed in Eddie's temple, his jaw ticking at the same rate. "You went through my laptop? Why are you violating my privacy? You don't trust me, Nadine?"

"I thought we didn't have secrets, Edward!" Nadine watched as Eddie put his head in his hands, shaking it back and forth. "Say something! Is that what you want? For me to be used like that?"

Eddie lifted his head to face his wife. "Used? Of course, not. I wouldn't want you to do anything you aren't comfortable with or consent to doing."

"Good," Nadine huffed.

"But," Eddie began. "What would be so bad about that?"

"Eddie! There is no way…"

"I am bored, Nadine!" Eddie interrupted with a shout. "Just fucking bored."

"Bored?!" Nadine held on to the column near the hallway. "You're jacking off to porn because you're bored? Bored with me?"

"It isn't all about you. The truth is that I have fantasies, Nadine. Just like every normal human being. Mine happen to be very specific ones that I am too afraid to even talk about with you."

"Fine. Talk to me. Tell me why you like watching *that* kind of porn? Cuckhold porn?"

Eddie sighed. "It's complicated. But to put it simply, all day I am in charge. In control. Making major decisions. Just like you. Sometimes, you want to relinquish that control. Revel in someone else's pleasure, which would give me pleasure. It turns me on. Does that make sense?"

Nadine squinted as if she was pondering Eddie's words. "But you didn't have to keep it from me. Jerking off in the dark like a pervert."

"Pervert?" Eddie rolled his eyes. "This is exactly what I'm saying. Deanie, I'd love it if we could create a safe space for each other where we can explore things. No judgment. Just freedom. But it's damn near impossible for you to not be judgmental. I forgot who I was talking to."

Nadine rolled her eyes. "That's not true."

Eddie chuckled dryly. "You know it's true, Deanie. When I try and get you to talk to me about what you want, hell, about anything sexual, you shut down. You put this wall up. I know you grew up religious but, you are over forty *and* married. Been married a long damn time. You can't use being sheltered as an excuse no more. It's like you're turning into your mother."

Nadine winced. That last part stung. "But…I…"

"And don't even bring up, Drew," Eddie warned. "That's the other excuse. Drew did this. Drew did that. It's been years, Deanie. Stop that shit. I don't know how long I have to prove to you that I'm not that sorry motherfucker. And I never will be."

Nadine tucked in her lips, embarrassed. He wasn't lying. Eddie, despite being in her life the last sixteen years, still lived in Drew's shadow at times. And yeah, despite her best efforts, maybe she was becoming more like Grace Davis. She didn't mean for that to happen, but trauma reared its ugly head sometimes.

Eddie, noticing her change in demeanor, softened his tone. "Baby, there has to be a compromise. I'm open to anything. Let's just talk about it."

"Anything?"

"Yes, anything."

"Ok. What if I wanted to peg you?" *Damn Alisa and all her pegging talk!* Nadine wasn't serious. She just wanted to see what he'd say.

Eddie shrugged. "I'd try it. Is that something you want to try?"

"No!" she squealed.

"Be serious, Deanie. What do you want? Do you want things to stay the same?"

Nadine waited for a beat. She thought about it, but…no…she could never say what she was really thinking. Instead, she shrugged. "Why can't we just be happy with the way things are?"

Eddie rose from the sofa and stood in front of Nadine. He gently lifted her chin with his finger. Her soft, hazel eyes met his deep brown ones. "Because it's not working, love. And we aren't happy. And I want to be happy. Your cousin Tate is happy. Alisa is surprisingly, crazy happy. Now, *they're* happy. I'm trying to be on that level…again."

Nadine bit her lip. She teased Alisa and Tatum about their poly situations, but the truth was she did admire their relentless pursuit of happiness, sexual and otherwise. It had paid off for Tatum and Alisa in major ways. She'd never seen the two of them so completely blissful and satisfied. She could admit that maybe she was a little jealous. But Nadine wasn't sure she could be so bold.

"You want me to bring another man in the mix?" asked Nadine, confused.

"I didn't say that. But we need to figure out what will work for us. We have to ask ourselves what happiness looks like for us?"

Nadine's eyes filled with tears. "And if we don't? If *I* don't? Will you leave me?"

"Never, love." Eddie bent down, kissing the top of Nadine's head. "I have faith we will figure out what works best for us. Whatever that looks like. This is our marriage. We make the rules. No one else. But we've got to talk. And be honest, ok?"

"Ok," Nadine said softly.

"You've got to talk to me Nadine. Please. I am begging you. You say I have secrets, but I feel like it's something you aren't telling me, either. But I'm here, ok? I'd never judge you."

Eddie kissed Nadine softly on the lips, then picked up his bag and headed downstairs to the basement. Slowly, Nadine walked around the room blowing out the flames of the candles, which had melted down significantly. She stared at the last candle, flickering in the near darkness, and watched as it eventually burned out.

CHAPTER 5
Vent Session

"He said he was bored! Can you believe that! Bored? With me!"

Nadine hadn't sat still since she walked into her therapist's office. She paced up and down the shag carpet, her heels snagging occasionally. She tried her best to keep upright. Falling on her face would probably be less embarrassing.

Dr. Flournoy held up her hands, pleading. "Nadine, I need you to take a breath, like we've practiced. Then let's slow down, and together we'll try to understand what happened."

Eventually, Nadine relented, easing herself down on the leather couch. "Sorry. I am just…angry."

"There's no need to apologize…it's okay to be angry. But let's talk about why Eddie's statement made you so angry."

"Because," Nadine's voice cracked on each syllable. "That means he's not happy. And he made it seem like it was all my fault. His rejecting me is my fault!"

"Is that what he said or how you interpreted it?"

Nadine blinked. "I…I mean…maybe."

"Maybe?" Dr Flournoy pursed her lips. "Maybe isn't definitely, Nadine. What I'm hearing is that Eddie is tired of routine. He is looking for excitement. Adventure. Sexual exploration. He wants you to be open to that as well."

"We've been together for sixteen years. Why all of a sudden?"

"Is it possible he was afraid that you'd judge him?"

Nadine winced. *Called out on her bullshit yet again.* "Yeah. He did say that."

"Once he expressed his sexual desires, about cuckold porn, what did you say to him?"

Nadine looked down at her hands, twirling her wedding ring around her finger. "I...called him a pervert."

Dr. Flournoy let out a deep breath. "Nadine, why do you think your first reaction was to call your husband a pervert?" she asked gently.

Nadine stilled, her throat feeling as if it was closing in on her. "Because...what I saw didn't seem...normal."

"Tell me more about that."

"It just isn't...something married people should be doing."

"Says who?"

"Says...I don't know...everybody."

Dr. Flournoy nodded, tapping her pen against her hand. "Nadine, sex isn't just heteronormative, missionary-positions. Between consenting adults, even married people, sex and sexuality isn't just one thing or another. You've been told your entire life that sex should be one way. That anything outside that dichotomy is wrong. Including how you felt about Allison."

"How many times do I have to tell you that the thing with Allison was just some childish thing?" Nadine sighed. "Just kids being kids!"

"I'm not sure that it was, Nadine. That moment in your childhood seems to have shaped how you feel about sexuality and morality today. It's possibly why you believe anything outside of heterosexuality is unacceptable, deviant even. And it's led you to suppress parts of yourself - because now your faith and your desires are at war. And they have been for a long time."

Nadine couldn't respond. She kept staring at her hands, willing her eyes to look up, but she couldn't. Dr. Flournoy went on.

"And now this inner conflict is resurfacing in your marriage today, influencing the way you perceive your husband and your shared intimacy. You think a good, Christian marriage shouldn't include fetishes or even bisexuality, or…

"Hold on," Nadine frowned. "Who said anything about being gay? I didn't say that about Eddie. Eddie isn't gay."

Dr. Flournoy gave Nadine a soft, gentle smile. "I didn't say gay, Nadine. I said bisexual. There's a difference. And I am talking about you, not Eddie."

Nadine scoffed. "Bisexual? I…over one kiss? Over thirty years ago?"

"It's not just about the kiss, Nadine. It's about all the things after it." Dr. Flournoy ran a finger through her locs. "It's about the crushes you had on your friends in high school that you dismissed as "fleeting." It's about you "experimenting" in college but brushing it off. It's about you rushing into your first marriage because you felt you had to do the expected. It's about you judging your friends and their polyamorous sexual choices. It's about your ambivalence towards sex with your husband. It's about…"

"Just stop," Nadine's lip trembled. "Please. Please, stop." Tears welled up in Nadine's eyes, rolling down her cheeks like a river. Every word Dr. Flournoy said stabbed at some part of her. The tender, hidden part of her.

"Okay." Dr. Flournoy moved over to the sofa, handing Nadine a tissue. "I am not trying to trigger you. I just want you to realize that this isn't about your husband. This is about you, Nadine."

Nadine nodded, wiping her eyes. "Maybe it is. I just…"

"Nadine, your belief system…these judgments you've placed on yourself…I want to explore with you whether they truly align with the fullness of who you are and the love you share with your husband. Let's unpack this together and work toward understanding how your faith and your authentic self can coexist in a way that feels healthy and fulfilling."

Nadine listened quietly.

"How would you feel about Eddie maybe coming to a session with you?"

Nadine's eyes widened. "I am not sure that's a good idea."

"Nadine, keeping this inside is only going to hurt you and Eddie even more. I think having Eddie here could help you open up more. Think about it, alright?"

"I will."

Dr. Flournoy patted her knee. "Good."

🗣

"I THINK ONCE WE HAVE A THOROUGH REVIEW OF THEIR PROFIT SHARING margins, our partnership with DigiCo can be sewn up within the month."

Nadine looked around the boardroom at the room full of nodding, white male heads. Her vice president, Mitchell Kersey, was the only one who had a slight scowl on his face. As her right hand, he should have been supporting her. Instead, he questioned her, undermining every decision every chance he got.

Nadine braced herself. *Here comes the bullshit.*

"And what if DigiCo counters? Are we prepared for that?" asked Mitchell.

Nadine inhaled a breath. *What a dick.* She gave a well-rehearsed smile. "Absolutely. Aren't I always prepared, Mitchell?"

Mitchell gave a curt nod. That garnered a few chuckles from people in the room. She loved sticking it to his privileged ass. Nadine was always going to be two steps ahead of that jerk.

"I think we're done here," said Nadine as she gathered her things. "I'll be expecting a report from analytics on my desk by Monday."

As everyone filed out, Nadine felt her phone buzz in her blazer pocket. She opened it and read the message.

Eddie: I need you to be home early. Before 6.

Before 6? For what? Nadine frowned as she texted Eddie back.

Nadine: What's wrong? Is it EJ? Alex?

After a few moments, a message appeared.

36

Surprise? Eddie wasn't one for surprises. But Nadine wouldn't question it. After her last therapy session, they had a long talk. He was adamant that they needed to make changes to prevent their relationship from getting stale. Routine was getting the best of them. Eddie pledged to be bolder and take more initiative to bring the sexy and fun back to their relationships. Maybe this was it.

Nadine went back to her office and pulled up her calendar. It was a little after 4 pm. She had a Zoom call with the South American team and another meeting with R&D. She pulled up TEAMS and sent her assistant Devi a message to move things to Monday. It was Friday, anyway. After that long ass board meeting, maybe she deserved to knock off a little early. She just hated giving Mitchell any kind of ammunition to use later.

As she shut down her computer for the day, her phone buzzed again. This time, it was an email from Dr. Flournoy.

To: Nadine Davis Moody <NPD.Moody@mail.com>
From:. Dr. Rina Flournoy, PhD <DrRFlournoy@Flournoy-
    Psych.com>
Subject: Homework

Nadine,
I am attaching a few exercises for our next session. I hope these
    will help you to open up more. Please give it a try.
Dr. F.

PS: And please, think about what I asked regarding a session
    with Eddie

Nadine pulled up the two PDF attachments and scanned them. The first one was about "Unpacking Childhood Trauma: A Journaling Exercise" and the other was about "Deconstructing Faith and Sexuality." *Nope. Not today.* That was entirely too heavy to get into on a Friday afternoon. Nadine closed the email and shoved her phone into her purse.

CHAPTER 6
Something New

Nadine made it to her home a little after 5 PM. As soon as she walked in the door, she heard the sound of tiny feet scampering across the floor.

"Mommy!" EJ, was all smiles as he ran to his mother's arms. His face was sticky with something rather viscous. There was no telling what it was. Kids were always sticky.

Nadine picked up her son and swung him on her hip. "Hey Junior! I am happy to see you, baby."

"Guess what? Daddy has a surprise!"

Nadine raised a brow. "Oh yeah? What's the surprise?"

"Me," a raspy, feminine voice said after clearing their throat.

Nadine looked up and smirked. "Well, if it isn't my wayward oldest child. What brings you by?"

Alex smiled, coming over to kiss her mom on the cheek. "Hello to you too, Mother."

"See," said EJ. "Alex is the surprise! And she's going to stay with me all night!"

Nadine furrowed her brow. "Is that right? Where is Glinda?"

"Daddy Ed sent her home early," Alex explained. "He called me and said I should spend the weekend with my little brother so the two of you can have some quality time. He even had Chef prepare all of

EJ's favorites for our sibling sleepover tonight. He's gonna be in a pizza coma for sure."

Nadine's heart squeezed. Eddie really had thought of everything. "Oh, really?"

"Yep. He told me to tell you to hurry up and be ready in…" Alex looked at her watch. "Shoot, you got about an hour before the car service comes. He's upstairs getting ready."

"Oh, shoot!" Nadine kissed EJ on the temple before putting him down. "Let me hurry and get ready then.

Nadine walked upstairs into her master bedroom. She called out for Eddie and ultimately found him in his closet. Nadine nearly drooled as she looked at him dressed in all black, his button down slightly open revealing his still toned chest adorned with a platinum and diamond chain. His slacks were tailored within an inch of their life on his long, toned legs.

"Well, you look good."

Eddie bent down to give her a kiss. "And you need to get dressed."

She folded her arms. "Are you going to tell me what this is about? Where are we going?"

Eddie adjusted his cufflinks with a smirk. "Can't a man surprise his woman?"

Nadine was still suspicious, but figured she'd just go along with it. "I guess. So what should I wear?"

"Actually, I picked you out something. It's on your mannequin in your closet. Get dressed, boo." Eddie smacked her ass, sending a spark down her spine. *What's gotten into him?*

Nadine walked into her massive walk-in closet and looked around. When her eyes landed on the mannequin, she froze. It was a dress… *barely.* It was satin with spaghetti straps, fitted in the bodice, with a very high slit. She was sure her ass cheek would be hanging out on the side. Eddie had also picked out a thong, no bra, and black YSL heels. It was definitely out of her comfort zone. Actually, that wasn't true. It was something she would have worn before they got married, when dating was fun and sexy.

Maybe Eddie's trying to get that old thing back…

Quickly, Nadine hopped in the shower, oiled her body, put on some perfume and slipped into the dress and heels. Her ass had swallowed the thong. She hadn't worn a thong in forever, so she had to adjust to the feel again. She decided to just let her naturally curly hair do its thing, running some product on her strands and drying with a diffuser to make her curls pop. As she was putting the finishing touches on her makeup, Eddie walked up behind her, staring at her in the mirror. Nadine took a quick glance up into his deep brown eyes. Something was different. His gaze was much more…*heated.*

"You look delicious, baby."

Nadine blushed. "Good enough to eat?" Honestly, all this build up was making her horny and if they skipped the surprise, she wouldn't be mad. Just the look in Eddie's eyes was making her wet.

Eddie let out a low chuckle. "Maybe later. I'm sure after tonight you'll definitely be on the menu." He bent down and kissed her shoulder. "See you downstairs."

Nadine quickly finished getting ready. When she met Eddie downstairs, he held a massive bouquet of white roses. She smiled, appreciating all of the effort Eddie had gone through already to make tonight special. Whatever this surprise was, she was sure it would be worth it.

"Ya'll have fun night, just don't make another kid," teased Alex, balancing her brother on her hip.

"Make a kid?" asked EJ, looking confused between his sister and parents.

Eddie chuckled. Nadine rolled her eyes. "Really, Alex?" The girl just refused to have a filter, sometimes. She definitely got that honest.

Alex winced. "Dang! Sorry." She tickled her baby brother. "Let's go watch cartoons and eat popcorn, Junior."

Once the kids left the room, Eddie extended his hand to Nadine. "Shall we go, boo?"

Nadine slid her hand inside his large, warm palm. "Absolutely."

❥

AFTER A FORTY-MINUTE RIDE, THE SUV CAME TO AN ABRUPT HALT. Nadine had been distracted by all of Eddie's flirtations to even take note of where they were going. When the driver opened the door, Nadine's eyes adjusted to the gold script on the dark tinted doors of the otherwise nondescript building.

"Secrets, Eddie! Really?" Nadine whispered, turning to her husband beyond annoyed. Had he lost his damn mind?

Eddie took Nadine's hand. She tried to wriggle her fingers free, but he held on tighter. "Deanie, just trust me, ok?"

Nadine was incensed. "So you want us to go in here and fuck other people?"

"Deanie," Eddie slowly exhaled, pinching the bridge of his nose. "Why are you jumping straight to that? Did I say anything about that?"

Nadine swallowed, feeling gravel in her throat. "No, you didn't. But there is only one reason folks come to this place!"

"No, it's not. Consider these baby steps, love." Eddie leaned over, kissing her gently on the cheek. "I wouldn't throw you to the sharks the first night. I don't roll like that."

Nadine raised a brow. "What you mean by "the first night?""

"Baby, you know what I mean! You've gotta trust me. OK?"

Nadine had her reservations, but Eddie was nothing, if not trustworthy. "Alright. But if I get a whiff of some fuck shit, I am out, Eddie."

"Fair enough. Just relax, baby. It's going to be fun. Trust me."

Inside, they were met by a well-dressed concierge at the front desk. To Nadine, he looked like someone's sweet grandfather who slides $20 in your hand at Thanksgiving. He gave them a warm smile before speaking.

"Mr. and Mrs. Moody. Welcome to Secrets. We've received your reservation for tonight. As this is your first time, if you would, please fill out the information and we will escort you back for our special event tonight."

Nadine squinted. *Special event?* If Eddie had her signed up for some kind of orgy thing, she would call an Uber, head home, and call a divorce attorney in the morning. *Baby steps my ass.*

She took the tablet from the concierge and her eyes widened as she scanned the screen. Biographical data. NDAs. STI questions. Financial queries. *What did they want next? A vile of blood?* She filled out her forms quickly. Once they both were done, Eddie slid his Black AMEX over for payment.

"That'll be $10,000. Plus our processing fee."

10k! The fuck. Nadine had to steady herself. Of course, they had it. Eddie had been quite smart with cash post-retirement, not to mention, he now hard a very lucrative D1 coaching salary. Nadine had major investments and had been very wise with her money. She invested every dime of alimony she got from Drew in their divorce settlement. But $10K seemed like an outrageous price to pay to potentially fuck people. She couldn't believe Tatum and Alisa had paid this amount of cash to get freaky. Especially Alisa. Nadine wouldn't call Alisa cheap, just frugal. With her salons and businesses, she was strategic in how she spent money.

I guess horniness makes you do financially wild shit, Nadine thought.

Eddie bent down to whisper in her ear. "It's just money, Deanie. Part of keeping it discreet. Don't trip, boo."

After they finished listening to a litany of rules, the concierge gave them a polite smile. "If you'll follow me, please." He pulled back the heavy black curtain, encouraging The Moodys to follow.

It was hazy in this area of the club. A few random lights shone as Nadine took in her surroundings. The concierge explained the layout. There was a dance floor, seating area, massive buffet on both sides, and a bar that wrapped around the back half of the club.

Nadine thought this was it, but the concierge led them past the bar and through another set of heavy, velvet curtains, down a narrow hallway that opened up into what looked like an intimate theater. It appeared that Secrets was much larger than she imagined. The concierge explained that this part of the club was meant for special events. He did a quick run-down of the other areas that Nadine deduced were for sex, including something called The Dungeon. She wasn't trying to find out what that was tonight.

"Here are your seats. Enjoy the performance," the concierge said, before turning to leave.

Performance?

Eddie held onto Nadine's hand. "Let's sit down and order a drink."

She blew out a breath. "Yeah, I definitely need a drink."

They slid into the half-moon shaped booth, upholstered in plush, green velvet not far from the stage. A small square table was in front of them. As soon as they sat, a shirtless man with locs pinned up in a bun approached the table. Nadine's mouth went dry as she took in the man in front of her. He was gorgeously dark, darker than Eddie. His face was framed with a gorgeous beard. She could smell the beard oil all the way from where she sat. *And the body, my god.* His chest and abs chiseled like a UFC fighter.

"Hello. I'm your personal bartender for tonight. What can I get for you?"

"I'll take a glass of Louis XIII." Eddie responded. "Nadine? What will you have?"

"Ma'am?" the bartender repeated. "Would you like anything?

Nadine hadn't realized she'd been staring. She'd been distracted by her pussy thumping in her thong. "Yeah, can you get me a French 75?"

"With pleasure," the bartender said, a slight smirk on his face as he headed back to the bar.

Nadine could feel Eddie's eyes on her as her own followed their bartender. As soon as he was out of earshot, he asked, "Did you think our bartender was attractive?"

"I guess." Nadine was downplaying her attraction. Lusting after another man in front of her husband was uncalled for. "I'm sorry I was gawking."

Eddie shrugged. "Why are you apologizing? You're married, not blind."

"Still, I shouldn't stare at other men like that. Especially in front of my husband."

"Would you fuck him?"

Nadine's neck nearly broke as she turned toward Eddie. "Why would you ask me that?"

"Because I'm curious." Eddie slid his hand at the split in Nadine's dress.

Nadine's eyes lowered as she watched Eddie's hand move higher and higher. When he got to the edge of her thong, right at the juncture of her thigh, she moaned.

"I asked you a question, Deanie, so answer me, love. I want honesty from you tonight. Would you fuck him?"

"No," she purred, biting her lip. "I wouldn't."

Eddie's finger went past her thigh and grazed her clit. "Really? I think you're lying, baby."

Nadine nearly bucked, the toe of her shoe hitting the edge of the table.

Her husband chuckled, softly. "Your pussy is telling the truth, so why can't you, Nadine? Would you fuck him?"

"Fuck," Nadine dropped her head to her chest. "Ok, yes. Fine. Yes, I would."

Eddie slid his finger out of her panties. "When he comes back, I want you to tell him that."

"What? Why?" Nadine was breathing hard as she stared at Eddie, wide eyed. He stared ahead as if he hadn't had his fingers in her pussy seconds before. Never had he done something like that to her. *What the hell had come over this man?*

The bartender slid their drinks onto the table.

"What's your name?" asked Eddie.

"Malcolm," the handsome bartender answered.

"Malcolm, my wife has something she wants to say to you." Eddie squeezed her thigh, hard, prompting her to speak.

"I'd fuck you," Nadine blurted out.

Malcolm looked up, a slight smile on his face. "Well, I appreciate that, beautiful." His eyes gave Nadine a once over, finally landing on her pushed-up breasts. "Trust me, I'd wear you the fuck out if I wasn't on the clock. With your husband's permission and your consent, of course."

"I'd certainly give it to you. She is beautiful, isn't she?" agreed Eddie, sipping his drink as his hand continued to squeeze.

"That she is," agreed Malcolm. "If you need anything else, please let me know. As for any *other* requests, I get off in about an hour." He winked at Nadine and made his way back to the bar.

Eddie released his hold from Nadine's thigh, picking up his drink. "See how easy that was?"

"Fuck," Nadine exhaled. Her whole body went hot, like molten lava. "Why did you make me do that?"

Eddie put down his cognac. "Because I want you to learn to demand pleasure. Ask for what you want. Say what you want. There is no shame in expressing desire. Ever." He took a finger, tipping Nadine's chin in his direction. "You're such a good girl, Deanie. But it's ok not to be sometimes. Don't do it for me. Do it for yourself. Think you can do that?"

"Yes," Nadine's voice felt so small, unrecognizable.

Eddie gave her a sweet kiss on her lips before letting go of her chin. "There's my good girl."

Fucking hell. That praise shouldn't have shot electricity to her pussy, but it did. She downed her drink, the hint of gin hitting her chest with a slow burn. If this was a preview of the night, she wasn't sure she could handle it. She was probably, no, *definitely,* going to need something stronger.

CHAPTER 7
Hot and Triggered

After upgrading her drink choice to straight Casamigos, Nadine was feeling loose. *Real loose.* She looked over at Eddie, who was more than pleased that she was relaxed. House music pumped through the speakers as the theater filled with more and more couples. She recognized a few people but dare not mention it. She was sure Secrets was probably like *Fight Club* in terms of rules. Cloaked in the relative darkness of their corner, Nadine thanked God that no one could see them.

"So what's supposed to happen?" asked Nadine nervously as she looked around the theater.

Eddie looked at his watch. "Patience, baby. It should be starting soon."

After a few minutes, a tall woman with blonde braids, dressed in a navy body stocking, heels, and nothing else, sauntered onto the stage with a microphone. To say she was stacked would have been an understatement. As the music lowered, a hush fell over the crowd.

"Beautiful people! Welcome to The Exhibition at Secrets. Our exclusive monthly live event meant to take you to sexual heights and unlock your pleasure. Tonight, you'll see scenes play out in front of you. Voyeurism on a higher level. Take note. Maybe it'll inspire you and your play later on..."

Nadine stared at Eddie. "Is this…?" They were about to live out Eddie's fantasy, front and center.

"No judgment," Eddie interrupted, squeezing Nadine's hand. "Remember?"

Reluctantly, Nadine squeezed back. "Ok."

The lights dimmed in the theater, and the curtain raised. The music, some song by PartyNextDoor that Nadine vaguely recognized, pumped through the speakers. On the raised platform was a large circular bed. Nadine watched as a bald plus size woman, dressed only in a lace thong, was led out on a leash by another woman in a red bob wig, heels, and leather corset. *And was that a dildo?* A big, black one that hung to her mid-thigh, harnessed right at her pelvis.

"On the bed, pet!" the woman said, tugging at the leash. "On your knees."

"Yes, mistress." The woman yelled, her large breasts heaving as she positioned herself on the bed, her ass high in the air.

Nadine looked at Eddie out of the corner of her eye. He was enthralled, completely wrapped up in the scene before him. If she was being honest, so was she. The women were beautiful with their round, full bodies and glowing skin. Nadine wished she could be as confident in her skin as they were. It'd been a while since she felt that way.

The woman rubbed the dildo with lube, then, without much warning, thrust into the woman. The moan that she released was so primal, so raw. It made Nadine's nipples stiffen. She grabbed another shot of Casamigos and downed it in record time.

"You, ok?" asked Eddie, a look of concern on his face. "If this is too much…"

Nadine coughed on the tequila as she waved off Eddie's concern. "Yeah. I'm fine… I am…"

As the woman continued to be fucked out of her mind, two men, totally nude, came out onto the stage. One was tall, all sinewy muscle and bronze skin. A diamond nose ring shone brightly, even in the dim light. The other was the epitome of a Mandingo warrior. He was huge, all over, with a dick so big Nadine thought it looked like CGI. Both of their dicks were as hard as concrete as they stroked.

The woman with the strap on, who was now glistening with a soft sheen of sweat under the lights, slowed her strokes. "Open your mouth wide, pet." The woman who was getting fucked did as she was told, completely obedient and compliant. Nadine looked at Eddie, who leaned forward, totally engrossed.

Is this what he wants? Unwavering obedience? Total submission? Nadine wasn't sure she had it in here to do that...not again.

The submissive opened her mouth wide as both men alternated gagging her with their dicks. Saliva and pre-cum dripped down her chin as she moaned in either agony or enjoyment. Nadine couldn't quite tell, but she admittedly liked the sound of it.

After a few languid licks, the men pulled out. The woman kept her mouth open as both men jerked their dicks, shooting cum all over her mouth and face. The stream seemed nonstop, like an aerosol can of whipped cream. One man rubbed the cum all over the woman's face, then she licked his fingers clean.

"Come, pet," the female dom demanded. And the woman did so, as she squirted all over the bed. The dom pulled out, rewarding her submissive with a few kisses, licking up any remnants of cum as the lights on stage slowly went dark and the curtain closed.

Nadine blinked a few times, her brain processing what she just saw. She turned to Eddie, who was staring at her.

"Before you ask, no, I don't expect you to do that." Eddie chuckled.

"But if that's something you want," Nadine began. "I mean, I guess I could."

Eddie rolled his eyes. "Baby, it's no fun if one of us wants it and the other doesn't. It's about mutual satisfaction. Get it out of your head about doing shit just because I'm your husband and I asked. I don't want that."

It's like he'd read her mind...

Nadine nodded, "You're right, babe." Blindly submitting to her husband was what was drilled into her from the time she'd gotten her period. God, her upbringing had really done a number on her. Maybe she needed to look at those exercises from Dr. Flournoy after all.

The emcee came back out with a wicked smile on her face. "I hope you all enjoyed that scene. As we reset for our next scene, we have some special entertainment for you all. We normally don't do this, but we had to pull out the stops for our VIPs. A few dancers from our sister club, Club Titanium, will be here for your viewing pleasure.

After their performance, if you'd like a dance later on tonight, please request one from these ladies. Enjoy."

The curtain pulled back, and the platform was replaced by one with a tall metal pole. Had the pole always been there? Maybe. Nadine wasn't quite sure.

The opening chords of Jhene Aiko's *Pu$$y Fairy* began as five women sauntered out. They were in neon G-string bikinis of various shades, all glowing against their skin. They were all beautiful. Stunning, really. But Nadine's breath was literally taken away when she laid her eyes on the curvaceous, dark-skinned beauty with the low fade in the neon green bikini. Against her skin, it glowed like jade. Everything about her said delectable. Her ass was natural, round and juicy with slight dimples at the top, her thighs were thick and a little cellulite laden. Her titties weren't too big and perky. Nadine could make out the imprint of hard nipples under her top. In her eyes, she was the perfect embodiment of beauty. No, it was more than that. She was a *goddess*.

"She's everything," Nadine said under her breath. She hoped she hadn't said that out loud. To her relief, Eddie was too laser focused on the stage to pay her any attention.

Two women were off to the sides of the stage, dancing and moving. The other three women all climbed the high pole and began spinning and moving. They were incredibly strong, moving their bodies in ways that rivaled a gymnast. Although she didn't frequent the clubs, Nadine thought strippers got a bad rap. This was a skill, an athletic pursuit that was just as taxing on the body as any other sport. Strong, curvy bodies that did amazing feats. In a few moves, the slimmer of the two held on to the pole straight out, and the goddess in the green stood on top of her, spinning around. The other girl, in pink swung upside down near the bottom of the pole.

A few people went up to the stage, throwing money at their feet in appreciation. Nadine rarely carried cash and only had $10 in her clutch. As if reading her mind, Eddie slid her a small stack of $50s.

"Go show your appreciation, Deanie," he smiled.

"Really?" Suddenly, she felt shy. Nadine was *not* a shy person.

Eddie nodded with a smile. "Go on, boo. Make it rain. It'll be fun."

Nadine took the stack of money, her palms sweating. As she made her way toward the stage, the women descended the pole, twerking, dancing and moving on stage with the other women. She was shaking, praying she wouldn't trip in her heels. *Why the fuck am I nervous?* Nadine made it to the edge just as the girl in the green bikini made her way over to her.

"Hey sexy." She smiled at Nadine, and it was like the earth stood still. This woman was the literal sun.

"Uhm…hey." Nadine stood paralyzed for a second, staring up at the woman in front of her. She could smell her. *God, she smelled so good.* Her perfume was like jasmine and cotton candy. Whatever scent she was wearing was making Nadine…*wet?* Yep. That was it. No other word for it. Nadine pressed her thighs together, pretty sure there was a puddle in her crotch. Between this woman and Eddie, she'd ruined her perfectly good thong. The dancer, who was rolling her hips in front of her, followed the movement with her eyes. *Fuck.*

In a panic, Nadine threw the cash, money flying across the stage in all directions, and hurried back to her seat in the booth.

"That was…" Nadine shook her head. "I need a drink."

Eddie signaled for their bartender, instructing him to leave the entire bottle of Casamigos. Nadine double fisted two shots with lime, downing them both in record time.

"Damn Deanie…slow down, boo." Eddie chuckled. "We've got all night."

"You wanted me to get loose," Nadine felt her words slur a bit. She was almost at her threshold for drinking. "So I'm getting loose."

The dancers finished their pole acrobatics and picked up their cash, collecting the cash in large trash bags with help from Secrets' concierge staff. They'd made a killing. Before the dancers headed backstage, Nadine locked eyes with the girl that had her enraptured. The dancer bit her lip and winked. Nadine felt heat crawling up her neck.

Once the stage reset, the show continued with various scenes, most involving men being flogged, teased, or humiliated in some kind of way. It was intriguing, albeit a bit unnerving at times for Nadine. She could admit some scenes were much sexier than others. Some seemed downright scary. Nadine tried to focus, but her mind kept going back to the dancers. *One dancer in particular.*

Eddie, however, was enjoying every bit of the show. He loved the scene with the men tied up, of course. His dick was hard the entire time, as he made no effort to tamper the tent in his pants. At one point, he pulled Nadine's hand to his crotch, placing his hand over hers as he pulsed underneath. She'd never felt him so hard in her life.

Courtesy of the tequila, Nadine was tipsy beyond belief. And a little horny. The music in the theater changed to *Cum Get It* by Tink. Nadine rolled her hips in time to the beat. Eddie enjoyed seeing this side of her. He wrapped his arms around her, glad that she was finally letting go.

She was in her own world, enjoying the music, when a shadow invaded her space and a smell enveloped her. *That familiar, sweet, intoxicating smell.* Nadine felt a lump in her throat as she looked up to meet familiar brown eyes.

"Hey there, gorgeous people. Would you all like a dance?"

Nadine tried to focus her eyes elsewhere. But the woman was so devastatingly beautiful that it was hard not to stare. Her eyes drew Nadine in. There was something about them. Something soft and sweet. Maybe a little...*dangerous*.

Eddie, noticing Nadine's shameless staring, decided to appease his wife's curiosity. He turned to the dancer, "Why don't you dance for my wife, sweetheart?"

"Sure thing," she smiled, then turned to address Nadine. "I'm Zen. What's your name, beauty?"

"Na...Nadine," Nadine stuttered. Was that her name? She didn't know who the hell she was at the moment.

"Well, Nadine. Hubby wants me to dance for you. You want me to dance for you, beautiful?"

All Nadine could do was nod slowly.

Nadine watched as Zen untied her bikini top, putting it on the table. When she stepped out of her panties, Nadine had to bit her lip to quell a moan. The girl was booty-hole naked, as her Grandma would say. Zen had the prettiest pussy she'd ever seen, with fat lips and a little strip of hair. And a barbell piercing at her clit. All Nadine could think about was flicking her tongue over it.

What the fuck was happening? Nadine hadn't eaten pussy in damn near twenty-five years. She hadn't thought about that...*until now.* Maybe it was the liquor. It had to be.

Zen put her hands on Nadine's shoulders and moved closer to her, breasts in her face. They were a perfect handful-size, with deep, dark nipples against a large areola. Nadine tucked in her lips because if Zen's nipples so much as grazed her, she'd explode.

I should get up. Right now.

She felt Eddie's hand on her thigh, silently steadying her.

"You're so pretty," Zen said, her voice husky and raspy. "All this curly hair." She twirled a finger in Nadine's natural curls.

Nadine swallowed roughly. The humming in her body was on a nuclear level. "Thank you. You are too. Pretty, that is."

Zen smiled as she turned her back to Nadine, moving her ass like water in front of her. It was mesmerizing. She bent over and Nadine took in a sharp breath. Fat ass. Tight asshole. Pretty pussy. Glowing, glistening skin. *Jesus, I may not survive this dance. Holy fuck.*

Nadine was in a trance, her nails digging in the velvet sofa as Zen moved in front of her. When she sat her ass on Nadine's lap, grinding, her hands instinctively went to Zen's thighs. *Shit, you aren't supposed to touch them, she thought.* When she tried to move them, Zen tightly held her hands in place.

In a whisper, Zen looked over her shoulder and gave her permission. "Touch me all you want, beautiful. I'm yours right now."

Zen loosened her grip and Nadine's hands felt the smoothness of her thighs, the softness of her skin, the ampleness of her hips. Every curve was worthy of being worshiped, not just touched. Nadine inhaled as she tried to subdue the aching in her core.

"I like how you touch me, beautiful." Zen purred as she turned around.

"I like how you…*everything.*"

Zen smiled, a slight twinkle in her eye as she bent down. Her nose grazed Nadine's, and she inched her lips closer to hers. "I feel like that deserves a thank you."

Before she could utter an objection, Zen pressed her lips against Nadine's. The kiss was soft at first. Sweet, innocent. Until Nadine parted her lips on a gasp, feeling Zen's tongue snake inside her mouth. She sucked and licked, pulling her bottom lip between her teeth. Nadine held on to Zen's hips as she kissed her back with everything she had in her. The exploration was mutually hungry, needy in a way that she hadn't felt in a while. Nadine was two seconds from coming, just from a kiss. She felt it.

She was close…so fucking close.

"Damn, beautiful." Zen smiled against her lips. She moved away slowly, giving Nadine a parting peck before slipping back into her bikini.

Nadine hadn't realized that the music stopped. She was breathing hard and wetter than ever. Eddie slid Zen a wad of $100 bills that she gladly stuck in her G-string.

"Thanks for letting me dance for you, mami."

Nadine watched Zen, her G-string disappearing between her ass as she glided away.

"Fuck, that was hot," Eddie said. "I'm hard as shit right now."

Nadine blinked, coming back to reality. She had forgotten her husband there. A five-minute dance had transported her, turned her brain to mush. *How could I forget Eddie was there? What is wrong with me?*

Guilt began to eat at Nadine, making her nauseated. The tequila was about to make a reappearance. "I….I gotta go to the bathroom." She jumped up from the booth and ran out of the theater.

Down the winding corridor, Nadine finally found the restroom. She pushed open the door, slamming it against the wall. She made a beeline for the stall. Luckily, the vomiting feeling subsided as she took a few breaths. She pulled up her dress and pulled down her panties. Sure enough, she was a wet mess in her thong. *Where did that come from? Actually, she knew exactly where it was coming from.*

What the hell was she thinking? Kissing a stranger? A woman? But goddamn it, it was one of the best kisses she'd ever had in her life.

It wasn't like the kisses I'd had before…

Nadine shook the thought out of her head. She quickly cleaned herself up with several pieces of tissue and made her way out of the stall. She stood at the sink, staring at herself in the mirror, touching her kiss swollen lips, a bit of liquid lipstick smudged just at her cupid's bow.

"You ok, ma'am?"

Nadine hadn't noticed the bathroom attendant handing her a towel. How long had she even been there?

"Thank you." She wet the towel, placing the cool cotton on her cheeks to try and calm herself. With shaky hands, she reapplied her lipstick and fluffed her hair. After a few minutes, Nadine felt like her feet could move. She slipped the attendant the $10 bill tucked in the bottom of her clutch, thankful that it was there.

Nadine exited the bathroom, heading down the dark corridor toward the theater. At least, that's where she thought she was going. The place was like a maze, every twist and turn leading somewhere else. She leaned against the wall, allowing a couple to pass. The man eyed her lasciviously as the woman gave her a slight smile as they turned down another hallway.

Where the fuck am I? Nadine looked around, trying to spot one of the staff or concierge, when a voice, seemingly out of the shadows, stopped her in her tracks.

"You lost, beautiful?"

Nadine turned to see Zen, leaning against a high boy tucked away in a corner. A slight plume of smoke from a vape in the air surrounding her. She was still in her bikini, illuminated against her skin only by the dim lighting of the hallway.

Nadine nodded. "Looks like I am."

Zen stepped forward, closing the space between them. There was a slight smile on her face as her eyes looked Nadine up and down. "You sure? Looks like you may be right where you need to be."

Nadine felt her throat tighten, her pulse beating rapidly under her skin. She felt like a trapped rabbit, and Zen clearly had the gun.

"I...I need to get back to my husband. If you'll excuse me..." Nadine stammered. But her feet would not move.

"What's the rush?" Zen moved a curl out of Nadine's face. "We could have some more fun."

Nadine could hear the faint pulse of music in the background. Blood rushed to her ears, obscuring the sound. It was dizzying.

"My husband..." was all that she could say in response. Zen's finger moved down Nadine's jawline, causing her to shiver as if she had a fever of 104.

A snicker bubbled up from Zen's throat. "That nigga can watch for all I care..."

He'd love that, thought Nadine. But she didn't say that out loud. "I just," Nadine swallowed, her breathing ragged. "I can't."

"Yes you can, pretty thing." Zen's lips pressed a chaste kiss on the underside of Nadine's jaw. "You ain't even gotta do nothing, mami. Shit, you can just let me handle everything."

The thumping between Nadine's thighs seemed to pulse in time with the music. The tightness of her dress wasn't allowing her to squeeze her thighs tighter, to quell the hunger and aching. Her thong was once again a sticky, utterly useless, mess.

Zen had pinned her in with one hand against the wall, next to Nadine's head. The other skimmed her side, making its way down her leg to the split in her dress. When she felt the edge of Zen's nails against her inner thigh, she moaned. Zen gave her a satisfied look.

Nadine's heels felt like toothpicks trying to keep her upright, but she knew, deep down, that this enchantress of a woman wasn't going to let her fall. At least, not onto the floor. *Into her pussy, maybe…*

"You're not letting me go?" Nadine didn't recognize her voice. It was so small, so nervous.

"You know you don't want to go, beautiful." Zen's hands moved inside her thigh, toward that sticky thong. One finger skirted her outer lips, causing Nadine to ball her hands up at her sides. *Fuck.* She wanted to touch Zen. Feel her. Pull her close, but she knew she couldn't. She shouldn't.

A voice called out from the shadows. "Hey Zen, a VIP is asking for a dance. You good?"

Zen moved away from Nadine, licking the finger that was near her pussy. "Coming." She leaned toward Nadine, whispering in her ear. "The theater is toward the left, down the hall, make a right. See you around, beautiful."

Nadine stood there, paralyzed for several minutes. She had to catch her breath and will her body to move. Her brain tried to remember Zen's directions as best she could. Eventually, she found her way back to their booth in the theater, trying her hardest to look normal.

Eddie looked at her, a worried expression on his face. "You ok, Deanie? I was about to come looking for you."

Nadine felt her liquor trying to make its way back up. She held her stomach. "Yeah, I think I drank too much. Can we go?"

Eddie's face was etched with concern. "Are you sure? We still have more of the club we can explore. If you need to take a break, we can even..."

"Yeah," Nadine shook her head, interrupting. "I'm sure, Eddie."

"Ok. I got us a room at the Ritz." Eddie finished the last of his cognac and pulled out a few $100 bills to leave on the table.

He held out his hand to Nadine, who took it. As they walked back to their SUV in silence, she tried to muster up a comforting smile, one that Eddie could find believable. She hoped that it worked.

❧

Nadine lay awake, surrounded by the plush pillows of the Ritz. Eddie's soft, post-coital snores and the hum of the air conditioner were the only sounds in the room.

She replayed the events of the night over and over. It was like the night was a constant highlight reel. She couldn't stop thinking about Zen at every moment. Not even when she was riding Eddie's dick. Not even when he was pounding into her from the back. She imagined his hand being that woman's hands, gripping her hips. His lips being her lips, searing her skin with kisses. She imagined Zen wearing a dildo just like the lady on stage, pounding deep into her pussy. Their mixture of moans belonged to *her*, the woman that had taken up residence in her brain. Eddie declared it was the best sex they ever had. She didn't have the heart to tell him it wasn't totally because of him.

With sleep evading her, Nadine reached over on the nightstand for her phone. She pulled up the email from Dr. Flournoy, reading the attached documents. She opened the first document on deconstructing faith and sexuality. Words such as "purity culture" and "shame" stood out. Nadine chewed her lip, pondering the words. So much of her life was about being a "good girl", being "pure". She remembers the messages at Sunday school about remaining virginal for your husband. About how her body belonged to her husband, and he was the head, along with God. God...husband...woman...child. In that order. So, when she kissed Allison...when she lusted after her fellow members of the cheerleading squad...when she let her Soror eat her pussy in her dorms after the frat party and blamed it on the alcohol. It was ok, wasn't it? She was still virginal. She was still pure. It wasn't with a man, so it didn't count, right? Like her parents said, she'd grow out of it. *Eventually.* As soon as she had a husband, these feelings would be replaced. The shame would be gone. She'd be a good girl again. *Their good, decent girl… the one her mother loved once.*

"Baby, you awake?"

Nadine place her phone back on the nightstand. "Yeah, just couldn't sleep .Just checking email."

Eddie turned to face Nadine, his fingers lightly stroking her bare shoulders. "What's wrong? Is it about tonight? Listen, if I pushed you too hard out of your comfort zone, then I am sorry. I just…"

"No," Nadine interrupted. "I enjoyed tonight. I did. Truly."

"Are you sure? Because when the dancer kissed you, you sort of freaked out." Eddie chuckled softly. "It's like you saw a ghost or something."

A ghost. A shadow. A fragment of a memory…

Nadine closed her eyes and took a deep breath. "I'm fine. I am."

"Are you telling me the truth?"

"I am sure that kiss was for better tips, that's all," Nadine chuckled nervously. "Eddie, seriously, it's all good." She turned, kissing him on the lips. "Go back to sleep, babe."

"Aiight," Eddie yawned. "But you can be honest with me, baby. Always."

"I know."

Nadine rolled over, squeezing her eyes shut as she tried to command her mind not to replay her time at Secrets. But like a video on pause, the loop restarted.

Nadine's lips tingled from the memory of the kiss. She pressed her thighs together, trying to ease the throbbing of her clit. Eventually, she grabbed a pillow, lodging it between her legs to relieve the pressure.

So much for honesty.

CHAPTER 8

Holding It In

Nadine stared at her computer screen, numbers starting to bleed into each other. The PharmaDigital acquisition of DigiCo was seeming to be going smoothly. Except the numbers. Nadine couldn't make heads or tails of the discrepancies between last quarter's sales and the previous ones. Something felt off, but she just couldn't put her finger on it. Math was never her thing, and she often relied on her forensic accountants for that kind of stuff. But there was too much riding on this. Like her reputation. She was the one who convinced the board that this merger was going to be lucrative. But now, the numbers were seeming very fuzzy. It was as if someone wanted to hide something. Nadine just wasn't sure what it was.

Work, for the past week, had become a pleasant distraction from things. After their weekend, Nadine had shut down, retreating into herself. Eddie tried to ask her a million times what was wrong and eventually gave up. Nadine didn't know how to even tell him how she felt. Each time she tried, her throat felt like it was on fire, closing in on her.

It shouldn't be this hard to tell the man you love the truth.

A knock on the door from Nadine's assistant, Devi, interrupted her thoughts.

"What is it, Devi?"

"I take it you haven't seen the email from the building manager."

Nadine raised a brow. "What email?" She closed her current document and went to her email. There, in bold letters, was an urgent notification from the building manager. Scanning the email, Nadine let out a sigh.

"Three weeks? Over an HVAC issue?"

Devi nodded. "Right. They're encouraging us to work from home until the issue is resolved. Three weeks is a conservative estimate. It could be longer."

Nadine scratched her head. "It's fine. Move all my meetings to Zoom or Teams. Let the folks at DigiCo know. Make sure Mitchell gets the invite." It wasn't ideal, but the building issue did give Nadine an excuse to be home to meet Glinda's replacement from the agency. They would be coming in the morning, and Nadine could be there to greet them, give them the lay of the land and the rundown of all of their schedules. Sure, the agency probably filled them in on most of the details. But the way Nadine's type-A personality was set up, she still wanted to integrate this new person to the way she liked things done. This morning, she'd given Glinda a big hug, wishing her sister a speedy recovery and to keep in touch. She'd slipped $10K in an envelope into Glinda's purse, knowing the woman would be too proud to take it. Glinda was the closest thing that EJ had to a grandmother, especially since her mother had died and they'd been long estranged when EJ was born. Then again, when Grace Davis was alive, she could be hardly classified as a doting grandmother.

Nadine stared at the photo of her family at her wedding on her bureau. Her mother had a scowl on her face, disapproving of her daughter marrying a "worldly athlete" who didn't go to church and had her and her grandbaby "living in sin". Living in sin was a stretch, given that she'd only moved in with Eddie about six months before the wedding. Nadine thought her mother would be happy that she got married, finding a wonderful father figure for Alex. But no choice she made was ever good enough for her mother.

"Don't run this one away like you did the last one," Grace had said on her wedding day, staring at Nadine as she stood there in her Vera Wang wedding gown.

"You must have forgotten I didn't run Drew away. He thought he could beat me and cheat on me! You wanted me to stay with a man that hit me! My own Daddy never laid a hand on me!"

Grace frowned. "You just never learned how to forgive! Drew was a Christian man from a good Christian home. Surely, he was sorry and repented for his sins. God forgives Deanie."

"Yeah, well, I don't. And you don't either."

"And what does that mean, Nadine Paulette?"

Nadine wanted to say more. Remind her mother that she'd treated her like a sinner and a mistake ever since she was a kid. But she said nothing. She adjusted her veil and picked up her bouquet. "Nothing. I'm going to marry the man I love, Mama. I don't need your approval."

Nadine's thought was interrupted by her cell phone buzzing. It was a text in her group chat from Alisa and Tatum. Nadine smiled, thankful for the interruption.

Alisa: I am officially over being on house arrest. Ya'll come break me out!

Tatum: It's bedrest, girl, not house arrest. You have a chef, a nurse and two doting husbands. Why are you complaining?

Nadine: Yeah you need to enjoy this time. Bedrest isn't fun. Trust me, I know. Would you rather be on your feet doing hair all big and pregnant?

Alisa: I mean, kind of. I miss work. I miss being in the shop with Shaunetta and Ritchie talking shit. I miss running my businesses.

Tatum: Tresses is doing great! No need for you to worry. Shaunetta and Richie are amazing managers. Allen is handling the barbering. They have it all under control.

Alisa: Still, I'm bored. All I do is watch TV. Kadeem and Chris won't even give me any dick.

Tatum: Unless you want those babies to come early, then I suggest you chill on the dick.

Alisa: But it's so good though. They can eat my coochie at least, right?

Tatum: Sometimes I wonder if we're related.

Alisa: Bitch me asking that is a clear indication that we are related.

Tatum: True. LOL

Nadine had to shake her head. Those two were ridiculous.

Nadine: Lis!! C'mon now! Can't you wait until the babies come? I mean at least another 8 weeks

Alisa: 8 weeks! 8 weeks without dick!

Nadine: Plus the standard 6 weeks post delivery

Alisa: Oh my god! You're fucking kidding me!

Tatum: You'll survive, you freak. LOL

Nadine: Says the woman who has three gorgeous men on rotation.

Alisa: Word, Deanie! She got a lot of nerve!

Tatum: Whatever. I got a meeting. TTYL.

Nadine stared at the phone. *What the hell was that about?* Tatum was moving really strange these days, and it was unnerving. Nadine winced because that was really hypocritical of her to think given her own issues. Before Nadine could respond, Alisa was calling her on FaceTime.

"What the hell was that about?" asked Alisa, as she munched on a carrot, frowning. Alisa hated carrots, no doubt, forced to eat them by her Daddy-Zillas. They were too controlling when it came to those babies. It was kind of cute, actually.

Nadine shrugged. "Tatum is being really weird when we ask her about the fellas. Have you heard anything? I mean, she would have told us if they broke up."

"I mean, now that Christophe is working at the firm with Miles, you'd think I'd get some kind of tea. Christophe isn't one for gossip, so he hasn't said shit. He's no fun. But something is up. Do you think she's unhappy? Is it about Frankie?"

"Maybe," Nadine shrugged. "Grief can come in waves and at any time. That could be the issue."

Alisa crunched on her carrot. "Well, I'm going to try and press Christophe. Even if I have to suck his dick."

Nadine shook her head. "You were gonna do that anyway."

"You're right. I was." Alisa chuckled. "And how are you?"

Nadine shrugged. "I'm fine I guess."

Alisa raised a brow. "I can tell in your voice you're lying too. What is wrong with y'all?"

Nadine didn't feel like this was the time or the place to get into the shit show that was her life. "Now isn't the time, Alisa."

"Fine. But you and Tate holding on to shit isn't healthy!" Alisa looked past her phone. "I gotta go anyway. I can hear the prison wardens coming now. Well, one of them."

"I done told you about calling me a warden!" yelled Kadeem in the background. "You better not be out of bed, Alisa! You know better, sweetness."

"What are you gonna do? Spank me?" The twinkle in Alisa's eyes told Nadine that her friend was definitely up for it.

"You would like that, with your bratty ass." Kadeem retorted. "Get back in bed Mrs. Bishop-Miller!"

Alisa rolled her eyes as she whispered into the phone. "See what I mean? Prison warden! Gotta go, boo. And listen, whatever it is, it'll be ok."

Nadine gave a faint smile. "I hope so."

CHAPTER 9
New Nanny, New Feelings

Nadine knelt down, straightening the collar on EJ's school uniform.

"Mommy! Why do you keep doing that?" he whined.

Nadine smiled. "Don't you want to look nice for your new nanny? We want to make a good impression, don't we?"

"New Nanny? Mama Glinda isn't going to take me to school?"

"No baby. Remember, she's in Florida taking care of her sister."

EJ looked up with sad eyes. "So she's not coming back?"

Nadine cupped EJ's chubby cheek. "No, baby. She's not."

It had been forever since Nadine had been home early enough to get EJ ready for school. She usually left before the sun rose to get an early start in the office. Since she was working from home, this morning was a rare treat. She enjoyed fixing his snacks, pressing his pants, and brushing his wild little curls into place. It made her feel less guilty about working so much, even if for a brief moment.

Eddie lumbered down the steps, dressed in slacks and a university polo. "Hey baby." He kissed Nadine on the cheek and tickled EJ until he was giggling. "I see you're up bright and early."

Nadine watched as he grabbed his messenger bag and keys. "Wait. You aren't going to stay and meet the new nanny?"

Nadine had gotten a thorough dossier from the agency. The new nanny, Zaire Baxter, seemed legit. She was twenty-six, a graduate student with an undergrad degree in early childhood education and had been a nanny for several years. She had glowing recommendations from previous employers, some stating that they wished she hadn't moved away for school. She was brand new to the agency, so her picture wasn't in their database yet. Her resume impressed Nadine enough for her to move forward with the selection. Besides, EJ probably needed someone with some youthful energy to keep up with him. Glinda was great, but EJ was indeed a handful.

"I'm sorry, babe. I got an early meeting with the athletic director today. It's mandatory. We're working on the budget for next year. Text me in case it's urgent or she doesn't work out." Eddie pressed another kiss to Nadine's temple and headed toward the garage.

Nadine sighed, turning to EJ. "I guess it's just me and you, kiddo. What do you think about pancakes and sausage for breakfast?"

EJ smiled. "Can I have waffles? And two sausages?"

"Absolutely!" Nadine picked up EJ and placed him on the barstool at the island. "Coming right up, Mister Moody!" Calling him "mister" always made EJ giggle.

Nadine moved around the kitchen, cooking up waffles and sausage for her little one and making a simple bowl of oats for herself. Nadine enjoyed actually taking her time for once, not rushing to scarf down a bagel and coffee to head out the door. As she and EJ finished their breakfasts, her front gate intercom buzzed, alerting her that the nanny was there.

"Hello?" Nadine answered, looking at the small monitor in the foyer. A small black sedan was parked outside the gate. She could only make out the top of the woman's head.

"Hi. Mrs. Moody? I'm Zaire. Zaire Baxter from the agency." A raspy voice said through the intercom.

"Yes. I'll buzz you in. Just park on the left side of the garage."

"Alright."

Nadine straightened out her casual Spanx loungewear set, smoothed back her ponytail, and quickly wiped EJ's syrupy face, much to his protest. Once the doorbell rang, Nadine grabbed EJ's hand and quickly walked down the marble laden hallway to the massive doors to meet Zaire.

When Nadine opened the door, her smile nearly dropped to the pit of her stomach. Standing on her front porch was the woman who had been haunting her dreams for the past few weeks.

Zen.

Nadine blinked a few times to be sure her eyes weren't playing tricks on her. No, it was definitely her, less makeup and toned down, but certainly her. Same dark, supple skin. Same gorgeously faded hair. She was a vision, standing there in a simple black tee, jeans that seemed poured on her, and Vans. *No way on earth that Zen is standing here in my doorway.*

When she felt EJ tug on her hand, Nadine snapped out of her thoughts.

"Hi. Hello. I'm Nadine. Nadine Davis Moody. Mrs. Moody." Nadine was a rambling mess.

"Hi. I'm Zaire." The woman, who appeared much younger without the sparkles or moody lighting, gave Nadine a panty wetting smile. She extended her hand, fingernails painted bright green. Hesitantly, Nadine took it and shook softly. *Jesus, her skin was still as soft as butter.* Nadine quickly removed her hand. She didn't need to embarrass herself further.

Zaire looked down at the little figure next to Nadine. "And this must be little EJ?"

EJ hid slightly behind his mother. Nadine looked down, shaking her head with a smile. "Sorry, he's a little shy. It's a big change for him."

Nadine watched as Zaire got down on one knee, eye level with EJ. "Well, EJ, this is a big change for me too. You're a new little boy I have to get to know. But I love making new friends. Especially ones that love Bluey."

Nadine smiled. Zaire had definitely read up on all the notes that Glinda left for her it seemed.

EJ gasped. "You like Bluey!"

"I *love* Bluey!" exclaimed Zaire. "So, I think we can start with that, can't we?"

EJ quickly shook his head, finally easing out of his mother's shadow. "Yes! Mommy, can I show Miss Zay-yay my Bluey toys?"

"EJ, it's Zaire," Nadine corrected, softly. "And maybe later, ok? We've got to get you to school."

Nadine looked up at Zaire, finding the woman smiling right at her. She couldn't help but smile back. *Damn, she was beautiful.*

Zaire moved her gaze back to EJ. "I know that's hard to say, but you can call me Miss Z. Since we're gonna be friends, ok?" She stuck out her hand and the pudgy little boy took it, shaking it like a big boy.

"Mrs. Moody?" the woman furrowed her brow. "Is everything ok?"

Nadine hadn't realized she was still staring. What had gotten into her? "Ah, yes. Can't have you standing out here the whole time. Follow me!" Nadine quickly ushered Zaire through the foyer. "I'll give you a quick tour. If you want, you can take your shoes off here and put them in the holder. In the future, you can come in through the garage. We have a mudroom to put your shoes. Glinda would keep slippers here, so you're free to do the same."

Nadine tried to put on some air of authority as the woman of the house, but internally, she knew she was failing miserably. She felt nervous, her pits sweating and her hands shaky. As she gave Zen a tour of the home, Nadine tried her best not to squeeze her son's hand to death. She could feel the boy squirming under her touch.

"And this is the spare bedroom," Nadine said as she opened the door, allowing Zaire to look around. "In the event, we may need you to stay overnight or something. You're welcome to bring anything you need to make yourself comfortable."

Nadine watched as Zaire looked around, her hands gliding up and down the linen on the bed. For a quick second, Nadine had a visual of Zen spread across her bedding, legs open, pussy dripping. Nadine shook her head. *Get it the fuck together, Deanie.*

"This is lovely, Mrs. Moody." Zaire nodded, her fingers fiddling with the scalloped edge of the comforter. "You have amazing taste."

Nadine watched, never wanting to be a duvet cover so badly. She smiled. "Thank you."

Zaire's eyes lingered on Nadine, brazenly moving down her body. "Seems like that's with everything, huh?"

Nadine swallowed, her breath caught in her throat. "I...I think we better get going. We'll take my car so you can familiarize yourself with drop off and pick up. It can be a beast at times."

"Sure thing, Mrs. Moody."

After buckling EJ into his car seat, Nadine opened the car door for Zaire. Nadine wasn't sure why she did that. But part of her just wanted to watch her slide that incredible ass across her leather seats.

"Thank you, Mrs. Moody." Zaire smiled as she slid into her seat.

"Of course." Nadine swiftly moved around to the driver's side and buckled herself in.

"Can I listen to the Sesame Street show?" asked EJ

"Absolutely, Junior!" Nadine said, way more enthusiastically than she should have. She usually hated listening to the Sesame Street podcast in the car but was entirely grateful for the distraction. Anything to take her mind off the fact that this fine woman was in her passenger seat. A woman she kissed weeks ago. The thought made her pussy hum like the engine of her car.

As she drove, Nadine peered at Zaire out of the corner of her eye. She was looking around, seeming to take in her surroundings, and putting notes in her phone. She wasn't paying attention to Nadine stealing glances of her profile. At least, she hoped she hadn't noticed. Full, glossy lips. High cheekbones. A barbell piercing in the helix of her ear. Nadine remembered the piercing she saw on her clit at the club. The thought made her salivate a little. She had to clear her throat.

Nadine pulled into the drop-off line at the posh Westmore School, just one of several luxury vehicles full of some of Atlanta's most privileged children from some of its wealthiest families. This hadn't been Nadine's first choice. She wanted EJ to go to a small Montessori school in the neighborhood, but the other athletes and coaches' wives insisted that it was the best place for kids "in their position". She was paying a fortune just for EJ to go to Pre-K for half a day. So she enrolled EJ, not wanting to seem ungrateful for the recommendation. She was always one to go with the flow.

When Nadine pulled up, she could see the other mother's eyes widen. She groaned at the sight of them in their Lululemon, holding their designer lattes as they plastered on the fakest of smiles. She braced herself for the barrage of questions from the stay-at-home moms who volunteered during morning drop-off or served on the PTA. Nadine was one of few women who had full time jobs. They rarely saw her. Instead, she'd relegated these duties to her nanny.

When it was their turn to drop EJ off, a perky, blonde woman came rushing to the car.

"Oh god, is that Nadine Moody? Oh my! I haven't seen you in ages!" said Ingrid Harrison, president of the PTA, her perfectly capped teeth showing. "When was the last time? The Christmas fundraiser, right? You're just always so busy, miss executive! That job at Pharma-Digital must be running you ragged."

Nadine knew there was going to be some jab about her not being seen at the school. "Hi, Ingrid. I know. I'm only here showing my new nanny, Zaire, the route."

"Oh, I was wondering where Glinda was," said Ingrid, invasively peering into the car. She turned to Zaire, extending her hand. "Hi, I'm Ingrid Harrison, PTA president."

"Nice to meet you, Mrs. Harrison. I'm Zaire," said Zaire, politely taking the woman's hand.

"Oh, she's so polite! And gorgeous! Oh Nadine, you better be careful having her around Eddie! We don't need another Sheila and Mercer scandal. Then again, Sheila did take him for half," the woman awkwardly laughed.

Nadine frowned. Ingrid was an incessant gossip, and Nadine couldn't fucking stand it. She wished the chick would mind her business. Before she could snap on Ingrid, Zaire replied. "Mrs. Moody has nothing to worry about in that department. Trust me."

Zaire's tone had a touch of annoyance and, dare Nadine say, slight aggression. A look of consternation spread across Ingrid's reddening face. Nadine smirked, pleased.

"Oh well, it was just a joke, hun. No need to get all serious. Anyway, let's get cute, little EJ out this car shall we!" Ingrid moved to open the car door.

When EJ was unbuckled from his car seat, he quickly leaned over, kissing his mom on the cheek. "Bye Mom! Bye Ms. Z!" he shouted, grabbing his book bag and lunch box.

"Remember, Miss Z is coming to pick you up this afternoon!" Nadine called out before Ingrid slammed her car door. *On purpose, no doubt.*

"I take it these aren't your friends?" asked Zaire, smiling at Nadine.

"Absolutely fucking not," Nadine said, pulling out of the school's circular driveway, heading toward the parking lot. "Sorry. Pardon my language."

Zaire chuckled. "It's cool, Mrs. Moody."

"And please, call me Nadine," Nadine corrected as she parked the car. Funny, she hadn't objected to Glinda calling her Mrs. Moody and Glinda was old enough to be her mother. But with Zaire, it just felt weird. It made her feel old. And she didn't want to seem *that* old to her.

Zaire turned, looking at her. "Nadine it is, then."

Nadine gave a warm smile. "Cool. Let's go inside. We'll fill out all the necessary paperwork for you to handle pickup and drop off. Then we'll be on our way. It shouldn't take too long."

After the necessary administrative task at EJ's school, Nadine pulled out of the parking lot like a speed demon. What should have taken twenty minutes turned into an hour-long ordeal, courtesy of Ingrid's nosy ass insisting on giving Zaire a tour of the school. To Zaire's credit, she skillfully avoided any personal questions which impressed Nadine. It was apparent that she wasn't new to dealing with moms like this. A definite plus for Zaire.

During the ride home, Zaire's scent was drawing Nadine in. She tried hard to focus on the road, but the softly sweet perfume was making her pulse race. When she finally pulled into her garage and made her way through the mudroom, Nadine felt a sigh of relief. She couldn't get out of the car fast enough as Zaire trailed behind her, trying to catch up.

In an attempt to focus, Nadine pulled up her phone, rattling off information. "I'll be giving you a key and the codes. The Audi SUV is at your disposal to drop off and pick up EJ, take him to his after-school activities, Karate on Tuesdays and Thursdays; swimming on Mondays and Fridays, you'll have to run a few errands if you don't mind. You'll be responsible for his breakfast and snacks, and…"

"Nadine," Zaire interrupted.

Nadine ignored her, continuing to rattle off things from her phone.

"After school, Glinda encouraged a lot of learning-based play, which is great. We just ask that you tidy up anything. EJ can be a tornado of messiness. I end work at about six or so, so I'd appreciate it if EJ had a bath after dinner. Bedtime is at seven. He really likes bedtime stories like…"

"Nadine," Zaire interrupted, again. "Are we really going to do this?"

"I'm sorry? Do what?" Nadine tapped away on her phone, not looking up. She was trying her best to ignore every thought she was having, and she couldn't face her.

Zaire came around the island, facing Nadine. She wrapped her hand around the phone, delicately taking it out of her grasp. Nadine's heart raced as the space between them grew smaller.

"Pretend that you and I haven't met before. Under different circumstances."

Nadine swallowed. She tried to move back, but Zaire gently grabbed her wrist, her thumb stroking softly. Nadine looked down at Zaire's perfectly manicured fingers, nails painted green. Her dark skin was a stark contrast against the creamy butterscotch tone of Nadine's. She tried to ignore the pulse in her wrist that was thumping double time.

"I mean, surely you don't think I could forget you. I never forget a pretty face." Zaire's eyes moved down Nadine's face, finally landing on her lips. The action made Nadine's nipples hard as hell under her shirt. If they got any harder, they'd poke a hole through the knit fabric.

"I…I think you're mistaken," Nadine chuckled uncomfortably, finally moving out of Zaire's grasp, her wrist still feeling warm from her touch.

"No mistake about it. I'd recognize you *anywhere*."

Nadine nibbled at the corners of her lips. Her poker face wasn't as good as she thought. The tingling twitch in her lips was telling on her. She thought she was doing a good job of acting like she didn't know Zaire, pretending that the night between them didn't exist.

Zaire sighed. "Listen, I know how to remain professional. I have five years' experience as a nanny. I'm here to take care of EJ…and anything else you may need. I'm here for you. I just wanted to get that out of the way. That's all."

It was the way that she said *anything* and *you* that made Nadine wet in the seat of her panties. Or maybe she was hearing things. *This was a bad idea. Seriously bad.*

Nadine wanted to say no, to tell Zaire to leave, that she'll find a new nanny. Hell, she could move meetings and things around at work and try to handle it all. Nadine didn't need the distraction that was Zaire Baxter in her life. Not right now. Her head was already screwed up enough.

"Listen," Zaire began. "If this is going to be awkward for you, you can find someone else from the agency. Other than now, I promise not to bring it up anymore. I swear…"

"Trust me, it won't," interrupted Nadine, holding her hands up. "Besides, I already know the agency has very few available nannies with your qualifications."

"Are you sure?"

Nadine looked at Zaire. Her face was etched in worry. That was the truth. The agency did tell her that they had very few nannies on standby. Getting Zaire on such short notice was a miracle in itself. Nadine could try to keep it together. Of course she could. This adjustment would only be for a few weeks until she headed back into the office. Her schedule would limit her interactions with her anyway. *At least, she hoped.*

"Absolutely." Nadine finally responded.

"I promise you have my utmost discretion." Zaire sighed, her shoulders finally relaxing. "Besides, I really need this job! "

Nadine gave a small smile. "Alright. In the meantime, I'll email you the schedule and any other information. If you have any questions, I'll be in my office working. It's right down the hall."

"Oh? You aren't going into the office?" asked Zaire.

"No. Unfortunately our building is having an HVAC issue that is extensive. So I'll be working from home for the next few weeks. It's temporary. "

"Oh, I see. I'll promise to be out of your way."

"I doubt you'd be in my way."

There was an awkward beat of silence between them. Nadine eventually began to move her feet, gathering her phone and moving to the other side of the island. "Well, again. My office is down the hall."

Zaire nodded. "Ok. Let me get started on the breakfast dishes while you work. If you need anything, let me know."

Nadine thought that maybe she sensed a bit of unease in Zaire's voice, but brushed it off, preparing to head into her office. Before she turned the corner, she pivoted back to the kitchen. "The agency said you're in grad school. What are you studying?"

Zaire gave a wide smile. "Oh, I'm getting my PhD in child psychology from Emory."

Well, fuck me. Another therapist.

Nadine plastered on a smile. "That's…great. Feel free to study or whatever during your down time. If you'll excuse me, I have a meeting."

Nadine power walked down the hall and sat at her desk in the office, staring at her computer. *Fuck. Fuck. Fuck.* This had the makings of a disaster if she ever saw one. She felt trapped and would be for at least three weeks with a woman nearly half her fucking age. Just that alone should have told Nadine's brain to shut off whatever thoughts she was having, but it wouldn't. How the hell was she going to keep her cool? Being in close proximity had Nadine so flustered. And Eddie.. *Fuck… Eddie.* What is he going to think?

"Nadine, you there?" Mitchell's nasally voice asked, interrupting her thoughts.

Shit. Nadine hadn't realized that her meeting had already started. She'd been staring off into the distance, on mute.

"Sorry Mitchell, I forgot I was on mute. Can you give me a summary of the meeting with DigiCo? Any explanation of the discrepancies?"

Mitchell rolled his eyes as he looked back down at his paper. "As I was saying…"

This asshole. Nadine put herself back on mute and shook her head. She tried her best to concentrate for the rest of the meeting, but it was difficult. She could hear Zaire moving around the house. Flitting like a butterfly in her orbit.

Nadine had to make it through the next three weeks. Three weeks and she'd be back in the office. In the meantime, Eddie knowing who Zaire was would probably put shit into a serious tailspin. What would he think? Would he ask her to quit? Would he even care? For now, she prayed that he wouldn't know. He couldn't.

Maybe Glinda would come back, and life could return to normal. At least that's what Nadine hoped. Given the state of Glinda's sister's health, that wish was far-fetched.

But was that what she wanted?

CHAPTER 10

Cookies

Nadine had very few vices. She loved her mimosas, no doubt. And she could run up a bag at the shops in Phipps Plaza. But when she was truly stressed, she baked. It had been a source of comfort since she was a child. If she was sad, she baked. If she got a bad grade, she baked. If her mother pissed her off, which was often, she baked. Her father often joked that she was part Keebler elf, eager to be her taste tester. Her mother just fussed that it would make her fat, and she was wasting her flour and sugar. The truth was that her mother was kind of jealous that she was a better baker than she was. It was the one thing that she always got right.

After her last meeting of the day and hours of pouring over reports, she needed to do something to expel the anxiety and stress that she felt. She'd tried her best to work, but knowing Zaire was in the house was making her pressure rise and her pussy wet. *Incredibly wet.*

It was shortly after 5 pm and Nadine could hear EJ and Zaire playing in the great room. By the sounds of things, it was going great. She'd never heard EJ giggle as much as he had with Zaire. Pick up had occurred without a hitch and the rest of the afternoon seemed to run smoothly. Zaire definitely heeded all her notes and stuck to the schedule, down to the timing and portion of snacks.

The smell of double chocolate chip cookies engulfed the kitchen.

Nadine pulled out the last batch, placing it on the cooling rack. She made her way back to her pantry to find her fleur de sel to sprinkle on top of her cookies before they cooled. It was the secret ingredient that made them so good. As she peered through the shelves, looking for the salt, a voice interrupted her search, nearly making her topple over.

"It smells amazing in here."

Nadine turned to find Zaire leaning against the doorframe. The pantry was massive, but suddenly, it felt entirely too damn small.

"Thanks. You're welcome to take a few."

"Oh, I'm good."

"Don't tell me you're on a diet. I mean, not that you need it." Nadine blurted out. She closed her eyes, regretting what she said. "Sorry."

"Thank you," Zaire chuckled. "No diet. I'm allergic to chocolate."

"Oh," Nadine breathed, relieved that she hadn't offended her. "That's too bad."

"I mean, if you bake something without chocolate next time, I'll surely have a taste."

Nadine had to quickly expel the thought of Zaire having a "taste" out of her psyche. "I'll keep that in mind."

Nadine almost forgot the salt and quickly grabbed it. As she tried to exit the pantry, Zaire stopped in front of her. Nadine watched as her tongue, adorned with a piercing, darted out, and licked the pad of her thumb. That same thumb traced a path dangerously close to Nadine's lips, moving slowly down to her chin.

"You had a little flour on your chin. Sorry, force of habit."

Nadine swallowed hard, her grip tightening on the jar in her hand. "Th...thanks."

"My pleasure. Can I take EJ a cookie? I know it's not a designated snack time, but he's been really good."

Nadine nodded her approval wordlessly. She watched Zaire's ass, ample and plump in her jeans, make its way back to the great room, a plate of cookies in hand.

"*Jesus Christ...*" Nadine whispered to herself. If she couldn't last the first day, three weeks was going to be fucking impossible.

Maybe she'd pour herself a mimosa after all.

The rest of the evening was a blur. Nadine stole glances of Zaire here and there as she played with EJ. She'd pretend to be looking at her phone or tablet if she felt she was staring a bit too long. It was entirely childish; she realized. It felt like fucking stalker ass behavior. For the most part, Nadine kept her cool, being as professional as possible. After going through EJ's bedtime routine, Zaire called it a night. Her first day was in the books.

"Hey, Nadine."

Nadine sat at the kitchen counter, nursing a glass of cabernet. She wasn't a cab girl, but it went well with the cookies. "Hey. Hope your first day with EJ wasn't too terrible."

"Of course not. He's an angel."

"Ha," Nadine laughed. "You ain't gotta lie, but I appreciate it."

"I definitely wouldn't lie. He's just as sweet as his mother. By the way, you didn't ask, but my day with EJ's mother wasn't so bad either."

Nadine felt herself blushing. *Hard.* "I appreciate that, but you don't know if I'm sweet or not."

"Well, I'm a pretty good judge of character. You know, kind of comes with the job. I wouldn't lie about that."

Nadine nodded. "I get that. See you tomorrow, then."

"See you tomorrow, Cookie." Zaire gave Nadine a wink and headed toward the garage.

Cookie?

Nadine sat at the counter, paralyzed. *Was she...flirting...with me?* She wasn't sure how long she was standing there until the sound of Zaire's car pulling out the driveway pulled her out of a daze. She was pretty sure that interaction was real and not a made-up scenario in her head, like all the scenarios had been in the weeks since Secrets. Nadine took the rest of the cab and downed it straight from the bottle.

By the time Eddie had come home, Nadine had polished off two bottles of Cab and five double chocolate chip cookies. He walked into the kitchen, finding his wife slumped over at the counter.

"Damn. Two bottles of cab and you baked double chocolate chip cookies? Your day must have been pretty shitty."

Nadine lifted her head, sighing. "I wouldn't say it was shitty, just... interesting."

Eddie put his bag down and sat at the counter. "I take it the nanny didn't work out."

At the mention of Zaire, Nadine's body heated. She hoped Eddie couldn't see her pressing her thighs together. "She's fine. A little young, but fine. EJ really likes her."

Eddie raised a brow. "Just fine? Fine isn't good enough for you, Deanie. Tell me what's up for real."

"I don't know if it's going to work out with her."

"Why?"

"She's just..." Nadine struggled to find the words as she twirled the wine glass in her hand. "She's just different from Glinda."

"But the agency said she was good, right?"

"Yeah, and there are no other last-minute replacements. Getting her was a God-send in the first place. But..."

"But what?" interrupted Eddie. "What is the real issue?"

Nadine stared at Eddie. She wanted to tell the truth. She really wanted to, but she just couldn't. "I just think I'm not used to change. It's just making me anxious."

"I know, baby. Have you talked to Dr. Flournoy about this? Change can be stressful."

Nadine rolled her eyes at the mention of her therapist. She still remembered her insistence that she talk to Eddie about her feelings and the emails with homework. "No. But at our last session, she suggested you come to therapy with me."

Eddie's eyes widened as he took a cookie from the domed cake stand. "Why? Is it something I did?"

Nadine leaned over, kissing her husband on the forehead. "Of course not, babe. It's just she wants me to let you in. Be honest about some things going on with me. That's all. It's...complicated."

Eddie took Nadine's hand, kissing the back of it softly. "I'll go. I'll do whatever you want."

"Really?"

"Of course, Deanie. You're my wife. I'm here for you. I'm your rock and vice versa. Nothing can make me not want to have your back."

Shit, you say that now. Nadine thought. "Ok. I'll let Dr. Flournoy know."

Eddie smiled, biting into a cookie. "In the meantime, give the nanny a chance. You never know, change may be good for you."

Nadine gave Eddie a wry smile. "Maybe." She tried to get up and wobbled a bit. She was fucked up. *In more ways than one.*

"Whoa, baby." Eddie took Nadine's hand. "Let's head to bed, love."

CHAPTER 11

Diving In

Nadine was on the step stool in her pantry, looking for the Madagascar vanilla. Although she used it all the time, she hid it from herself constantly. Was it behind the brown sugar? The cinnamon? As she stepped down from the stool, she heard the creak of her pantry door closing, and then the snick of it locking.

"Why'd you lock the door?"

Zaire came close to her, smelling like wildflowers and juniper berries. Every spice in Nadine's pantry didn't smell nearly as delicious as Zaire smelled right then.

"You know why, beautiful. Come here." Her short, green nails beckoned her closer, drawing Nadine in like a flashing green traffic light. Her feet were moving on command. She stood in front of the woman. They were nearly the same height, so she could do nothing but stare into her big, brown eyes.

"Do you want me?"

"I want you so badly," Nadine breathed, her hands going to the back of Zaire's neck. Her skin was so soft, so smooth. "So badly it hurts."

"Show me where it hurts. I'll kiss and make it better."

Nadine fisted the hem of her sundress, lifting it to reveal that she was bare. She hadn't worn panties just for this possible occasion. Her pussy was dripping and her arousal mixed with the smell of spices and Zaire.

Zaire dropped to her knees, her hands gripping the back of Nadine's *thighs. She pressed her face against Nadine's pussy and inhaled, making her whole body shake.*

"This should never hurt, baby. Never."

Zaire's tongue took its time, parting her swollen pussy lips, savoring the flavor. The ultimate goal of her perusal being her even more swollen clit. As soon as her tongue swiped against it, Nadine cried out. She lifted her foot, placing it on the edge of a pantry shelf. The only thing she could see was Zaire's heart shaped part in her hair as she tasted her.

"More, Zen…please…I need more."

Another swipe of her tongue and then another. And another. That fucking barbell piercing tapping her over and over until Nadine couldn't take it anymore.

Zaire looked up, face covered in Nadine's juices. "Hmm.. Cum for me, beautiful…cum all over me…"

Nadine held on to the shelves in the pantry for dear life.

"Fuck…fuck…fuuuuccccck!"

Nadine woke up, sweat drenched and her heart beating a mile a minute. She tapped the lamp on her nightstand and downed the glass of water that sat next to it.

This is crazy…I'm losing it. Clearly losing it.

She'd had the same dream, or some iteration of it for the past week. At first, she thought it was a fluke. But they started the night after she and Zaire had the encounter in her pantry. The dreams were becoming progressively dirtier, and Nadine knew it was her subconscious snitching on her. She felt the edge of her nightgown, which was now damp from her pussy, and her clit ached to be touched. Nadine felt terrible. Lusting after a girl old enough to be her…well… *niece?* She couldn't think about her being in the same age group as Alex. This was weird enough.

"Deanie? You ok?"

Eddie turned on the lamp on his nightstand and turned to face Nadine, who was now sitting up in bed, staring at the walls.

"Huh? Yeah. I am fine, babe. Go back to sleep."

Eddie sat up, adjusting his pillows. "You're lying. You've woken up every night for the past few days. Is it a nightmare? Worried about the merger, maybe?"

"No," Nadine sighed. "I mean, I am worried about the merger, but that isn't it. It's…just really disturbing dreams."

"Do you want to talk about it?"

Nadine's eyes widened. "Hell no…I mean….no. It's too embarrassing."

Eddie gave Nadine a slight smirk. "It must have been a really nasty dream. Is it about the mayor? You know, ever since you met him at that fundraiser, I knew you had a thing for him."

"First off, I do not have a crush on the mayor. I just said he was handsome. Secondly, what makes you think that it was a sex dream anyway?"

"Uhm, you have that look. You know, like you came. You're glowing."

Nadine felt her face. It was clearly flushed. "That's sweat and I'm perimenopausal."

Eddie rolled his eyes. "Deanie, you ain't gotta lie. It's nothing to be ashamed about. You know about my fantasies. Why can't I know about yours?"

"Who said anything about shame? Or fantasies? I'm not talking about this with you…just…go to bed."

Eddie sighed, frustrated. "Fine." He roughly pulled the duvet over his shoulders and rolled over.

Nadine waited a few beats and turned off the lamp on her nightstand. An awkward silence now filled the bedroom. She sunk into the covers, willing her brain to chill for the rest of the night so she could face Zaire in the morning. She peered over to look at Eddie. He wasn't asleep. She knew it.

"Are you going to therapy with me Friday?" she asked, softly.

"Do you want me to? Or are you going to not talk then either?"

The sting in Eddie's voice made Nadine wince. "I promise I'll be more forthcoming. It's just…it's hard sometimes to tell the truth."

Eddie turned, facing Nadine. His eyes, barely visible via the soft moonlight in their room, were sympathetic. "The truth can set you free, Nadine."

"That's what Dr. Flournoy said."

"She's an expert. She would know." Eddie leaned over to kiss Nadine's shoulder. "I promise to be there if you promise to be open."

Nadine nodded. "I will. I promise."

"Good. Now please, get some sleep. You don't want to be wired when the nanny comes."

More like Horny.

"Right. Goodnight."

☙

ZAIRE'S FIRST FULL WEEK WAS ENDING. FOR THE MOST PART, IT HAD GONE smoothly. She'd done drop-off and pick up flawlessly. She shuttled EJ to karate and swim classes. She made cute snacks in the shape of animals. EJ was truly smitten with her. Nadine could say the same for herself.

Unless it was about EJ, Nadine tried to avoid Zaire as much as possible, staying holed up in her office, even when she wasn't busy. It was silly, but she didn't know if she could handle being so close to Zaire. One touch, one stare...she wasn't sure what she'd do. It was useless. Because Zaire found a way to just...appear. If Nadine was in the kitchen to get a snack, Zaire was there too. They ran into each other in the laundry room. Zaire even refilled Nadine's coffee cup, placing it on her desk when she wasn't paying attention. Ok, so that was actually quite thoughtful. That wasn't part of her duties at all.

Nadine was on the call with her team, getting the rundown on the negotiations with DigiGo. Things were not going great. DigiCo insisted that their last quarter numbers were accurate, but Nadine wasn't so sure. Something felt off. And she wanted to get to the bottom of it.

"Nadine, we've gone over the numbers with a fine-toothed comb," sighed Mitchell. "What more do you want? We need to be moving forward before DigiCo pulls out altogether."

Nadine pinched the bridge of her nose. "Mitchell, If I say something feels off, it feels off. I am trying to assess our risk here. We could be losing money, not gaining it. It's like you want this to fail."

Mitchell didn't reply, instead decided to defer to Justin. "Back me up here, Justin. What do you think?"

Justin was a VP of marketing and social media. He had nothing to do with numbers. Nadine knew why Mitchell called on him. He just wanted another white guy to back him up. Justin wiped his eyes under his glasses. "I think that's beyond my scope. So I am with Nadine on this. Let's just make sure things are square before we move forward. I trust her expertise."

Nadine could see Mitchell literally fuming, seething through the screen. She couldn't help but gloat a little. *That little troll.* No matter what he did, Mitchell could never knock her off her game.

Nadine turned to her assistant. "Any word on when the HVAC situation will be fixed, Devi?"

Devi sighed. "I hate to report that the situation is worse than expected. Three weeks may be turning into a month. Or two. There are some corroded pipes that's an issue. Then the county has to come inspect. It's a whole thing, according to the building supervisor. As a courtesy, I attached his report. I know this isn't what you wanted to hear."

You've got to be kidding me. A month or two? How the entire hell was she going to deal with working from home for two months...*near Zaire.* Nadine's head was pounding. She looked at the time. It was way before lunchtime, but she could use a break. "Thanks Devi. Actually, let's table the rest of this discussion after the R&D meeting at 3 pm." Nadine logged off the computer and sighed.

"You ok?"

"Shit!" Nadine nearly jumped out her skin as she looked up and saw Zaire at her doorway. Today, she wore sweats slung low at her hips and a crop top with Whitney Houston on it. No matter what she wore, she couldn't hide any of her curves. *Deadly, deadly curves...*

Zaire held up her hands. "Sorry. I didn't mean to scare you. I just noticed that you looked stressed."

"I am," Nadine scratched her head. "A lot of things are not going as planned."

"What do you do to relax?" asked Zaire.

Nadine frowned. "Other than baking? Read. Ok, that's a lie, I haven't read a full novel in years. Uhm, I used to swim in our pool every morning." Nadine actually loved to swim. But lately, she hadn't had time to even stick her toe in the pool.

"So let's do it!"

"Uhm, do what?"

"Take a dip in your pool."

Nadine's eyes widened. "Uhm, I don't have time to take a dip in the pool. I have a meeting in a few hours. My hair will get all jacked up. Besides, me? In a swimsuit right now? I don't think so."

"It's just us. Trust me, your body is fine."

Nadine watched as Zaire's eyes traveled down the length of her body. *I know I'm not crazy. She's checking me out. Fucking hell…*

"Do…do you even have a swimsuit?" stuttered Nadine.

Zaire shrugged. "No. Panties and bra are cool, right? It's just us. Besides, you've got a washer and dryer. C'mon. I'll meet you out there." Before she could object, Zaire had turned the corner, heading for the pool.

Nadine ran upstairs to her bedroom and into her closet in search of a swimsuit. She rifled through the drawer, pulling out tons of swimsuits until she settled on a modest white one piece to don. Nadine took one look in the mirror and groaned. *What the hell was she thinking?* She could see stretch marks, cellulite, and a soft middle. She could also use a bit of a trim on the bikini line. Not to mention, this was crossing so many employee/employer lines. Clearly, she was thinking with her pussy and not her head, because all she could think about was seeing Zaire half naked again.

Nadine grabbed a towel and made her way to the back patio. She had a Junior Olympic size pool that Eddie insisted be heated year-round. Nadine stood at the edge of the pool and just stared.

Zaire's clothes were in a pile on the side, and all she wore was a thin, *very thin*, Savage x Fenty bralette set, which cupped her firm, perky tits. She had areolas so big and nipples so dark that they reminded Nadine of dark chocolate truffles. Zaire was breathtaking, but a *wet* Zaire was intoxicating.

"Are you getting in?" asked Zaire as she floated closer to the stairs. "I had no idea this pool was heated. The water feels amazing."

With trepidation, Nadine made her way down the steps, into the water. The water did feel amazing, instantly easing the tension in her muscles. Slowly, she floated toward Zaire, who glided through the water like a mermaid. With her body wet and glistening, her skin was as gorgeous as dark silk. It was baffling that this woman was so fucking beautiful and walking around in Nadine's world.

"You're right, this is maybe what I needed." Nadine declared, enjoying the feel of the water on her skin.

"See, I told you. I think I know what you need."

Nadine's eyes narrowed on Zaire. "Do you? You barely know me."

Zaire gave a slight smile. "Like I told you before, I'm a good judge of character. But I'd like to get to know each other."

Nadine was hesitant, but her resolve faded away when she looked into Zaire's eyes. "You go first. Tell me about yourself."

Zaire swam closer. "Let's see. I was an Army brat, so no one place is home. Spain., Kuwait. Germany. I've lived all over the world. I speak three languages, French, Spanish and German. I'm the eldest out of three and the only girl. I speak to my brothers, but me and my folks aren't that close. I went to Rutgers undergrad. I started being a nanny then. Made some mistakes, got caught up with wrong folks. Came to Atlanta to start over."

"What does "made some mistakes" mean?"

Zaire seemed to tense up. "Fell in love with someone I shouldn't have. And paid the price for it."

"Oh, I see." Nadine was curious but didn't push further.

"But, I did manage to graduate. And I got into grad school at Emory, so I moved to Atlanta. New York is expensive, but hell, so is Atlanta. I only got partial funding for my degree. So, that's why I have so many, uhm…professions."

Nadine understood. "When did you get into pole dancing?"

Zaire swam in a semi-circle. "I actually used to do it for fun, you know, exercise. But the girl I was taking classes from said I was really good and should consider working at the club. This was back in undergrad. In NJ, you only get topless. Since you can get fully naked here, I knew I could make better money in Atlanta. Again, Atlanta and Emory is fucking expensive."

Nadine finally moved away from the ledge. "I hear you. When I first moved to Atlanta, from a small town in Georgia, I had complete sticker shock. That was over twenty years ago, but still."

"Twenty years ago? Wow, you've been here a minute."

Nadine winced. "You make me sound so ancient."

"You aren't ancient. You're vintage. Like a fine wine."

Nadine let out a loud laugh. "That's a nice way of calling me old. You're very sweet."

"No, *you're* sweet. Don't thank me for calling you what you are."

Zaire swam closer, coming within inches of Nadine. Nadine could feel her heart racing as if it was lodged in her throat as she backed up.

"You keep saying that. You just met me." Nadine dealt with Fortune 500 CEOs and executives. She never backed down from anything. Yet, she couldn't look this woman in her eyes.

"You are sweet. I know what you taste like, Cookie. Sweet as fuck. Or did you forget?"

Zaire moved a strand of hair out of Nadine's face. She seemed to like doing that. Nadine bit her lip, trying not to whimper.

"I thought you said you wouldn't bring that up. *And why was she calling her "Cookie?"*

"I lied." Zaire shrugged.

"You were just giving me and my husband a fantasy. It wasn't real. It was just for a night. One night."

Zaire smirked. "First off, I'm very real. I also don't kiss customers. Secondly, respectfully, fuck your husband. I was there for you. I'm still here for you. So it wasn't just for a night or a fantasy."

"But you…you don't know me."

"You keep saying that, Cookie." Zaire sighed. "We can change that."

Nadine knew now what she was feeling, what she was assuming, wasn't in her head anymore. She'd been out of the dating game for decades, but clearly, this girl was applying pressure. Or shooting her shot, as Alex would say. This was out of bounds. She was her employee, for God's sake.

"Please," Nadine begged. "Stop calling me nicknames."

"I won't." Zaire smirked, teasingly darting out her tongue a little. *Her pierced tongue.* "Cookie fits you."

"If you can't respect boundaries, then I'm getting out. This was… out of line in the first place. Enjoy the pool." When Nadine attempted to swim back, Zaire caught her by the leg. Nadine flailed, screaming and yelling for her to let her go. But she wouldn't. Zaire's hand went up to her waist, and she pushed Nadine back against the ledge of the pool.

"What are you doing!?" Nadine couldn't move. Zaire pressed the weight of her body against hers. Nadine could feel her hard nipples against her own and it made her traitorous clit come alive.

"You felt something that night at Secrets. That's why you ran…"

"I…"

"You felt something the other day in the pantry, too. That's why you've been avoiding me. Tell the truth, Cookie."

"Yes," Nadine breathed. "I felt wrong then…fuck… this is wrong, now…"

Zaire moved one hand up to Nadine's neck, bending it slightly to the left. She replaced her hand with her lips, soft and warm at the curve, sucking gently. Nadine tried not to moan, but she couldn't help it. It felt so good.

Zaire licked up the curve of her neck. "I can't stop thinking about how you tasted that night. Let me taste you again," she whispered.

Nadine turned her head, her lips crashing into Zaire's. Their tongues tangled, reacquainting with each other. She tasted so fucking good, remnants of the caramel iced coffee she'd seen her drinking earlier still on her tongue. Nadine licked and sucked her tongue, feeling the cold metallic of the barbell piercing, which sent shock waves straight to her pussy.

"This is fate," Zaire breathed against her lips. "There's a reason I showed up at your doorstep. I'm supposed to be here. It's a sign, my sweet Cookie."

Fate? Maybe it was fate. Or maybe Nadine had willed this to be. Her obsessive, intrusive thoughts had done this.

She might as well give in…

Nadine's hands gripped Zaire's ass, pulling her closer to her. She'd been wanting to feel that juicy ass for days.

As soon as Zaire was in her hands, Nadine finally spoke. "You been teasing me with this ass all week." She wasn't sure where that thought came from. This type of sexual boldness wasn't innate to her, but something about this girl made her this way.

Zaire smiled against her lips. "You've been teasing me with every-thing." She put a wet hand through Nadine's hair, pulling her deeper into their kiss. Shaunetta was gonna kill her for messing up her silk press already. But this was worth it. *So worth it.*

Zaire licked Nadine's bottom lip. "You taste so fucking good. All of you taste good." With that, she moved a hand to the crotch of Nadine's swimsuit, pulling it to the side. The rush of water against her pussy did nothing to cool the heat she felt between her thighs. As soon as Zaire's fingers breached the lips of her pussy, she let out a deep moan.

"We…*mmhmm*…I shouldn't…" Nadine's eyes were closed. If she looked at this girl, she would combust. She was sure of it.

Zaire's fingers explored, moving through Nadine's slick folds, teasing her swollen clit. "You've got a fat little pussy. Hmm.. I knew you'd be perfect, Nadine. Let me see you cum, beautiful."

Nadine threw her head back, gripping the sides of the pool. She lifted a leg and instinctively wrapped a thick thigh around Zaire's waist. When Zaire pushed two fingers inside Nadine, she let out a scream so loud she was sure her neighbors would hear.

"That's it. That's what I want from you." Zaire strummed, fingering Nadine's slick pussy and swollen clit until she felt as if she was leaving her body. Tears were streaming down her cheek. Her breathing was labored. She felt as if her body was so hot it would make the water boil. She had to get out of there.

Nadine's obvious apprehension did little to stop Zaire from her mission at hand. Her fingers had begun an agonizingly slow pace. Nadine didn't know which was worse— furiously finger fucking her or the slow strokes of her nimble fingers.

"Why are you running? You want me to stop?" Zaire kissed the inside of Nadine's thigh. "I don't think you do." She eased her fingers back inside Nadine, curling them to hit right at her G Spot.

Nadine didn't want her to stop. But guilt mixed with an impending orgasm was crashing down on her, coming in fast like a bullet train. She was a married woman, lusting after a woman half her age, letting her finger fuck her in her pool. *What was she thinking?*

"Oh, my fucking God!" A mix of her squirting juices and creaminess flooded Zaire's hand. She had a satisfied, euphoric look on her face. So fucking proud of what she'd done to her.

Nadine lifted herself out of the pool and onto the ledge, easing away from Zaire. She looked down at the impressions in the dimples of her thighs from the hold the girl's wet fingers had on her. When she bent down to grab her towel, Nadine saw her licking her fingers with enjoyment. The moan that escaped her lips almost made Nadine have second thoughts to go back in for more.

I definitely need to get the fuck out of here.

Nadine scurried back into the house as Zaire called out to her. She couldn't face her. She wouldn't. She quickly dried off, changed into an uncharacteristically un-chic tracksuit, went into her office and locked the door.

After a few minutes, she heard a soft knock.

"Nadine? Are you ok? Can we talk?"

Nadine refused to answer. Refused to open the door. After a while, she could hear footsteps moving down the hallway. Relieved, Nadine exhaled. If she had to hole up in her office the rest of the day…the rest of the weeks…she would. Otherwise, there was no telling how far things would go. Because after that one moment, Nadine knew there would come a time when resistance would be futile.

And that was dangerous.

CHAPTER 12

Hall Pass

Nadine's leg bounced incessantly as she glanced at the clock on Dr. Flournoy's wall. Eddie was late. He'd promised to show up to her session. In some ways, Nadine hoped that he wouldn't. Then maybe she wouldn't have to deal with the shit show that was now her life. She glanced at Dr. Flournoy, who didn't seem to have a worried or exasperated expression at all. She was the epitome of calm. Nadine needed to learn how to be that calm.

"I'm sure he'll be here, Nadine," Dr. Flournoy assured. "In the meantime, have you been doing your homework like I asked?"

Nadine nodded. "Yes. Definitely. I have been journaling. I read the articles."

"Good. I hope they were helpful."

"Actually, they were."

Initially, Nadine was resistant to writing down everything. But after the incident with Zaire in the pool, she had journaled...*a lot.* At first, it was to avoid Zaire. When she wasn't in her office, she was journaling, anything to avoid speaking to her. What was initially an avoidance tactic was quickly becoming a cathartic cataloging of her emotions. Her guilt. Her anguish. Her arousal. Her disgust with herself. Her anger with her mother. The incident had triggered an avalanche of memories for Nadine, beginning with Allison, her divorce from Drew, her relationship with her mother, church, and her withdrawal from Eddie. It was starting to make sense why and how she did the things she did. Nadine was broken, never made whole, and had resorted to being a judgmental hypocrite to fill in the gaps and keep anything she felt buried in a tomb of her own sorrow.

A soft rap at the door broke the silence. Dr. Flournoy went to the door, ushering Eddie inside. He kissed Nadine on the cheek before sitting down.

"I'm sorry I'm late. Practice ran pretty long."

Nadine nodded. "It's ok. We still have some time."

Dr. Flournoy nodded. "We do. And I want to make the most of it." She turned to Eddie. "Eddie, do you know why Nadine asked you to come to therapy today?"

Eddie smoothed his hands down his slacks. "I guess it's about whatever is bothering Deanie, and how I can help. She hasn't really said much."

Dr. Flournoy turned her attention to Nadine. "Nadine, before we begin, are you alright? I want to allow you to set the pace right now."

Nadine let out a ragged breath. "I am ok. I am."

"Ok," Dr. Flournoy began, folding her hand across her lap. "I've been working with Nadine almost four years now. Initially, it was about her stress with her job, balancing things, figuring out the post-partum depression. She said that she's told you this."

Eddie nodded. "Yes. She has."

"Good. As you know, therapy sometimes gets into the weeds of why things are the way they are. Sometimes what seems surface level has deeper, more tangled roots."

Eddie reached out for Nadine's hand. "Yes, I understand."

"Good. Nadine, are you ready to speak to Eddie? This is a safe space, and I am here to support you. So, whenever you're ready."

Nadine swallowed, her throat feeling like sandpaper. "I love you Eddie. I love you with all that I have. I need you to know that."

Eddie moved closer to her, his long legs brushing her knee. "I know, baby."

Nadine's eyes darted to Dr. Flournoy, who gave her a soft smile of reassurance. She let out a deep breath and continued. "All my life, I've been feeling like I was damaged. Or that there was a missing piece of me. My parents, especially my mother, made me feel like I was going to hell for feeling the way I felt."

Eddie's brows knit. "Felt how?"

Nadine looked down at her fingers twirling her massive ring. *Fuck. Might as well rip the Band-Aid off.* "Felt like it was wrong to like women."

Eddie let out a rough scoff. "Wait...what do you mean, *like*? As in?"

"As in sexually," Nadine continued. "I'm attracted to women."

"Hold up?! For how long?" he asked, completely flabbergasted.

"I guess forever. When I was younger, I fell in love with a girl. I was almost ten, definitely tween. My mom found out, caught us making out, and told me I was going to hell. She made me feel so ashamed. My dad said I'd grow out of it. But...I didn't. I messed around with girls in high school and in college...thinking it was a phase. Then I married Drew, hoping I could put it behind me. It just made shit worse."

"So why the hell did you marry me?"

Eddie's tone was sharp. Nadine felt his body stiffen next to her. His eyes searched hers for some sort of understanding. "I love you, Eddie. That's why I married you."

"Deanie, I feel like these past fifteen years have been a lie! Where's the fucking trust!"

Nadine's eyes filled with tears. "It hasn't been a lie. I love you, Eddie."

"Bullshit!" Eddie countered, shaking his head. "Love isn't hiding something like this from me!"

"Okay, you two. Let's take a breather for a second," suggested Dr. Flournoy.

Nadine watched as Eddie leaned back against the sofa. She could tell that his brain was going a mile a minute, cataloging the last sixteen years of their life together. Their life...their love...it wasn't a lie to her. Yet, something was gnawing at her to where she couldn't be her whole self. And now she realized what it was. He had to feel that, sense that. Maybe he didn't.

"I don't want you to be upset with me, Eddie," Nadine's voice cracked on every syllable.

Eddie rubbed his hand down his waves and let out a breath. "Nadine, I am not upset that you're bisexual. I am upset you hid this from me. To be honest, I am kind of relieved. I knew there was something off. Now I know I wasn't crazy or making up something in my head. Shit, I thought there was another man. But women? You've held this inside for years? And you judged *my* fantasies? Your friends' relationships? It all just seems…"

"Hypocritical," Nadine finished. "I know that. Dr. Flournoy helped me to realize that."

"I cautioned Nadine to not judge you for your sexual fantasies," Dr. Flournoy explained. "We're working on her having healthier responses."

Eddie's eyes widened. "You talked to your therapist about *my* fantasies? But you couldn't talk to me?" He balled his fist up, pounding his knuckles on his thigh. "I swear, unless it's a complaint or something, you won't open up to me about shit!"

Eddie's voice sounded as if it was breaking into millions of pieces. It wasn't anger. It was betrayal. Deep, gut-punching betrayal.

His leg bounced, a clear indication that he was upset. "God, shit is starting to make sense. After the stripper kissed you at Secrets, you flipped out."

Nadine shook her head. "I know. I'm sorry. It's just…"

"No, Nadine. Don't be sorry! Be better!" yelled Eddie. "All I asked is that you talk to me. Share with me. You been keeping shit from me for our whole relationship. It's like I finally have the final piece of the puzzle. It's why you won't fuck me worth a damn. Or want to try new shit in the bedroom. Fuck!" Eddie stopped, staring at Dr Flournoy. "I'm sorry, I didn't mean to…"

"It's alright Eddie," Dr. Flournoy assured. "It's understandable that you're hurt. You can express yourself freely here."

Eddie closed his eyes and inhaled. "Still, I shouldn't blow up like that. This isn't Nadine's fault. Deep down, I know it. But…the fucking self-righteous judgement has been suffocating! Yet this whole time you've been bisexual? I…I feel like I don't know you anymore."

Nadine threaded her fingers with Eddie's. "Please know that me judging you…or Alisa and Tate…was all because I was hiding. I was too afraid to open up fully, body and soul."

Eddie pressed her hands against his beating heart. "But I should be the one person you can do that with. Always, Deanie. Forever and Always."

There was several minutes of silence, nothing but the sounds of the ticking clock on the wall and the soft waterfall sculpture filled the air.

"Is there someone else?" Eddie finally asked, his voice much softer. "Do you want a divorce?"

Nadine's eyes widened. "No, I don't want a divorce!"

"But you didn't answer my question. Is there someone else? Another woman?"

Nadine blew out a breath, her chest feeling as if bricks were on top of it. She looked cautiously at Dr. Flournoy, who also seemed to want to know the answer.

"Yes. I am attracted to someone. But, I love you Eddie. This changes nothing."

"Deanie, this changes a lot…like…so much. This is about who you are. What you like. Right now, it isn't me and I can't give you that missing piece that you want."

"Eddie," Dr. Flournoy began. "Nadine's sexuality isn't the totality of who she is. Her sexuality is a drop in the bucket. I want to caution against reducing Nadine to just that."

Eddie nodded. "I get that. I'm sorry. But right now, that's what we're talking about."

"I know," Dr. Flournoy turned her attention to Nadine. "But I want to circle back to something you mentioned. You all visited Secrets, the private adult club. For what reason?"

Eddie sighed. "I thought we could just spice things up."

"Did it?" asked Dr. Flournoy.

Eddie looked at Nadine. "I supposed it did. You fucked my brains out…better than you ever have. It was because you were thinking about her, weren't you? It ain't have shit to do with me."

When Eddie brought up Zaire and that night at Secrets, Nadine flinched.

"Was the kiss triggering for you? He says you ran out," asked Dr. Flournoy.

Nadine nodded. "Yes. It was."

"Why didn't you tell Eddie the truth then?"

Nadine sighed. "I was ashamed. Especially since, like he said, we'd had some amazing sex afterwards."

"And fantasies are normal, even during sex", reminded Dr. Flournoy. "How are you navigating this attraction to this woman you mentioned?"

"I mean, I'm not. And given the circumstances, I shouldn't be."

"What are the circumstances?"

Nadine knew she should tell the truth, but there was absolutely no way she could tell Eddie that the nanny who was also the stripper from Secrets finger-banged her in the pool. Or that she'd been secretly lusting yet simultaneously avoiding her for fear she'd give in to her every desire.

"We work together," she said, giving a half-truth. "And she's a bit younger than me. It's foolish, really. Maybe it's just a crush."

"I see." Dr. Flournoy took some notes. "This is the first time you've expressed a recent attraction to a woman. How do you feel when you're around this woman?"

"Like, intrigued. Curious."

Dr. Flournoy crossed her legs. "Are you aroused by this woman?"

Nadine bit the inside of her jaw. Saying this in front of Eddie made her uncomfortable. "Yes. I was…I am."

"Eddie, how do you feel hearing this?"

Eddie's shoulders slumped as he leaned back against the couch. "Shocked. She's feeling things for this woman she hasn't felt for me in ages. What am I supposed to do with that? It fucking hurts."

Nadine closed her eyes, tears rolling down her face. This is what she feared would happen. Eddie felt rejected. It pained her to think she was the reason.

He turned to Nadine. "I have to ask. Did Drew know you were…?"

Nadine shook her head. "No. Besides, I was too caught up in trying to save that train wreck, thinking I'd cured myself. He would have probably twisted it into some sick fantasy for him. Or tried to beat it out of me."

Eddie nodded. "Yeah. I can see that. He was a punk ass bitch. Sorry, Doc."

Dr. Flournoy waved her hand. "It's fine. I've heard all about Drew. He deserves it." She looked at the time on her watch. "Do you all need a break before I continue? We can extend the session a few extra minutes if you need to?"

Eddie and Nadine looked at each other, then shook their heads.

"Alright. But if at any time you want to stop, we can." The doctor pulled out her stylus and tapped on her iPad. "Have you all heard of the term consensual non-monogamy?"

Nadine and Eddie shook their heads in the negative.

"Well, couples who are consensually non-monogamous have relationships with other people outside of their marriage, with the consent of their partners, of course."

"So, polyamorous?" asked Nadine.

Dr. Flournoy nodded. "That is a term that would fall under that category, yes."

Eddie frowned. "Honestly, I'm not interested in dating anyone else."

"Then, Nadine can be in what's termed mono/polyamorous dynamic. Meaning, she is the person in the relationship that has polyamorous relationships, not you."

"Like a lifelong hall pass?" asked Eddie.

"Not quite a hall pass," Dr. Flournoy chuckled, adjusting her glasses.

"But," Nadine blinked. "How is that fair to Eddie?"

"If Eddie is consenting to this, it is totally fair to him. He knows you are bisexual. He knows you really haven't had a chance to explore that in a healthy, safe way. It would give you the opportunity to do so, with your partner's knowledge. Some couples find this arrangement helpful. It makes their own bonds stronger. It's a suggestion, not a commandment, Nadine."

Nadine looked at Eddie, who was biting the corners of his lips. "How would we even do this? I mean, we're married."

Dr. Flournoy shrugged. "Open lines of communication. Explicit rules. Honestly, it is how you define it. Marriage, contrary to your beliefs, Nadine, is just a contract between two adults. Nothing more. Nothing less. It isn't and shouldn't be wrapped up in all that religious dogma that has destroyed you endlessly."

Eddie nodded. "Actually, I said something similar. We define what we want. We can be a safe space for each other. I was talking about spicing up the sex…I didn't think it was *this,* though."

Dr. Flournoy smiled. "Nadine, are you receiving what Eddie is saying?"

"I am," Nadine said, tears spilling from her eyes. "But I also want Eddie to know that I want to be that safe space for each other. Whatever that means. But exploring this…finally being who I've always been…I'd like to try and do that without hiding it anymore."

"And I get that," Eddie said, squeezing Nadine's hand. "I do. I'll do whatever to make you happy. Even if it means letting you explore this. But I can't be in the dark about things moving forward. I just don't want you to ever keep something as major as this from me again. I love you. I don't want to lose you, Deanie."

"I promise I won't," Nadine said. "And I don't want to lose you, Eddie." She meant that. Every word of it. She practically melted as Eddie kissed her forehead.

"I love you Deanie. I just need a minute to wrap my head around this. You understand, right?"

Nadine nodded, the tears streaming down her face like Flournoy's waterfall sculpture.

Dr. Flournoy handed Nadine a tissue. "Nadine, I am proud of you for being honest and opening up with Eddie. That was really brave."

Nadine smiled, dabbing her tear-streaked cheeks. It did feel good to tell Eddie the truth, even if it was just *part* of the truth.

"In the meantime, I'll email some literature about mono/polyamory and straight-presenting relationships. Let you all read about it. Come up with questions for our next session. You all need support during this time."

"Wait," Nadine asked. "What do you mean by 'straight presenting'?"

"Ah, yeah." Dr. Flournoy scratched her head, looking up from her tablet. "Let me explain that. Because you're bisexual and Eddie is straight, folks will assume on the surface that the two of you are just heterosexuals. But, you're not."

"So we fake straights?" Eddie chuckled. Nadine cut a side-eye at him. *That was funny though.*

"No," Dr. Flournoy laughed. "But realize that if you choose to be open about your relationship, many folks won't understand, given that you're married. They'll ask invasive questions because folks seem to only care about genitals and not feelings. People can't wrap their brains around something other than the hetero dichotomy."

Nadine nodded with understanding. She had judged Tatum and Alisa harshly for seeking relationships outside the norm. Now, she'd be in a position of being judged too. At worse, misunderstood and ostracized. At work? In her mom groups? Hell, what if Alisa and Tatum stopped being her friend, too? Shit, what if Eddie's colleagues found out? Would this jeopardize his career, too? It didn't feel that great to have the shoe on the other foot, but it was necessary.

Dr. Flournoy reached for both Eddie and Nadine's hands. She squeezed them softly. "It's not about coming out, Nadine. It's about letting folks in. And the most important person you did that with is here today. Supporting you. Loving you. Pledging to be there for you. Eddie has said that he will be supportive but definitely needs better understanding of this changing dynamic. Be patient with him. He'll be patient with you. This is the first step to redefining what happiness is for you both. I hope you realize that."

Nadine looked at Dr. Flournoy, then at Eddie. The corners of his full lips returned a soft smile. She did the same.

"I do."

❧

THE CLACK OF NADINE'S HEELS AS THEY WALKED TOWARD THE ELEVATORS was deafening. Eddie hadn't said a word since the end of the session. Now Nadine was internally freaking out.

Nadine pressed the button for the elevator, and they walked on. Nadine looked up at the numbers as they decreased.

"That was…lot." Eddie blew out a breath.

"I know. And I am sorry."

"Stop apologizing. But damn…almost sixteen years, Deanie. I just…" Eddie shook his head. "Even though I'm your husband, I'm also your best friend. I wouldn't have judged you."

"I know. I guess I was afraid what would happen if I gave you this information. Would you hate me? Would you leave me? I wasn't sure."

Nadine reached out for Eddie's hand. "Ed...we don't have to do this. It's a suggestion, that's all."

"Deanie," Eddie sighed. "I'd be a terrible partner if I said you can't explore this. Continuing to deny and hide who you are? Do you think that's healthy?"

Nadine sniffed, staring up at the elevator's ceiling. "No. But this feels so wrong. A marriage is..."

Eddie interrupted her thought, tipping her chin upward toward his face. "Dr. Flournoy said a marriage is what we define it to be. I'm unhappy, partially because I know you're unhappy. Shit, I'm starting to think we never were happy."

"Eddie, that's not true."

"Maybe. Maybe not. But I'm willing to focus on the now. And baby, like I said, I'm willing to do whatever it takes to be happy."

"But this?" Nadine blinked back tears.

Eddie rubbed Nadine's chin gently with the pad of his thumb. "Whatever it takes, Deanie." He kissed the top of her nose, then pressed his forehead to hers. Nadine inhaled him, thankful to God that she had this beautiful, gentle giant of a man in her life.

The ding of the elevator doors opened, pulling them out of their embrace.

"See you at home, Deanie."

"Ok."

Nadine pressed her back against the cold elevator glass as she watched the doors close slowly.

CHAPTER 13
Changing Tides

"Wow, this is absolutely breathtaking."

Nadine, Tatum and Alisa stood inside the nursery for the twins. Draped in shades of gold and purple, it was like something out of a fairytale. Even the rocking chairs look like miniature thrones. Toys and Black children's books lined the built-in shelves. Murals were painted on the walls and a starry night was painted on the ceiling. It was clear the Bishop-Miller's had spared no expense for their bundles of joy.

Nadine was grateful for the distraction. It had been a crazy couple of days since therapy. She and Eddie were talking, unpacking her budding attraction to her "co-worker" and how to navigate it. He was more supportive than she thought he'd be, telling her she needed to face it head on. Yet she was still avoiding Zaire. It felt so tense as they danced around each other. But Zaire didn't push. She kept her distance, yet Nadine still felt her eyes burning holes into her, searing her skin as if she was touching her all over again. Nadine could admit that she missed the feeling of her body pressed against hers. Her fingers strumming her clit. Torment felt like the right word for how she was feeling, but it still felt too small.

Alisa smiled, taking in the room. Dressed in an Oscar de la Renta kaftan, she looked like a goddess. "I know. The decorator really did her thing. I told her I wanted Wakanda meets fairytale, and she really delivered."

Nadine picked up a stuffed lion. "I swear you can fit two of my bedrooms in here. It's gorgeous, Alisa."

"So are you ready, Alisa? Just a few more weeks!" asked Tatum excitedly.

"Well," sighed Alisa as she sat down gingerly in a rocking chair. "As ready as I am going to be. I just want these jokers outta here so I can get my body back. I want to fuck my husbands like I used to. And I wanna stop peeing so much."

"That ain't gonna stop," declared Nadine. "Actually, it's probably gonna get worse."

Alisa's eyes widened. "Why didn't y'all tell me the truth about pregnancy!? Both of you made it look so easy! Ya'll were just glowing and stuff. And here I am, looking like a dressed turkey!"

Nadine rolled her eyes. Alisa always had a flair for the dramatic, but pregnant Alisa was on ten. "Uhm, we told you, but you didn't listen. Girl, I was swollen all over with EJ. Shuffling in slippers most of the day. Or you don't remember? Alisa, you're far from a turkey! You've never looked more beautiful. Your hair is all flowing down your back. You're glowing!"

"I agree," said Tatum "You *are* glowing! My skin got so dark with Morgan I looked burnt. Frankie was so concerned that he took me to a dermatologist. Not to mention…"

"Alright, enough you two," interrupted Alisa. "I didn't ask y'all to come over to talk babies. Y'all both been acting weird and I need to get to the bottom of shit." Alisa pointed to the two plush ottomans nearest the rocking chairs. "Sit! And you all better not move until you both tell the damn truth."

"Wow, you really are in your motherhood phase," mumbled Nadine as she slowly sat, followed by Tatum, who gave her a smile.

Alisa adjusted her back pillow, settling in to read them down to their socks. "What is it with you two? Is it because Chris and Kadeem took over the shower and stuff? I know y'all wanted to be involved." Tears pricked the corners of Alisa's eyes. "It's me? I know it is. I feel so disconnected from you all. I'm just stuck in this big ass house, all big and can't do shit. I can't even see you all like I used to."

"Oh, Lisa..." Tatum rubbed her knee. "It's not like that at all."

"Not at all," Nadine assured. "But it definitely isn't about you or the shower. Truth be told, I'm glad they took charge. With the merger at the job and adjusting to the new nanny, I don't even have the time."

"Same," agreed Tatum. "This new chair position has been a lot."

Alisa wiped her tears. "Ok, because I was so worried. So, Deanie, how is Glinda? Her sister ok?"

"Glinda is ok. Her sister is still on the mend. I didn't know the two of you sent her something too. That was really sweet of y'all." Glinda had checked in with Nadine a few days before, asking about EJ and the new nanny. Her sister was actually doing a lot worse than she realized. She'd received Zelle payments from both Tatum and Alisa. Nadine was so grateful to have such kind friends.

Alisa smiled. "Of course, she's practically family. I don't remember a time when she wasn't around."

"Right, so I know this new nanny is a serious adjustment." agreed Tatum.

"Yeah," Nadine twirled the fraying hem of her designer jeans. "So, the new nanny is...she's...different."

"What does that mean?" Tatum squinted. "She better not be treating EJ harshly. This is a new adjustment for him too, with Glinda gone."

"Oh god, no! Not that. EJ loves her. And I..." Nadine's eyes fell to her knees. She willed herself not to clam up or cry. Her friends, like her therapist said, deserved to know the whole of who she was. And how she felt. It's not about coming out, it's about letting people in. "I like her too."

"Well, that's good." said Alisa. "Because I am sure it's not easy to have a new person in your space."

"No," said Nadine, blowing out a breath as she looked up at the painted ceiling. "I...I *like* her."

Alisa and Tatum looked at Nadine wide-eyed but said nothing, allowing their friend to have the space she needed to talk. Nadine was grateful, because she needed a few more beats before she could speak again.

"Zaire is young. She's beautiful. Gorgeous. I've never had someone care for me the way she does. Like I said, EJ adores her and…I'm very attracted to her."

"How young?" interrupted Tatum, her perfectly arched brow raised to the heavens.

"Twenty-six."

"Whoa," Alisa said. "That is young. And does Eddie know?"

Tears fell from Nadine's eyes. "He knows I'm attracted to women… now. We kind of had it out in therapy." She looked at her friends, who were so quiet that you could hear a pin drop. "I've always been attracted to women. I just finally had the courage to actually admit it."

"Have you and Zaire, you know, had sex?" asked Tatum

"I mean, we've touched and kissed. But…" Nadine looked up, confused. "Wait, y'all don't seem that surprised by the fact that I am attracted to women? We just gonna skip over that like it's nothing?"

Tatum smiled. "Deanie, we've been your friends since we were old enough to ride bikes to Miss Lula's corner store. We've always known."

"Really?" Nadine's eyes nearly bulged out her head.

"Please! Remember that time you got caught with Ally in the dirt after Girl Scouts?" said Alisa. "That was a big red flag. You stopped coming to Scouts, and you stopped being friends with Ally. We were kids, but we definitely could put two and two together. Not to mention, Mrs. Alston called you all kinds of "unseemly dykes" in church. I had to go to the dictionary to find out what a dyke was."

Nadine sighed. "Yeah. She and my mama weren't too happy about that."

"And when we were on the cheer squad, you sure did like being a base and look up skirts." Alisa shrugged.

"Hold on now," Nadine protested. "I liked being a base because it was easiest."

"So you weren't looking up Shamika Parker's skirt?"

"Ok…maybe…Shamika did have a big ass."

"True," laughed Tatum. "And those skirts didn't leave much to the imagination."

'My point exactly," Alisa rolled her eyes. "Then, I remember that time we came and visited you on campus at Spelman. You were all flush in the face when your sorority sister left your dorm room."

"Yep, it was very clear to us that you were uhm… a little busy," Tatum nodded.

Nadine remembered that day. She and her soror, who had a boyfriend, would fool around on occasion. When Tatum and Alisa popped up on her, she lied and said they were practicing step routines. She had no idea they saw right through her ruse.

"Why did you two never say anything!?" screeched Nadine, looking between the two. "You two coulda saved me so much heartache. Especially when I married Drew. I realize now that I married him to just squash those feelings. To seem normal."

"As your friends that wasn't our place," Tatum reached out for Nadine's hand. "This is your journey. Some people realize their sexuality later in life. You're one of them."

Alisa rocked slowly in her chair. "We know you, Nadine. You were probably making up excuses about why you felt the way you did in the first place and couldn't tell us."

Tatum nodded, agreeing. "You had this visceral reaction when both Alisa and I started our relationships. You said bisexuals were "selfish", remember? I know all of that was because of how you were raised."

Nadine's face flushed with shame. "I did and I am sorry I ever said that. I just I always thought it was a phase. That's what my parents kept telling me. But then I met Zaire at Secrets with Eddie and those feelings rushed back to me all at once…"

"Back up," Alisa held up her hand. "I thought Zaire was the nanny."

"And you went to Secrets, girl? With Eddie?" Tatum asked, shock registering on both her and Alisa's faces. "Thought you said I was a bad influence, and you'd never be caught dead there."

"It was Eddie's idea, actually." Nadine went on to explain how she initially met Zaire and the kiss that they shared. How it freaked her out, yet she couldn't stop thinking about her. How she went straight to therapy about it. And how she ended up on her doorstep weeks later.

"Whoa," Alisa said, leaning back. "I knew you were holding on to some shit, but never this. Damn…Deanie…and you think you know your friends?"

Nadine had to smirk at Alisa using her lines back on her.

"Does Eddie know that you're attracted to your nanny?" asked Tatum. "You gotta tell him, babe."

Alisa nodded her head in agreement.

Nadine rolled her eyes. "Sort of. Well, not really. He just knows I'm attracted to women."

"What did the therapist say?" asked Tatum. "How are you supposed to navigate this attraction?"

"Dr. Flournoy suggested to take this time to explore this."

"Like a hall pass?" asked Alisa

"Sort of like a hall pass. Eddie agreed. I just…didn't tell them it was with the nanny."

"Well, sleeping with the help! You got more in common with them funny acting, rich, white women at EJ's school after all," Alisa bemused.

"Really, Alisa?" Nadine rolled her eyes.

The three of them burst out laughing. Nadine needed to laugh. She needed to release all the tension and angst she was feeling about everything.

"Stop making me laugh before I wet myself," Alisa declared, wiping her eyes.

The sound of someone clearing their throat interrupted them. They looked up to see Christophe leaning against the doorframe, smiling. From the loosened tie and rolled up sleeves, it appeared that he was coming straight from the office.

"I see the crew is back together," Christophe moved around, leaning down to give Nadine and Tatum hugs.

When he got to Alisa, Christophe lifted her chin and kissed her with so much passion, Nadine and Tatum swooned. That man knew he loved some Alisa and Kadeem and had no problem showing it. Audience be damned.

"Hey, princess. You look beautiful," Christophe rubbed Alisa's stomach. "Are my babies behaving? And by babies, I mean all three of my babies?"

Alisa laughed. "Christophe, please. You know I don't behave. So neither are your children."

"That is so true. This is the first time I'm seeing you sit down willingly. So I have Tate and Deanie to thank for this," Christophe teased.

"Tate, I haven't seen you around the firm in a minute. Miles is a cool lunch partner, but I think I'm just a poor substitute for you."

Tatum gave a weak smile. "Yeah. I've just been super busy with the new department chair stuff. Miles knows. It's fine."

Nadine and Alisa looked at each other, confused. That was a super weak excuse, even for Tatum. She'd move heaven and earth to be with Miles, Deacon or Cassidy. Something was off for real. Christophe looked at Alisa, clearly sensing her confusion. She shook her head, letting him know to drop it.

"Well, enough about work. Princess, did you ask Tatum if what we discussed was cool?"

Tatum furrowed her brow. "Ask me what?"

"I was going to get to that, babe." Alisa looked up at Christophe with a smile and he nodded, urging her to continue. "Well, we wanted to know how you'd feel about naming our son Franklin? We hadn't decided if it should be a middle or a first name yet..."

"Yeah," Christophe added. "I know he meant a lot to you all. I see how much he meant to Miles and Deacon. And in some strange way, he's responsible for all of this. Kadeem and I wouldn't have found our Alisa without him."

Tatum's eyes immediately filled with tears. "Seriously? Oh my goodness! That would be wonderful." She jumped up, hugging Christophe and Alisa. "Wait, so you're having boys?"

Alisa smiled. "Actually, we are having a boy...and a girl."

Nadine squealed and jumped up to give Christophe and Alisa a hug. "Yes! I knew at least one baby was a girl! And Nadine is a wonderful name for a girl."

"Hey now! So is Tatum," Tatum interjected, pointing a finger at Nadine playfully.

"We haven't settled on a name for the girl yet," chuckled Alisa. "But trust me, you two are their godmothers so, some part of you will be there. Trust me."

All three of them began crying and hugging, squealing with delight and talking over each other.

"So that's my cue to bounce." Christophe chuckled. "Let me go see what the other prison warden is doing." With that, he kissed Alisa on her forehead and left the ladies alone to celebrate.

Tatum pulled back, her eyes still brimming with tears. "Alisa, I can't wait to hold these babies. A little Frankie! Gosh, Franklin would be so happy if he were here."

"Speaking of happy," Alisa tipped Tatum's chin up, her eyes meeting . "What is going on, cuz? Clearly, you aren't happy these days. And stop telling me and Nadine nothing."

Tatum shook her head as she sat back down. "They asked me to marry them."

"Who?" Nadine and Alisa asked in unison.

"Miles and Cassidy. They both asked me to marry them. On two separate occasions. It was a lot."

"Who had the better ring?" Alisa asked, garnering a pinch from Nadine. "Ouch! Stop assaulting pregnant women!"

"Well, what did you say?" asked Nadine. "Did you say yes to one? Turn one down? Yes to both? How did they take it?"

Tatum wiped her tears with the pad of her thumb. "I haven't given either one of them an answer."

"Why not?" asked Alisa. "Don't you love them?"

"I do." Tatum sat back down on the ottoman. "That's the problem. I love Miles. But…" There was a long pause. In the silence was the answer.

"You're in love with Cassidy, aren't you?" surmised Nadine.

Tatum nodded. "I am. Fuck. I can't even explain how that happened. I thought my heart was big enough to love all three of them equally. Miles is great and there is a level of familiarity that gives me comfort. Deacon is so funny, fine and caring. He caters to me like no other. But the more I time I spent with each of them, apart from the group, I realized that Cassidy is the one that makes my heart flutter. We read books together. He gets the stress of being an academic and Black. Cass gets that part of me that neither Deacon nor Miles understands. But that's also complicated because now we also work together."

"Uhm, in different departments," reminded Nadine. "No conflict there."

"Besides, working together means he can come into your office and bend you over anytime you want," Alisa waggled her brows.

"It always comes back to sex with you, huh?" asked Nadine.

"I know you ain't talking when your old ass is trying to scissor your nanny!" Alisa shot back. "And that's no shade because I've been with my fair share of girls too."

A slight shiver went down her spine as Nadine thought about Zaire. "I mean, I wouldn't put it like that. "

"We'll circle back to you, Nadine." Alisa smirked, turning her attention back to Tatum. "Ma'am, you ain't answer my question. Are we getting bent over the desk or nah?"

"Yes, Lis, there's been plenty of getting bent over the desk. Which Jesus…is so hot." Tatum's face went flush as she fanned herself. "But I can't risk getting caught with my skirt literally down. I don't need a scandal at work. I avoided one already, remember? That shitty little student could have cost me my job. It was years ago, but still…I really am working my ass off to prove that I deserve this chair position. I'll be the first Black woman to be head of the English department at Decatur Tech. A lot is riding on it."

Nadine nodded with understanding. From her first day at Pharma-Digital, she'd worked hard to prove she wasn't some affirmative action hire. "I get it. Trust me. You don't want to seem like you didn't earn this job. "

"Exactly, Deanie. You get it."

"And what about Deacon?" asked Alisa. "Surely, he has to have some feelings about this."

"That's the thing…he's the one most hurt. He feels left out. He doesn't want the group to break up. Like we're The Temptations or something. But he has made it very clear that he doesn't want to get married and loves both Miles and me. He just doesn't want to be shut out. If I marry Miles, what if Cassidy hates me? If I marry Cassidy, what if Miles hates me? And Deacon, he's left out in the cold either way."

"That's so tough." Nadine reached for Tatum's hand. "Follow your heart. Isn't that what you'd tell me? Or Alisa?"

Tatum nodded. "It is. But I don't want to hurt anyone in the process."

"An honest answer is like a kiss on the lips," said Nadine.

"Nadine, I feel like you made that shit up," quipped Alisa.

Nadine laughed. "I did not. That's from Proverbs, you heathen. Imma make sure I take the babies to church."

"Oh you ain't gotta worry about that. Mother Miller is going to make sure the babies know the lord."

"Excuse me," Tatum's eyes widened. "Did you say Mother Miller? I know you're lying!"

Alisa raised her hand. "Hand to God, I'm not. The old bird is coming back around. When she heard I was pregnant, she said she couldn't miss out on seeing her grandchildren. Bishop Miller hasn't had a change of heart, though."

"Wow, look how the tides have changed," said Nadine.

Alisa looked between her friends. "That's certainly an understatement."

Nadine had to agree. She never thought that she'd be telling her friends that she was attracted to someone else, let alone a woman. In retrospect, the fact that she'd been afraid to be honest with her friends felt so silly.

"Let's promise not to keep secrets from each other anymore," Tatum declared, putting her hand out. Nadine and Alisa put theirs on top.

"I promise," said Nadine. "I honestly feel better that it's out there."

"And I'm glad I told the two of you how I feel," said Tatum. "It was tearing me up inside to keep this from you both."

"But the two of you know you've gotta be honest with your men, right?" Alisa looked between Tatum and Nadine with a slight frown on her face.

"We know," they both said.

Alisa patted their hands. "Good. Now help me up from this chair so I can sneak and order some Popeye's from the delivery app."

"I heard that," Kadeem boomed from the doorway. Dressed in sweats and a tank, he was so big, his head was near the top. Nadine marveled that Alisa could handle all that man let alone *two* of them. Nadine peeked down at the sweats. *Damn.* Yep, she got why Alisa was losing her mind being on dick restriction.

"You ain't feeding our babies no greasy fried chicken," Kadeem fussed. "Your blood pressure is already a little high. You know that, sweetness."

Alisa pouted. "That's not fair. You never tell me no!"

"Well, life ain't always fair, babe," Kadeem rolled his eyes. "Chef made baked chicken, roasted sweet potatoes, and lots of other veggies you hate, but you *will* eat. You ladies are welcome to stay for dinner."

"See what I am saying, fucking prison wardens," groaned Alisa, easing out of the rocking chair.

"Call me that one more time, and Imma put you over my knee," Kadeem frowned.

Alisa bit her lip, slowly repeating herself. "Prison…warden…"

"Bad girl," Kadeem shook his head, a smirk on his face. "I forgot who I was dealing with. Dinner will be ready shortly, ladies." With that, he headed back toward the kitchen.

Tatum and Nadine laughed out loud. Alisa may have been annoyed, but secretly they knew she loved being doted on. She deserved it. H*ell, they all deserved it, thought Nadine.*

"I am definitely staying for dinner," Tatum said. "I really want to see Alisa being force-fed vegetables. Ever since we were kids, she only ate green beans and collard greens. A Brussel sprout may kill her."

Alisa rolled her eyes. "You ain't shit, Tate."

Nadine waved her head. "Thank you for the invite, but I think Imma go home. I need to go talk to Eddie."

"I am proud of you, Deanie." said Tatum. "Live your truth."

"Welcome to the dark side," declared Alisa. "I knew you'd come around."

Nadine laughed. "I love you both."

"We love you too," Tatum and Nadine chimed in, circling Nadine with a hug that felt like it closed a hole in her heart. She was so lucky to have them. Men and women would come into their lives, but their love was forever.

CHAPTER 14
Applying Pressure

Nadine made it home in time for EJ's bedtime. She stood at the doorway quietly, watching Zaire tell jokes to EJ until he was in fits of giggles. The two of them were in their own world.

"Ok. No more jokes. Good night, sweet boy."

"Nooooo. Don't gooooo," EJ whined. "You have to sing our song! Please!" For good measure, he pouted and batted his impossibly long lashes. Nadine had to stifle a chuckle. That was his go-to move to get folks to succumb to his cuteness. Zaire was a goner.

Zaire sighed and shook her head. "You're relentless, you know that? With your cute self." She adjusted herself at the edge of the bed and she began singing "Orange Moon" by Erykah Badu. Nadine's heart nearly stopped beating. Zaire's voice was absolutely breathtaking, completely arresting.

Eventually, EJ's eyes grew heavy, and he fell asleep just as Zaire was rounding out the chorus.

When she got up from the bed, Zaire froze, hand over her heart. "Shit! I didn't hear you come in," she whispered.

"Didn't mean to scare you," Nadine smiled. "I just got in. Seems like just in time for a mini concert."

Zaire shrugged. "Just doing my job, Mrs. Moody. Good night."

The way she said her name made Nadine's heart ache. *I guess we're back to square one.*

Zaire began to move past her until Nadine reached for her arm, holding on to her wrist. She looked down at Zaire's delicate fingers, painted another shade of vibrant green.

"Z, can we talk? Just for a moment."

Zaire sighed. "Now you want to talk? Sure you don't want to go run to your office and close the door and pretend I don't exist?"

Nadine let go, leaning against the opposite side of the wall. "I deserve that. I am sorry."

"Let me guess, you've never been with a woman before?"

Nadine chuckled dryly. "Uhm, I've been with a woman before. A few. None as fine as you...and that's the problem."

Zaire squinted, folding her arms. "What does that mean?"

"Ugh," Nadine rubbed her tired eyes. "It's complicated."

Zaire leaned against the opposite wall. "I can handle it. Tell me."

The light from EJ's starry night light twinkled in the hallway against Zaire's skin. Like beams of fairy dust against her dark skin. It was too beautiful. Too much.

Nadine had to look away for as she spoke. "Baby girl, you're so pretty that it hurts. You feel so good to kiss. To touch. The thoughts I have about you are consuming me. But I'm *married*, Zaire. And you're too young for me and..."

"I'm almost thirty, Nadine. I am not a child."

"But you *could* be my child. Shit, you're just a little older than my daughter, Alex. Still, I shouldn't feel the way I do. Married or not. You work for me."

"I know," Zaire blew out a breath. "I was being selfish. I wasn't really caring about that in the moment."

"Neither was I. I just told my husband of almost two decades that I'm bisexual and we are still working through that."

Zaire's eyes widened. "Wait? Your husband didn't know you liked women?"

Nadine shook her head. "No. I was trying to bury all of that in the past...until the night I kissed you. Then you showed up on my doorstep. And that just added heat to something that was already bubbling to the surface."

"This isn't all on you, Nadine. I was applying pressure."

Nadine smirked. "Yeah, you were. I may be old, but I caught on."

"Not old, Cookie. Just vintage, like I said."

They both softly chuckled until their laughter died down, and their eyes met.

"I told him about you…sort of," Nadine confessed.

"What do you mean, sort of?"

"I told him I was feeling someone. Someone younger that I work with. I mean, that's not a total lie."

Zaire's eyebrow raised. "Uhm, that's a definitely stretching the truth, Nadine."

"I know. Being your employer makes this worse. Even if he's ok with me exploring my attraction."

Zaire's mouth was slightly agape. "He is?"

"Yeah."

"How does that even work?"

Nadine shrugged. "We haven't exactly worked out the details. But this is messy. Seriously. So fucking messy."

"It is, but, honestly," Zaire moved, closing the gap between them. "I didn't give a fuck how messy it was. I wanted you. From the moment I saw you at the club…"

"Zaire," Nadine breathed out her name like a whisper. "We shouldn't."

Zaire nipped at Nadine's neck, eliciting a whimper. "You just said you want me. You're feeling me, Cookie. Let me *feel* you."

Nadine's eyes went past Zaire, looking toward EJ's room where he was still sound asleep. Without a word, she grabbed her hand and led her down the hall toward one of the guest rooms. As soon as the door closed, Zaire pushed Nadine up against it, kissing her until she could barely breathe. Nadine moaned into her mouth, opening wider to invite her tongue to explore. Zaire tasted better than she remembered, felt better than the first time. Nadine palmed Zaire's ass, the thin material of her leggings feeling like a second skin.

"This ass," Nadine moaned. "So fucking juicy."

Zaire smiled against Nadine's lips. "I know you've been looking. Why do you think I wore these?"

"Such a tease," Nadine grumbled. "Come here."

They walked backwards, tumbling toward the bed, their mouths never disconnecting. Nadine inhaled every fiber of Zaire. The feel of Zaire's body over hers, the plushness of all her curves, made Nadine heat with desire. Their hands simultaneously found the top of their waistbands. Through a small tuft of hair, Nadine's fingers found Zaire's clit, slick and swollen, as she teased it. Stroking and caressing it as the piercing at the hood flicked across her fingers.

"Fuck..." Zaire mewled, writhing against her fingers. "That's it, right there."

Nadine wanted to make her moan like that again and again. But before she could, she felt Zaire's fingers do the same to her, stroking her clit. It was good. So unbearably good. Nadine's eyes rolled to the back of her head as she felt an orgasm coming. But the pressure wasn't coming on strong enough. She felt restricted.

Swiftly, she removed her hand from Zaire's leggings and pulled down her own slacks and soaked panties. With her pussy was fully exposed, Zaire pushed Nadine's legs open wide as she explored with her fingers. She squeezed her sensitive clit between her fingers, which made Nadine let out a slow hiss. She didn't have to look down to know she was drenched and dripping all over the sheets.

"Look at you, Cookie. Dripping all over my fingers. You gonna come for me?"

Nadine looked up at Zaire through wet lashes, tears pooling in her eyes. The sight of Z kneeling between her legs, one hand in her pussy, the other in her own was too much.

"Yesss...fuck yess..." Nadine replied.

"You better," Zaire demanded. "You and this pretty pussy owe me."

With that, Zaire pressed the heel of her palm against her clit as two fingers drove into Nadine. Reflexively, she arched her back off the bed and cried out, grabbing the sheets as she braced herself for an orgasm.

"Z...fuck...I'm coming."

Nadine's essence shot all over the bed, onto Zaire's hand. Nadine's heart raced and her head throbbed as she felt her pussy contract and continue to suck Zaire's fingers harder into her pussy. *What the entire fuck?* She'd never come so hard in her life.

Zaire looked down at Nadine, a slight smirk on her gorgeous face. "Oh mami, you made a mess. I gotta clean it up for you."

Before Nadine could fully regulate her breathing, Zaire replaced her fingers with her hot, wet mouth. Her full lips sucked in Nadine's clit, licking and rolling the sensitive nub until Nadine's legs were shaking. Zaire pressed her palms against Nadine's thighs, splaying them open as she sucked her dry. The barbell in Zaire's tongue was sending her into orbit. She was young, so fucking young, but ate pussy like she'd been doing it for ages. She was, in a word, beyond qualified.

"Come for me, Nadine…"

"Shit…I'm… coming…."

Nadine palmed Zaire's head, feeling her waves as she pressed her deeper into her pussy. She feared she was cutting off the girl's circulation, but when Zaire looked up, lips covered with her wetness, Nadine could do nothing but smile.

"I need to taste me on your lips." Nadine grabbed Zaire by her shoulders, pulling her up to her face. She grabbed her by the throat, licking and sucking her lips until she consumed every drop of her from those beautiful lips. The moan that left Zaire's lips only made Nadine kiss her harder, deeper until her lips felt numb and her tongue tired.

Zaire looked at her, eyes hazy. "Now that was a real kiss."

Nadine smiled. "Were those not real kisses before?"

"Hmm," Zaire licked Nadine's full bottom lip. "At the club? No. By the pool? We were getting there."

"Guess we are." Nadine smiled as her eyes traveled down the length of Zaire's body. Her eyes stopped at her crotch where she could she the faint dampness as the imprint of her fat pussy lips swallowed up the seams of her leggings. "But I didn't get to kiss where I really wanted to. "

"Is that right? Let me give you a sample then." Zaire reached into her leggings, swirling her fingers in and out of her pussy. Nadine's nipples throbbed at the sight of her. When she pulled out her green polished fingers, they were beyond soaked. She rubbed her juices all over Nadine's lips, which she greedily devoured. Zaire did it repeatedly, clearly pleased with Nadine's willingness to please. That was a bit out of character for Nadine. But these teases were doing nothing but stoking the fire that was burning in her. She had to get Zaire's pussy on her face immediately.

Furiously, Nadine tugged at the waistband of Zaire's leggings, getting them over her thick ass and thighs. Once they were near her ankles, Nadine didn't waste time and pulled Zaire to hover over her face. For a moment, Nadine just stared. The glistening lips of Zaire's pussy, swollen and aroused, called to her. Her clit was large as it peeked from under its pierced hood. Her eyes shifted to her thighs, slightly dimpled and deep brown. Zaire's scent had Nadine's mouth watering. She hadn't tasted another woman's pussy in nearly twenty years. Maybe it was like riding a bike. Could she remember how to please…how to bring another woman to climax? She needed to show her pleasure in the same way that Zaire'd done to her.

Slowly, Nadine gripped Zaire's ass, lowering her onto her mouth. She flattened her tongue to part the swollen lips, gaining access to her ripening bud. Nadine teased the piercing, sucking and flicking her tongue until she could taste Zaire's juices overflowing. She had her right where she wanted her. And she wanted to taste her, experience her, forever.

Nadine could hear the rustle of Zaire gripping the comforter. "Oh my god, shit, Cookie you feel so fucking good."

Nadine tried to hold on, to steady herself as Zaire writhed against her lips. She knew her moaning was sending shock waves to Zaire's clit. Nadine wanted more, needed to have the woman succumb to her. She moved one hand from her ass to further part Zaire's pussy, sliding a finger inside as she steadied her sucking. Nadine pumped her fingers faster and faster and sucked her clit harder until Zaire's pussy clenched around her fingers and a steady, warm stream trickled down Nadine's lips, chin and chest. She licked every drop that she could, satisfied that she could bring Zaire such pleasure.

Nadine released her grip of Zaire and allowed her to slide down, their bodies meeting. Zaire kissed Nadine on the cheek softly.

"You're so perfect, Nadine."

Nadine smiled, warmth blooming in her chest. "I'm not, but I appreciate that."

Zaire cupped her chin, forcing their eyes to meet. "What did I say? You're perfect. Don't fight it."

Just as Nadine was about settle into the warmth of their embrace, she heard the familiar alert of the alarm.

Eddie was home.

"Fuck," Nadine's eyes widened in panic. "We gotta get up."

"Seriously? But I thought you said…"

"I know but, c'mon!" Nadine turned away. She couldn't allow Zaire to look at the slight hurt on her face. It wasn't rejection, she had to know that.

Zaire and Nadine moved quickly to set themselves right, pulling up their pants and fixing their tops. Nadine stripped the bed, tossing the wet comforter in the closet. Nadine went to the mirror, smoothing down her hair. As her fingers went to her lips, she felt Zaire come behind her and grab her by the throat, turning her to face her.

"Don't you fucking wipe my shit off your lips, Cookie. When your husband kisses you tonight, I want him to taste what you do to me. How fucking wet you get me, you got that?"

Nadine's clit throbbed at the command, and she nodded. "Y…yes."

Zaire pressed a kiss to her temple. "You're so good to me, beautiful. Such a good girl."

Such a good girl. Nadine swallowed thickly at the familiar phrase that played in the background of her mind. But it made her want to be anything but good.

As Nadine exited the bedroom, the sound of heavy footprints stopped her dead in her tracks, with Zaire on her heels.

"Hey babe. I was looking for you downstairs. Already turning in?" Eddie approached his wife, placing a kiss on her lips. Nadine didn't have to turn around to see the smirk that was on Zaire's face. She could *feel* it.

Nadine gave a slight smile, her nerves rattling like a set of janitor's keys. "Hey. Was just talking to Zaire about a few things with EJ's schedule"

"Cool." Eddie extended a hand to Zaire. "Sorry we haven't met formally yet. We seem to keep missing each other. I'm Eddie."

Zaire shook Eddie's hand. "Nice to finally meet you, Mr. Moody. "

"Don't make me feel like my Pops! Please, call me Eddie."

Nadine looked between the two of them, trying to notice if Eddie recognized Zaire from Secrets. But he just gave her his usual warm expression.

"Well, Eddie, Nadine sings your praises all the time," continued Zaire. "You two have a lovely home. And EJ is so sweet."

Nadine tried her best to hide her shocked expression because that *so* wasn't true. She could count the number of times Eddie came up in conversation. Instead, Nadine put on her fakest of smiles at the compliments Zaire was laying on thick.

Eddie smiled. "Well, she's the one who really keeps the ship running. We'd drown without her."

Zaire nodded. "Right, and who wants to get wet, right?"

Nadine nearly choked as she stifled a cough. Zaire wasn't slick with the thinly veiled innuendo.

"Right." Eddie raised a brow with a chuckle, turning to Nadine. "She's funny, Deanie."

Yeah. Real fucking funny.

"Well, if you all will excuse me, I have to get home to study for my midterms. Goodnight. See you bright and early tomorrow."

"Goodnight," Eddie and Nadine said in unison.

Zaire walked past them. Nadine watched her ass, an ass she was face deep in minutes before, bounce down the hallway toward the steps. She looked up at Eddie, who was also looking at her ass. Nadine couldn't even be mad. The girl was fine as hell.

As if realizing that he was staring, Eddie cleared his throat, turning his attention back to Nadine. "Well, she seems nice. Very cordial. You still want to fire her?"

Yeah, so I can fuck her, she thought. Nadine shook her head. "No. EJ loves her. And she's been super great around the house. Invaluable, actually."

"That's great. She's super pretty. I bet EJ has a crush too."

Nadine groaned. "Ugh. That's inappropriate, Ed." She really didn't like when people talked about kids like that. Besides, the only person in the house crushing on the nanny was *her.* And from the looks of it, maybe Eddie too.

Eddie chucked. "My bad." He paused for a second, looking down at Nadine with a serious face. "So, I was thinking about what Dr. Flournoy said at our last session. About allowing you to take some time to explore this attraction to women fully."

Talk about timing! Nadine folded her arms nervously. "What about it?"

"If we're going to do this, I think we need to establish some ground rules."

Nadine furrowed her brows. "What kind of ground rules?"

Eddie extended his hand toward Nadine's. "Let's grab a bottle of wine from the cellar and talk. I'm sure we can hash it out over one bottle."

One bottle was probably a very optimistic estimate.

Nadine let out a sigh as she laced her fingers with Eddie's. "Sure. Let's talk."

Suddenly, the idea of drowning didn't seem so bad.

CHAPTER 15
Boundaries

Nadine woke up with a throbbing headache. One bottle had turned into three as she and Eddie sat in the wine cellar, discussing the rules of her "exploration" as Dr. Flournoy so eloquently put it. Eddie hadn't required much, but what he required gave Nadine pause. In her office, Nadine rubbed her temples as she replayed the conversation over and over in her head.

"I am not asking for much, Nadine. But if this is going to work, as a couple, we need to set some boundaries."

"What kind of boundaries?"

"I don't think I need details of everything that you all do."

"Ok. I can respect that and..."

"I'm not done, Deanie..."

"Oh. Sorry. Continue."

"If you start to develop feelings, real feelings, let me know."

"Feelings? As in fall in love?"

"Yes. If you feel a deeper connection, I need to know because you falling in love requires a different type of space and a different conversation."

"I mean, what would that mean for us?"

"We'll cross that bridge if it gets that far."

"Would you want to meet them? If it gets that far...I mean."

"Eventually, but not right now. Nor do I want them around, EJ. I don't

need the confusion for him. Not saying you're confused...shit...you know what I mean."

"Yeah. I know."

"This is about us. Our marriage. No one and nothing else."

Nadine had already broken two out of the three rules. Zaire was around EJ every day. And now Eddie had officially met her. Surely, this was too close for comfort on so many levels. But Zaire was irresistible. Even if she was miles apart, she'd want her. Nadine was like a moth drawn to a flame, more than willing to get burned. Was that the "feelings" Eddie warned her about? If so, Nadine was going to be fucked.

Nadine's stomach was queasy, and she couldn't be bothered to eat breakfast. She tossed back two ibuprofen with some water as she logged into her first meeting of the day. Mitchell was already looking annoyed as the team gathered to talk strategy.

"Good morning everyone," Nadine said. "You too, Mitchell."

Mitchell snorted as he rolled his eyes. He looked as if he just rolled out of bed. "I'm just not a morning person, that's all. Sorry if I seem so unpleasant."

You're unpleasant any time of the day, thought Nadine.

Nadine gave a weak smile. "Well, thank you anyway for taking this meeting. I know early morning strategy meetings are unusual, but I want to get to the bottom of things before we move forward with DigiCo. I am glad to have a representative here. Thanks Clyde."

Clyde Waters, current VP at DigiCo nodded. "Sure thing, Nadine. We want this merger to go through smoothly so any questions you have, I am here, along with my team."

"Great. Let's discuss last quarter's numbers."

Just then, Nadine's office door opened. Quietly, Zaire came in, bringing a cup of coffee on a saucer, along with a spice cake muffin. Nadine had baked them earlier in the week during one of her stress-induced fits. She tried to focus on the meeting on her screen, but her eyes perused Zaire quickly, taking in her wide hips, joggers, and Emory t-shirt that did little to hide her hard nipples. Now that she knew what Zaire had under those clothes, all she wanted to do was get them off of her.

Fuck. Focus, Deanie.

Nadine blinked, trying to replace her lust with some type of neutral expression. Upon second glance, she noticed a Post-it on the cup.

You need to eat, beautiful.

Nadine looked up as Zaire was giving her a wink as she headed back out the door. Nadine smiled.

"Nadine? Did you hear what Clyde asked?" Mitchell's annoyed voice broke through her thoughts.

"Sorry. Could you repeat, Clyde?" Nadine was embarrassed that she wasn't paying attention. It's what Zaire did to her all the time, it seemed. Distract her until she was flustered.

Clyde graciously continued. "Nadine, I am not sure what the issue is. We've sent you our numbers for last quarter and our projected numbers. We wouldn't mislead you."

Nadine nodded, taking a sip of her coffee. *Oh, my god. She even put the right amount of hazelnut creamer.* She had to stop herself from moaning in delight and refocus on her meeting. "I understand that, Clyde. But that's not the report I have. It is way over what you said."

Nadine watched as Clyde looked through his notes, then sighed. "Nadine, I don't know what to tell you, but the numbers on my end are right on target."

Devi chimed in. "Mr. Waters, I also double checked, and this isn't what I received to forward to Mrs. Moody."

Clyde frowned. "Well, maybe it was an error on my assistant's part..."

"It wasn't," chimed Agnes, Clyde's assistant. "I ran it twice and checked before sending it over to Devi. I also cc-ed Mitchell."

"And Mitchell replied back that everything seemed ok," Devi confirmed. "Then I uploaded it to the cloud."

Nadine flared with anger but kept her cool. *Mitchell has access to the cloud. He probably switched it on me.* She flashed a smile. "I see. No harm, no foul. Agnes, from now on I am alright with you sending me things directly. No need to CC anyone. No need to upload to the cloud."

The meeting continued without much incident. But Nadine had made it up in her mind: Mitchell had to be dealt with. At the conclusion of the meeting, Nadine asked Devi to stay on. She took a huge bite of the muffin to try and calm her nerves. Before she could say anything, Devi began to rail.

"Mitchell switched the reports. I know he did. Mrs. Moody, I'd never upload the wrong report. You have to believe me." The young woman was utterly frantic. She'd been Nadine's assistant since returning from work and had been nothing but stellar.

"Devi, I believe you." Nadine rubbed her temple. "But I need to prove that Michell did this. Without a doubt."

Devi was typing furiously. "On it. Let me give a call to IT and get some logs. I'll keep you posted."

"And not just his logs to the cloud. I think we need a deeper dive. Be discreet." Nadine felt it in her gut that something was going on more than just misplaced reports. It wasn't about embarrassing Nadine. It was about making her seem utterly incompetent. Mitchell was gunning for her.

Nadine ended her call, then moved on to her meeting with advertising. She was still furious but kept her composure. When she finally had a break, Nadine stormed into the kitchen and headed straight to the pantry. She grabbed sugar, flour, vanilla and other seasonings to bake. What was she going to bake? She had no idea. She just knew she was pissed and other than eating the rest of the muffins, this would calm her down. She was in her own world, sifting flour when she felt a pair of arms around her waist. Nadine looked down and smiled.

"Let me guess, you're stressed," Zaire said as she leaned into give Nadine a kiss to her neck. Instantly, she felt the tension release. Nadine thought Eddie was the only person who could do that to her. Zaire seemed to have a magic touch, too.

"Dude at work is trying to pull some shit. I just…I can't catch a break." Nadine turned to Zaire. "I appreciated the coffee and the muffin, by the way. That was really sweet."

Zaire smiled. "Anything for you, Cookie. I'm always going looking out for you." She moved Nadine's hand away from the sifter. Her heated, brown eyes narrowed in on Nadine's. "But I can think of better ways to help you decompress."

Nadine chuckled. "I'm sure you can, baby girl. But I have to work."

She looked at her watch. "Besides, you'll have to pick up EJ in a couple of hours."

"Aren't you the boss? And I don't need hours to get you off..." Zaire was untying Nadine's apron, slipping it off her waist.

Nadine shook her head. "Mighty confident aren't we?"

"I can show you better than I can tell you."

Zaire grabbed Nadine's hand, leading her up the steps toward the bedrooms. Before they could enter the guest bedroom, they were tearing each other's clothes off. First, Zaire removed her t-shirt, then her joggers. Nadine drank in the sight of Zaire as she stood dressed in only lilac panties and bra. The color of the bra against her skin reminded Nadine of her favorite taffy candy. She was, in a word, perfection. Sweet perfection.

Nadine moved forward, slipping the straps of Zaire's bra down, pulling the flimsy cups to reveal the tight, dark buds of her breasts. She bent down, taking one into her mouth, sucking and licking, delighting in the taste of Zaire on her tongue.

"You taste so fucking good," Nadine moaned around the nipple, the vibrations of her voice stiffening them further. She felt Zaire tug at her hair as she moved from one nipple to the other, teasing her with her hot, wet tongue.

"Nadine," Zaire breathed, her back against the dresser. "Kiss me."

Nadine smiled against her breast as she released the nipple with a wet pop. Zaire pulled her up by her neck, crashing her lips onto hers. Their tongues danced and tangled as if they were fighting for dominance. In the end, Nadine won, as she sucked Zaire's tongue, marveling at the feel of the piercing against her lips. As she kissed, Nadine snaked a hand into Zaire's panties, parting her puffy, wet pussy until she found exactly what she was looking for.

"Fuuuuck," Zaire cried as Nadine's fingers teased and flicked her pierced clit, her fingers slick with the moisture she gathered from her heated center.

"Tell me you like that," Nadine demanded. "Tell me, baby."

"I like it," Zaire moaned. "Fuck. You know I do."

Nadine moved from Zaire's clit and plunged her fingers deep inside her pussy, curling them until she could feel her walls tighten around her. She was so close to coming. Nadine burned with desire, spurred on by the satisfaction of being the one to make her come. She moved her fingers faster, the sound of Zaire's wet pussy and moans being all that she could hear.

"Come for me, pretty girl," Nadine begged as she increased her pressure. When she curled her fingers deeper, Zaire's squirt ran down her hands and onto the floor. Satisfied, Nadine removed her hands, licking them, savoring the taste. She beckoned Zaire to open her mouth, sliding her fingers inside so she could taste herself.

"See how good you taste? Better than anything I could ever fucking bake," declared Nadine. She slowly moved back, easing onto the bed. She removed her bra, freeing her breasts as Zaire gazed hungrily. "Come here, love."

Zaire's panties were soaked. She slipped out of them as she followed Nadine to the bed. She pulled down Nadine's panties, the seat of which was a wet, creamy mess. Nadine watched as Zaire took them off and proceeded to lick the seat of them clean. Her pussy clenched at the sight of her devouring her that way.

"Damn, you're wild," Nadine said with a slight chuckle.

"Only for you, Cookie. But I need a better taste." Zaire knelt down and parted Nadine's legs. Worried, Nadine placed a gentle hand on her shoulder.

"Uhm, I haven't shaved in a minute."

Zaire's quirked a brow. "And? I think maybe you've forgotten that I actually like pussy. Especially *your* pussy."

"Fine," chuckled Nadine. "But you can't have all the fun. I want to get to taste you too."

Zaire smirked. "You read my mind."

Nadine moved to the middle of the bed, laying horizontally across it. Zaire climbed up her body, peppering kisses along the way until she turned her body to position her pussy over Nadine's face. A pretty pussy and a juicy ass in her face? Nadine was in heaven. She inhaled, the scent of Zaire making her wetter by the second. She could see the glint of the barbell on Zaire's hood, beckoning her to feast.

Zaire lowered herself onto Nadine's hot, wet mouth as she bent down and began simultaneously sucking her with a fury. Nadine gripped Zaire's ass, spreading her cheeks apart and dipping her tongue into her center. She tasted like pure honey, raw and sweet. She sucked, slurped, and hummed against Zaire's pussy, juices of her arousal dripping down her face. But she wanted more. Needed more.

Nadine swiped her ravenous tongue near Zaire's asshole, and she bucked against her face with a moan. She had to smile to herself that she had that effect on her. She did it again, and Zaire let out a scream.

"Fuck, Cookie, you nasty bitch!"

Nadine chuckled. She'd never been called that before. *If it's nasty that she wanted, I could give it to her.* Nadine focused her tongue and lips on Zaire's clit, teasing the pierced pearl until she could feel it engorge on her tongue. That wasn't enough for Nadine. She wanted her to feel her. To own to her. Claim her. She pushed her finger inside Zaire's hot box, pumping and sucking until Zaire's task of eating her pussy was all but forgotten.

But Zaire reminded her that she knew how to take care of her while being taken care of as soon as Nadine felt her sex being breeched by her adept fingers. They were meeting each other stroke for stroke, the sounds of their equally wet pussies creating a heated soundtrack of lust, want, and need.

"Come for me, Z," Nadine begged. "Come for me, pretty girl."

As if Nadine had the magic words, Zaire squirted all over her tongue and fingers. She devoured it, relishing the thrill that she was the one to bring her to ecstasy. Zaire's body stilled as she came down from her orgasm, her thighs and ass shaking. It was a glorious sight. She moved to lay next to Nadine, seeming to catch her breath, then looked over at her with a smile.

"Are you good?" asked Nadine.

"Perfect," Zaire answered. "But we ain't done till you come too."

Zaire got up, then straddled Nadine sideways. She watched as Zaire spit on her hand, then rubbed her already throbbing pussy. Nadine's breath hitched as she anticipated what was going to happen. Tribbing was something she hadn't done in decades. Internally, she was thanking God her old bones weren't on top. She wasn't sure if she'd be effective.

"I wanna make you feel so good, Nadine," Zaire said as she began to rock her hips. "I want to feel you come like this."

Nadine moaned, feeling the slickness between them. She could hear the sound of them together, their breathing in time, with the squelching of their juices pooling between them. Their clits, their bodies rubbing together, was driving Nadine crazy. She loved Eddie, God knows she did. But he could never make her feel this way or this good.

"Shit, I'm coming," Nadine cried, feeling the heat pool in her belly as her orgasm rocketed through her. Her body shivered as if ice and heat were both running through her veins. When she calmed down, Zaire lifted off of her. She looked down, swiping a finger through Nadine's pussy, which was glazed like a Krispy Kreme donut.

"We taste so fucking good together, Cookie," moaned Zaire, as she sucked her fingers. "Don't you want a taste?"

Nadine said nothing, simply opened her mouth to receive Zaire's fingers. "More," she said, once she'd licked her digits clean. And Zaire obliged. Nadine didn't know who or what she'd become. But she knew she'd never be the same again.

With their bodies slick with perspiration, Nadine and Zaire settled onto the bed, pillows nestled around their heads like white clouds.

"That was…incredible." Nadine sighed as she lay her head on her shoulder. She inhaled the scent of Zaire, now cotton candy mixed with the saltiness of their sex. The last time had been rushed, in a frenzy, to just get each other off. But this time, it was something else.

"It was." Zaire kissed the top of Nadine's wild curls. Her fingers gently circled Nadine's deep brown areolas, making her shudder. "You should pierce your tits," she said as she playfully pinched Nadine's still hard nipples. "You'd look amazing with some gold hoops. Maybe a barbell like mine?"

Nadine moaned. "Hmm…I've breastfed two kids with these. And they hang to my knees, I don't think so."

"Stop," Zaire sucked her teeth. "They are still juicy as fuck. I could suck 'em 24/7 if you let me."

Nadine looked up at Zaire with a frown. "I hope you don't think this is all I want from you. Sex, that is."

"Well, I mean, someone has to pick EJ up from swimming," Zaire joked.

"I'm serious." Nadine raised up, looking into Zaire's eyes. "This isn't just about sex."

"So what you trying to do? Date me?" The way Zaire said it was laced with incredulousness.

Nadine nibbled at the corners of her lips. "I mean, I guess. Why not?"

Zaire sighed. "Listen, you don't have to do all of that. I know you said you and Eddie have an understanding. I'm cool with that. Besides, I don't really date. We can just do our thing."

"Yeah, but I am not trying to reduce us to just the physical," Nadine insisted. "Why are you hesitant? Didn't you say it was fate that you ended up here?"

Zaire stopped her stroking. "Listen, I'm ok being your fun, fling on the side. I'm not trying to get hurt again."

Understanding slowly registered with Nadine. "Would this have anything to do with your last situation? Something about getting caught up?"

Zaire nodded. "Yeah. Something like that. Not trying to uproot my life again for heartache."

"I'm sorry." Nadine lay her head back on Zaire's chest. She didn't say anything for a while. She simply listened to her heart beat.

Zaire's fingers circled Nadine's cheek softly. "What are you sorry for, Cookie? There's nothing to be sorry about."

"I don't want this situation with me and Eddie to cause you heartache," Nadine sighed. "We have rules in place. And I am hoping these rules will prevent all of that."

"Oh yeah, what rules?"

Nadine tried to explain what she and Eddie had discussed the night before. "But like I said, you working here. It makes it difficult."

"Breaking rules already, huh, Cookie?" Zaire smirked.

"I know," snorted Nadine. "You're amazing. Having you around with EJ these past weeks, I don't know what I'd do. Having you near is a win for me too."

Zaire chuckled dryly. "I bet it is."

Nadine lifted up. She grabbed Zaire by the back of her head, kissing her slowly. Softly. "Stop downplaying this. All I want to do is have you near. I want to make sure you're good. With you near, I know you are." Nadine was surprised at her candor, but she felt like Zaire deserved an honest, unfiltered answer.

"Nadine," Zaire breathed. "You don't have to."

"I will. If you let me..."

Zaire stared up at Nadine, her fingers caressing the folds at her waist. "I can't say no to you. I'm already addicted. I told you, I don't give a fuck how messy this is."

"Good, because I wasn't going to take no for an answer. So, our date..."

"Our date?" Zaire laughed. "I didn't say yes. Plus, I'll have to check my schedule at Club Titanium."

Nadine rolled her eyes. "I mean, can't you take off one night?"

"Yeah, but one night helps pay my tuition...my rent...my car note..."

"Z, I got you."

Zaire narrowed her eyes. "Nadine...I can't let you do that. And I damn sure don't want you to think this thing between us is me trying to come up."

"You aren't letting me do anything," Nadine declared. Honestly, Nadine had more money than the law should allow, and she rarely spent it. "And I don't think that. I told you. I want to make sure you're good." Nadine didn't know why, but she felt compelled to do whatever this girl wanted her to. To please her. To treat her as sweet and softly as she felt. She leaned down and kissed her again. "Ok. Let's get up. Chef is about to arrive, and I can ask him to fix an early lunch before you pick up EJ."

"Wait," Zaire held Nadine by her wrist. "What about Eddie?"

Nadine sighed. *Fuck.* "I'll tell him. I promise." She slipped her tongue back over Zaire's lips until they parted, and she kissed her again, tweaking a nipple simultaneously, which made her moan.

"Well, we can skip lunch," breathed Zaire, her hands moving down Nadine's stomach.

"You sure?"

"I'd rather eat your fine ass, Cookie."

Nadine smiled against her lips. "Open up, baby."

Yeah. She'd tell Eddie.

Eventually.

CHAPTER 16
Far From Ideal

Dr. Flournoy stared at Nadine, barely able to mask the disappointment in her eyes. "The nanny, Nadine?"

"Yes."

"The nanny who also happens to be the stripper at the club?" recalled Dr. Flournoy.

Nadine closed her eyes. "I know. It's not ideal." She wasn't sure what she expected Dr. Flournoy's reaction to be when she told her she had been intimate with Zaire. It wasn't this. It felt uncharacteristically judgmental. And as someone who was always judgmental, it didn't feel good to be on the receiving end.

"Far from ideal!"

Nadine frowned. "But you said you wanted me to explore this."

"I did." Dr. Flournoy ran a hand through her locs. "But this woman is your employee, caring for your son. There is a power dynamic here that could lead to disaster."

"It's not like that..."

"So let's talk about what it's like, Nadine," challenged Dr. Flournoy.

Nadine didn't know for sure. But in her heart, she felt like Zaire wouldn't take advantage of their relationship. And neither would she. She liked her. Cared for her. She wanted this.

"I just feel I can trust her..."

"But can you trust yourself?" Dr. Flournoy sighed. "Nadine, when I suggested you explore this, I didn't think it would be so close to home. You weren't truthful in our session with Eddie. You told us the young woman you were attracted to worked with you. Not that she worked *for* you."

"I know." Nadine felt heat crawl up her neck to her scalp. She wasn't prone to lying like this, not to Dr. Flournoy, of all people. "But telling Eddie the truth was too hard then. It felt easier to just say that."

"Does Eddie know that the woman in question is the nanny?"

Nadine shook her head. "No. I don't know how he'd take this. Especially since it violates the rules we established." It wasn't simply a violation, it was a betrayal.

Dr. Flournoy's perfectly arched brows lifted. "So you all have already talked about the rules of your sexual exploration?"

As Nadine slowly explained to Dr. Flournoy the rules they had discussed, her eyes followed the movement of the doctor's pen against her tablet, her brows furrowed the entire time. That wasn't a good sign.

Once she was done, Dr. Flournoy pinched the bridge of her nose. "Can't tell you what to do, but I am going to warn you. You violated part of the agreement you've established with Eddie with regards to your mono/poly exploration. Not telling him may only deepen the chasm between the two of you. Is this young woman worth that to you?"

Nadine stared down at her wedding ring, twisting it around and around. "I don't know. Fuck, that shouldn't be my first answer."

Dr. Flournoy smiled softly. "It was an honest answer."

"I don't want to hurt Eddie. But I also don't want to stop being with Z. I want them...both."

"Now that's a change of heart." Dr. Flournoy nodded encouragingly. "Go on."

Nadine knew that she probably sounded like a big ass hypocrite. Especially given that she had everything to say about her friends' poly relationships. She held up her hands with a chuckle. "I mean, I'm not saying that's what I want..."

"What do you want then, Nadine? Because what you're describing sounds like a polyamorous relationship."

"I don't know." Nadine was becoming frustrated with this line of questioning. "Why do I have to call it anything? Like, why do I have to call *myself* anything?"

"Nadine," Dr. Flournoy softened her tone. "Terms like bisexual or polyamory aren't here to hurt you, but it seems that you're feeling uncomfortable accepting that you might be-- "

"But you want me to be defined by them!" Nadine interrupted with a yell. "Why can't I just be me? Why can't I have what I have? Love who I love?"

"You can, my dear. You can. I'm only concerned that your choice to not "put a label on it," as you say, might keep you from fully embracing who you are and what you want, which strips you of your agency and diminishes your power. It's like crawling back into a hole. That same hole your parents tried to put you in when you first expressed desire for a girl. That same hole that made you judge your friends and their relationships. Why go backwards?"

"Because," Nadine started and stopped her sentence several times, trying to stop the cry that was bubbling up, but it was no use. She hiccupped and tears streamed down her face. Through a blur of tears, she watched Dr. Flournoy press a tissue into her hand and squeeze.

"Nadine, I see you're really having a strong reaction to what I'm saying. Can you share what's coming up for you right now?"

Nadine wiped her tears, upset that her makeup was streaked. "I don't know. I just thought…I thought I was there. I thought I was free from all that."

"You're getting there," Dr. Flournoy patted her hands. "But true freedom is being honest about your desires and not keeping folks in the dark. Including Eddie."

"I just am scared he's going to react like… "

"Like Andrew?" Dr. Flournoy finished Nadine's thought.

Nadine nodded. "Yeah."

"Has Eddie, in fifteen or so years, ever given you any indication that he'd react violently towards you?"

"No."

"Has he reacted negatively since telling him that you're bisexual?"

Nadine shook her head. "No." She hadn't felt as safe in her life as she did with Eddie. He cared deeply for her, even when he was frustrated or didn't understand her. He was the most patient man there was.

"I do not think he's going to hurt you, Nadine. Actually, you have the power to hurt him. Emotionally. So please, talk to him."

Nadine nodded. "I will."

Dr. Flournoy leaned back. "Good. I hope you do this before our next session and before you decide to pursue anything with Zaire. I mean it, Nadine. You can't keep hiding. Not like this."

Nadine shook her head. She'd never heard Dr. Flournoy speak so forcefully about her issues. She knew she was serious. "Okay."

Dr. Flournoy waited a few beats before she asked, "Now Nadine - let's talk about your attraction to Zaire. Tell me about that."

Nadine smiled softly. "She's sweet. Incredibly beautiful. A little aggressive, which I like, I suppose. Very sexy."

Dr. Flournoy nodded. "Anything else?"

Nadine chewed her bottom lip. "Part of me just wants to care for her."

"Care for her?"

Nadine shrugged. "Yeah, because she seems a little wounded. Her job is literally to care for other folks' kids, but who is caring for her? So all I want to do is care for her."

"I see." Dr. Flournoy wrote something down in her iPad. "Is it because you see yourself in Zaire?"

"Uhm, Zaire is nothing like me. I don't understand."

"She's a young, queer Black woman. Estranged from her family, right?"

Nadine nodded. "Yes, but..."

"So, in some ways you're trying to heal both of your wounds by being together. Is it possible you're unconsciously drawn to one another as a way of healing the unresolved wounds from your relationships with your mothers?"

Nadine's eyes widened. "What does my mother have to do with anything? Are you trying to say I want to fuck my mother?"

Dr. Flournoy tented her hands under her chin. "Well, according to Freud..."

"Stop right there," Nadine said, holding up her hand.

"It's not meant to be literal, Nadine," chuckled Dr. Flournoy. "It just means we look for partners to heal and affirm the parts of us that our parents wounded. In your case, it was your mother. She lacked empathy and warmth. She was cruel to you. She used religion to justify her treatment of you. Therefore, in this relationship, you want to give Zaire all the things neither one of you had. It makes sense."

"So what about Eddie?" countered Nadine. "Am I with him because I have father wounds or whatever?"

"Well, your father certainly was kinder and more empathetic. It's very possible that you were drawn to Eddie because he encompasses your father's positive characteristics…that is, without the religious dogma that informed his life."

"I see." Nadine pondered the doctor's words. "That makes sense."

Dr. Flournoy leaned forward. Her brows creased with concern. "Nadine, we've been working so hard to break you out of your old habits. If you hide this relationship from Eddie, you'll be taking steps backward. And I just don't want all your hard work to be in vain."

"I understand." Nadine's voice broke into tiny pieces. "I do."

"Intimacy isn't just about sex, Nadine. It's about letting people in. Letting people know the real you. You told me you tell Tatum and Alisa almost everything. But not your husband? Of all the people that should know the real you, shouldn't it be Eddie?"

Nadine shook her head. "You're right."

Dr. Flournoy looked at the clock on the wall. "Our time is up. But before our next session, and certainly before you're intimate again with Zaire, I urge you to tell Eddie the truth."

CHAPTER 17
Shameless

After therapy, Nadine decided to make a detour. She couldn't go home. She didn't want to face her job, the meetings, and the bullshit that was Mitchell's alleged sabotage. She didn't want to be tempted to fuck Zaire until she could think of nothing else. Instead, she stopped by Alon's Market and had them pack a gourmet lunch basket for herself and her Tatum, and had one delivered to Alisa while she was on bedrest. Surprising her girls was a surefire way to cheer her up and get her mind off her life. She made her way down to Decatur Tech to surprise Tatum so they could catch up and would FaceTime Alisa during lunch so she could feel included.

Nadine parked and made her way to campus. She had to ask a student which building was the English department because she'd only been on campus twice and always got turned around. When she finally made it to Grover Hall, Nadine was slightly out of breath from hauling her bag and the food.

"Hello there," greeted the English department's receptionist. "How can I help you?"

Nadine caught her breath, balancing the lunch. "Hi! I'm looking for Dr. Simmons' office."

The receptionist frowned as she looked at the computer. "Is Dr. Simmons expecting you?"

"Oh, no! I'm her best friend, Nadine. I was in the area and decided to surprise her with lunch."

"That's so sweet! Doc sure could use it. She's been so stressed!" The receptionist said with a smile. She looked back at her computer. "Well, it looks like she's finishing up a standing meeting. She should be done now. Her office is number 216- A. Down the hall, to the right."

Nadine navigated the long corridor to Tatum's office. She balanced the bag and drinks in one hand as she knocked.

"Tate. It's Deanie!" she announced. "Thought I'd surprise you with lunch."

Nadine wasn't sure, but she swore she heard a low moan, followed by a chair or something scraping the floor. Nadine was about to knock again when the door flew open. Standing before her was a super fine, slightly sweaty astrophysicist.

Nadine smirked. "Well, hello Dr. Valentine."

Cassidy cleared his throat, adjusting his crooked glasses and tie. Sweat dotted his forehead. "Hey Nadine. Uhm, Tate and I were just… talking."

"Uh huh, I bet." Nadine peered around Cassidy's broad shoulders to see Tatum adjusting the hem of her skirt. She shook her head. Cassidy gave Nadine a sheepish smile and hug, taking the bag from her hands and placing it on a table.

Tatum cleared her throat as she tried to maintain her` professionalism. "Dr. Valentine and I were just finishing our meeting."

Nadine raised a brow, then leaned in to whisper. "Oh, is that what we call fucking in the middle of the day, Professor?"

"Really, Deanie." Tatum's dark skin flushed as she shook her head.

"Man, your girl knows what's up." Cassidy turned to Tatum and smacked her on the ass, then kissed her lips. "See you later, mama. Later, Nadine."

"Later Cass," Nadine said as she watched him walk out the door, closing it behind him. Nadine turned to her very embarrassed friend. "Well, so much for not getting caught with your skirt around your ankles."

"First of all, you showed up without calling," chided Tatum. "Secondly, can you blame me? That man is fine as hell. He can get it anytime he wants." She kissed Nadine on the forehead before sitting at the table. "Thank you for lunch, Deanie. This is a pleasant surprise! You must have known I'd work up an appetite."

"Ugh, gross." Nadine chuckled, moving to the table to take out their lunch. "I take it that you've given him an answer. Oh, before we get into that," Nadine pulled out her tablet to FaceTime Alisa. She answered on the first ring, teary eyed. It was clear she'd been ugly crying.

"Why are you crying?" asked Nadine. "Oh god, is it the babies? They alright?"

"The babies are fine," sniffed Alisa. "It was just so sweet that you had our monthly lunch delivered to me, so I wouldn't feel alone. I've been crying ever since. Fucking hormones."

Tatum and Nadine laughed. Babies had turned Alisa into a total softie. It was too cute.

Alisa wiped her eyes, adjusting her phone on the table. Her belly took up most of the screen. "Ok. I got my lunch set up. What's tea? And why does Tate look all sweaty?"

Tatum's hands flew to her face. Before she could answer, Nadine replied. "Because she was in here rearranging the furniture with a certain astrophysicist. Do you know they have a standing meeting to bone?"

Alisa laughed, a mouth full of food. "Damn! Do you all give it a rest?"

"I know you aren't talking," Tatum rolled her eyes. "Didn't you, Kadeem and Christophe christen your new salons *before* they opened?"

"Yeah, but they are *my* salons, and it was empty!" Alisa said, pointing a fork at the camera. "But we ain't talking about that. If you boning, that must mean you gave the man an answer."

"Nope," Tatum sighed. "No answer just yet. Trust me, the man is trying to get an answer from me any way possible. So is Miles."

"Is Miles rearranging furniture to convince you, too?" asked Nadine with a chuckle.

Tatum laughed. "No. His approach is to shower me with gifts until I say yes." She lifted her arm, showing off a gleaming tennis bracelet. "See?"

Alisa moved closer to the screen. "He has very good taste. I mean, Kadeem woulda picked bigger diamonds, though."

"Really, Alisa?" Tatum shook her head, admonishing her cousin. "Anyway, I'm just afraid."

"Why are you afraid? Do you think things will change for the worse?" asked Nadine.

"I'm afraid because I've been married once before and…" Tatum's voice cracked a bit, but she pressed on. "I don't know if I can handle it."

"What does that mean? Is Cass or Miles tripping?" asked Alisa.

Tatum shook her head. "No. They're fine. Perfect as ever."

"So why think the worst?" asked Nadine. "You can't go into any relationship thinking that."

"That's true," Tatum sighed. "I guess part of me also doesn't want things to change. What if marriage makes things weird?"

Nadine chewed slowly. "How so?"

Tatum shrugged. "I dunno. People change when you get married. I mean, all change isn't bad, but…change still happens."

Nadine swallowed, feeling a lump in her throat. *People change. I've changed.* She looked up to see Tatum squinting at her. "I've changed," Nadine confessed. "I'm sure Eddie doesn't know who he married anymore."

"Why do you say that?" asked Tatum.

"I slept with Zaire," Nadine blurted out. She dropped her head in her hands. "Shit, a few times."

Tatum whistled. "Well, damn."

Alisa gasped. "And how was it?"

"Hot, sexy…fucking amazing," Nadine sighed. "But now, I'm having second thoughts. I told my therapist, and she nearly lost it."

"Why? I thought she wanted you to explore this?" asked Alisa, who had moved on to the brownie.

Nadine scratched her scalp. "The thing is, I didn't tell her the woman I was attracted to was the nanny. So she's bringing up this thing about power dynamics and stuff. And how I didn't tell Eddie the truth. I feel like I've fucked up."

Tatum winced. "I mean, I *did* say that. She has a point, Deanie. What if this goes south? Then what?"

"I feel confident that Zaire wouldn't be malicious. She wouldn't hurt me."

After her therapy session, Nadine was, in fact, not so confident about that anymore. But she wanted to believe it.

"That's nice and all, but respectfully," Alisa chimed in. "We are talking about *you*. I know how you are, Nadine. Are you willing to take that chance on someone you haven't known long? If some shit goes wrong, you'll scorch the earth. "

Nadine frowned. She couldn't even contradict what Alisa said. She was right. Nadine could be not only judgmental but vindictive at times. It was part of the reason why she went no contact with her mother towards the end. And when her father called to say that her mother died, she felt only a little pain. She could hold a grudge like no other. She couldn't see herself doing that with Zaire. She wanted her around forever.

Maybe Dr. Flournoy was right. This situation with Zaire was about something deeper.

Nadine took a long sip of her drink before responding. "I know, but I don't see myself doing that. Not with Zaire."

"Damn, the pussy musta been good." chuckled Alisa, to which Tatum gave her a scolding look. She waved her off to address Nadine. "So what really has you worried?"

"What worries me is everything with Eddie. He's just wrapping his brain around me being attracted to women and exploring this attraction. We talked about it, established some rules and being with Zaire clearly violates a few…shit…maybe more than a few rules."

"What are the rules?" asked Alisa.

Tatum and Alisa went quiet as Nadine went on to explain the rules that she and Eddie outlined for her mono/poly exploration. Nadine tried her best not to freak out, thinking about how Eddie would react to this.

"Well," Tatum pushed back her nearly empty container. "Speaking from experience, anytime you open your relationship up, there needs to be communication and boundaries. And Eddie was very clear with you about both."

Nadine bit the corners of her lip. "I know."

"And you need to be clear with Zaire too."

Nadine frowned. "What do you mean?"

"You're willing to risk a lot for Zaire," Tatum sighed. "Is this just about sex? Or something more? I haven't heard you say a thing beyond…"

"Beyond bumping beans." interrupted Alisa. "Is there anything else to this relationship?"

Nadine rolled her eyes. "Of course it is, Alisa. I like her. She's funny. Considerate. Sexy. I want to get to know her. I mean, I asked her out on a date."

"A date?" Tatum and Alisa said in unison.

"Uhm yeah, a date. To get to know her. Maybe do something nice for her. I want to spoil her. You know? She hasn't said yes, though." She stared back at her friends, who were a little taken aback. "Why is that so strange?"

"It's not," Tatum shrugged. "Just never took you for the spoiling kind."

"Yeah boo," Alisa chimed in. "You're the one usually being spoiled."

"Well," Nadine smirked. "Maybe I want to do the spoiling for a change."

"Well, before you start trickin', you need to tell Eddie about Zaire," warned Alisa.

"Yes, please stop keeping this man in the dark," Tatum added. "A half-truth is still a lie."

Nadine nodded. She'd been operating so much of her life in half-truths. About her feelings. Her sexuality. Everything. She wasn't sure who she was protecting or why she was doing this. Actually, she knew why.

She let out a deep sigh. "Sometimes I still feel like that ten-year-old girl. Trying to protect myself…my parents. Always trying to save face to not bring disappointment or shame upon my family."

Tatum grabbed Nadine's hand. "Deanie, the only thing you need to protect is your heart in all of this. Whatever that looks like for you."

"Baby, we don't do shame over here. Not anymore," declared Alisa. She raised her glass of water, motioning for them to do the same. "I wanna make a toast."

"To what?" asked Nadine, amused.

"To not giving a fuck anymore. If we wanna marry two men. Have three boyfriends. Have a boyfriend and a husband. Shit, a husband

and a girlfriend. We can do whatever we want because we are happy, free Black women."

Tatum nudged Nadine, and they both raised their plastic cups, angling them toward the iPad.

"To not giving a fuck."

CHAPTER 18
Another First Date

Nadine stared at herself in the mirror. She adjusted her top a second time, making sure she wasn't spilling over in the corset that she was wearing. Maybe she was doing too much? Was this outfit too "sexy" for a first date even though she'd seen her naked? Was she too old to be wearing this? Maybe she should change. She was second guessing everything. She looked down in her jewelry box for her earrings to distract herself.

"Stop second guessing yourself. You look beautiful."

Nadine looked up to see Eddie standing at the entrance to her walk-in closet, his tall frame leaning against it. It felt so strange to have him staring at her, getting ready to go out with someone else. But this was their new normal, she supposed.

"You don't think it's too much?"

Eddie walked over to her, placing his hands on her shoulders, massaging them. "Absolutely not. Why do you think it's too much?"

Nadine shrugged. "I don't know. I feel silly. I've never been on a real date with a woman. And I haven't been on a first date in…"

"Seventeen years," Eddie finished with a smile. "I remember that day like it was yesterday. I was the nervous one."

"You brought Alex and me flowers." She giggled. Nadine remembered, fondly. "I still have a rose from the bouquet pressed in a book somewhere." She sighed, placing her hands on her vanity. "Maybe this is a bad idea. Maybe I'm too old for this shit. I shoulda done all of this in my twenties."

"But you didn't. You're finding out who you are. Isn't this what this is about?"

"Ugh," groaned Nadine. "That's easier when you're younger and prettier."

"Baby," Eddie leaned down, kissing the curve of her neck. "You're allowed to find yourself at any age. You are prettier than all the flowers I've ever bought you. And if she can't see that, or appreciate that, come home to the man who does."

Nadine turned around to look up at her husband. She rubbed her hand over his soft waves and watched as his eyes closed. "What did I do to deserve you?"

"Nothing but being you." Eddie kissed the delicate skin of her wrist, inhaling her scent. "Go have fun, love. Don't keep her waiting."

Nadine arrived a bit early at Bastion, a quaint tapas restaurant in the heart of downtown. She picked it because the vibe seemed intimate and chill. It was the perfect place for them to talk and get to know each other beyond their obvious attraction. Not to mention, she wanted to spoil Zaire with the good wine, food, and amazing music that the place offered.

The waiter, an older gentleman, sat Nadine at a small table near the windows, not too far from the entrance. She wanted to be able to spot Zaire when she walked in. She ordered Sangria and sipped as she enjoyed the Bossa Nova music playing in the background. As the waiter came over to refill her water glass a second time, Nadine looked up to see Zaire coming through the door.

"Jesus," Nadine said under her breath.

Wearing a short, strapless, black dress that barely covered her ass, all eyes were on Zaire as she glided through the room toward Nadine. Her skin was glistening, as if she was dipped in diamonds. It was a far cry from the sweats, leggings, and joggers she wore most days. Zaire made it to Nadine and smiled. Nadine rose out of her seat, leaning in to give Zaire a hug. She smelled so good, like cherries and cinnamon. It took everything in Nadine not to lick her.

Zaire gave her a quick peck to the cheek. "Hey beautiful. Damn, you look good."

"I definitely can say the same for you. All eyes were on you when you walked in here."

Zaire slid into the chair across from Nadine. "Well, as long as the most important eyes that were on me were yours, then I am fine."

Nadine shook her head, smiling. "You can't help but flirt, can you?"

"You know you like it, Cookie. Besides, any opportunity to make you blush is so worth it. You should try it sometimes."

The waiter returned, smiling as he brought the menus. "Hello ladies, you both look lovely. Welcome to Bastion." He turned to Zaire. "Can I interest you in a drink while you peruse the menu?"

"I'll have a Sangria too," said Zaire.

"I'll have another," Nadine chimed in.

"Very well," he said in a thick Spanish accent. "I'll be back with your drinks and to get your orders."

Nadine watched as Zaire took in the atmosphere. Bastion also had a small dance floor where folks also salsa danced later in the evening. She turned to Nadine, giving her a sly grin.

"So, are you going to take me for a spin on the dance floor too?"

Nadine chuckled softly. "Honestly, I have two left feet, but if that's what you want. I can make an exception."

"Good," Zaire crossed her thick legs, Nadine watching the movement as the dress rode up her thighs. *Did she even have on underwear?* Nadine was curious to find out. She took a quick sip of her Sangria, trying to focus on something else.

"I'm glad you were able to make time to do this," Nadine began. "I really appreciate it."

"I'm glad I did too. Besides, this morning, a little birdie sent me $2k via Zelle as some incentive to say yes."

Nadine smiled behind her glass. "Well, you said was you were missing out on money at the club tonight. Just letting you know I value your time."

"You didn't have to do that."

"But I did. It got you here. And that's all that matters."

Zaire slid her hand across the table, taking Nadine's hand into hers.

"I was going to say yes regardless. You know I'm not with you because you have money, right?"

Nadine traced Zaire's sparkly green painted nails with her index finger. "Oh yeah, then why *are* you with me?"

"You're beautiful, kind, and got the sweetest tasting pussy on the planet. Plus...you make amazing pastries. My taste buds thank you for both."

Nadine laughed so embarrassingly loud that the neighboring table was looking at her. She could feel her face heat. "Stop it."

"Seriously, Nadine. You're a whiz when it comes to baking. Why aren't you doing that instead of slaving behind some desk looking at numbers? I know you're making bank, but you seem so unhappy."

Nadine shrugged. It wasn't the first time someone had asked her about her passion for baking. Eddie included. "I guess I was just playing it safe. I thought having a bakery was taking a huge risk. Plus, my mother said I would have been wasting all her and my dad's hard-earned money that they sacrificed for my education. I'd be throwing it away to make treats. Her words."

Zaire gave Nadine a soft, sympathetic smile. "I think your parents have gotten their monies worth in terms of your degree. It's time you do stuff on your own. I see how miserable you are at your desk most days. What are you trying to prove?"

Nadine sighed before sipping her Sangria. She *was* miserable. And knowing that Mitchell was probably trying to sabotage her didn't help. It was making her question why she had returned back to work in the first place. Zaire was right. She didn't have shit to prove to those people. Not anymore.

The waiter returned with their drinks. "Ladies, have you all decided on what you'll start with?"

Nadine glanced at the menu. "I think I'll start with Manchego mushroom croquettes."

The waiter turned to Zaire. "And for you lovely daughter?"

Nadine's eyes widened as she looked at Zaire, whose brow was furrowed with anger. She and Zaire didn't resemble each other in the least. They were literally like night and day in terms of appearance.

"Daughter? You think this fine ass woman is my mother?" scoffed Zaire

"Z, it's ok," Nadine said, waving off the comment. She didn't want to cause a scene.

The waiter motioned between the two women. "Oh. Is it not? I just assumed."

"Sir, it's fine. We..." Nadine attempted to explain, but Zaire wasn't having it.

"Would I do this to my mother?"

With that, Zaire leaned across the table, cupped Nadine's chin, and slipped her tongue into her mouth nastily. Nadine moaned, enjoying the taste of Sangria mixed with Zaire's gloss on her lips. She attempted to pull back, but Zaire held on tighter, tangling her tongue with hers until they parted with a wet smack to their lips. Nadine could feel the wetness pooling in her panties. She could hear a neighboring table say *"damn"* as she adjusted herself in her seat.

"Oh," the waiter, who was turning redder by the second, began to apologize profusely. "I am so sorry for assuming."

Zaire adjusted herself back into her seat. "And I'll have the grilled octopus."

Nadine watched as the waiter scurried away. She tried her best not to laugh and just shook her head. "You didn't have to do that to that man."

"Yes, the fuck I did," Zaire declared. "I had to let him know this was a date. I mean, you're Big Mama, but not *my* mama."

Nadine held up a hand. "Ugh, do not call me Big Mama. That definitely makes me feel geriatric."

Zaire chuckled. "Nah, not like that. I am not talking grandma status. More like...big boss energy."

"I see. I guess I'll take that. Even though I'd argue you're the one with all the boss energy."

Zaire looked down, fiddling with her napkin. She was silent for a few beats before responding. "I guess it's a defense mechanism in a way."

Nadine didn't understand. "What do you mean?"

Zaire exhaled a few times before continuing. "Growing up with dark skin, nappy hair, and hand me down clothes. Shoes from Walmart. I got teased a lot."

"I see. I'm sorry that happened to you."

"It's cool. I see it as character building now, but back then, not so much. What those folks failed to see was that I loved myself fiercely. I probably could psychoanalyze myself, but I won't." Zaire leaned closer to Nadine, smiling. "I am sure you had everybody tripping over you. Curly hair. Hazel eyes. Caramel skin."

Nadine shook her head, dismissing Zaire's comment. "It wasn't even like that. Just caused me more trouble than anything. Men thought I was arm candy. Girls thought I wanted their man and was stuck up. Shit, the whole time I was probably staring at the girl, not the dude. Too scared to say anything."

"So, how does it feel now?"

Nadine put her napkin in her lap. "How does what feel?"

"Not hiding who you are. I mean, I just tongued you down in a restaurant full of folks and you didn't run."

"You didn't give me much of a choice," laughed Nadine. "But honestly, I feel whole. Happy in my skin for the first time in a while. I guess I have Eddie, my therapist, and you to thank for that."

Zaire waved her hand. "Please! Don't thank me. I didn't do anything."

Nadine placed a hand on Zaire's thigh. "Stop that, baby girl. Seeing you that night at Secrets reawakened something in me I didn't know was missing. I'm definitely glad you showed up on my doorstep."

Zaire looked at Nadine, lips pursed. "You sure you don't regret not sending me back out the door?"

Nadine moved her hand up and down Z's warm thighs. She could smell the scent of her body oil as she inched closer. "Granted, the situation isn't that ideal, but it is what it is. I can promise you I won't take advantage of it. No power tripping over here. I will take care of you, Zaire. In so many ways…if you let me, love."

Zaire leaned forward, pressing her lips against Nadine's. She could feel her smiling. "See, that's Big Mama energy right there."

With her other hand, Nadine grabbed Zaire by the back of her neck, a delicious gasp escaping her lips. "Then give Big Mama a real fucking kiss."

After feeding each other various tapas and drinking damn near a pitcher of sangria, Nadine found herself on the dance floor, with Zaire grinding on her. It was supposed to be a salsa lesson, but it was turning into something extremely hot and slightly scandalous. At one point, Zaire's dress began riding up, damn near exposing her fat ass to the world. It was then Nadine confirmed her date *definitely* wasn't wearing any panties. An audience had gathered near them, encouraging them and being generally voyeuristic. Nadine would normally be a bit self-conscious, but she didn't care. Let them stare. Granted, she was tipsy and totally out of her element. It was also the most fun she'd had in a long time.

Zaire was with her. She was going to enjoy this completely.

The DJ changed to a slower song. Nadine thought that was the perfect time to catch her breath. But Zaire had other plans. She pulled Nadine close, holding her around the waist at first, but eventually, her hands traveled lower to palm her ass. They were chest to chest, damn near melting into each other on the dance floor as they swayed to the beat. Through the thin material of Zaire's dress, she felt her hardened nipples against her exposed skin. *So no bra either…damn.*

"You just want to grind on me? You don't want to slow dance?" Zaire asked in a low, seductive voice. It made Nadine tingle and her nipples stiffen.

"Of course I do, but baby, I am not as young as you. I need to take a breather. And I gotta pee."

Zaire rolled her eyes. "Fine. Go on and handle your business. I'll be waiting."

"Thank you, baby." Nadine giggled as she placed a quick peck on her lips and made her way to the bathroom. She snaked down the hall until she finally found the single-stall unisex restroom. She was entirely too grateful because that Sangria was running through her. Nadine relieved herself and was reapplying her lipstick when she heard a knock at the door.

"Coming. I'll just be a second," she called out.

But the knocking wouldn't stop.

Annoyed, Nadine threw her tube of lipstick back in her clutch and snatched open the door.

"What!"

Zaire was standing there. She opened the door wider, pushing past Nadine. The snick of the door locking echoed off the walls was so loud that Nadine jumped a bit.

It was like deja-vu.

"What are you doing?" Nadine laughed nervously. "Don't tell me the sangria got you too?"

"No mami," Zaire shook her head. "You were gone too long."

"I was literally gone less than five minutes."

"Five minutes apart from you, Cookie? Way too fucking long."

Zaire pushed Nadine up against the sink, her mouth finding hers. Her kiss was warm and hard, her tongue laying claim to Nadine's mouth. It was less of a kiss and more of a warning to never kiss anyone else again. When Nadine moaned, Zaire grabbed her by the throat, teeth sinking into her bottom lip. The pain stung as a slight metallic taste filled her mouth, but Nadine loved it. She grabbed Zaire's waist, pawing at her dress until her ass was exposed. Nadine cupped her cheeks, spreading them apart until a finger teased her back entrance.

"Fuck, Nadine," moaned Zaire. "You trying to go there, mami?"

Nadine didn't respond. Instead, she moved her hand and plunged two fingers into Zaire's pussy, moving in and out, collecting her essence all over her fingers. Nadine delighted in hearing Zaire's pussy talk and grip her fingers with such force. Before Zaire could come from the feeling, Nadine pulled out, took her wet fingers, and gently guided one into Zaire's asshole.

"Shiiit!" Zaire cried out as she lifted a knee slightly on the sink to give Nadine better access. Nadine moved gently at first, then faster, careful to make sure Zaire could balance on her heels. She took her other hand and played with Z's throbbing clit. Zaire, unable to speak, stared up at the ceiling. Nadine knew she had her where she wanted her.

"Don't you want to come for me, pretty girl?" asked Nadine, her fingers working in both places. "You look so pretty when you come for me."

"Shit, yes Cookie. I wanna come for you. Fuck." Zaire's head fell to Nadine's shoulder as she braced herself for an orgasm.

"Look at me, Z," demanded Nadine

Zaire's eyes met Nadine's in the mirror. They were glassy as she tried to breathe through her orgasm. When she came, her juices squirted all over Nadine's perfectly manicured hand. Nadine removed her fingers and placed them in Zaire's mouth, letting her savor the taste of herself.

When she was done, Nadine kissed her, enjoying the taste of them. *Together.* It was so perfect Nadine wished she could bottle it up.

"See, you're so pretty when you come," Nadine praised. "So fucking pretty."

Zaire let her leg down and stepped back. Nadine smirked as she turned back to the sink to wash her hands.

"I know you don't think we're done." Zaire said, her breath hitching.

Nadine looked up at her through the mirror. "Sweetheart, you can barely stand up."

"No, I'm talking about you, Nadine."

Zaire came behind Nadine, lifting her skirt and tugging down her lace boy shorts. Nadine stepped out of them, careful not to snag her heels on them. Zaire bent down, spreading Nadine's ass and licking and sucking her pussy from the back.

"Shit Z," gasped Nadine as her fingers splayed against the mirror. If Zaire licked her anymore with that lethal tongue of hers, Nadine was liable to be sent to an early grave.

Eventually, Nadine was given a reprieve when Zaire came up for air. "Put your knee up on the fucking sink, Cookie."

Nadine didn't argue and did what she was told. She watched through the mirror as Zaire went into her clutch.

"Look straight ahead," Zaire instructed.

Nadine playfully rolled her eyes and looked in the mirror. Z was so bossy, but it was cute. Before she could utter another word, she heard buzzing.

"Goddamit!" Nadine screamed as the tiny bullet vibrator assaulted her clit.

Zaire smirked. "I know you didn't think you were gonna make me come and me not do the same for you, Cookie." She said, placing a kiss on the underside of Nadine's jaw as she increased the speed of the tiny but powerful toy.

Nadine couldn't take it. The bullet was alternating between Nadine's clit and gliding between her slick folds, making the entire ordeal almost torturous. Her legs were about to give out on her as an orgasm ripped through her. Zaire held her up, one arm around her waist.

Her hand moved from her waist to Nadine's throat, where she squeezed as the bullet steadily rang her bell. "Look at you, Cookie. Coming for me. You're so nasty, mami."

Nadine could hear knocking at the door. She had no idea how long they'd been in there, but she wasn't about to leave until she got hers. She grabbed hold of the sides of the mirror, praying she wouldn't rip it down from the goddamn wall. If she did, fuck it, she'd pay for it.

"Oh god! Z…" Nadine said through gritted teeth as the wave of satisfaction poured over her and its evidence all over the bullet. Nadine watched through the mirror as Zaire pulled the vibrator away, licked it clean, and dropped it back in her purse.

"Hey, we trying to pee here!" someone yelled from outside as they banged again on the door.

Quickly, they freshened up with paper towels and set themselves right again.

Nadine took Zaire's hand. "C'mon baby. Let's go have dessert."

CHAPTER 19

Debrief

The night had indeed ended with *actual* dessert. Nadine and Zaire fed each other flan as they got to know each other better. Nadine told her all about her life living in Waycross, and even about her first crush on Allison. Zaire told her about being an Army Brat living on bases all over the globe and how it was hard for her to make friends. She was thankful for college, which gave her a sense of stability.

Once the date ended, Nadine took Zaire home. She looked around as she parked. Not the safest neighborhood, but she understood Z was counting her coins. They sat in her car outside of her apartment, listening to the old school quiet storm music on the radio. Nadine had to chuckle at Zaire, not knowing some of the artists but being more than willing to up her music game.

Nadine looked at the time on her console. "Tonight was nice. But..."

"Yeah," Zaire nodded, understanding. "You've got to get home to Eddie."

"Trust me, I'd stay longer. I really would."

Zaire shook her head. "No, I understand. This time I know what's up in advance."

Nadine squinted. "What do you mean by that?"

Zaire lifted her head, looking up through the moonroof. "Remember, I said I fell in love with someone I shouldn't have? Well, this was my Junior year at Rutgers. I was nannying for a family in the city, trying to balance school and my job. My parents weren't speaking to me. Cut me off when they found out I liked women. I was nearing academic probation, and I needed some help. There was a professor in my department who really liked me, looked out for me. Soon, I started seeing that same professor. It got really intense. I feel for her, hard. She told me she loved me, and it was all good…until she went back to her husband. She'd told me they were separated, going to divorce. But it was just a lie." Zaire turned toward Nadine, running her finger against her cheek. "At least I know you'd never lie to me, Cookie. You been straight up from the jump. I appreciate that."

Nadine took Zaire's hand, turning to kiss her warm palm. "I'd never hurt you or lie to you. I can't predict the future so I don't know what will happen between us, but at least I can promise that. Can you say the same for me?"

"I'd never." Zaire smiled. "Now, kiss me so I can dream about your fine ass tonight."

When Nadine got home, she was floating. It had been one of the sexiest, best dates of her life. She took off her heels before making her way through the mudroom and down the hall. Before she could turn to head up the steps, she heard soft jazz playing from the great room. Nadine peeked inside to see Eddie sitting on the sofa, in just his basketball shorts, staring at the fireplace. She was surprised that he was up so late. He'd spent all day with EJ and had an early practice with the team in the morning.

"Did you have a good time?" he asked, still staring ahead at the fireplace as he sipped something dark and brown from a glass.

Nadine paused. She wasn't sure if disclosing this violated their agreements. She answered truthfully, but cautiously. "It was great. One of the best dates I've had."

"Best?" Eddie huffed, as he put his drink down on the ottoman coffee table. He turned to look at her. "Come here, Nadine."

Nadine was startled at the tone of Eddie's command. It wasn't angry, but gruff. Was he offended that she said it was one of the best dates? That didn't mean the dates that they had were bad at all. She walked slowly, her heels in her hand, toward the sofa. She stood next to him, and he grabbed her arm, pulling her down to straddle his lap.

"Are you drunk?" asked Nadine. She'd only seen Eddie drunk a few times, but he was certainly not himself.

Eddie leaned back, taking her in. "No."

Nadine wasn't sure she believed that. "You didn't have to wait up for me. Why aren't you asleep?"

Eddie didn't answer, he just stared up at her. It was unnerving.

"I...I should check on EJ." Nadine tried to move, but Eddie held on to her waist.

"Tell me everything that happened."

"But I thought you said..." Nadine frowned. She wasn't expecting to debrief Eddie, especially given his parameters regarding boundaries.

"Fuck what I said," Eddie quickly spat out. "What happened?"

Nadine swallowed. "We went to Bastion. Drank Sangria. Had some tapas. Danced."

Eddie's brow raised, amused. His face finally relaxed. "Really? *You* danced?"

"Yes, Salsa. Well, sort of. She was twerking on me. Well, we were kind of twerking on each other. I was tipsy."

Eddie's eyes grew dark as he listened. "And then what?"

"We had dessert and then I took her home." Nadine couldn't hide the slight warble in her voice.

"Hmm, is that all? You're leaving something out, aren't you? Tell the truth, Deanie."

Nadine sighed. "Eddie, you said you didn't..."

"What...happened..." he asked, pausing to stroke her heated skin between each word.

"I...I went to the bathroom to freshen up. And she followed me inside. And locked the door."

"Hmm," Eddie grunted. Nadine felt his hands moving up and down her torso. "Go on."

"Then, we kissed." Nadine felt Eddie's hands go to the back of her corset, slowly unzipping it. Once it was removed, she felt a shiver go down to her toes. She could feel his dick pulsing underneath the weight of her. This was turning him on. Tremendously. Since he wasn't there to satisfy his fetish to watch, Nadine knew he was settling for a play-by-play from her.

"How did she taste?" asked Eddie. His large, warm hands cupping and massaging her breasts, her nipples growing hard under his touch.

"Like…sangria…and…salt."

"She sounds delicious. Just as delicious as you."

Nadine closed her eyes, enjoying the feel of Eddie's hands on her body. His breathing quickened as if he was trying to get a hold of himself.

"What else?" asked Eddie, before taking a nipple into his mouth. Nadine moaned as he licked her until her nipples were stiff peaks. Underneath her, she could feel his erection growing hard as stone.

"Fuck, Eddie…"

"Go on, Deanie, baby," Eddie encouraged. "Tell me more."

Nadine's head pounded from being dizzyingly aroused and still a little tipsy. "I pulled her dress up and fingered her pussy."

"Was she wet?"

Nadine closed her eyes, trying to concentrate. "She was so wet for me."

"Fuck," Eddie groaned as he lifted slightly, pushing his shorts down. His dick, thick and veiny, was standing at full attention. It bobbed and slapped against his stomach, the tip of it leaking. It turned Nadine on that he was so aroused by just her words. She reached out and began stroking him, pre-cum leaking down her fingers. Eddie hissed through his teeth, enjoying the pressure and feel of her hands against his dick.

"I took my wet fingers," continued Nadine, "and played with her asshole."

"Shit, you did that?" asked Eddie. "Bad girl…"

"Uh huh," Nadine kept her stroke steady and firm, just like he liked it. "She came all over my hand, then licked my fingers clean."

"She's a nasty fucking girl." Eddie pushed up Nadine's skirt, then pushed her soaked panties to the side. "Where did she touch you?" His fingers went between her wet, swollen folds. "Did she touch you here, baby?"

"Yes," moaned Nadine. "She did…with a bullet". Her hands were now fully coated with Eddie's sticky pre-cum. She put her index finger in her mouth, savoring the taste of him. He always tasted so good.

Eddie watched, never taking his eyes off of his wife. His fingers moved to Nadine's clit. He strummed her swollen bud until her body was humming. "Did it feel good? Tell me."

"So fucking good." Nadine was on the verge of tears as an orgasm began bubbling to the surface. "Eddie, please. I'm gonna come. "

"Hold on, baby."

Without time to adjust, Eddie moved Nadine onto his dick. He stretched her to capacity, filling her up and hitting her spot. Pumping into her, he held her by the throat. "Did it feel good?"

"Yes, it felt so good. So fucking good." Nadine could barely get out the words. His hands were so tight around her throat. Eddie had always been a safe, relatively routine lover. Mostly because she asked him to. He certainly never talked this much or was one for breath play. Tonight, Eddie had become possessed by something more passionate.

"I bet you were so wet, baby. Just like how you are right now." Eddie lifted up, angling his dick just to the right spot. Nadine cried out, her pussy spasming all around his girth. Eddie's fingers stroke her clit until her wetness was dripping down his dick and balls.

"That's a good girl, Deanie. Soak my shit up."

"Eddie, please, fuck me!"

First Zaire, now Eddie. Nadine was losing it. The entire night was overstimulating and at that moment, she felt as if her body would combust. But Eddie kept on with his questions as he pounded into her, every stroke harder and more forceful after each answer.

"Did she make you come?"

"Yes…"

"Did she eat your pussy? Fucking answer me…"

"Yessss…"

"Who's fucking you right now?"

"You are Eddie…you are…"

Eddie grabbed a fistful of Nadine's hair, pulling her to face him. Tears rolled down Nadine's face as she whimpered. "Whose pussy is it?"

"Yours, dammit!"

With a guttural yell, Eddie drained his dick inside of Nadine. Even after he came, he stayed inside of her, not caring that his cum dripped all over his lap. Nadine collapsed on his chest, her body wrung out. Eddie grabbed a heavy throw blanket and wrapped it around them. He cradled Nadine in his arms, kissing her damp forehead. Their combined breathing was as ragged, slightly crackling like the sound of the fireplace. After a few silent moments, Eddie spoke.

"Sex on the first date, huh? Wow, the old Nadine would never," he teased.

Nadine settled into the warmth of his bare chest. "What happened to me not telling you details?"

"I can't lie. It turns me on to see you reclaiming this part of yourself. Knowing someone wants you as bad as I do, I fucking love that shit."

Nadine lifted her head, surprised. "Really?"

Eddie nodded. "Really. I admit it, at first I was hurt. This entire idea seemed wild, but when I took myself to the equation and put myself in your shoes, I understood."

Nadine kissed Eddie's chest. "Thank you."

"So," Eddie began. "Are you going to see her again?"

"I really like her, so yes."

Eddie smiled. "That's good. You deserve to be happy."

Nadine wanted to say more, wanted to delve into what happiness was like for her…what it could be like for them both. But the night had been perfect, and she didn't want to ruin it. She'd been pleased by both of the people she adored. Soon, her eyelids became heavy, and she eventually drifted off to sleep in the comfort of Eddie's arms.

It had been the best night of her life.

CHAPTER 20

Have It All

The week was going from sunshine to shit in record time. Nadine's calendar was full of meetings to the point of her having to eat standing up at her desk. The tension with Mitchell was also at an all-time high. She tried her best not to snap at the guy, especially after Nadine's assistant said that it was inconclusive that Mitchell switched her data in the cloud.

On top of the madness of work, Nadine had committed to attend EJ's school play. He'd come home every day reminding her about the play and she couldn't break his heart. This is why she was up at the crack of dawn the day of the play, making cupcakes for the entire class. It wasn't enough to just be there; she had to make her presence known to the stay-at-home moms that judged her endlessly. Her motherly guilt was getting the best of her.

Ugh. Dr. Flournoy would not approve of this behavior.

She was taking the last tray of cupcakes out of the oven when Zaire entered the kitchen. Nadine bit her lip as she took her in. She wasn't sure what was more enticing, Zaire or the warm cupcakes. She was pretty sure Zaire wore leggings most days to drive her crazy with the way her ass jiggled.

Zaire rounded the island. The smell of her perfume mixed with the sweetness of the cupcakes. "I should start calling you Little Debbie, the way I'm always catching you stress baking at odd times of the day."

Nadine shook her head. "Sometimes baking is just that. Baking. These are for EJ's class."

Zaire raised a brow. "So you are coming to the play? He's going to be so happy."

"Yeah, I had to shift some things around this afternoon, and I am sure my team isn't pleased, but I am tired of missing things in my kids' lives." Nadine sighed as she began piping icing on the cupcakes. "I shouldn't have to keep doing this."

"So quit," Zaire said.

Nadine paused icing. "If I quit, then what would I do all day?"

Zaire looked Nadine up and down, her eyes lingering on her lips. "Trust me, we can think of plenty of things to occupy your time." She swiped her finger in the bowl of icing and licked. "Oh my god, this shouldn't taste so good."

Zaire reached for a finished cupcake, but Nadine playfully tapped her hand. "Get out of there, girl!" She turned to the counter, picking up the half dozen caramel cream cupcakes that were under a cake dome. "These are just for you. They have all the sugar and good stuff. Not the gluten free, sugar free, organic nonsense I am taking to the school."

"Aww! Thank you, Deanie."

Nadine watched as Zaire carefully lifted the top of the cake dome and inhaled the sweet scent of the cupcakes. She gave Nadine a soft smile, eyes a little misty. "Like I said, you're definitely the sweetest."

Nadine was about to lean in for a kiss when heavy footsteps snapped her out of it. She almost forgot that Eddie was still here. He had a late morning meeting and decided to sleep a little later than usual. He was dressed in a suit, looking as handsome as than ever.

"Looking good, Mr. Moody," Zaire replied, admiring Eddie's suit.

Eddie visibly blushed. "Thank you, Zaire. I thought I smelled something sweet." He smiled as he came over to place a kiss on Nadine's cheek. "I see you've been baking up a storm."

Nadine wiped her brow. "Yeah. It's just a little something for EJ's class."

Eddie looked at Zaire, who was now devouring a cupcake. "I see you can't resist Nadine's sweets either."

"I sure can't! I swear, anything she makes, it's irresistible." Zaire licked her lips slowly, then licked the remnants of icing off her fingers. The act made Nadine press her thighs together as she watched. She was clearly making a show of it.

Nadine peered at Eddie, taking notice too. He cleared his throat, then adjusted his tie. She bet if she felt his slacks, she'd feel a hard as a brick dick.

"Yeah, I get it," Eddie said with a slight chuckle. "Her pastries are pretty irresistible."

Zaire smiled and gave a wink. "Definitely. Well, you have a nice day. Let me get EJ ready for the day."

Nadine and Eddie both watched her leave the kitchen and head up the steps.

"She really likes leggings," Eddie mumbled, trying his best to tear his eyes away from Zaire's jiggling ass. "Sorry. No disrespect, Nadine."

Nadine shook her head. "Nah, I get it. The girl is thick. If I had a body like that, I'd live in leggings too. Thank God you're such a good guy. You'd never fuck the nanny." Nadine had to pause at her words, picking up her coffee cup to take a sip. *She was one fucking the nanny. What a cliché.*

Eddie shook his head as he poured coffee in a travel mug. "I'm not trying to blow up my life over some ass. I mean, even if it is a nice ass." He paused, staring curiously at Nadine. "Just wondering…would Z be your type?"

Nadine nearly choked. "Uhm, she's a little young, don't you think?"

Eddie shrugged. "True, but I mean physically? I am trying to get to know what you like. What you're attracted to in women. We never really discussed that."

Nadine was trying to carefully think of what to say. Zaire was definitely her type, but she liked all kinds of women, if she was being honest. She thought about it. "I mean, I messed around with mostly femme women. Maybe one soft stud. I think that's how she identified. Not sure we called it that back then. I honestly am still learning."

That was the truth. When Nadine was younger, she hadn't thought about the type of women she was attracted to until she discussed it with her therapist. Now, she had the language to really talk about the specifics of her attraction. If she had to categorize Zaire, she was a "stem". Some days she was ultra femme, other days she was very tomboy. Nadine loved the way she changed it up.

"Interesting," Eddie mused. He looked at his watch, then grabbed his coffee. "Shit, I gotta go, babe. Meeting about NILs and our athletes. I am going to try and make it to the play if I can. See if I can move stuff around."

Nadine was surprised. "Really? You sure you have the time? You have a lot going on." This was Eddie's first year coaching collegiate basketball. He had a lot riding on his rookie season as a coach. If he missed this play, Nadine understood. There would be others.

"Yeah. I realize that I can't miss out on EJ's life either. Like you said, time is flying. And you can't be the only one making sacrifices. That's not fair." Eddie gave Nadine a peck on the lips, grabbed a cupcake, and headed out the door.

Nadine felt a shit-ton of guilt at Eddie's words. Eddie was such a good man. A great husband and a tremendous father. She needed to tell him the truth about Zaire soon. He deserved it.

💋

NADINE AND ZAIRE HADN'T STEPPED TWENTY FEET INTO THE AUDITORIUM when Ingrid was making a beeline toward them.

"Wow, Nadine! I didn't think you'd actually show up! Imagine my surprise when I heard you were coming and bringing cupcakes! How sweet!"

This phony, bottle-blonde bitch.

Nadine gave a tight smile. "Well, I can't be all about work. Besides, someone has to bring the kids a sweet treat for all their hard work. I'm sure they're tired of rice cakes and stale granola bars." That was a direct jab at Ingrid. For someone who had money, she was incredibly cheap. She always brought stale, store-bought snacks for the kids that were no doubt days old and close to expiration.

Ingrid huffed as she attempted to plaster on a smile. "Well, we all can't be as talented as you." She turned her attention toward Zaire, who had been quietly observing their exchange. "I see you brought your nanny. EJ just adores her. You better be careful, Nadine. She might steal the hearts of all the men in your life."

Nadine was sick of Ingrid's shit. "Trust me, I am not worried about that." She seductively curled her hand around Zaire's waist. "Z, can you find us some seats, sweetie?"

Zaire gave a slight smirk. "Of course, love." Nadine watched as Zaire deliberately sauntered down the narrow aisles toward the seats. Every nosey adult in the place was staring at her and those goddamn leggings, ass moving like ocean waves. Nadine was pretty sure Z didn't have on any underwear. She never did. Nadine made a mental note to buy her leggings in every single color imaginable.

Ingrid's eyes widened as she looked between the two women. "Wha...what is *that* about Nadine?" she stammered.

Nadine gave Ingrid the fakest of smiles. "Ingrid, I say this with the utmost respect. But go fuck yourself." She gave the blonde a cute little pat on the shoulder and walked toward her seat next to Zaire. With the way that gossip traveled, she was pretty sure that she was going to have to find EJ another school by tomorrow.

Zaire leaned over, chuckling. "You know, you just made that bitch's head explode."

"Please! Fuck her," Nadine sucked her teeth. "I am sure by the time I sat down in this seat, the entire school is going to hear a rumor that I am fucking you."

"Do you care?" Zaire asked sincerely.

"I should, but I don't." Nadine looked around the auditorium. A few eyes stared at her. "Let them think whatever they want."

Zaire nudged her playfully. "See. That's Big Mama energy, Cookie."

Just as the lights began to dim, Nadine spotted Eddie coming through the auditorium doors. She smiled, waving him over to the empty seat next to her.

"Got here in the nick of time," Eddie said, placing a kiss on Nadine's forehead.

Nadine returned a warm smile. "You did. The play is about to start."

The crowd hushed and camera phones began to flash as the children made their way onto the stage. Nadine beamed with pride as she saw EJ in his Big Bad Wolf costume. Nadine quickly snapped a photo. He was too cute for words.

In the darkness of the auditorium, she felt Zaire link her pinky with hers, pulling her hand between their touching thighs. On the other side, she felt Eddie place a firm hand on her other thigh. Feeling them both touch her sent tingles down her spine and heat pooling in her belly. Nadine brushed off the sensation, trying to concentrate on the play instead. Yet, her mind replayed the same thought over and over.

Maybe I can have it all.

CHAPTER 21
Euphoria

After the sugar rush of cupcakes and excitement of the play, EJ eventually crashed. He was fast asleep by the time they'd made it home. Nadine carried him up to his room to put him down for the night.

"I guess all the excitement wore him out," Nadine said as she stared at her son, peacefully sleeping. "He could barely keep his eyes open during dinner."

Nadine turned on the nightlight and closed EJ's door. She began to walk downstairs when Zaire caught her arm.

"Where are you going, mami?" Zaire asked.

Nadine sighed, frowning. "I need to get back to my office. I missed two late afternoon meetings and need to see what notes Devi has left for me. Besides, shouldn't you be finishing your term paper, anyway?"

"All that can wait until the morning, Cookie." Zaire whispered as she pulled her closer. "I have something special for you."

"Something special?" Nadine was curious. "Like what?"

"Come find out."

Nadine watched as Zaire slowly pulled away from her, pulling her Emory sweatshirt over her head as she walked back toward the guest bedroom. Nadine's sharp intake of breath stung at the sight of Z's bare breasts. Like a sailor heading a siren's call, Nadine was powerless when it came to Zaire. *This girl is going to be the death of me,* she thought as she followed her down the hall.

As soon as she was in the room, Zaire was pawing at Nadine, eager to take her clothes off.

"What's the rush?" Nadine giggled, watching Zaire damn near rip off every button of her blouse. There was a hunger and a need in her that she hadn't seen before.

Zaire bit down on Nadine's shoulder, and she moaned at the sting. "I just need you naked and on the bed as soon as fucking possible."

Nadine obliged, slipping out her navy boy shorts and bra, laying across the bed. Her nipples hardened and her pussy began pulsing as soon as Zaire stripped out of those goddamn leggings. She wasn't wearing any fucking panties. *Just as she suspected.*

"So you've been fully naked under your clothes all day?" Nadine breathed out, captivated by the mahogany beauty in front of her.

"Why wear panties or a bra? My nipples stay too hard, and my pussy stays wet when I'm around you. Why ruin them?"

"Oh," Nadine exhaled, a little more than aroused that she was responsible for Zaire's lack of underwear.

Zaire walked over, placing a soft kiss on her lips. "I'll be just a minute, beautiful." She walked into the ensuite bathroom and closed the door.

Nadine could feel her heart beating hard in her chest. She wasn't sure why she was nervous. But Zaire was on some new energy. She felt it. And it intrigued her.

When Nadine heard the lock of the bathroom door release, she looked over and her eyes widened at the sight of Zaire, wearing a thick, blue strap on harnessed to a black straps around her waist.

"Oh shit," Nadine whispered lowly. She hadn't expected that at all. It was like that night at Secrets all over again. Except Nadine was the pet, held captive by Zaire's gaze.

"Don't worry, Cookie. This strap is just for you. It's new." Zaire smirked as she stroked the dildo slightly.

"I…I wasn't even thinking that. It's just…I've never done that before."

Zaire frowned. "Really? But I thought you've been with women?"

"I have but, it was more manual stimulation and things. Not this."

"Oh," Zaire looked down. "Should I take this off?"

"No," Nadine quickly responded, sitting up on her elbows. "I want to try. I'm open."

"Cookie, you sure? We really don't have to."

"Z, I want to. I trust you." Nadine was willing to try, to give this woman part of her she craved. Zaire had given herself to Nadine in so many ways. Why not give her lover what she wanted?

Zaire walked over to the bed. She stroked Nadine's face, gently at first until she grabbed her by the chin. Her eyes were dark and stormy. "So I'm gonna be the one to pop your strap cherry, huh? Imma make you cum all over this dick, mami." When Zaire released her chin, Nadine let out a whimper. *What was she doing to me?*

Zaire moved closer, stroking the blue dildo. Against her dark skin, it was like a flame drawing Nadine in. She was officially under a spell. Zaire placed it against Nadine's lips, tapping slightly. "Get her wet, baby."

Nadine opened wide, her tongue wrapping around the dildo slowly. She sucked, licked, spit trailing down the base and between her breasts. *Yes, she was completely spellbound.*

"You look so fucking good doing that," moaned Zaire. She pulled Nadine's hair. "Look at me."

Nadine's eyes flicked up to see Zaire biting her lip, her face enjoying every moment. Her face made Nadine's skin burn with desire. She wanted to please her, the need for Zaire's approval fueling her to suck that dildo with a frenzy.

Zaire drew back, and Nadine released her lips. Zaire rubbed her thumb across them before leaning down to give her a kiss. Her tongue painted the inside of Nadine's mouth, sending electric ripples down her spine. "Lay back," the dark beauty commanded, and Nadine did so, her head cradled between the pillows. Nervousness coursed through her body, and she tried to tamper it down, taking deep breaths.

Zaire got on her knees on the bed, between Nadine's legs. Their combined weight dipped the mattress slightly. "Don't be nervous, Cookie. I'd never hurt you."

"I know. And I'd never hurt *you*," Nadine repeated, her voice shaky.

"I know, gorgeous." Zaire smiled. "You're too good to me to hurt me." She kissed Nadine, sucking and licking her full lips until she was wet with anticipation. Zaire's fingers slipped between her legs, and as she parted her wet folds, Nadine let out tiny, quick gasps. She was so sensitive already, so needy. One stroke and Nadine would probably come all over her hand.

Zaire licked her fingers, savoring the taste of her. "Wet already, baby? I need you wetter." She gripped Nadine's thighs, sliding down to suck on her clit. She blew on the sensitive nerves and Nadine felt all her senses crashing into her all at once. *That mouth…that tongue…that fucking tongue.* She gripped the sheets as Zaire's fingers moved to her nipples, pinching and tweaking them until they were painful, sensitive points. Wetness was running down between the crack of her ass as the mixture of Zaire's mouth and her essence made a mess of the sheets.

"Fucccck!" Nadine cried, her nails nearly breaking from gripping the duvet so hard.

Zaire looked up, her lips and chin totally wet. "That's it Cookie, come for me just like that."

Nadine felt like a geyser on the precipice of eruption. She closed her eyes tightly until it felt like starlight was bursting throughout her body. Her legs shook as she came, and Zaire was there to drink her fill of her.

"So fucking sweet, baby." Zaire praised as she rose, hovering slightly over Nadine. She moved a sticky curl from her forehead as she leaned down, kissing her softly. Nadine could taste her arousal on her lips, which she hungrily devoured. She finally let go of the sheets, grabbing Zaire's ass. The tip of the dildo rested against her thigh. Nadine looked into her eyes, silently signaling that she was ready. Even though Nadine was extremely wet, Zaire reached for the small bottle of lube she'd brought out and slathered the dildo until it was coated generously.

Nadine let her legs fall open as Zaire eased between. As soon as the dildo breached her pussy, Nadine's back arched off the bed. Her nails dug into Zaire's ass, pushing her deeper into her.

"You're so fucking greedy," chuckled Zaire lowly. "Let me fuck you how I know you need it, Cookie." She pumped into her slowly, methodically. Nadine felt her body heat as if at any minute she'd combust. The combination of steady stimulation and Zaire's softness was euphoric. *God, this was everything she could ever want and more.*

With one hand, Zaire held on to the headboard and with the other, tweaked Nadine's taut nipple over and over. Her hips thrusted into her repeatedly, the sound of her pussy squelching from the strap was too much to bear. She shut her eyes tight.

"No, look at me, Nadine," Zaire panted between thrusts. "Open your fucking eyes, beautiful."

Nadine's lashes fluttered until her vision focused. She looked at Zaire, her body glistening, her breasts heavy. They called to her, and she lifted up slightly, focusing all her attention on them. She heard Zaire hiss, then moan as Nadine's lips circled the dark areolas, then teeth graze the hardened peaks. She could taste the faint hint of cherry and jasmine perfume on her skin, mixed with the saltiness of her sweat. It was an intoxicating elixir. As wet as her pussy was, it was working. She licked and tasted her skin, over and over. Fuck selling drugs at PharmaDigital, Nadine thought. If she could bottle this up as a sexual stimulant, she'd be a quadrillionaire.

With every stroke, Zaire was fucking her as if she was staking her claim on her pussy. When her hand moved to stroke Nadine's clit, she wasn't sure if she could take another orgasm. They were rolling in fast, back-to-back. Nadine was moaning loudly. She prayed to God that she wouldn't wake EJ. Zaire didn't give a fuck how loud she was; she was going to pull every orgasm from her that she could.

"That's it Cookie. You like how I give it to you?"

"Yesss…" Nadine moaned.

Zaire's fingers moved furiously over Nadine's clit. "Give me another one, baby."

Nadine felt heat coursing through her veins as tears ran down her face. She pulled Zaire's face closer to hers as she kissed her, trying to breathe through her orgasms.

Nadine was in bliss, drowning in a state of orgasmic nirvana. She was so zoned-out that she didn't hear the alarm beep nor the footsteps coming up the steps. It wasn't until Zaire's stroking slowed that she focused on the present. Zaire's eyes were looking past Nadine's, wide with recognition. Nadine followed her gaze until her own eyes met

Eddie's as he stood in the doorway. She hadn't heard the door to the room open.

Shit.

"What the fuck," he breathed out, standing paralyzed in the doorway.

Nadine lifted up, trying to move her body from underneath Zaire's, but she was pinned. She looked at her mercifully. "Let me get up, baby. Please," she whispered.

"Baby?" Eddie questioned, incredulously.

"No," Zaire said, indignant as she continued to fuck her. "Let him watch you get fucked how you deserve."

"Zaire, please." Nadine begged. Zaire sucked her teeth, finally slipping out of Nadine.

Nadine stood, trying to grab her top to throw it on quickly. Before she could fasten a single button, Eddie was there, quick as lightning. He grabbed her by the neck, pushing her up against the wall.

"You don't have to do that!" Zaire exclaimed.

Eddie ignored Zaire, his eyes still focused on Nadine. "The nanny, Nadine? Really?"

Nadine attempted to swallow. She'd never seen Eddie like that in her life. She had flashbacks to Drew and her blood ran cold. "Eddie, please, let me explain." She watched as Eddie's eyes took her in, and her body, then looked over at Zaire, who was nearby, eyes wide.

"Is she what you want? What you like?" he asked, his voice low and gravely. "Do you like how she fucks you? Don't fucking lie to me! Answer me!"

"Yes," Nadine whispered, a tear rolling down her cheek.

Eddie's eyes were dark as a summer's midnight. "She made you come?"

"Please, Eddie, we can talk about this," pleaded Nadine. She didn't want to have to call the police on her husband, but she would. She could see the headlines in the paper now. Her eyes quickly scanned the room, but she remembered that her phone was downstairs. *Fuck.*

Nadine's eyes went back to Eddie. His chest rose with each breath, eyes narrowed in on her. His hands felt hot and sweaty against her skin. She could hear the faint sounds of Zaire shakily breathing in the background. *What the hell was she going to do?* He had more than a foot and fifty pounds on her. Paralyzed, Nadine could only pray for mercy. He'd trapped her like a bird in a cage.

"Y'all *been* fucking, huh? That night I met Zaire, I bet y'all were fucking."

Nadine said nothing, just blinked as she tried to mentally formulate an escape plan.

"Did she make you come?" Eddie repeated as he leaned forward, inhaling her scent.

Nadine felt his grip slightly loosen as his face pressed close to hers. When she looked up into his eyes, the anger he'd had was replaced by something else. Something heated…something…*carnal.* He pressed his body against hers, and she felt the unmistakable hardness of his dick.

Trying not to anger him further, Nadine swallowed before answering. "Yes. She did."

Eddie's tongue darted out, licking at the seam of Nadine's lips. "Is this how she tastes on your lips?" He groaned, then licked at her lips again, this time forcing his tongue to part her lips as he kissed her fully. Nadine, even though she'd been terrified just minutes before, opened her mouth wider to receive it. Her brain was officially scrambled like old school cable television.

Eddie pulled back with a satisfied sigh. "You looked so good getting fucked. Both of you looked… so beautiful."

Nadine watched as Eddie crossed the room, sitting on the chaise. She could still see the traces of a strained look on his face. She knew that look well. He was aroused. His erection was probably painfully hard. She gave Zaire a quizzical look, to which she only raised her brow in similar confusion.

"I…I just want to watch." Eddie confessed, his voice softer now. "Please. I won't interrupt again. Unless you ask me to. But…" He looked between the two women. "Just…please let me."

This was Eddie's fantasy come true. The fantasy that had been consuming him for months. The very thing that Nadine had made him feel ashamed about. A simultaneous strain of guilt, fear, and arousal plagued her in the moment. Should she deny him? Thoughts percolated through her brain until she felt Zaire close the space between them.

Nadine swallowed. "Eddie, baby. Let's talk about this. I don't think this is a good idea. I just..."

"Cookie," Zaire interrupted, turning Nadine's chin to face her. "Let him."

Nadine's eyes widened. "Wait...what?"

"Let him watch." Zaire placed a soft kiss on her lips. "Let him see how good we are together." She moved her lips up her neck, to the shell of her ear, making Nadine's flesh have goosebumps. "Let him see how I make you cum, Cookie...how you make me cum."

Nadine turned to face Zaire, then looked at Eddie, who was leaning back against the chaise, watching. He rubbed his hands down his legs, nervously anticipating an answer. Nadine bit the corners of her lip. She shouldn't be this intrigued or...*turned on.*

"Are you ok with this?" asked Nadine. This wasn't part of her and Eddie's agreement. She didn't want Zaire to feel coerced in any way. Nadine knew how that could be.

Zaire nodded, a hint of a smile on her face. "It's clear he wants this. And looking at you, you want this too. You can't hide it. I see the look of desire on your face. Honestly, I've had the same thoughts of us all being together since the first time I saw you two. Both of you are sexy as fuck. But I want to fuck you. *Only* you." Zaire grabbed a fistful of Nadine's hair, pulling her closer. She kissed her, swallowing her moans and devouring her tongue until Nadine was panting.

They continued kissing as they moved back toward the bed. Zaire fell back as Nadine eased on top of her. She was still wearing the strap and Nadine ground against it as she continued kissing her. She was slick with heat and wetness, gliding up and down the shaft of the dildo. The stimulation was wholly gratifying. When she heard Eddie let out a slow moan, it made her grind even harder against it. This felt so wrong, but so right. *Oh, so right.*

"Put it in," Zaire whispered hoarsely. "Ride me, Nadine."

Nadine lifted off Zaire slightly as she spit in her hand, sliding it up and down the dildo before seating herself on it. This angle stretched her fully, hitting her G-spot at just the right angle. Her curly hair flopped down in her face as she looked down at Zaire, who looked up at her as if she'd given her the world. Nadine wanted to be that reason for that look on her face forever.

She rode slowly, her ass bouncing on Zaire's lap. Zaire cupped her tits, pulling her cola-colored nipples hard. She moaned as she slammed down on her. She could hear her own wetness as she rode up and down.

"Open your eyes. Look at us, Deanie. Please."

Nadine hadn't realized her eyes had been closed until she'd heard Eddie's voice. When she opened them, she saw Eddie with his hands down his slacks, jacking his dick furiously. Something about it made Nadine hungry for him and Zaire. *Together.*

"Come here," she beckoned to Eddie. He was next to her in two steps, his hand still down his pants. Nadine gave a slight smile as she looked at him. He was so eager to please. "Let me touch you, Ed."

Eddie quickly pulled down his slacks and boxer briefs, his dick springing forth. He was hard in a way that Nadine had never seen. She could see every ridge and vein of his thick, curved dick. He was already leaking pre-cum in anticipation. Nadine had to taste, to ease her craving and relieve Eddie's growing pressure. She leaned down, licking the tip of his dick slowly. At the first lick, Eddie groaned. If she wasn't careful, Eddie would come right then and there. Nadine knew she had to take her time. She looked down at Zaire, who winked, giving her a little encouragement.

Nadine focused on Eddie's thick tip first, licking and sucking around it until her tongue slipped into the hole. Eddie let out a slow hiss of relief as Nadine licked a little before moving down his shaft. She slurped and sucked until spit was spilling out of her mouth, onto her chest. Nadine felt Zaire move her hands up, gathering some of it before moving down her torso to her clit. Nadine nearly let Eddie's dick slip out of her mouth as she felt an orgasm slowly building, but he steadied her head, grabbing her by the hair. Nadine tried to concentrate on the tasks at hand, but the dual stimulation was too much.

"Keep sucking me Deanie. Fuck! You feel so fucking good."

Zaire slapped her ass. "I didn't say stop riding me, Cookie."

Nadine's body hummed with excitement, the rush of an impending orgasm fueling her desire. She groaned around Eddie's dick as she felt sweat trickle down her brow. She could barely breathe as his dick pumped in and out of her mouth. Nadine braced herself for Eddie coming down her throat. He was close, she could feel it, but suddenly, he pulled out.

"I don't want to come like that. I…" he hesitated, looking between the two women. "I want to come inside you, baby."

Nadine looked down at Zaire, who nodded. She lifted off the strap, which was now coated in every last drop of her. Zaire began to remove it, but Eddie stopped her.

"Can I…" His eyes looked down at the strap on, heated curiosity in his gaze. Nadine was confused, but apparently Zaire was very aware of what his half-formed question meant. Still on the bed, the obsidian beauty got on her knees to give Eddie what he wanted.

Nadine let out a slow breath as she watched Eddie, bending down, licking the strap clean. She blinked, then again, making sure she was seeing what she was seeing. He devoured it, licking every single inch of it. She'd never known Eddie to express any desire to do something like this, so the image shocked her. Aroused her. Zaire was steady, her hands on her hips as she let him explore the strap with his tongue. The look on her face told Nadine that she seemed entirely too pleased with the scene. Seemed like this didn't shock her one bit.

When he'd had his fill, Eddie licked his lips. Zaire removed the strap and harness, laying it on the nearby nightstand.

"Fuck, you taste so good, baby. Even better." Eddie breathed against Nadine's lips, coaxing a kiss from her. "I just wanted to taste what she did to you." He deepened their kiss. The faint taste of her pussy on his tongue made Nadine moan into his mouth. That moan made Eddie kiss her deeper, harder, until they were both clawing at each other.

When they broke free, Eddie snatched off his shirt, leaving him totally naked. For his age, Eddie had a body that would rival any of his players- lean, muscular, sculpted. He pulled Nadine by her legs toward the edge of the bed. She squealed as a chuckle erupted from her lips. But it died quickly when she looked at Eddie, who was already fisting his dick, which was getting harder with each stroke. He reached for the lube that Zaire had used and put some in his hand, gliding it up and down his shaft. He gave Nadine no warning, no time to breathe as he entered her swiftly and forcefully. She gasped, and as she did, Zaire was there to capture her mouth and kiss her through it.

Zaire leaned down at Nadine's side, kissing her at the curve of her neck. "Look at you taking your man's dick. Your pussy is devouring him."

Eddie lifted Nadine's legs, wrapping them around his waist as he stood at the edge of the bed. He pounded into her, filling her pussy to the hilt with every inch of his dick. Tears pooled in her eyes as he rammed into her. It had been a while since Eddie had fucked her with so much vigor. It was violent, passionate, and too wild to be fully constrained.

And Nadine was loving every second of it.

"Creaming his dick up just like you did for me, baby," praised Zaire. "You wanna come don't you, Cookie?"

"Yessss," Nadine moaned. The intensity of the pleasure they were giving her was too much. Her hips tried to meet Eddie stroke for stroke. But it was damn near impossible. He and his dick were in the zone. She felt Zaire's hand move between them, stroking her sensitive clit. Between Zaire's praise, her stroking, and Eddie's dick, Nadine knew she wouldn't last.

"I'm coming, Deanie, baby," Eddie announced as his strokes finally slowed. She could feel him coming inside her, hot, pulsing and furiously. He had to steady himself to calm down from how hard he'd come. As he relaxed, Nadine could still feel the relative hardness of his dick inside her.

When he pulled out, Zaire eased herself between Nadine's legs. Nadine watched as Zaire licked, gathering every drop of cum that was leaking from her pussy. Satisfied she'd gathered it all, Zaire crawled up toward Nadine's face. She pulled Nadine's bottom lip with her thumb, opening her mouth wide as she deposited every drop of cum from her lips. Nadine swallowed, then kissed Zaire until she was fully satisfied.

"Damn," Eddie said as he watched the scene playing out before him. He tucked himself back into his pants before heading into the bathroom, leaving Zaire and Nadine alone.

When Zaire pulled back, Nadine blinked, as if coming back to reality. *Her husband? Zaire?* What just occurred between the three of them hit her like a ton of bricks.

Zaire noticed the strain on Nadine's face. "Why are you stressing?" she asked, curling up to Nadine. "It's just us having some fun."

"Yeah but, this changes everything."

"It doesn't have to," Zaire said, kissing Nadine's damp forehead. "Just enjoy the moment, mami."

Eddie came back into the bedroom with two warm, wet towels. "Let me take care of you, both of you. Please." He carefully began to wipe Nadine down, cleaning her gently. He did the same to Zaire, careful to ask if it was ok, or could he touch her there. Eddie had always been attentive, but this was tenderness in a way Nadine had never experienced. It made her love him even more.

Once Eddie was done, Nadine and Zaire slipped on their clothes and sat on the bench in front of the bed. Eddie slipped on his slacks and leaned against the dresser. Nadine wanted to say something, but she didn't have the words. What could she possibly say?

Zaire looked between the couple. "Maybe I should head home."

"No," Eddie began, holding up his hand. He sighed, rubbing his low-cut Caesar. "Please, stay. We need to talk."

CHAPTER 22

Aftermath

Nadine, Eddie, and Zaire sat at the dining room table. He'd opened a bottle of La Fete Du Cotes Rose' for the ladies while he opted to pour himself a bourbon on the rocks.

They sat quietly, sipping for a few minutes until Eddie spoke, turning to Nadine.

"That was…amazing." Eddie said, a shy smile gracing his face.

Nadine felt her face heat as she remembered what happened just hours ago. "It was."

"Yeah, I don't really fuck with couples or men like that, but you two are too hot to not want to," Zaire said as she bit her lip, staring at them.

"Thanks," Eddie and Nadine said in unison. They were more than enamored by the compliment.

Eddie took a sip of his bourbon before turning to Nadine. He reached out for her hand, squeezing gently. "I want to say I am sorry. I shouldn't have reacted initially the way that I did. Putting my hands on you like that? I know your history with shit like that…I'm so fucking sorry."

His voice was shaky and so small, so unlike the Eddie that Nadine knew.

Nadine patted his hand. "It's ok, Ed. I know you wouldn't hurt me.

I know it was a shock to walk in on us like that."

"Shock or not, that was a fucked-up reaction, and I can't apologize enough. My emotions were all over the place. I was so turned on, yet so upset. It was…confusing." Eddie looked down at his glass. It was clear to Nadine that he was completely ashamed.

Nadine closed her eyes and sighed, trying to shake off the memories that his reaction brought up for her. "I get it. About the emotions all over the place."

"You and Zaire…how long has this been going on?" Eddie asked, motioning between the two women.

Nadine took a larger sip of wine before answering. She felt the burning chill of the rose slide down her throat. "A couple of weeks."

"Weeks?" Eddie repeated, astonished. "And you didn't think you could tell me? Why?"

"Given the circumstances and our rules we established, I didn't know how to."

"Yeah, but," Eddie sighed. "I thought we were going to be honest, Deanie. I am ok with you exploring this. You didn't have to lie about any of it."

Nadine looked at Zaire, hesitation in her eyes. But Zaire nodded, encouraging Nadine to continue. "There is more to it than Zaire being the nanny. I…well…we've met her before."

Eddie furrowed his brows, confused. "We have? Where?"

"The night you took me to Secrets."

Eddie looked at Zaire, eyes slowly widening with recognition. "The dancer. The one that you kissed…"

"I'm very much a qualified nanny, if you're wondering," Zaire interrupted before Eddie could continue. "The agency can definitely back that up."

Eddie's mouth dropped open, and his eyes were still wide. "I thought you looked familiar. I thought I was tripping but…wow. This is wild." He smoothed his hand down his goatee. "Nadine, really?"

"I know," Nadine sighed. "I didn't plan for any of this to happen, but it has. And it did." She reached out for Zaire's hand. "I don't regret any of it."

Eddie sipped more of his bourbon. "She's bad as hell. I totally understand the attraction. A little young but…"

"I'm almost thirty, Eddie. Old enough to know my way around pussy as good as your wife's." Zaire quipped.

Nadine nearly choked on her wine. Eddie narrowed his eyes, giving Zaire a stare that could cut glass. But instead of lashing out, he started to chuckle. "That you do. And Nadine damn sure has good pussy. That we can agree on." He held out his glass and Zaire clinked it.

Everyone started to laugh. Somehow, that dissipated any tension that could have been lingering between them.

Nadine reached for Eddie's hand again. "Eddie, seriously, if this makes you uncomfortable…"

As much as she cared for Zaire, she loved Eddie. He was her heart, the love of her life. She wouldn't throw away sixteen years of marriage because of her own desires consuming her, even if it was integral to understanding who she was. She was a different Nadine. She had Zaire to thank for that. She was part of her heart. But Eddie was the reason that Nadine even had a heart to give to Zaire.

Eddie shook his head, interlacing his fingers with hers. "No, baby. If Zaire makes you happy, then I am happy. But I think we need to re-establish some ground rules for this mono/poly dynamic you got going on. EJ…"

"He's barely four, Ed." Nadine didn't think it necessary to bring EJ into this.

Zaire waved her hand. "And I'm the nanny. Just Miss Z to him. That's all. Cookie knows I'd never do anything to make him uncomfortable."

Eddie nodded, understanding. "Ok. And what about Alex?"

Nadine's eyes widened. "I…I mean…I'll talk to her. I promise." She and Alex were on shaky ground as is. She was going to have to have a long session with Dr. Flournoy to tackle her approach. Her therapist was going to be sick of her.

"By the way, Z. Why do you call her Cookie?" Eddie asked, curious.

Zaire bit her lip as she smirked. "One, she's a beast with baking. There's nothing she can't make. And two, that pussy. I've never tasted pussy as sweet as hers. Don't you agree?"

"Damn," Eddie chuckled. "I've been married to her ass for sixteen years. Why didn't I think of that shit?"

"Because," Zaire smiled. "I see your wife in a whole new light. You don't have fresh eyes like I do."

Eddie looked at Nadine and smiled. "You're right. I don't. But I see you now, Deanie. I do."

Nadine's eyes filled with tears. "And I see you too."

"Aww," Zaire teased. "Ya'll are too cute. But, uhm, can we get back to these rules? Because I'd like to continue fucking my girlfriend in peace."

❦

THE THREE OF THEM TALKED FOR ANOTHER HOUR MORE BEFORE HEADING TO bed. Eddie made it clear that he was fine with Nadine and Zaire continuing to be together.

Zaire wasn't opposed to being exclusive but stated that if Nadine met someone else or either party wanted to end this, they would be honest. Nadine promised to keep lines of communication open with both of them if her feelings were to change. Zaire said she had absolutely no desire to have sexual intercourse with Eddie and he agreed, which surprised Nadine. He was very clear about his boundaries sexually, going into detail about what he would consent to and what he was comfortable with. He explained in great detail his cuckold fantasies to Zaire, who simply nodded with understanding, asking him questions about his boundaries, safe words, and the like. Nadine wished she'd had done that initially instead of judging. Zaire was way more mature than she was when it came to sex. She could learn a thing or two from Z.

In the end, they all agreed that, if invited, Eddie was more than willing to participate with Nadine or simply watch. Eddie had very specific needs in terms of his voyeurism fetish that Nadine, surprisingly, didn't flinch at hearing. She'd come a long way in terms of acceptance. This was the first time they'd been completely open and non-judgmental about sex in their marriage. It felt good.

Zaire kissed Nadine softly before retiring to the guest room, and Eddie kissed Zaire on the cheek. It was the first time he'd kissed another woman since marrying Nadine, and she wasn't even upset about it. This was definitely a new normal.

When she made her way downstairs the next morning, Zaire was with the chef, getting EJ to eat a bite of eggs. He was shaking his head in absolute protest, arms folded, with a frown plastered on his face. Zaire sighed as she looked at Nadine. "Morning, our EJ won't eat his eggs."

"Cause they smell like poopie!" EJ yelled.

Nadine laughed. "Come on, Mister Moody. One bite, please? For Mommy?"

"Yes," Zaire added. "One more bite and I'll let you listen to all the Elmo podcasts you want in the car on the way to school."

"Fine," EJ huffed.

They watched as he held his nose and took a bite. It took everything in them not to laugh. Nadine was so amused at EJ's antics that she almost missed the two massive bouquets, filled with assorted roses, lilies and orchids on the opposite end of the island. Nadine nodded toward the miniature garden. "What's that about?"

Zaire smiled. "Go read the card, Coo...uhm...Nadine." She playfully winced at the gaffe, nearly forgetting about EJ sitting there eating begrudgingly.

Nadine walked to the counter and read the card in the bouquet.

"Something beautiful for two beauties. Thank you both for last night's experience- E.

Nadine smiled, holding the card to her chest. That was so unexpected that she was tempted to skip work, drive down the Eddie's job, and drop to her knees to suck his dick in appreciation As she was rereading the card, her phone buzzed with a text message from her assistant.

Devi: Good news! The HVAC is all fixed. Sending a message to everyone that they can come in today. Moving all meetings back to in-person.

Nadine groaned. The old Nadine would have been more than eager to get back to the office. After the night she'd had, she didn't want to be away from home. She'd enjoyed working from her home office, having Zaire near, and feeling her comforting presence. Grudgingly, Nadine fired off a quick text.

Nadine: Good. I'll be in the office by 7:30.

Devi: By the way, new developments. Will inform you in person.

Don't want to text.

Nadine looked at the phone, puzzled. *That was ridiculously cryptic.*

Nadine slipped her phone into her bag. "Well. Looks like I'm heading into the office today." She went to kiss EJ on his forehead. "Have a good day, my love."

"You too, Mama!" EJ beamed with a smile.

Nadine looked up at Zaire, giving her a heated glance. She licked her lips. "You have a good day too, Miss Z."

"You too Mrs. Moody. We'll miss you. Isn't that right, EJ?" said Zaire, returning an equally heated glare at Nadine. Nadine felt her coochie dancing in her panties. *Highly inappropriate so early in the morning.*

❧

As soon as Nadine stepped off the elevator, Devi was there, tablet and coffee in hand. She handed the coffee to Nadine, who took a sip and winced. She missed Zaire's perfectly made coffee already.

"Good morning, Mrs. Moody. Your 9 am meeting was cancelled. The pharmaceutical sales team wants to talk recruitment strategies. They're asking you to be a guest speaker for one of their training sessions. And…"

"Slow down, Devi," Nadine chuckled. "Can we ease into things? We've been virtual for over a month now. Gotta ease back into the groove."

Devi closed her tablet and nodded. "Right. I'm sorry. I just wanted to get a jump on things."

"I appreciate that." Nadine gave her a pat on her shoulder. "So, what was up with the last text you sent?"

Devi looked around cautiously. "Uhm, let's talk in your office." She opened Nadine's office door, ushering her inside. She closed the door behind her and sat in front of Nadine's desk.

Nadine shrugged off her jacket and sat down. The theatrics were a bit much, but she appreciated Devi's discretion. She folded her arms across her chest. "Devi, what is really going on?"

"Well," Devi sighed. "Mitchell isn't the one that's been messing up your reports."

Nadine's eyes widened. "Really? Then who?"

Devi tucked her lips into her mouth, then took a deep breath before speaking. "It was Clyde Waters, Mrs. Moody."

Nadine's eyes widened. Clyde, she thought, was a stand-up guy and quite eager to make the merger successful. He'd been a staunch ally during meetings and really had her back when it came to the snide remarks Mitchell was making. "Are you sure?"

"I'm positive," Devi nodded. "I had to basically promise Gerald down in IT that I'd go out on a date with him. I am not proud to say that I agreed to that to get this information. Even if the girls say he is hung like a circus elephant."

Nadine raised an eyebrow. Not sure if she wanted to know about Gerald's dick, but Devi going out of her way to get this information was beyond the scope of her duties. She definitely was getting a bigger Christmas bonus than usual.

Devin straightened in her chair. "Sorry. Long story short, Clyde Waters is manipulating the numbers. He's trying to make you look bad so that he can come for the CEO job once the merger is complete. In all honesty, DigiCo is doing terribly. In the toilet, actually. Yet, they want to seem like their numbers are great as this merger completes and have PharmaDigital take on a greater financial burden. It would line their pockets tremendously."

Nadine was stunned. She knew she wasn't going crazy when she thought things weren't adding up. She had no idea it was because of this. "Well, I certainly appreciate it, Devi. But you didn't have to do that. I'm sure I could have found out another way. Even if Gerald is… blessed."

Devi cleared her throat. "Well, Mrs. Moody, there's more."

Nadine squinted. "More than Clyde fudging the numbers?"

"Yes. This isn't easy for me to say, Mrs. Moody, but Clyde hates you. They all do. The whole being supportive thing is an act. Apparently, a few of the exec team from both DigiCo and PharmaDigital have a secret Discord channel where they are bagging on you."

Nadine's jaw was on the floor. A secret Discord just to shit on her? She couldn't believe it. True, she knew that she and Mitchell had tension. But to go this far? That was disgusting. What a waste of brain cells and energy.

Devil continued. "They're calling you incompetent. Saying you're just a rich woman playing CEO. Wondering why you're working when you don't have to. Not to mention the memes. Some of them made when you were pregnant calling you a "Real Housewife reject". Now, those were made mostly by Mitchell. It's terrible."

Nadine smoothed down her hair and straightened her back. It was a tale as old as time. No matter how competent she was or how much revenue she earned, she'd always be a joke to them. Always had been. Always will be.

Nadine tried to regain her composure. "When is the meeting to close the merger, Devi?"

Devi looked at her calendar on the tablet. "Uhm, it's next Tuesday."

Nadine's phone buzzed in her pocket. She opened a text message to see a photo of Zaire, completely naked, fingers deep in her pussy as she sat at Nadine's home office desk.

> Zaire: Because I miss you.

She was about to close her phone when another text came through, this time from Eddie. It was a photo with the print of his dick in his slacks in his office at the university.

> Eddie: My dick is hard just thinking about you
> right now. I should come home and fuck you
> on my break.

Jesus, those two. Nadine smiled, then cleared her throat, almost forgetting that she was at work. She turned her attention back to Devi, who was staring at her, curiously.

"Sorry, Devi. Again, thanks for this information. In the meantime, this stays between us. And seriously, you do not have to go out with Gerald."

"But the girls in advertising say his dick is magical. And I've been celibate like six months now…never mind, sorry. That's TMI. I'll see myself out." Devi quickly left Nadine's office.

Nadine drummed her fingers on her desk. She didn't have a plan… yet. By the time she had her next meeting with the team, she would. They wouldn't get away with this shit.

CHAPTER 23

Letting Them In

D r. Flournoy gave Nadine a smile. "Wow, Nadine. It's like a brand-new woman stepped foot in my office.

Nadine moved her freshly silk-pressed hair from her shoulders. "I feel great."

"Would any of this have to do with the nanny? I'm sorry, what was her name again?" Dr. Flournoy looked through her notes on her tablet. "I know it's a country in Africa. Zimbabwe? "

"Zaire," chuckled Nadine. "Yes, part of its Zaire. But the other part has been Eddie. It's been great." Nadine was glad she had requested an emergency telephone session with Dr. Flournoy last week and filled her in on everything. She didn't want the revelation of what had occurred between the three of them to come as a shock to Dr. Flournoy during this in-person session.

"Oh yeah, what has Eddie done?"

"Well, he's been really…" Nadine hesitated to go into depth but felt like she owed it to Dr. Flournoy. "He's been very open. This is also helping him to explore his own fantasies as well."

Dr. Flournoy looked surprised. "Consensually, I hope."

Nadine nodded. "Of course. We talked about it, created new boundaries, and modified our rules. He mostly watches us if we allow him to. He participates with only me, if I want that. Otherwise, my interactions with Zaire are on my own terms and with her consent."

"And he hasn't abused the access he has?"

Nadine furrowed her brows. "What do you mean?"

Dr. Flournoy leaned forward, worry clearly on her face. "Meaning, he isn't strong-arming you into letting him in your sexual space with Zaire. Or demanding that sex only occur when he's there. Remember, this is your time to explore things. Not his exclusively."

"Oh no," Nadine shook her head. "He doesn't do that." It was true. After the first night, Eddie never intruded. Nadine was the captain of the ship. She said when and if he could come into their space, and only if Zaire agreed.

Nadine thought about the day she came home after finding out that her team was trying to sabotage her. Once EJ was settled and in bed, she and Zaire talked, cuddled, kissed, and finger fucked each other until she came so hard she nearly forgot about her problems. When Eddie came home later that night, he ran her a bath, poured her a glass of wine, and put on some smooth jazz. He gave her a full body massage with hot oil and ate her pussy until she blacked out.

Eddie and Zaire cared for and respected her. It felt powerful to be the center of that, if she was being honest.

She was in heaven. Now she understood why her friends enjoyed having multiple lovers. They served multiple purposes. They were becoming her safe haven. Their adoration was a reprieve these days because the little power and respect that she did have in her professional life was dwindling.

"Why the frown, Nadine?"

Nadine's hands flew up to her face. "I was frowning?"

"Yeah," Dr. Flournoy leaned back. "What else is going on?"

"It's work." Nadine sighed. "I got some disturbing news recently." Nadine told Dr. Flournoy about the internal coup that Clyde was trying to stage and the Discord channel.

"Wow, Nadine, I am so sorry."

Nadine shrugged. "I don't know what to do. Do I report this to the EEOC? Do I file a lawsuit? Do I stay and ignore it? I don't even know why I'm fighting so hard for a company that doesn't want me or respect my position of authority. Maybe I'm wasting my time. Maybe I should quit."

"Quitting is certainly one option. Have you put any thought into what you might do if you quit?"

Nadine bit her lip as she thought. "This sounds ridiculous, but I would probably open a bakery."

"Oh please," scoffed Dr. Flournoy. "Totally not ridiculous. I remember when you told me all the moms at the PTA were gushing over your cinnamon and pecan tarts and asking you for more when you brought them to the last meeting."

Nadine laughed, feeling warmth that she remembered. "Yeah, I remember that. I enjoyed making them. Especially because they couldn't believe that CEO me had made them."

"I wonder why your first response to the idea was to think it was ridiculous?"

Nadine shrugged. "I don't know. I graduated summa cum laude. Interned for several Fortune 500 businesses. I clawed my way to the top to get where I am. Seems like it would be a waste of a degree."

Those weren't Nadine's words or how she really felt. She was repeating, verbatim, what her mother had told her when she considered going to culinary school instead of graduate school. Her mother's words were ringing loudly in her head.

So you gonna just waste that Spelman degree me and your daddy paid for to go bake cakes? You are ungrateful, little girl!

"I see," Dr. Flournoy nodded. "Well, let me ask you this– how do you feel when you bake?"

Nadine gave a slight smile. "Other than being with my family and friends, baking seems to be the only thing that sparks pure joy."

Dr. Flournoy nodded. "It's important to do what truly brings you joy, Nadine. Whether it's coming to terms with your sexuality or quitting your seven-figure salary job to bake cakes and pies for a living, this is your life to live, no one else's. That's what I've been guiding you toward these past four years."

Nadine's leg began to bounce. "What would people think?"

"Who are *people?*" challenged Dr. Flournoy.

Nadine thought long and hard about that simple question. Almost instantly, her leg stopped bouncing. "Actually, there isn't anyone. I am sure Eddie would support me. Zaire too. Tate and Alisa definitely would. The kids would love it. My dad…maybe? But…" she stopped mid-sentence.

"She's gone, dear." Dr. Flournoy reminded, recognizing the hesitation in Nadine's voice. "Your mother can't judge you for any choice you make anymore. Ridiculous or not. No one has that power over you anymore."

Nadine nodded. "I know." It was almost like muscle memory to bring up her mother's name. She'd been dead at least five years, yet she still was seeking her validation. She was haunting her like a judgmental ghost.

Dr. Flournoy took a sip of her tea then spoke. "Have you given any thought to what I asked about last session?"

Nadine twirled her ring around her finger again. "I…I don't know about that, Dr. Flournoy.

"Why not?"

"Do they *need* to know?"

Dr. Flournoy continued. "You don't think coming out to the other two most important people in your life, your daughter Alex and your father, isn't necessary?"

Nadine's hazel eyes widened. "That feels…strange." Nadine knew what it was. It felt intrusive, honestly.

"It's about welcoming people in, not you coming out," Dr Flournoy reminded. "Nadine, given your and Eddie's high-profile status, they may find out before you have a chance to tell them. You mentioned before that you don't want a scandal like your friend Alisa had in the media."

Nadine shuddered, thinking about the madness that surrounded Alisa, Kadeem and Christophe and the senate race. She thought about Morgan catching Tatum in the act with the fellas. Every secret was exposed, and it threatened to tear them apart. For a brief while, it almost did. Luckily for her friends, love was able to prevail and win.

Nadine ran a hand through her hair. "Alex is my child. My entire life, I've told her to save herself for marriage and all the same shit my mother told me. And to spring something like this on her? We barely talk as it is. She's going to hate me."

"Or she may extend grace and understanding. Give her a little credit. From what you've told me, she's really smart. Like her mom." Dr. Flournoy countered with a smile.

"She is," Nadine agreed. "But telling my Dad? I just..." Nadine thought back to that day when she got caught fooling around with Ally. Her dad had been sympathetic yet told her what she was feeling was just a phase.

"The natural order of the world is that a man and a woman be together."

Nadine attempted to swallow back tears, thinking about her father's words. With Zaire and Eddie, she'd disrupted the order of her life. Yet, being loved by them had been the most "natural" feeling she could ever imagine. Love like that could never be wrong.

"What's coming up for you right now, Nadine?" Dr. Flournoy handed Nadine a tissue. She hadn't realized that tears had been steadily falling. She dabbed her face and tried not to disrupt her makeup.

"I don't want him not to love me anymore," Nadine whispered softly.

"Despite someone loving you or not, you need to have enough love for yourself to move forward." Dr. Flournoy said, taking Nadine's shaking hand into hers. "Maybe I pushed you too hard. Let's take a step back. I think we need to try some more exercises before you do that. "

"What kind of exercises?" Nadine asked.

Dr. Flournoy paused a bit, looking up as she tried to gather her words. "I think it's time for you to close one chapter and open another."

Nadine shrugged. "Maybe."

"I have a suggestion. Write a letter to both your father and Alex, telling them about the new Nadine and how she's found herself. Once you read over it a few times and feel ok with it, I want you to try and say those same words to them in person. Finally, I want you to write a letter to your mother, telling her about everything. How she made you feel, etc. Go to her grave and leave it there. Let your words rest with her eternally."

Nadine nodded. She could do that.

"I see the change in you, Nadine. Let others see it too, ok? But only when you're ready. I'm here to support you through this." Dr. Flournoy patted Nadine's hands before leaning back in her chair. "That's our time for today. I'll see you next time."

CHAPTER 24

Generational Curses

Nadine stood in the hallway of the Alex's college apartment. The smell of weed and God-knows-what-else filled the hallway air. She coughed and rang the doorbell. *Again.* The music was blasting so loudly she wasn't sure if they'd heard her at all.

Just as she was about the ring the bell for a third time, the door flew open.

"Oh! Hey Mrs. Moody," said Britt, one of Alex's suite mates. "Sorry. I didn't hear the bell at first. Please tell me that is one of your world-famous cakes in that container you're holding. My period synched with Raina's this month and my hormones are raging!"

"Indeed. It's Death by Chocolate, y'all's favorite." Nadine smiled, shaking her head. Britt reminded her of so much Alisa, down to the ever-changing hairstyles. The girl had zero filter. She could see why she and Alex got along so well. Their other suite mate, Raina, reminded Nadine of a mix of Tatum and herself. It was crazy how Alex had carbon copies of her aunties as her own friend group.

Nadine walked into the apartment. "You know, I'm forgetting my manners. I didn't even ask if Alex was home."

Britt was already cutting a large slice of cake. "Oh yeah, she's here. She's been holed up in her room studying for mid-terms for hours. Won't even take a break."

"With this loud music going on?" Nadine motioned to the thumping sounds coming from the Bluetooth speakers.

"Please," snorted Britt as she licked icing off her finger. "Alex can study during a hurricane. This noise is nothing to her. I think she's used to it by now."

Nadine shook her head with understanding. As a kid, Alex could read a book during one of Eddie's loud and raucous playoff games. It didn't even phase her. Seems like that hadn't changed.

Nadine made her way down the hallway toward Alex's room door, which was decorated in their shared sorority letters and photos on a cork and whiteboard. Nadine stared at the photo where she got to pin Alex at the induction ceremony. They both looked so happy. The whiteboard read, "Studying so DND". Nadine knocked hard, hoping Alex could hear over the music.

Alex's face when she opened the door was annoyed until she realized it was her mother standing there. A soft smile graced her face. "Oh! Hey Mom! Sorry, I thought you were Britt or Raina trying to get me to do...well...who knows what." She moved to the side, inviting her mother in.

Nadine sat at the desk. She watched Alex reposition herself on the twin XL bed strewn with papers and open textbooks. It was like looking in a mirror. Other than being a few inches taller, Alex was her mother's twin- same hazel eyes, light brown skin, and sandy-brown curly mane. *Except...*

"Is that a tattoo, Alex?" Nadine raised a brow. It seemed to be some sort of shield or something.

Alex tried to cover her ankle. "Yeah. It's a Supergirl symbol. We all dared each other to get tattoos one night. Long story. So what's up, mom? What brings you by?

"Can't I just come and check on my daughter? I mean, it's not like I know how you are. My text go unanswered, and you blocked me from your social media."

"My phone is almost always on DND, but I blocked you on socials because you make weird comments like "Why are you wearing that?" or "Is this what you really want to post?"

Nadine winced. *Jesus Christ, she was more like her mother than she real-*

ized. "If I promise to stop doing that, will you unblock me? I really want to be part of your life. Don't shut me out, Lex."

Alex shrugged. "Sure. I guess."

"Thank you," Nadine smiled, then took a deep breath. "But this isn't about being blocked. I came by because I have something important to talk to you about."

Alex went wide-eyed. "Oh God! Don't tell me you and Daddy Ed are getting a divorce!"

"No Lex…"

"Oh, my God! Is something wrong with EJ?"

"No, he's fine. They're all fine, baby. It's about me."

Alex grabbed a pillow and clutched it to her chest. She sniffed. "Ma, please don't tell me you're sick! I don't know if I can handle that. Shit, I'm sorry for blocking you, if that's the case. I was being a brat, I know…"

Nadine held up her hands. "No, I am fine, sweetie. Just let me talk, Alexandria. Please, baby."

Alex sat up straight. The use of her full first name always did that to her.

Nadine let out a breath. "There are things about me, about who I am, that I've hidden from you. Mostly out of shame. Mostly because I didn't have the vocabulary for it."

"Things like what?" Alex's brows were knit tightly, confusion in her eyes.

"I've been going to therapy lately," Nadine began. She felt her phone vibrate and saw it was Alisa. She quickly silenced the call. She'd call her back. She had to get through this. "And I've been learning things about myself. And about my…sexuality."

Alex looked bewildered. "Your sexuality?"

"Yes. I'm bisexual, Alex."

Alex blinked a few times as if she was pondering the word over in her head. "Say what now?"

"I'm bisexual. That means…"

"Ma! I am twenty! I know what that means. I go to college and my roommate is a lesbian! But *you*? Bisexual?"

Nadine nodded. "Yes."

"And how do you know this? Did you just wake up one day and realize it?"

"Of course not. I've always known. Since I was young, actually. I just felt like I had to hide it. Your grandmother wasn't the most tolerant person in the world. So I just hid it. I hid it so well that I thought marrying your dad would rid myself of the feeling. Honestly, the only good thing I got out of doing that was you."

"Ugh, please don't mention my father." Alex made air quotes around the word *father*. "He's been trying to get me to meet his latest girlfriend and come down to St. Croix for Christmas. I'm not interested. Not sure why he thinks I'd want to do that."

Nadine had never interfered with Alex's relationship with her father. It wasn't until she was well out of high school that she told her the real reason why she divorced Drew. Her dad had proven years before that he was a deadbeat. He never showed up for birthdays or holidays. He'd make elaborate plans and always break them. When Nadine remarried a wealthy NBA player, Drew felt he was off the hook monetarily and emotionally as a parent. Nadine was grateful that Alex had Eddie. He'd been the father she never had.

"So you and Daddy Ed *are* getting a divorce? You're cheating on him?!" Alex looked at her mother as if she was a common whore. The look of disgust on her face made Nadine wince. She didn't like being on the receiving end of that vitriol from her child.

"No, we aren't, baby. It's complicated, but he knows. I just wanted you to know before you heard about it or saw something. I didn't want you asking questions now that I'm seeing someone…a woman."

Alex was quiet for quite some time. Nadine nibbled the corners of her lips, worried that this was a mistake and that Dr. Flournoy's suggestion was foolish.

"So let me get this straight, no pun intended," Alex began, arms folded. "You're bisexual or whatever? With a side chick? Yet, you're the same woman who looked down on Auntie Tate and Auntie Alisa's relationships? Who kept telling me sex was sacred, between one man and one woman. Who told me that "good girls" didn't have multiple partners. Who told me to wait until I got married."

"I know honey, and I am sorry. But…"

"You barely talked to me about sex," interrupted Alex. "You made it feel so secretive. And now this? Now, overnight, you've become this liberal thinking bisexual woman?"

Nadine could feel herself flush with utter shame. "I know, and that was entirely hypocritical of me. Your grandmother, the way I was raised, it did a number on me and everything. I'm not making an excuse, because that is just wack and doesn't hold me accountable. But I know I dumped my trauma on you. And it was totally wrong."

"You're damn right. It was more than wrong. It was misogynoir. Hypocritical. Patriarchal," Alex said. Nadine narrowed her eyes. Alex tucked her lips in. "Sorry, mom. I am just saying. My whole life you made sex seem kind of dirty and barely talked about it. And it was all because you felt guilty about it?"

"I know. Forgive me for that. Please."

Alex went silent for several minutes, her arms still folded.

Nadine couldn't tell if she was pissed or confused. But she pressed on. "Alex, I know this is a lot to process. But…are you ok?"

"I mean, I guess. It's your life." Alex scratched her head. "So, you've got a girlfriend and Eddie knows. Is she Eddie's girlfriend too?"

"Yes and no."

Alex's full lips turned up into a smirk. "Oh, so you get to have all the fun, and he just sit backs and watches, huh?"

Boy, Alex had no idea how accurate that statement was. Nadine simply sighed. "I don't think getting into the dynamics is…well…it's between me and your father."

Alex snickered. "And here you were, calling Auntie Tate a bad influence. My, how the tables have turned."

Nadine had to laugh. "I know. Trust me, I've apologized to them too for how I acted. And your Auntie Alisa won't let me live it down." Her eyes softened as she looked at her daughter, nibbling her lip. "Alex, seriously, I know this was a lot. Are you ok with this?"

Alex got off the bed and wrapped her arms around Nadine, taking her by surprise. "Mom, I am glad you're living in your truth and being happy. You don't have to hide anymore. I love you."

Nadine felt tears roll down her cheeks and onto Alex's ratty college sweatshirt. "Thank you, baby," she said, her voice breaking like shards like glass.

Nadine's phone rang again, and she saw Alisa calling. This time on FaceTime. She rolled her eyes. "Let me answer this before your aunt drives me crazy." She pressed the button.

"Alisa, I am not bringing you any American Deli wings." Nadine's eyes widened as she saw Alisa on her screen. Her skin looked dull and her eyes watery with tears.

"Alisa? What's going on?"

"Nadine, it's the babies. Something's… wrong."

CHAPTER 25

All I Need

Nadine was going ninety down the highway toward Alisa's house. She called Alisa from the car, encouraging her to stay on the phone until the ambulance arrived. She'd told Nadine that she tried calling everyone. Christophe was in court. Kadeem was at the studio. Tatum wasn't picking up. She'd called her doctor's office and was put on hold. Nadine had done the same and gotten no answer, either. It was a clusterfuck of bad shit all at once.

"Alisa, talk to me, honey. I am on the way."

"It's too early. They are coming too early." Alisa looked panic-stricken. Nadine could tell she was on the floor, leaning against either a counter or a dresser of some sort. The babies weren't due for another two months.

"Honey, sometimes twins come early. It happens."

Alisa was crying, her hair sticking to her face. "I don't want to be alone. Oh, God…"

"Where is the nurse, Alisa?" Nadine asked as she weaved in and out of traffic. She prayed to God she wouldn't get a ticket or hit anyone.

"She…she went to get my nausea meds. Something is wrong, I feel it." Alisa let out a wail that made Nadine's blood run cold. It was terrifying. She'd never heard Alisa in pain like this.

"I am almost there." Nadine looked at her GPS on her console. "It says I'll be there in 5 minutes. I got the codes to get in the gate and door. I'll make sure it's open. You just say calm." Kadeem had the foresight to give both Tatum and Nadine the app that controlled access to the mansion. Kadeem and Christophe were so overprotective. She never thought she'd have to use them.

Alisa's voice was drifting in and out. Nadine had to keep her alert. She had to talk about something, anything.

"Keep talking to me, sweetie. Did you decide on names for the babies?"

"No…not yet. Uggggh.. It hurts!" Alisa screamed, her hands shaky. Nadine knew she was going to drop the phone at any second. She had to get to Alisa. She had to make sure she was ok.

Nadine pulled into the driveway at the same time as the EMTs. She barely put her car in park before she was running up the circular driveway to the house.

"Ma'am?" said one of the paramedics. "Do you live here?"

"No, but I am the one who called 911! That's my sister!" Nadine screamed. "Please, she's pregnant with twins! It's high risk!"

"OK ma'am. We're just heading in. Stay calm."

Nadine followed the paramedics inside the mansion, where they found Alisa, lying in the kitchen in a pool wetness. Nadine gasped when she saw a trickle of blood on the floor and on her caftan. She ran to Alisa, kneeling down. She looked as if she passed out.

"Alisa!" Nadine's voice cracked. "Wake up, baby! Wake up!"

Alisa's eyes barely fluttered open. "Deanie?"

"I'm here," Nadine said. "The EMTs are here to check you out."

Nadine stood back as she watched the team of paramedics examined Alisa, taking her vital signs and giving her IV fluids. Nadine closed her eyes, praying that Alisa and the babies were going to be ok. She hadn't been to church in a while, so she hoped God still knew who she was.

"Ma'am. We need to get her to the hospital immediately," one of the medics announced. "Her blood pressure is through the roof and her water broke."

Nadine nodded, her eyes watery. "Ok. I'll follow you there."

Nadine sat in the waiting room, her stomach doing flips. She shot a text to both Eddie and Zaire, telling them what was going on and to expect her late. Zaire understood, saying she'd prepare to spend the night if necessary and would make sure EJ was settled in for the night. Nadine decided against telling Alex. She didn't want to stress her out, given it was her midterms. Nadine hadn't been there too long when she looked up to see Christophe and Kadeem barreling through the labor and delivery doors.

"Nadine," Christophe said, tie undone and his eyes red-rimmed. "Where is she?"

"Is she ok?" Kadeem was out of breath. "Fuck! I was prepping before going on-air. I knew I shouldn't have turned off my phone."

Nadine stood. "She's in the ICU. They are trying to get her blood pressure down and stabilize her. The doctors are preparing to deliver the babies. When I found her, she was lying on the floor. She'd lost a lot of amniotic fluid."

"ICU?" Kadeem's eyes widened. "Jesus."

"And where was the fucking nurse? She knows she's not supposed to leave her alone. She's supposed to call if she leaves her alone." Christophe was furious.

"Calm down, Christophe," Nadine said, rubbing his arm, but he snatched it away. She understood his anger. "The nurse had gone to get Alisa's nausea meds and got caught in a bad accident. She called me as soon as she got home and saw that Alisa was gone. She called you all too, but your phones were off."

"Still," Kadeem fumed. "Still, she could have…if we lose her…lose them…" Kadeem's voice broke as Christophe embraced him.

"The doctor said she'd be back out shortly. It's going to be fine. Alisa is so strong. You know this." Nadine was trying her best to reassure them, to calm them down, but it was utterly useless. She had no idea if Alisa would be fine, and they didn't either.

"The doctor needs to bring her fucking ass out here now!" Christophe yelled as onlookers stared at them. Out of the corner of her eye, she saw someone snap a photo of Kadeem. She tried her best not to curse them out because someone had to remain calm.

"Kadeem. Chris. You've both got to remain calm. For Alisa," begged Nadine.

Kadeem and Christophe both took deep breaths, trying to regain their composure. "We gotta find out something," Kadeem said, motioning toward Christophe. "Come on, babe."

Nadine watched as Christophe and Kadeem marched to the nurses' station, trying to get answers.

Minutes later, Tatum rushed in, with Miles, Deacon, and Cassidy trailing behind her. Nadine raised a brow. By the way Tatum was scantily dressed, it looked like she was out with her men having adult fun. Nadine could only imagine *where*.

"Oh my God, Deanie!" Tatum rushed over, wrapping Nadine in a hug. "I am so sorry. I didn't have my phone. None of us did. We were uhm…"

"Occupied?" Nadine asked, brow raised. "Already? It's barely evening time!"

Tatum sighed. "We were trying to blow off some steam. It's midterms and well. You know the establishment doesn't allow phones, so…that shit doesn't matter right now. What matters is Alisa."

"Right," Miles said, rubbing his bald head. "Is Alisa ok?"

Nadine sighed. "I hope so. She'd lost a lot of amniotic fluid. There was blood. They can't get her blood pressure down."

"She…she was bleeding?" Christophe said, coming back over. "Oh my God." He looked as if he was going to pass out. Deacon and Cassidy quickly led him back to the chairs.

"I'll go grab him some ice water," Miles announced as he headed in search of the ice station.

Tatum let out a shaky breath. "Is she gonna be ok? Be honest, Deanie."

Nadine shrugged. "It's been a minute since I've seen the doctor. I have no idea what is going on."

A tall, slender Black woman with shoulder length locs came to the waiting area. "Is the family of Alisa Bishop-Miller here?"

Nadine motioned toward everyone. "That's the doctor."

Everyone got out of their seats.

The doctor smiled. "Ok, let me clarify. Is her next of kin here?"

Kadeem and Christophe both stepped forward. Puzzled, the doctor looked down at the paperwork and back up at them. "And which one of you is Mrs. Bishop-Miller's husband?"

"We are," they said in unison.

The doctor's eyes widened. "Uhm, ok." She looked back down at the paperwork. "But who is her *legal* husband?"

Christophe cleared his throat. "That would be me. Christophe Bishop. But..." He looked at Kadeem, who shared an equally distressed look on his face. It was breaking everyone's heart, including the doctor's.

The doctor nodded. "I understand. But I can only discuss this with Mrs. Bishop- Miller's legal spouse."

Kadeem folded his arms across his chest. "Like we said, I'm also her husband. Those babies are also...*my* babies." He could barely get the words out.

Miles stood up. "There should be a medical directive on file with this hospital that lists both Mr. Miller and Mr. Bishop as her health care proxies. I know because I am the one who drafted it. Now, if you would, please share the status on Mrs. Bishop-Miller to *both* of her husbands before I have to call the hospital board and make a complaint."

Nadine smirked. She loved that Miles could push his weight around like it was nothing. She could see how Tate was drawn to that. That type of power and authority was appealing.

The doctor's facial expression was tight as a drum. "Very well. If you would, let's discuss it over here, shall we?" She motioned toward both Christophe and Kadeem, who huddled with her in a corner.

Nadine and Tatum sat holding hands, watching as Kadeem, all brawn and muscle, was reduced to tears. Christophe nodded, as he tried to listen to the doctor and literally support his man. It was too much to bear witness to.

"She's going to be fine," Tatum reassured, squeezing Nadine's hand. "My cousin is too strong-willed to not fight for her babies or herself."

Nadine nodded. "I know. She's too fucking stubborn to give up."

Tatum chuckled softly. "Yep. That she is."

Cass knelt down in front of both of them, his hand resting on Tatum's leg. "Ya'll want anything? Coffee? Candy? Shit, weed?"

Tatum rolled her eyes. "You know damn well you don't have weed."

Cass shrugged. "I bet I could find some. This is a hospital."

"Shit, I've got some," Deacon said, a little too loudly. "Some edibles too."

"Deacon, seriously," Tatum said, shaking her head. "Coffee is fine, Cass."

Cassidy smiled. "Sure thing, mama. What about you, Deanie? Coffee?"

Nadine nodded, even though she didn't really want it. "Yeah. That's cool. Just black."

"Got it." Cassidy kissed Tatum on her shin before rising and heading toward the vending machines. As soon as Cassidy left, Deacon was there to rub Tatum's shoulder. Nadine smiled. Tatum was so well cared for. Franklin knew exactly what he was doing. Her mind flashed to the two people waiting for her at home. *She wondered if she could have that with Eddie and Zaire.*

Tatum and Nadine sipped the terrible vending machine coffee, hoping it could soothe the anxiety that they'd felt. Christophe and Kadeem made their way back toward the group. Everyone turned their attention towards them.

Christophe rubbed his head. "Doctor says they've stabilized Alisa's blood pressure. She was nearing stroke level due to her preeclampsia. The babies are fine. But they aren't taking any chances. They are preparing to deliver the babies within the next half hour, then they'll be transported to the NICU. By the grace of God, she got to the hospital just in time."

"Praise God," declared Nadine, clasping her hands.

"Listen," Kadeem rubbed his eyes. "Ya'll can go home. I know you all had things to do. Places to be."

Nadine shook her head. "Absolutely not. Alisa is our family. You're our family. We will be staying until we know the babies are here safely." Everyone agreed, shaking their heads.

Christophe and Kadeem looked at each other and smiled. The group settled in for the night on the uncomfortable waiting room chairs and prayed.

It was almost 1 a.m. when Nadine finally made it home. She was exhausted and hungry, having eaten nothing but a vending machine chicken salad sandwich and more stale coffee. Deacon had offered to grab decent food for everyone, but they all declined. Everyone was too anxious to eat anything substantial.

To Nadine's surprise, Eddie and Zaire were both at the kitchen island, talking and sharing a laugh. She smiled, seeing the two people she adored enjoying each other's company without her.

"Hey you," Zaire said as she came up to Nadine, kissing her on the temple. "How are things with Alisa and the babies?"

Nadine blew out a breath. "Well, the babies are here. A boy and a girl. They delivered them about two hours after we brought Alisa to the hospital. They were barely three pounds each. Their lungs aren't the greatest so...they'll be in the NICU for a while getting treatment and a battery of tests to make sure they are fine. As for Alisa..."

Nadine's eyes watered as she tried to get the words out. Eddie rushed over to put a hand around her shoulder, guiding her to the chair. He sat next to her and Zaire brought over a glass of wine for Nadine, sitting down on her opposite side. She took a sip before continuing.

"Even though she delivered the babies, her blood pressure wouldn't come down. They think she had a clot somewhere, maybe her lungs because she said her chest hurt. They think it was something called HELLP syndrome, and they are praying they got it under control. She'll be in the hospital for a while. I just...I can't lose my best friend. This is too much."

Eddie rubbed gentle circles on her back. "It's ok. You got her to the hospital. Plus, Christophe and Kadeem are there. They'll move heaven and earth before they let anything happen to her."

"And what if I hadn't picked up her call? She would have bled out on the floor of her kitchen and those babies...." Nadine shook away the thought. "Black women die all the time in childbirth. Shit, she could die now. We're never in the clear. Doesn't matter if Christophe or Kadeem are there or how much money they have. The stats don't lie."

"But the devil does! So don't listen to lies swirling around in your head. Alisa's not dead," Zaire reminded her. "She isn't. She and the babies will be fine. You've got to think positively."

Nadine drank more of the wine, then frowned as the taste soured her stomach. "Maybe I shouldn't drink anymore. I haven't had much to eat."

"Chef made ratatouille and grilled chicken. Would you like some?" asked Eddie, moving toward the fridge, but Nadine stopped him.

She looked between Eddie and Zaire, the heat of her gaze increasing by the second. "I just want you." She placed a soft kiss on Eddie's lips, then turned to Zaire, doing the same. "And you."

Zaire looked at Eddie, then back at Nadine. "Are you sure, baby? You've been through a lot tonight. I mean, this seems like a family thing."

Nadine looked between Eddie and Zaire, her heart breaking, if they'd say no. "You *are* my family. I need you…*we* need you."

Eddie grabbed her hand, pulling Nadine off the bar stool. "Let's go, honey."

They walked a few steps. When Nadine didn't feel or hear Zaire next to her, she stopped. She turned to find her at the island, looking hesitant. Nadine stretched out her hand. "Come, love." Slowly, Zaire walked toward her and took her hand.

All three of them made their way toward the master bedroom.

CHAPTER 26
Together, Finally

Tonight felt...different. The slower, sensual pace made Nadine's flesh pebble, and her nipples tighten. She wasn't sure what to feast her eyes on first.

Her eyes darted to Eddie, who was already fully nude, lazily stroking his dick to hardness. Then to Zaire, who was in a beige bra and panties, unbuttoning Nadine's top as they kissed. Her nipples, dark as blackberries, peeking through the mesh material of her bra, pressed against Nadine's now bare flesh. It made Nadine's mouth water, craving to suck them until they were plump, and Zaire was begging for relief. For now, she'd give her the next best thing.

She moved her hands toward Zaire, pulling down the cups of her bra and tweaking her nipples between her fingers. The hum that she let out reverberated against Nadine's lips and sent sensations to her clit. She loved the way that they kissed. It was its own language. Between kisses, they'd completely undressed each other, admiring the lushness between them. Nadine could hear Eddie moan in admiration.

"You both look so beautiful," Eddie admired, his long legs spread wide as he sat in the chair. The head of his dick was slightly coated with pre-cum. And he was hard, painfully so. But Nadine knew Eddie wasn't going to approach. Not until they wanted him to. This was about the ladies. His pleasure was their pleasure and vice versa.

"Tell me what you need, Nadine," Zaire said, her tongue licking at the seams of Nadine's lips. It surprised her that she was calling her by her name, something she rarely did these days.

Nadine groaned as Zaire's tongue made its way down her neck toward her clavicle. "I want to come so hard I forget about everything."

Zaire chuckled softly. "Cookie, you were gonna do that anyway. Come on." She led her to the Alaskan king bed that she shared with Eddie. They'd never shared their bed with someone other than their kids. When she looked over at Eddie, the sight of him enjoying the scene put all her nervousness at bay. It was pure pleasure, unfiltered passion. *The marriage bed is undefiled.* It was an inconvenient thought in the moment, but it reminded her that she wanted this. She deserved this. No questions asked.

Nadine lay back on the bed as Zaire settled over here. They kissed, moaning into each other's mouths and grinding softly against each other. Nadine could feel the wetness leaking from Zaire's pussy as she ground down on her thigh. She bent down, taking a nipple into her fingers and rolling slowly. She loved the way they felt between her fingers and tugged a bit, eliciting a hiss from her lover.

"No, Cookie," Zaire moaned. "You gotta get yours first. Let me take care of you." She reached between them, parting Nadine's pussy with her fingers. She moved between her folds, collecting her wetness as she moved toward Nadine's clit. Nadine could feel her clit pulsing and swelling with each touch.

"Don't make me cum like this," Nadine begged, still grinding against Zaire's fingers. Clearly, her body was betraying her mouth. It felt too good to stop.

Zaire smiled. "You don't tell me what to do, Cookie. I'm getting you off." She looked over toward Eddie. "Look at your husband. He wants to see you get yours, baby."

Nadine's eyes darted toward Eddie. His face was strained as he stroked his dick faster. Nadine could hear the slickness as he motioned his hand up and down his thick shaft. He looked so fucking sexy. He wanted to come, but she knew he wouldn't. Not until she did.

"Not until you come," whispered Zaire, as if she read Nadine's mind. She abruptly stopped the movement of her fingers until they slid down her body, her pussy leaving a trail of wetness down to her knee. She parted Nadine's legs and pushed two fingers inside her, curling toward her G-spot. Nadine's hips bucked, her pussy noisily and greedily sucking in Zaire's fingers as she stroked.

"Shit, Nadine, your pussy is always so tight," Zaire praised. "So tight and wet." Nadine was seeing stars. She was about to come all over Zaire's hand.

"With such a fat little clit too," added Eddie. "I love sucking on that motherfucker."

"Me too." Zaire agreed. "I think I need a taste." Her tongue darted out, licking and sucking at Nadine's clit. That was all it took for Nadine to erupt like a geyser all over Zaire's face and fingers. She wouldn't let up until she'd drank every last drop of Nadine's essence.

Once she'd had her fill, Zaire moved up to kiss Nadine, letting her taste the remnants of her arousal. Nadine never knew she could taste so good, especially on someone else's lips.

"Where are your toys?" asked Zaire.

Nadine nodded toward her nightstand. "Bottom drawer." Nadine didn't have that many toys, but she knew Zaire would find whatever it was she was looking for. When she produced Nadine's thickest, biggest black dildo and lube, Nadine knew exactly what time Zaire was trying to be on.

Before she could truly say anything else, Nadine felt herself being pulled to the edge of the bed. Her head dangling close to the edge. She looked up to see Eddie standing above her, his dick all but pointing right where he wanted to be.

"Suck my dick, Deanie," Eddie begged as he stroked. "Suck it while Z fucks you with your toy."

Nadine opened her mouth, and Eddie dropped all the inches of his dick deep into her throat. Eddie pulled her up by her hair, cradling her head as he fucked her mouth. She gagged as he pumped methodically into her mouth. She sucked and slurped, tasting the saltiness of his pre-cum coated dick. Nadine had always loved the taste of Eddie but tonight turned her on even more. She reached down to stroke her clit, only to find her hand being moved.

"No, let me handle that for you, baby." Zaire said. She spread lube inside Nadine's aching pussy that was begging to be filled. Slowly, she felt Zaire move the dildo up and down her slit, letting the vibration settle right on the clit. Nadine moaned around Eddie's dick as Zaire increased the vibrations.

"You feel so fucking good, baby," Eddie praised. "That mouth is so wet...so good."

Inch by inch, Zaire pushed in the dildo. She teased Nadine at first, pumping slowly, letting the dildo fill her up only to take it out. Nadine opened her legs wider, the emptiness of her pussy begging to be filled.

Zaire chuckled. "You're so greedy, Cookie. Mouth full of dick and your pussy still wants more." She pushed in deeper, harder into Nadine's pussy. Zaire increased her pace, and it took everything for Nadine to keep focused. Between the sounds of her slurping on Eddie's rock-hard dick and her pussy being rammed over and over, Nadine was about to come, riding a high that she'd only imagined having.

When she felt Eddie's hips slow down, Nadine knew he was going to come. And in three short bursts, his cum slid down her throat, hot and salty-sweet. She swallowed, and Eddie leaned down, giving her a satisfied smile.

"Such a good girl, Deanie," Eddie repeated as he slowly kissed her over and over.

"She sure is. Look at the mess you made, Cookie." Zaire held up the dildo, covered in creamy release. Nadine's clit throbbed and her nipples tightened as she watched Zaire lick the dildo clean.

"You're so nasty, pretty girl," Nadine teased. "I need to thank you for taking care of me." She sat up and stalked toward Zaire on the bed. When she got to her, Nadine pushed her down slightly and dove head first between her legs. She focused her attention on the delicious piercing, flicking and sucking until Zaire was riding her face. If Eddie was salty-sweet, then Zaire was so sweet it would give you a cavity.

Nadine licked and sucked, moving her tongue in and out of her tight hole. Zaire gripped the sheets, moaning and writhing in pleasure.

Nadine looked up slightly to see Eddie, his dick still surprisingly hard as he leaned near the chest of drawers. She began to play with her pussy as she ate Zaire, hoping that the action would entice Eddie to come and fuck her from the back. She wanted to taste and feel them both at the same time. She moved her fingers in and out of her pussy, then used her index finger to tease the rim of her asshole. When she felt the weight of the bed dip, she knew Eddie was behind her. She loved that he knew her non-verbal sexual cues so well.

Nadine felt his tongue, hot and stiff, eat her pussy from the back. She moaned around Zaire's clit, which only made Zaire pull Nadine further into her pussy, her nose rubbing against the hood of her clit.

"Shit, Nadine, eat that pussy baby," Zaire mewled, as she was coming close to her peak.

Nadine felt Eddie spit into her asshole, and a finger slightly press against the tight space. She moaned, pushing her hips toward the wet digit.

"Can I fuck you here, Nadine?" asked Eddie. "I wanna come in your ass while you eat Z's pussy." His voice was so heated, Nadine barely recognized it.

Nadine turned slightly to look back at Eddie. "Yes," she breathed out. No sooner had she said the word that she felt the coolness of lube sliding down the crack of her ass. When she felt the bulbous head of Eddie's dick breech her asshole, she let out a strangled moan.

"Fuck Eddie," Nadine screamed. "Ugh, baby, go slow. Please…"

"I got you, baby. I got you."

Eddie gripped her hips, which pushed Nadine further down into Zaire's pussy. Nadine took the opportunity of that angle to lick between Zaire's pussy and asshole. A moan tore through Zaire's clinched teeth as she came from the action. When she tried to move, to give herself a reprieve, Nadine pressed down on her thighs, sealing Zaire between the bed and herself. There was no way she wouldn't have Zaire come again on her face while she was getting fucked by Eddie. If she was going to have this opportunity, this moment, she'd have her fill both ways.

Eddie slowly drilled into Nadine's ass, his fingers digging into her plump ass cheeks. She knew her skin would be red in the morning from the force of his grip. The slight sting of pain turned her on. She settled into the rhythm as she licked and sucked Zaire's pussy. Her clit was so swollen that the slightest lick made Zaire's legs shake. Nadine loved being the one to do that. When she latched on, sucking hard as she could, she knew that Zaire would explode.

"Fuck, I'm about to…" Zaire held onto Nadine's hair and squirted her juices all in her face. Nadine loosened her grip on her thighs as she licked her clean.

"Goddamn," Eddie grunted, his sweat trickling down Nadine's back. The sight of Nadine getting squirted on had Eddie coming hot and deep in her ass in record time.

Nadine lifted off of Zaire. She laid between Eddie and Zaire, catching her breath. She was drenched, her muscles sore, but she'd never been so satisfied in her life. Zaire trailed her fingers down Nadine, right to her pussy. She gathered the cum and put her fingers to Nadine's lips. She licked them clean.

Eddie chuckled, shaking his head at the two of them. He never thought he'd see the day that Nadine would do something like that. Zaire had definitely brought out the nasty little freak in Nadine. And for that, he'd be eternally grateful.

Once they were done, Eddie grabbed two warm washcloths and cleaned up Nadine and Zaire, taking his time to admire and care for them. It touched Nadine deeply that he was so tender toward both of them. He'd told them both that aftercare was his job and his job alone.

"How're you feeling, baby?" Zaire asked.

"I'm perfect," Nadine smiled, satisfied.

Eddie kissed her temple. "You *are* perfect. But are you happy?"

"I'm more than happy." Nadine tried to will her tears not to fall, but they did.

Eddie wiped them away with the pad of his thumb as Zaire kissed her shoulder. "What are you feeling right now, baby?"

"Nothing. Just..." Nadine said nothing as she finished her sentence in her head.

"Free."

Eddie seemed to register the answer in her silence and simply pulled back the duvet. He slipped in and nodded toward Nadine and Zaire to join him. They did, slipping into the bedding and finding their desired positions. Eddie's arms wrapped around Nadine; Nadine's arms wrapped around Zaire. Soon, a quiet cacophony of snores filled the air.

It was the best sleep Nadine had in her life. She was truly at peace.

CHAPTER 27

New Chapter

Nadine power walked down the hallway toward the conference room. She wore her favorite red Veronica Beard suit and Louboutin heels, ready to face the board. Devi was on her side, trying her best to keep up.

"And I have your presentation ready to go on the computer," Devi handed Nadine a coffee as she looked down at her tablet. "Are you sure about this?"

Nadine turned to Devi. "Devi, don't second guess me."

For the first time in a very long time, Nadine was resolute and confident in what she was going to do. *Well, for the most part.* The full board of DigiGo and PharmaDigital was meeting today to close the merger. The entire office was buzzing about the magnitude of the merger and what it meant for the company Nadine would be the first Black CEO to broker such a massive deal in her industry. She had never felt more confident.

Nadine entered the boardroom, and the chatter seemed to cease. Mitchell rolled his eyes, whispering to his counterpart at DigiCo. *Smug bastards.* She had to smirk to herself. She took one last sip of coffee, straightened her jacket and stood at the head of the impossibly long conference room table.

Nadine smiled. "Good Afternoon everyone. This is an exciting day for DigiCo and PharmaDigital. Joining forces officially to become the largest online pharmacy, delivering medical supplies and prescriptions to people nationwide. This day has been a long time coming. Let's go over the final numbers, corporate restructuring, and the proposed calendar for the advertisement rollout."

Nadine went through her presentation as usual, taking questions from the team. Of course, Mitchell had to agitate her, but Nadine didn't allow him to grate her nerves. She was used to him. What was most difficult was trying to not be phased by Clyde Walters. His faux sense of allyship was what irritated her the most. Every time he smiled at Nadine, she simply smiled back, pretending to appreciate his supportive nature.

Once the presentation wrapped up and the celebratory handshakes were given, everyone began to quietly pack away their things to leave, but Nadine interrupted the shuffling.

"Actually, I almost forgot. There is one more section I'd like to present. It won't take long, I promise."

"To end the meeting?" questioned Mitchell.

"Trust me, it'll be fun," Nadine assured. "Think of it as team morale booster as we move forward as one company."

There was a bit of grumbling, but everyone stayed in their seats. Nadine nodded to Devi, who then moved the presentation to the next set of slides.

An audible gasp was heard as everyone looked up to see the unfavorable meme of Nadine from the Discord. Someone had put her face on the old Aunt Jemima pancake box, calling her a "corporate mammy."

"I love memes. But, I'd have to say, Mitchell, if you were going to pick a photo of me to put on a pancake box, you could have picked a better one."

Nadine moved to the next side and read out loud

"Now, this is interesting. "Nadine is such a bitch. It's a wonder she has two kids. Who would fuck her frigid ass?" Wow, Doug, and you call yourself a feminist. I had no idea you felt that way."

Doug Parsons, senior VP of Human Resources, was turning bright red. "Nadine, I didn't mean…"

"Save it," she interrupted, as she continued to read. "Nadine doesn't even need to work. She's taking up space for someone more qualified. Nadine shouldn't be representing this company. Her salary is a waste."

Nadine moved to the next slide and read. "But this is my favorite one, courtesy of Clyde Waters. It reads, "She's such a simple, dumb bitch. Just another DEI hire. She needs to go back to sucking NBA dick." Attached was an A.I. created photo of Nadine, on her knees, naked, sucking off her jersey clad husband.

The board room was now in pure chaos. Clyde was about to head toward the door, but Devi was there to stop him.

"Sit your ass down, Clyde." Nadine ordered, pointing to the seat. The man slowly moved back to his seat.

"Nadine! How did you even get these?" asked Michell. "These were private conversations! You had no right!"

"Nothing is ever private on the internet. You really think I wouldn't find out, you asshole!" Nadine shouted. "You are the idiots who decided to create a special Discord to talk about me and share dirty memes. You all hate me that much, huh? Why? Because I'm competent? Because I am good at my job. Or is it just because I'm Black, a woman or both?"

Mitchell scoffed. "That's what you think?"

"That's what I know," Nadine said. "And I cannot wait to present all of this in court when I sue this company for a ridiculous sum. The EEOC is going to love this!"

"Nadine, seriously think about this," Clyde begged. "This could bankrupt us and put the merger in jeopardy."

"You should have thought of that before you decided to make that Discord," Nadine fumed.

"What do you want, Nadine?" asked Michael Josephs, one of the lawyers helping with the merger. "Let's talk about this. Maybe schedule a meeting. I can get our other mediators on board."

Nadine held up her hand. Her body was shaking with anger. Once the room was silent, she put down her hand and took a deep breath. "I've given my all here for the past seven years, even working while dealing with a really tough pregnancy. I gave my all to this place. For what? To be a joke? Doesn't matter if the company has high sales each quarter or was well praised for the advertising and community outreach. I was just a joke to you all. No amount of money, sensitivity training, or apologizes is going to help this situation." Nadine took a deep breath. She closed the presentation on the laptop. "I quit. You'll be hearing from my attorneys at Dawson and Simmons in the morning. Let's go, Devi."

Nadine smoothed down her jacket and exited the board room with Devi. She knew they were probably sitting there dumbfounded, but Nadine didn't bother to look back.

Nadine finally exhaled when she got back to her office. She turned to her assistant. "Devi, make sure you make a copy of those slides for me on a thumb drive."

"Already done. By the way that was so boss!" Devi squealed. "You're my hero. Pretending like you're going to quit! Genius. Please think of me when you get even bigger bucks."

Nadine gave a soft smile. "I wasn't pretending, Devi. I'm quitting. I know that wasn't the plan. I just wanted to embarrass them. Get them fired, maybe. But they can have this job if they want it so bad. They're right. I don't need it. I love what I did and hit every goal imaginable. What else is left? What am I trying to prove?"

"Uhm, that this company is going to go to shit without you, pardon my language," Devi said sadly.

Nadine gave Devi a gentle pat on her shoulder. "I am not going to go down with this sinking ship. I suggest you find something else, too. If they can treat me this way, I imagine they'd treat you even worse. You're a wonderful assistant. You'll get nothing but glowing recommendations from me. Too bad you can't bake. I'd hire you."

Devi raised a brow. "Bake?"

Nadine nodded. "Yeah, thinking about opening a bakery. I don't know. Just a thought."

"Well, I appreciate the job offer, Mrs. Moody," Devi laughed. "But all can do is boil an egg and I am terrible at that."

Nadine glanced at her watch. "Speaking of eggs, why don't I take you out to a late brunch? I am done for the day. I am sure they are scrambling since shit hit the fan."

Devi was truly surprised at Nadine. "Are you sure?"

"Absolutely. And please, call me Nadine. We're friends, now."

Devi's dark eyes sparkled. "Ok Nadine. One request, though?"

Nadine's eyes narrowed. "What's that?"

"After that meeting, I need a drink. I could definitely use a mimosa."

Nadine whispered. "Oh, we're *definitely* ordering mimosas. On the company card, too. I dare them to say something."

AFTER SEVERAL MIMOSAS AND A LOVELY BRUNCH WITH HER FORMER assistant, Nadine felt at least twenty pounds lighter. Sure, she'd put gasoline on an already burning shit storm, but she had zero regrets. Silently, she kept chanting her own personal mantra that had carried her through these past few months:

"I'm free. I deserve to be free."

When Nadine got home, she found Zaire at the kitchen island, papers strewn around and her laptop open. She was bobbing her head to something in her earbuds as she typed away. Nadine paused near the mudroom, taking her in. This week's leggings were flesh colored, and it looked like she was totally naked against the cream color of the barstool. Her ass was spilling around the sides of the seat. Nadine made a mental note to buy her a shit ton of those same-colored leggings to add to her growing collection.

Nadine softly padded over to the island and placed a kiss on Zaire's forehead. Startled, she jumped, placing her hand over her heart.

"You scared the shit outta me, Cookie! Be glad I don't carry that thang on me," Zaire laughed. She looked at her watch. "Wait, what are you doing home so early?"

"Well, it appears that I am without a job now."

Zaire's eyes widened. "Did you get fired?"

"Nope," Nadine shook her head. "I quit. In glorious fashion, might I add. You should have seen their faces. Especially Mitchell's."

Zaire smiled. "I'm proud of you, baby. So, what did Eddie say when you told him you'd quit?"

Nadine froze. "Shit." In her rush to get home, she hadn't told him yet. Currently, he was in the middle of practice for the upcoming tournament. He didn't need the drama and distraction. She'd find the right time to break the news.

Zaire let out a long whistle. "Wow, looks like y'all got a lot to talk about."

Nadine ran a hand through her hair. "I know. I'm not worried, though. Honestly, he will probably be relieved. He knew how that job stressed me out. In the meantime, I guess I'll be trying to figure out what to do next."

Nadine watched as Zaire's smile slowly faded. She tilted her chin toward her gently. "Why the sad face, pretty girl?"

"I mean, you're going to be home more. What's the point of me being here?"

Nadine laughed, loudly. "Do you seriously think I'm going to let you go?" She rubbed her thumb gently across Zaire's plump bottom lip. *Such pretty lips.* "I need you. And as I try to figure out my next steps, I'll need you more than ever now. You have no idea how much of a support you've been for me. Not just with EJ. As a matter of fact, why don't you just move in?"

Zaire raised a perfectly arched brow. "Move in? As in, live with y'all?"

"Why not? To be honest, I wasn't too fond of your apartment's location. It isn't that safe of a neighborhood."

"You really are a leaning into being a lesbian, huh?" chuckled Zaire. "A couple of months in and you trying to move a chick in."

Nadine rolled her eyes. "This house has eight bedrooms. I just want you close to me. Always. I feel at peace when you're near." She stroked her cheek, softly. "You're safe with me, Zaire. Seriously, think about it."

Zaire's dark skin flushed at the sentiment. "That's a very generous offer. I'll think about it."

Nadine leaned down and pressed her lips to Zaire's. "Good. Right now, I'll let you study. I need to get out of this suit and relax. I'm going to hop in the shower and think about how I'm gonna to break this news to Eddie."

Zaire pulled Nadine by her hips, rubbing her thumb under her silk camisole. "I could join you. I could use a study break. I don't have to pick up EJ for another hour."

Nadine licked her lips. "Then let's go get wet, baby."

216

IN THE SHOWER, THE WATER FROM THE MASSIVE WATERFALL SHOWER HEADS rained down on them. Steam enveloped them as if they were in a rainforest. Their bodies were slick with soap, pressed against each other. Nadine kissed Zaire until she was breathless. Her hard, sensitive nipples rubbed against Zaire's. A touch, a light flick of Z's fingers against them, had her pussy thrumming from the sensation.

"Your titties are everything," Zaire said before she bent down to take a nipple into her mouth. She sucked hard, her teeth grazing them slightly. Nadine moaned, throwing her head back.

"Shit," Nadine whispered, her voice already hoarse from screaming in pleasure. Zaire had made her come twice in a short amount of time. She grabbed the back of Z's head, riding the wave of pleasure she felt coursing through her.

Zaire finally released her lips from the hardened buds. When she did, Nadine grabbed her by the back of the neck and pushed her up against the glass doors of the shower.

"Put your leg up," Nadine commanded. Zaire steadied herself and lifted her leg onto the built-in bench. Nadine leaned down, whispering in her ear. "You think you can make me come like that and me not return the favor?" She grabbed Zaire's neck harder, eliciting a moan from the woman. "I'm going to make that pussy talk to me, Z."

Nadine slid two wet fingers between Zaire's pussy. Nadine wasn't sure if it was the heat of the shower or Zaire's own body, but her pussy was so fucking hot. She toyed with her clit for a minute, rubbing back and forth until Zaire was writhing with pleasure. But that wasn't enough for Nadine. She could admit, sex with Zaire had made her brazen, demanding in her need to give and receive pleasure. Zaire's sexual confidence was rubbing off on her.

Nadine curled her fingers inside Zaire's tight, wet pussy, reaching for the spot to give her exactly what she wanted. She pumped furiously with her fingers. "You gonna come for me, pretty girl?"

Zaire splayed her fingers against the glass. "Yes Cookie, Imma come for you, mami."

"Give me what I fucking want then, Z."

Nadine moved her hand down, holding on to Zaire's waist as she continued her assault on her pussy. Before she knew it, Zaire was squirting all over her hand and onto the shower floor.

It took a few minutes for them both to come down from their orgasmic high.

"You're getting too good at this," Zaire remarked, breathless.

"I had a good teacher." Nadine kissed her neck, a smirk forming on her face as Zaire's breathing finally returned to normal.

Zaire turned to face Nadine. She moved a wet strand of hair from her cheek and cupped her face. She stared at Nadine for what seemed like minutes. Her mouth opened and closed, as if she wanted to say something but didn't know how. Nadine didn't have to guess. She knew.

"You don't have to say it, sweetheart. I know."

Zaire smiled, tears pooling in her eyes. "Ok." Nadine was surprised that was all that she could say. The normally bold Zaire was timid and of few words.

"Good." Nadine gave her a soft peck. "Let's get out before all this pretty skin gets wrinkly."

She playfully slapped Zaire on her ass before turning off the shower.

Had she really asked Zaire to move in? If their days were anything like this, Nadine could get used to this.

CHAPTER 28
Waycross... Now

Nadine pulled her car up the gravel driveway. She smiled when she caught sight of her father in his natural habitat. Under the hood of an old car, tinkering away.

As she exited her SUV, the early autumn winds blew through her hair. She swore it was always a few degrees colder in the country than the city. At least, it always felt that way when she came home. Maybe it wasn't the breeze. Maybe it was her unease at setting foot back in her little country town. She never felt like she fit in there, no matter how hard she tried. Now she knew why.

The gravel crunched under her boot as she approached her dad. He stopped his tinkering and smiled widely as he looked at her, wiping his greasy hands on his coveralls. He had Dickies coveralls in every single color. Nadine was pretty sure she'd only seen her father in a suit once, and that was at her mother's funeral.

Paul Dee wrapped his arms around his daughter. "Deanie girl! You looking good, sugar. What brings you by in the middle of the week?" His smile was replaced by a worried look. "Everything ok with the Alex? EJ? What's going on?"

Nadine inhaled the familiar scent of Old Spice and motor oil and pulled back to inspect her father. "I just came to look at my old man and see how he's doing. I went by mama's grave and paid her a visit too."

Nadine had taken Dr. Flournoy's advice. She wrote a letter to her mother, telling her that her judgment was no longer going to define her life. She read the letter out loud, tears falling to the ground. Once she was done, she buried it in the dirt near her headstone.

"That's nice." Paul pulled out a rag and wiped his forehead. "Well, I'm fair to middlin', sugar. I can't complain. Gout got me in my toe, but other than that, I am fit as a fiddle. Just wish I could get them damn developers off my back."

"Developers?" Nadine frowned. She had noticed on her drive into town that it was teeming with new business and activity. It was different from the very segregated, very sleepy town that she grew up in.

"Yeah," Paul continued. "Every day I get a call about the land. I tell them no thank you. This here is my inheritance. My great-great grandaddy ain't work himself to death to buy himself outta freedom for nothing. I'm leaving it you or PJ if y'all want it."

Nadine smiled. She knew her baby brother, with his fancy corporate tech law job in the Bay Area, wasn't interested in coming back to Waycross. As for her? She wasn't sure. Country life could be a respite from the noise and chaos of her life. Especially now that she was without a job.

"How much they asking for the land, Daddy?"

Paul scoffed. "Enough for me to never work on a car ever again and maybe retire. I mean, I wouldn't be rich as you and Eddie, but I'd be good."

"You can always come and live with me. I've got plenty of extra bedrooms."

"Ha! Girl, now I know you're talking every bit of crazy. What Imma do in that big old house? Besides, city life don't suit me. Atlanta is too crowded and too fast for my taste." Paul eyed his daughter suspiciously. "Deanie, I know you didn't drive all this way to talk living arrangements. What's going on? Something going on with the job?" He motioned to the metal folding chair that was near the toolbox.

Nadine sat quietly, fiddling with the sleeves of her cardigan before answering. "Actually, I quit my job last week."

Paul's eyes widened. "Really? Well, you ain't need to work anyway. You got Eddie to take care of you. You just always wanna be an independent woman or whatever."

Nadine rolled her eyes. Her father was so old-fashioned. "Daddy, I didn't come to talk about my job. I came to talk about something else." She paused before asking, "Do you remember Allison Alston?"

Paul nodded. "Yeah. I remember the Alstons. Lived not too far from the cemetery. Why?"

"I...we...." Nadine paused, trying not to cry and get her thoughts together. "You all made me stop being friends with her."

"Did we? I don't recall that." Paul turned his attention back to his car and tinkered with the oil cap.

Nadine rolled her eyes. She knew her daddy was lying, but she didn't dare call him one. She played along. "You don't remember? Me and Allison were kissing in the woods and our mamas caught us. I got kicked outta Scouts that summer and Mae Alston forbade me and Ally from being friends. Ally avoided me all through middle and high school. Told everyone I was weird, even though she was the one who would always kiss me first."

Paul scratched his head. "Why you bringing this up, Deanie? Stuff happened over thirty years ago. Ya'll was kids."

"Because Daddy, it matters. It just does...I..." Nadine took a few deep breaths, recalling her tools she'd learned in therapy. "I am telling you this because after thirty years, I realized that was a pivotal moment for me. It made me realize that I liked girls. Just like I liked boys. And when I told you I liked Allison, you said I'd grow out of it. You said I'd learn to like boys more."

"But you did, didn't you?"

"No, I didn't!"

Paul Dee looked at Nadine like she had two heads. "You been married twice now and got two kids. You trying to tell me all these years you been gay?"

Nadine sighed. "I didn't say I was gay, Daddy."

"Then what is it?"

"I'm bisexual. I like both men and women. I always have been. It just took me thirty years and some change to realize that."

"Bisexual?" Paul held up his hands. "Hold on now, you saying *now* you bisexual. What the hell going on down in Atlanta? Tatum got three boyfriends. Alisa got two husbands. Now you a bisexual?"

"This has nothing to do with Alisa or Tatum."

"Then what the hell this about? What Eddie got to say about all this?"

"He's supportive and just wants me to be honest about who I am. And before you ask, no, we aren't getting a divorce. There are plenty of folks who are bisexual in straight presenting relationships?"

"Straight presenting? What the hell that mean?"

Nadine pinched the bridge of her nose. She knew she was probably throwing around terminology that was going straight over Paul Dee's head. "It just means on the outside looking in, folks think we are both straight when one of us isn't."

Paul grunted as he tinkered with the engine. "See, I knew maybe sending you down to Spelman around all them girls…"

"Daddy! This has nothing to do with Spelman."

"Then what?"

Nadine blew out a ragged breath. "I'm just putting a lot of pieces together realizing who I am. That puzzle started with Allison. I've always felt different. I realized my whole life I've tried to bury it because I felt ashamed. You all made me feel ashamed, especially mama. Me being a dyke, her words, was worse than being a murderer."

"Well, your mama was always one for exaggeration." Paul pulled out an old washcloth and dabbed his forehead. "Deanie, you blaming this on me and your mama, god rest her soul? What we got to do with how you feel about women?"

Nadine looked up at the pecan trees, willing her tears not to fall. "No. But you all pushed religion down my throat, made sex seem like a bad thing. Had me thinking my body and who I was was dirty. And when I did like a girl or had feelings, I shoved it down, told myself I'd grow out of it. But not anymore, Daddy."

"What done brought about all this change?"

Nadine didn't think she could mention Zaire without giving her father a heart attack. "A close friend and therapy. A lot of therapy. I felt like if I said who I really was…you'd turn your backs on me. Tell me

I'm going to hell. Say you never want to see me again. And that woulda broke my heart."

The tears Nadine held back finally ran down her cheeks. Her father stepped to her, bending down to wrap his arms around her. Her shoulders shook as she sobbed onto his coveralls. She felt transported back to that same little girl in dirty Keds and a Girl Scout uniform.

Paul wiped Nadine's face, cradling it in his calloused hands. "Deanie, I would have never said I never wanted to see you again. You are my child, baby. You will always be welcome here."

"But Mama.."

Paul Dee shook his head. "Your mama would have had to let shit go. We was raised a certain way, good or bad, we tried to do the same with you. You gotta eat the meat and spit out the bones from it. What we said about you and liking girls, that was the bones. I'm sorry for that."

Nadine nodded. "It's ok. You don't have to apologize."

"Naw, apparently it's not, ok. We done messed up your life, Deanie." Paul let out a breath. "I know some of them bones was also the reason you stayed with that no, good Drew for a second too long."

Nadine nodded. "Yeah. I was trying to be the good Christian wife and mother you all raised me to be. Also, I was marrying Drew to bury who I was. When I said I wanted to leave him, Mama kept telling me to pray on it. You said he'll grow up, eventually."

"That's all on me. Like I said, generations were different. I was wrong. When he put hands on you..." Tears welled up in Paul's eyes. "Just glad you got out of that and found your happiness. Whatever it looks like to you."

Nadine smiled. "Thanks Daddy."

Paul Dee squinted. "So what this mean? Being bisexual? You gonna have a girlfriend and a husband?"

Nadine blinked. Now, she wasn't trying to go there with him, even though he was sort of right. The details of that were none of his business. It might just give him a heart attack. "Daddy, I don't think..."

"Hell," Paul interrupted. "Ain't that the next logical step? Tatum got three boyfriends now. Alisa got what? Two husbands? Lord, Eddie probably living the dream then." He chuckled under his breath.

Nadine rolled her eyes. She stood up, giving her dad a peck on the forehead. "Daddy, chill. Let me take you to lunch while I'm here. I'll try my best to explain things."

"Good. Now, let me change into my *good* coveralls."

Nadine smiled.

AFTER STUFFING THEMSELVES WITH FRIED CATFISH AND SHRIMP AT CAPTAIN Joe's, Nadine took her father back home. Over lunch, she tried her best to explain her arrangement with Eddie, but all her father said was "Well, y'all are grown." And left it at that.

Paul Dee was disappointed, hoping her visit would be longer. He tried his best to get her to stay, even promising her that he'd cook his famous salmon croquettes for breakfast. As tempting as that was, Nadine declined, insisting that she wanted to get home before dark to say goodnight to EJ. Her father understood, but his hug lasted far longer than normal. Nadine practically melted into his arms, promising to come see him more often. Paul Dee pulled back, staring into his daughter's watery eyes.

"You're the best part of my heart walking around on earth. You know that, don't you, sugar? Don't matter who you are. What you do. Who you love. You my child. Don't ever forget that."

Nadine nodded, tears brimming in her eyes. "I won't Daddy. I promise."

"Tell Alex to call me sometimes and next time, bring my EJ down to see his Pappy. Boy gotta learn how to fish and hunt. Eddie shole ain't gonna teach him, lest he grow up too citified and spoiled. "

"Daddy," Nadine chuckled, "He's barely four. He can't barely wipe his butt, let alone hold a fishing pole."

"Well," Paul Dee flashed a wide grin, showing his gold crown. "Ain't never too early to learn, Deanie. Or in your case, too late."

Nadine made her way onto the highway, blasting the best of Mariah Carey for her nearly four-hour trip back home. About halfway through MCs catalog and her ride, Nadine needed a break. She made a detour toward the Buc-ees gas station in Warner Robbins. Nadine had been obsessed with the chain of massive gas stations ever since a work trip took her through Texas. It was the perfect place to fill up her tank, stretch her legs, and get some snacks for the rest of her trip home.

Nadine made her way inside, the smell of fudge and savory treats making her mouth water. After grabbing a much-needed cup of coffee, Nadine decided to wade through the crowd to stand in line to grab the fudge and peanut brittle that she didn't need but was calling her name. Just as she was about to grab an extra bag of popcorn for EJ and Zaire, she swore heard someone call her name. Nadine froze, clearly dismissing the sound as exhaustion until she heard it again.

"Nadine? Nadine Davis?"

Nadine turned and nearly dropped everything in her hands as she stared at the woman standing before her. She was older, curvier, yet it was still unmistakably her. Same deep, dark skin. Same full lips and deep-set brown eyes.

Allison Alston. Ally.

Those big, brown eyes were staring back at Nadine through simple, brown frames, a slight smile on her face as she came closer. Nadine could hear her heart thumping in her ears.

"Ally?" Nadine managed to say, her voice cracking on the last syllable. Had she conjured up this woman after talking to her daddy? She had to have done that. This couldn't be real.

Allison stepped closer. Dressed in jeans and a simple V-neck sweater, she looked effortlessly chic. "Hey! I would give you a hug but..." She nodded toward Nadine's full hands "Still got a sweet tooth, huh?"

Nadine smiled bashfully. "Yeah. Some things never change." She watched as Ally's eyes took her in. She caught her reflection in the door of the beer cooler. A hand flew up to her hair, up in a messy bun. "Sorry. I look a mess."

After a breath, the woman replied. "You look as beautiful as always. Like I said, some things never change."

Nadine felt her cheeks heat at the compliment. Never in a million years would she have thought she'd see Allison again. And here she was, in the middle of a Buc-ees in middle Georgia. A crowd of patrons began to get annoyed because they were blocking the counter near the brisket sammies. Nadine and Allison maneuvered to get out of the way, moving to the end of a less crowded aisle.

"What are you doing here?" asked Nadine.

"I was stopping for gas. Just dropped my kids off in Savannah to visit their father. I had to wrap up some things in Charleston, so that was good midpoint."

Charleston? Did she remember that she lived in Charleston? "Oh, cool." Nadine nodded, trying her best not to sound affected by that bit of information.

"I don't live there," offered Allison with a sigh. "Well, not anymore. Just dropping my youngest off to spend the weekend with their father. We got divorced last year."

Nadine's eyes widened. "Wow, I'm sorry to hear that."

Allison waved her hands with a slight smile. "Girl, I'm not. It was a long time coming. It was years in the making. We just realized we are better as friends." She paused, staring at Nadine with a smile. "I still can't believe I ran into you here, of all places."

Despite Nadine being in boots, they were eye level now. When they were kids, Ally seemed to tower over her. Ally's eyes hadn't once stopped staring directly at Nadine. Nadine tried to divert her eyes from such an intense stare, but she couldn't. It was like looking into the sun.

Nadine finally spoke. "Yeah, I was just stopping here for snacks on the way back to Atlanta. I was coming back from Waycross seeing my Dad."

"Oh yeah, I hadn't been back home in years. Me and my folks… long story. Has it changed much?"

Nadine was curious about Ally meant by "long story." She didn't want to pry. Instead, she answered her question. "Other than a few more chain stores, the vibe is the same, I guess. Developers are trying to scoop up land, my dad says. I took my dad to Captain Joe's, and he told me all about it."

"Wow. That place still standing?" chuckled Allison. "I'm shocked Mr. Davis let you treat him to lunch."

"He's getting soft in his old age, I suppose," mused Nadine. "I'm surprised you remember my Daddy?"

"He's kind of unforgettable. A Waycross legend. Him and his cars."

They laughed a bit until they both quieted. The noise of the gas station seems to fade into background noise all around them as if they were in their own world.

"You still friends with Tatum and Alisa? Man, I heard all about that drama with Alisa, the Senate candidate and that football player. It was all over the news."

Nadine nodded. "Yeah, but those are her husbands now. She has gorgeous twins too."

"Whoa," chuckled Allison. "Seriously?"

"Yep. And Tatum, well…she's happy and doing well." Nadine didn't think she needed to blow Allison's mind any further with her best friends' love lives. *Or her own.*

"So, "Allison began. "How are things with you? Last I heard through the grapevine, you were married to some baller, and you were some big time CEO."

"Ex-baller," Nadine nodded. "He's coaching on the collegiate level now. And I *was* a CEO. I quit last week."

Allison's eyes widened. "Really? You gave up a big C-suite job?"

Nadine shrugged. "It was a long time coming."

"And you have a daughter, right?"

Nadine wondered how she knew any of this. Being married to Eddie, her life was semi-public. Just ripe for gossip, especially in her small hometown. *Or maybe she'd be keeping tabs on her too.*

"My oldest, Alex, is a freshman in college. And we also have a son, EJ. He's four and I want to spend more time with him. You've got kids too, right?" Nadine knew she had kids. She'd stalked her Facebook page far too many times over the years.

Allison nodded. "Yep, three. My oldest son is 22 and a senior at the Citadel. My middle baby is 18 and a freshman at SC State. Super smart girl. And my baby girl is fourteen. I was a principal for many years, so I could keep a decent schedule. But now that they're older, I am shifting gears now that I've moved to Atlanta. Time to do me."

Nadine's breathing nearly stopped. "Oh, you're in Atlanta, now?"

"Technically, in Lawrenceville, but you know how it is. Just started an educational consulting business. So I'm my own boss now."

"That's awesome, Ally," Nadine beamed, truly proud. "I'm happy for you."

Allison smiled, large dimples showing as she ran a hand through her grey streaked bob. "Thanks. I appreciate that." She moved closer to Nadine, closing the space between them. "Listen, I…I saw your Facebook request. I'm sorry I didn't accept it. I will, though, if you want me to."

Nadine shrugged. "It's ok. No big deal."

"No, let me explain." Allison sighed. "Seeing your name pop up just flooded me with so many memories. It took me right back to when we were ten and…" Allison blinked rapidly, looking up at the fluorescent lights. "Our mamas had no business doing and saying what they did. Calling us names. We were kids."

"I know," Nadine said. "They overreacted. Like you said, we were kids and…"

"I loved you,' Allison interrupted, her voice trembling. "You were my first love, Deanie. Shit, you might have been the only person I've ever loved."

Nadine felt like her world had flipped upside down. "Ally, I loved you too. Times were different. Again, we were kids."

"And kids don't know about love?"

"Of course they do," Nadine blinked. "Ally, yes, but still…"

"No," Allison grabbed Nadine's free hand. "I gotta say this. I have been waiting thirty years to say this. And honestly, the divorce has given me the courage to be honest with myself. We might have been kids, finding our way, not fully understanding everything, but I felt love every time I kissed you. Every time I was with you, I felt happiness. It was a love hadn't felt before. Not with my parents. Not with my siblings. No one. Then our parents just tore us apart, called us names. We couldn't do anything but take it."

Nadine swallowed thickly as she digested Ally's words. "Like I said, it was a different time. Not giving them excuses but, they just reacted the way they were taught. Grace Davis and Mae Alston were too religious for their own good."

Alison rolled her eyes. "Yeah, but still, we were the ones who got hurt by it. Then, we got to middle school, then high school and just drifted apart. We pretended like it never happened, but I could never stop thinking about you, Deanie."

"I couldn't stop thinking about you too. You have no idea." Nadine squeezed Allison's hand a little tighter. Yes, to reassure her, but to also make sure that this moment was real.

"Even when I was lying and calling you weird?" asked Alison

Nadine smiled. "Even when you weren't checking for me, I always knew deep down that maybe you didn't mean it."

"It was just my hurt talking. Hurt because I couldn't have you. And I couldn't be myself. I'm sorry for that. Please forgive me, if you can."

"Of course I forgive you." Nadine felt hot tears roll down her face. "Can you forgive me?"

Tears rolled down Allison's face. "Already done."

They briefly wiped their tears away before intertwining their hands again. Nadine didn't expect that a pit stop at a gas station would have her in tears. It was like they were kids again. Nadine didn't necessarily believe in soul mates. But if she did, Allison would come damn close.

"You know," Allison smiled, a twinkle in her eye. "Even in a busy place like this, I could spot you in a sea of hundreds. Guess I had years of practice. In school, I'd see you in the halls in your cheerleading uniform and it took all my might to pretend like I didn't notice you."

Nadine chuckled, brow raised. "You remember me in my cheerleading uniform?"

"Who didn't? I mean, clearly Shamika Parker and her ass got a lot of attention on the squad, but you definitely were a close second."

"It wasn't even close." Nadine rolled her eyes, chuckling. "Shamika definitely was the star."

"You're downplaying yourself as usual, Deanie. You've always been a star. At least in my eyes."

Nadine's eyes took in Allison's face as she said the words. It made something warm flow inside Nadine and a pulsing ache nearly cave in her heart. Gosh, she'd missed Allison.

Allison shook her head. Her teeth nibbled at the corner of her lip. "Tsk. It's a shame, though."

Nadine's eyes went straight to the movement of Allison's teeth against lips. *I wonder if she still tastes the same...kisses the same.* Nadine blinked, trying to refocus. "What is?" she asked.

"Well, I'm single and back out here. But now the one person I'd want to ask out is married. Such is life, I guess." Allison chuckled dryly.

"Well," Nadine smirked. "I'm flattered, but I am kind of seeing someone."

Allison frowned. "I thought you were married?"

"I am. It's…complicated," Nadine confessed. "I can explain, but I feel like the candy aisle in Buc-ees isn't the right venue for that."

Allison chuckled. "It probably isn't. I've already done enough confessing in these aisles to last a lifetime. Next time, confessions should be over cocktails and appetizers other than fudge and corn dogs"

"True," agreed Nadine, balancing her snacks. "Let me check out so we can walk back to my car and exchange numbers. I don't think we should wait another thirty years to talk to each other."

Allison smiled. "I'd like that. I'd love to catch up when we get back to the city."

"Me too." Nadine smiled. As they moved down the aisle, her eyes locked in on a familiar-colored pack of gum. She grabbed a pack of Bubblicious, adding it to her already full bounty of snacks.

For old time's sake.

CHAPTER 29
The Last Session

Nadine watched as Dr. Flournoy bit into a batch of fresh blueberry scones. Watching someone take the first bite of anything she'd made was Nadine's favorite part of baking.

"Oh my god, Nadine," Dr. Flournoy said, between bites. "I am losing my manners here. These are amazing!"

Nadine smiled. "Thank you. I figured I should bring a parting gift."

Dr. Flournoy wiped her hands on a napkin. "You know, I cannot believe this is going to be our last session."

"For a while," Nadine clarified. "I am sure I'll need a mental tune up here and there but not like before. I think you've given me the tools to handle problems if things arise. Right now, I think it's time to take a break."

Dr. Flournoy smiled. "I understand. Therapy is a process and a journey. You've concluded this part of the journey."

Nadine rubbed her hands against her jeans. "I am super grateful for everything, too. I know I was difficult at first, especially with opening up. But I've learned so much about myself over these past few years. Especially about accepting who I am. I feel, well, I *know* I'm in a good place."

"I wouldn't say difficult," laughed Dr. Flournoy. "But I'm glad that you allowed me in."

"Me too," chuckled Nadine.

"So what's next for you, Nadine?"

Nadine shrugged. "I don't know. And for the first time in a long time, I am relieved."

"Why is that?"

Nadine smoothed the top of her bun down as she thought. "I think it's because I've always had an answer for everything, felt like I had to have a plan a, b, and c if things didn't work out. When my first marriage didn't work out, I threw myself into work. When I got pregnant, I threw myself into motherhood, not once, but twice. When I felt like I couldn't be myself, I threw myself into crafting the perfect image of myself. I am so fucking tired of being perfect. And I am tired of having plans."

Dr. Flournoy nodded with understanding. "So how does it feel to let go of the idea of perfection and plans?"

"Freeing," Nadine responded. "My friend Alisa says Black women have the right to do whatever they want. Be whatever they want. Without judgment. I spent so much of my life judging everyone around me without looking internally at myself. I was locking myself in a cage of my own fear and anxiety. I finally understand that."

"Good for you. And that Alisa seems like a wise woman."

Nadine rolled her eyes. "Oh lord, don't have her hear that! She'll think she's The Oracle from the Matrix."

Both women laughed until Dr. Flournoy gently steered the conversation back to Nadine. "So, how are things with Eddie? And Zaire?"

Nadine could feel the smile forming across her face. "Things are incredible actually. Eddie's given me the space to see where this goes. Z and I are also giving Eddie space to also explore his own sexual desires. It's been pretty easy to balance, but so far no issues."

"I take it this has changed your mind on polyamorous relationships now."

"Absolutely. Can't judge my friends anymore. I see how love isn't just one thing."

Dr. Flournoy paused as she looked down at her notes. She scrolled a few times, tapping her pen against the tablet. Nadine was curious about what she was looking for, but didn't want to interrupt.

"When we last met, we talked about what it would be like opening up to your father and daughter, and it was something you needed to think about. Where do you stand with that now?"

"I had those conversations," Nadine sighed. It was a sigh of relief, no doubt, that Dr. Flournoy noticed. She nodded, encouraging her to continue. "Alex has been understanding, but a little resentful. I understand. I gave her a lot of mixed messages over the years. My father, bless him, still can't wrap his brain around any of it, but he's trying. So, that's all I can ask for."

Nadine bit the inside of her jaw. Dr. Flournoy noticed her change in demeanor. "Is there something else, Nadine?"

"I saw Allison." Nadine blurted out.

Dr. Flournoy's eyes widened. "Really? When?"

"Coming back from Waycross visiting Daddy. In a gas station, of all places. I wasn't exactly looking the cutest," chuckled Nadine. "But it was still…seeing her was…amazing."

"Amazing? Tell me about it."

"Well, we caught up on our lives. Said some things we'd been waiting to say for like thirty years. It was wild."

Dr. Flournoy was genuinely surprised. "Things like what?"

Nadine recalled her conversation with Ally, the apologies, the confessions. At the conclusion, Nadine felt as if she was telling her and Allison's secrets, but she knew she was safe with Dr. Flournoy.

"We even made plans to go out to lunch. So, that's nice."

"How do you feel learning that she's out as well?"

Nadine looked up at the ceiling, trying to choose her words carefully. "Relieved," she confessed. "Knowing someone was on a similar journey as I let me know this isn't so crazy. And I'm not alone."

"Nadine, coming out late in life happens more often than you think. Trust me."

"I know that now," Nadine smiled. "You've helped me to see that."

"Well, I'm glad you got a sense of closure, Nadine," Dr. Flournoy patted her knee. "But you have to promise me something?"

Nadine's forehead wrinkled. "What's that?"

"That you stop by and bring me at least a dozen of these scones once a month." Dr. Flournoy picked up another scone and took a big bite. "Mercy! They[are just heavenly!"

Nadine laughed, happiness blooming deep within her soul. "Will do."

Epilogue

FOUR MONTHS LATER

"**O**h my god, they are absolutely gorgeous." Tatum cooed as she and Nadine stared down at the tiny, brown bundles swaddled in matching Dior layettes.

Nadia Tate and Nicholas Franklin lay sleeping side-by-side in a massive, custom bassinet, a gauzy material canopy hanging from the ceiling draped over it. They didn't stir or move an inch as family and friends peered at them in awe.

Since Alisa had gone into labor so early, she and the twins had to spend a significant amount of time in the hospital. In lieu of a baby shower, the family opted to have a sip-and-see just for family once the babies came home and were settled. Alisa swore she would keep it simple. Tatum and Nadine knew that was a lie as soon as she declared it. It wouldn't be a Bishop-Miller function without some level of lavishness.

There was a full buffet spread, flower arches as far as the eye could see, and massive photos of the babies on easels all over the house. Alisa laughed as she told the girls about Deacon stopping every five minutes to wipe his teary eyes between shots of the kids.

Christophe's parents, Ambassador Valencia Bishop and her husband, Clayton flew in from Kyoto, armed with unique Japanese gifts that the babies didn't need. Christophe tried to tell them to chill,

235

but they refused, saying that they were going to spoil their only grand-kids. Even Mother Miller, despite the objections of her husband, the Bishop, came. At first, she was her usual stuffy self. She was more than perturbed that the babies had two last names. But once she laid eyes on the twins, she couldn't stop crying and hugging Kadeem, Christophe, and Alisa, declaring the little miracles to be a blessing from God.

"I swear, they get more gorgeous every time I see them," admired Nadine as she gently adjusted the hat on her goddaughter's head.

"Nadine, quit fussing over the baby," admonished Alisa, who came to stand next to them. "This is a sip and see. You're supposed to be relaxing, enjoying them, not babysitting. You are relieved of your godmother duties to Nadia and Nicky for today."

Nadine rolled her eyes. "Please. I'll never be relieved of my duties. The spoiling will never stop."

Tatum huffed. "You are forgetting that they have *two* godmothers."

"No, I'm not," Nadine smirked. "I am just the best one."

All three of them started laughing just as Cassidy brought over several glasses of champagne.

"Thank you baby," Tatum said, taking the glass from Cassidy.

"You're welcome, mama." Cassidy said, before placing a searing kiss on her lips.

Nadine and Alisa looked at each other, wide-eyed and amused. Tatum and Cassidy kissed as if there weren't a house full of people around them.

"My bad," said Cassidy, finally pulling back from their kiss. "I mean, look at her. She's too fine not to kiss."

Tatum's dark brown skin went flush at the compliment. "He's exaggerating."

"Nah, he's not, cuz," teased Alisa. "Being a fiancé again looks good on you. You've been smiling a lot these days. Props to Cassidy for picking the perfect ring. It's totally you."

Tatum held up her hand. It was basically a meteor on her finger. Very fitting.

Cassidy scratched his fluffy beard. "Actually, Miles helped me with the ring. He basically threatened me and said that if I didn't get her something perfect, don't even do it at all. He acted like I had no clue about rings. I study rocks for a living."

"Space rocks," clarified Tatum with a chuckle to which Cassidy shrugged.

"So I take it he took the news of the engagement well?" Nadine asked.

"Yeah," Tatum said. "Especially when we explained that nothing has to change. Well, except living arrangements. After the wedding next spring, we'll be looking for a new place. Just Cass and I."

"You're selling the house?" asked Alisa, surprised.

Tatum looked at Cassidy, then Nadine and Alisa with a smile. "Yeah. It's time."

Nadine and Alisa knew that Tatum must really be in love with Cassidy for her to sell the home she shared with Franklin. It was a place that held so many memories, good and bad. Change was good. Something they all realized.

"I bet Deacon was elated," Nadine nodded toward the corner. They all turned to look at Deacon, who was snapping pics.

Deacon looked up from his camera. "I sure was. Ya'll wasn't about to break up my happy home. I can't deal with a miserable ass Miles. And he can't deal with a miserable me either."

Everyone laughed at his admission, but he was right. Miles and Deacon, though together, were miserable without Tatum. It was an unconventional yet symbiotic relationship that was only balanced with Tatum being there too. Alisa could relate. And now Nadine understood what they meant as well.

"He's downplaying it. He and Miles had to show me...*all night*." Tatum laughed as Cassidy shook his head.

Alisa whistled. "Wow, so Tatum gets to have her cake and eat it too. Lucky girl."

"Ain't nobody eating cake, but I am eating..." Cassidy began before Tatum put her hand over his mouth with a giggle.

"Don't you dare finish that sentence," she warned.

Miles and Christophe walked up, curious about what all the laughter was about.

Christophe put an arm around Alisa. "What y'all over here

laughing about? It better not be my babies. They'll grow into their heads."

"No," Nadine laughed. "We were talking about cake…"

Miles pushed up his glasses, confused as he looked over at one of the dessert tables. "But I thought Nadine brought cupcakes? There's a cake?"

Tatum smiled, kissing Miles on his cheek. "Honey, please don't pay these nuts any attention."

"And thank you, Miles, for releasing my husband back to me," teased Alisa as Christophe kissed her on the lips. "You two have been holed up in a corner talking all afternoon. I know it was about work."

"My bad, princess," Christophe said. "Miles and I were discussing a case. It's our biggest one since he made me a partner. And I just wanted to go over the logistics."

"Chris and I were getting our plans together, Alisa. That's all. We got this." Miles gave Chris a fist bump.

Miles making Christophe a partner was such a natural progression. With the way they ribbed each other over schools and fraternities, one would have thought they had been friends for years. In a short period of time, they'd become close. They got along great, bouncing ideas off of each other, and winning tons of cases. Miles said Christophe was a valuable asset, especially after he was able to lure his buddy Dedrick over to the firm. Miles said that Christophe wasn't a replacement for Franklin, but now that Deacon left the firm for good, he was grateful to have a close friend. He said Franklin would have loved him. Everyone agreed.

"Not today, sir," Alisa pouted as she poked Christophe. "Today is about your son and daughter, not work."

Christophe smiled. "You're right. But why am I getting all the smoke?" He nodded toward Kadeem, who was chopping it up with Eddie. "Eddie and Kadeem have been talking sports all day and sneaking off to watch the game in the theater room."

Alisa's neck snapped in their direction. "Is that right?"

Christophe pinched his brow, instantly regretting snitching. "Alisa, baby, seriously, let the man have a friend to talk sports with. God knows I damn sure don't wanna talk about sports all day."

"Hmpf," Alisa handed Christophe her champagne glass. "Hold this."

The group watched as Alisa marched over to Kadeem and pinched him on his arm. All he could do was laugh as he picked her up, gave her a quick peck, whispered something in her ear, and put her back down as if she was a petulant child. Alisa shook her head and giggled as he smacked her on the ass as she walked away. It still baffled Nadine that not one, but *two* men had been able to tame the very feisty Alisa. Like her father would say, every pot had its lid. In Alisa's case, she had two lids that fit her perfectly.

Nadine shook her head in amazement. "Alisa is just so blessed and happy. I love this for her."

"I can say the same for you, sis," Tatum nudged with a smile. "You look much happier and lighter these days."

"I am." Nadine's eyes found Zaire in the crowd. She watched as Zaire teased EJ, making his icing-covered face giggle. When their eyes met, Zaire winked. Nadine calmed the heat she felt simmering before continuing. "Now that I've quit PharmaDigital, I can focus on the things that truly make me happy."

"Like the bakery!" Tatum excitedly said. "I am so glad you're finally doing it! About damn time!"

After telling Mitchell and PharmaDigital to kiss her ass and settling her discrimination case for an undisclosed amount of money, Nadine had a long talk with both Eddie about the next phase of her life. Eddie was more than supportive, totally thankful that she was finally putting herself first. Two weeks after their conversation, Nadine met with a realtor and found a small, commercial kitchen space in an industrial area not far from Deacon's photography studio.

Zaire was also on board, too. It took some convincing, but Zaire quit her job at Club Titanium and moved in. She could focus on school and help out with EJ when necessary. Zaire hadn't had stability and a sense of family like that in a really long time. "This feels like home," she declared. And Nadine agreed.

Deanie's Decadent Desserts was still in its infancy but gaining some popularity. She was a viral sensation on social media, her posts on Instagram getting thousands of likes and reposts. Nadine was nervous, but with Eddie and Zaire's support, she knew she would be fine.

"Thanks," smiled Nadine. "The bakery is just a small part of that happiness. Everything's changed so much, though. I feel...a lot. But in a good way. I can't explain it." She bit the corners of her lip.

Tatum, observing the change in Nadine's mood, grabbed her hand. "Wanna go into the solarium to talk?" she suggested. "Just us girls." Tatum signaled for Alisa to follow them. Alisa gave a wink of acknowledgement, excusing herself from a conversation with her in-laws.

The three of them grabbed another glass of passed champagne and entered the jungle-like solarium of the mansion. The sun gave the space a comfortable warmth as they settled themselves on the wicker couches.

"So, the dark side isn't so bad, huh?" asked Alisa as she plopped down on the couch. "I saw the way Zaire looked at you."

Nadine smiled. "She makes me very happy."

"So, are you all dating? Exclusive? Or what?" asked Tatum. "You've been kind of radio silent about it."

"I mean, we aren't defining it. She's young. She has her studies to focus on. I'm not trying to tie her down, but I am enjoying our time together. And she's a godsend with EJ. It's been an adjustment with him at the new Montessori school, but without Zaire, I am sure I'd be a wreck."

"And what about Eddie?"

Nadine smiled. "Eddie is happy that I am happy. We are in a good place. Therapy helped. Talking is helping..."

"And letting him watch you get your coochie ate is also probably helping," quipped Alisa.

"Jesus, why are you always so freaky?" laughed Tatum, shaking her head.

"Because it's probably the truth! Deanie, am I lying?" asked Alisa.

Nadine shrugged. "I mean, Alisa isn't lying. The sex has been everything, but it's more than that. We're fulfilling our fantasies and desires in a safe, healthy way. This whole thing forced us to really talk about things. I am happy and so is he."

"And that's all that matters," Tatum said, placing a hand on Nadine's knee. "You deserve it."

"*We* deserve it all," Alisa said, putting her hand on top of Tatum's. "And we got it!"

"We sure as hell did," Tatum smiled.

There was a soft knock. All three ladies looked up to see a plume of graying curls peaking around the corner. Tatum's face instantly lit up.

"There you all are," said Deacon, camera in hand. He walked over to Tatum, placing a soft kiss on her lips before turning to Alisa. "Everyone is looking for you, proud mommy!"

"Deacon, I just needed a little breather," Alisa sighed. "Besides, it's about the babies, not me."

"Yeah, Deek, can't we slip away for a little girls' time?" asked Tatum.

"Darling, y'all always have plenty of girls' time. Besides, I haven't gotten all my shots of the prettiest people in the room yet."

"And who's that?" asked Alisa, brow raised.

Deacon smirked, adjusting the lens of his camera. "You three, that's who." With the quickness, he took a candid shot of the ladies mid-laugh. Nadine made a mental note to ask him for a copy of that. She knew it was something she'd want to treasure.

Alisa rose from the sofa first. "Come on, before the wardens come looking for us."

"You know, Chris and Kadeem hate when you call them that," teased Nadine.

Alisa rolled her eyes. "It's foreplay for them at this point."

"Girl, with that talk, you'll be pregnant again in no time," teased Tatum. "Six weeks be damned."

Alisa whipped her honey blonde bob in Tatum's direction. "Please do not wish that on me. I love my babies, but nearly dying during childbirth woke me right the fuck up to any thought of having more. I am too old. I got my tubes tied immediately afterwards. If either one of their super sperm bypasses all that to make another kid, I am going to have to renegotiate my prenup."

The three of them howled with laughter.

Eventually, the ladies made their way back to the main atrium to their family and friends. As she took in the scene, Nadine spotted a familiar face in the crowd, holding a massive bouquet of flowers and a large box from Tiffany and Co.

Tatum nudged Nadine. "Deanie, is that who I think it is?"

Inexplicably, Nadine's heart skipped a beat, maybe two. She could feel herself smiling like an idiot.

"Don't just stand there, girl, go over there and say hello!" Alisa whispered.

The trio of friends walked over to a very nervous Allison. Nadine extended her arms first, inviting her in for a hug. As they embraced, she kept willing herself not to embarrass herself by holding her too long. Eventually, they let go, and the other ladies quickly embraced Allison as well.

"Ally Alston! It has been ages, girl!' exclaimed Alisa. "I am so glad to see you!"

"Me too," Allison smoothed down her shirt dress. "Nadine invited me when we met for lunch the other day. She said she put me on the list. I hope you don't mind."

Alisa waved her hands. "Of course not! It's all family and friends, and you are both." She took the box and flowers from Allison, handing them to Kadeem's assistant, Bresha. "Anyone who brings my babies Tiffany's is alright with me."

"I just wanted to give you my congratulations in person. I got a quick peek at the babies before their grandmothers scooped them up. They are beautiful, Alisa."

"Thank you," beamed Alisa. She motioned toward Nadine to say something besides standing there looking like a mime with a smile plastered on her face.

"Yeah, so glad you came Allison," Nadine eventually said. "Uhm, would you like a glance of champagne or anything?"

Alison shook her head. "No, thank you. But I sure would love one of these cupcakes I've seen folks devouring. Please tell me they're yours, Nadine."

Nadine's smile could light up a Christmas tree. "They are. Is your favorite flavor still red velvet?"

"Wow, you remember that?" Allison's brown skin blushed. "That was forever ago."

"Of course, I mean, you always devoured two slices of Mother Jenkins' cake on first Sunday after church. My cupcakes may not be as good as hers, but I think they are damn close."

"Well, I'll be the judge of that. Let me have a taste." Allison winked and Nadine bit her lip, trying not to focus on the phrase *"have a taste."*

Tatum put her hand on Allison's shoulder. "Unlike Mother Jenkins, Nadine isn't stingy with the icing. Let me take you over to the dessert table so you can get a couple before folks devour them all." Sensing her friend's awkwardness, Tatum looked over her shoulder, mouthing *"be cool"* to Nadine, who simply shook her head.

Alisa turned toward Nadine, who had a very pointed look on her face.

"What?" asked Nadine, feeling her face redden with embarrassment.

"You still got it bad for that girl."

Was it that damn obvious?

Nadine shrugged. "It was a childhood crush, Alisa. We're friends now."

"You know, you could date her too," Alisa suggested. "I mean, if Eddie and Zaire are ok with that. Like I said, the more the merrier."

Before Nadine could object, she felt a pair of arms wrap around her waist, and the smell of jasmine and sweetness engulfed her. She relaxed into the feel of familiarity.

"Date who?" Zaire asked, kissing Nadine on her nape.

"Well, on that note, let me go look for my babies before Mother Miller tries to baptize them," said Alisa, winking at Nadine.

Nadine gave Alisa a stare down as she watched her swiftly move out of her vicinity. She could kill her for being messy for no fucking reason.

"No one," Nadine said, turning to Zaire. "Alisa was being messy."

"Uhm, if she is talking about that thick, fine sister with the bob and glasses you keep staring at, then I approve," said Zaire. "Who's that?"

"Allison."

Zaire's eyes widened. "Wow. So, that's *the* Allison? Shit, I understand the obsession. She's fine as hell."

Nadine's eyes watched Allison take a bite out of her cupcake and seem to moan in delight. *Best review of her food to date,* she thought. "Yeah, she's still very beautiful."

"Yeah, I can't even be mad if you want to ask her out, Cookie."

"Oh, really?" Nadine chuckled. "I'm still new to this polyamory thing and can only handle one woman and one man at a time. Besides, Eddie may combust."

Zaire raised her brow. "How do *you* know? He may like the variety. Besides, I think the three or four of us could have some fun."

"You got a thing for older women, huh?" asked Nadine, wrapping her arms around Zaire's waist.

"Maybe," Zaire teased. "But right now, you're the only vintage wine I want to drink right now. Remember that."

Nadine kissed Zaire on the lips, tasting the faint hint of caramel icing on her lips. "I better be, baby girl."

Eddie joined the two of them with EJ on his hip. "Hey baby," he leaned down and kissed Nadine. "You two behaving?"

"For now," Nadine winked. She let Zaire go, taking a glimpse at her watch. "Have you seen Alex? She should have been here by now."

"Yeah, she came in a few minutes ago. But…" Eddie's voice trailed off, his face twisted.

Nadine frowned. "Is the new boyfriend that bad?"

Alex told her parents that she'd be bringing her new boyfriend to the event. Nadine wasn't entirely comfortable meeting him in this setting, but Eddie assured her it would be fine. Alex had five other "uncles" who could vet this dude. Christophe had become especially fond of Alex and said he'd beat the dude's ass if necessary. Kadeem backed him up with a similar sentiment.

"Uhm. That ain't it." Eddie sighed. "Here she comes."

Nadine looked up to see Alex walking hand in hand with a very handsome, full-bearded, dark-skinned guy with locs up neatly in a bun. When they got closer, Nadine's eyes widened with recognition, but she tried to play it very cool.

"Hey Mom, sorry I'm late. I wanted to introduce you to my, I mean, Malcolm."

Nadine blinked, trying her best not to throw up the rest of her champagne as she stared at the face of the bartender from Secrets. The one that she declared she'd fuck. Right in *front of him*. "Uhm, hello. Nice to meet you, Malcolm." She extended her hand toward him, and he shook. Nadine wasn't sure, but it seemed like there was a glimmer of *something* in his eyes. He definitely recognized her.

"Nice to meet you too, Mrs. Moody." Malcolm flashed his signature panty-wetting smile.

"Please. It's Nadine.", she stared at Malcolm as she roughly swallowed. "So, how did you two meet?"

Alex looked at Malcolm, a bit hesitant. "Oh, he's my...history professor."

"Excuse me?" asked Eddie with a frown. "What did you just say? Because I swore you said...*professor.*"

"He said fesser," EJ chimed in, as he looked between the adults.

"Daddy, please don't be weird," Alex declared. "I'm an adult. There are no rules against dating professors."

"There may not be rules against it, but it isn't really favorable," Eddie declared. Nadine looked at him out of the corner of her eye. He was fuming.

There was a beat of silence between them all before Malcolm cleared his throat.

"I understand your hesitation," interrupted Malcolm. "But if it's any consolation, I'm only thirty. I graduated with my PhD at 26."

So what the hell was he doing working at Secrets? Nadine pushed the thought out of her mind. "Well", Nadine guffawed. "Alex is barely twenty-one."

Alex sighed. "Mom, seriously. Do not make a scene! And you got a lot of nerve." She motioned toward Zaire, who threw her hands up.

"I am grown," Nadine said through gritted teeth.

"And so am I," Alex shot back. "What happened to not being judgmental? What happened to the new Nadine?"

"I know you didn't just call me *Nadine!*"

"Don't fight," EJ whimpered. Eddie bounced him and tried to quiet him down.

"We aren't fighting, baby," Nadine said, rubbing EJ's back, trying to soothe him. "Just talking."

Nadine sighed because she knew Alex was right. Nadine had no right to judge. She *was* a new person and Alex was an adult. This was an old pattern of behavior, as Dr. Flournoy would say. Honestly, the old Nadine would have pitched a bigger fit. She needed to get her shit together.

"I'm sorry. It's just," she looked at Malcolm, biting her tongue. "Me being a mom. Listen, why don't you two go get something to eat. There are drinks at the bar. Malcolm looks like he knows his way around a bar."

Ok so maybe old, petty Nadine could come out every now and then.

Malcolm chuckled, rubbing his beard with a knowing smirk. "Actually, I do. I appreciate the offer. It was nice meeting you all." With that, he took Alex's hand and headed toward the bar.

When they left, Eddie leaned down to whisper. "You don't think…"

Nadine whipped her head, daring Eddie to finish that sentence. "I do not want to think about her going *there* to meet men and doing God knows what. She is grown, but that is still my child."

Out of the corner of her eye, Nadine could see Tatum making a beeline toward her. Before she could say a word, Tatum whispered. "Listen, I know my eyesight is bad, but I could have sworn that was Alex with Malcolm from Secrets. "

"It is, and I damn sure don't want to talk about that."

"You don't think…"

"I pray to God, *not*. She says he's her history professor." Nothing about that man said professor to Nadine. Then again, nothing about Cassidy said astrophysicist to Nadine when she first met him. Looks can be deceiving.

"Wow, a professor," Tatum looked over Nadine's shoulder toward Alex and Malcolm. She was feeding him one of Nadine's cupcakes. "What is it with these kids and their teachers? First my Morgan, now Alex. How old is Malcolm anyway?"

"He's thirty," Nadine threw up her hands. "But I am not going to pry any further. New year. New Nadine."

"Uh huh," smirked Tatum. "I already know as soon as this is over, you're going to do a background check."

Nadine laughed. "I am. You know me too well."

"Of course I do," nudged Tatum. "You're my best friend."

The soft jazz that was playing in the background lowered, and Christophe began to gently clink his champagne glass.

"Now that I have your attention, I'd like my lovely wife and husband to join me up here."

Alisa and Kadeem, each with a twin in their arms, made their way next to Christophe. He leaned over and kissed them both sweetly.

Everyone cooed and swooned. The babies had captured everyone's hearts.

Christophe cleared his throat. "Thank you all for coming. Alisa, Kadeem and I are so blessed to call you our family. So much has changed over the years. Never would we have thought we'd be parents to gorgeous twins or have Alisa in our lives. Their arrival symbolizes the beginning of a new chapter in all our lives."

"Right," said Kadeem, trying his best not to cry. "We never would have thought we'd have you all as our extended family." He turned his attention to the audience. "Shaunetta and Ritchie, thanks for holding it down as managers of Tresses franchises and making our Alisa's dreams come true. I know it wasn't easy holding down the fort while Alisa was on bedrest and in the hospital. You all know how she is."

"What does that mean?" Alisa snapped.

"Princess, you're a bit of a control freak," said Christophe.

"Takes one to know one," Alisa mumbled.

"She is, but we'll do anything for our boo," yelled out Shaunetta, who had been dipping into the top shelf liquor all afternoon. She was faded.

As was Ritchie, who added, "Don't forget Allen, the best brother-in-law, who is bad as hell with a pair of clippers."

"Hell yeah," Allen chimed in. "Big sis knows what's up." Everyone laughed, and Allen nodded proudly. Since his commutation, he'd become a licensed barber, holding down the Tresses barber shop space in Brookhaven. Alisa was so proud of her brother. They all were.

"True," Christophe laughed, continuing. "We want to thank our parents. Mom, Dad, I know at first this was all hard to understand but thank you for realizing that families can be formed in an abundance of ways."

"And," Kadeem turned his attention to Mother Miller. "Mother, I know it's been a journey for you. You've come so far, and I love you. And for that, I appreciate you."

The grandparents said nothing, simply wiped their tears and nodded their heads in appreciation.

"And we want to thank our chosen family. Miles, Deacon, Cass, Nadine, Eddie, our niece Alex, and now Zaire. You mean the world to us. Miles, I haven't seen Chris as happy and fulfilled as he's been working with you. You're the brother he never had. Cass and Deek, you're amazing friends and your love for Tatum, and even for us, knows no bounds. Nadine, you were literally there when our babies were born. And I...we..." Kadeem's voice broke, tears flooding his eyes. "We cannot say thank you enough. They or Alisa may not even have been here without you."

Nadine wiped her tears as she felt both Eddie and Zaire wrap their arms round her. She blew Kadeem a kiss and mouthed. *"Love you."*

"Finally," Christophe motioned toward Tatum. "Tatum, if you would, can you come up here and join us?"

Tatum looked confused as she made her way next to her cousin. Alisa, with her free hand, squeezed Tatum tight.

"Don't tell me you're going to rescind my godmother duties," joked Tatum. The wait staff began passing out fresh glasses of champagne to everyone in the room. Alisa tried to take one, but Kadeem swiped it fast, giving her apple cider instead. Everyone laughed, and Alisa rolled her eyes in mock protest.

"Tatum," Alisa began. "I would have never thought the love that our dearly departed Franklin had for you, and his selflessness after death would be the reason for all these people gathered in this room today. In some small way, the love that the two of you had has influenced the myriad of love stories in this room, including your own. Look at us, babe. You have a new fiancé and two boyfriends who adore you and each other. I have twins with two amazing men who spoil us endlessly. And even Nadine… " Alisa turned to Nadine and gave her a big smile. Nadine felt the tears overflowing once again. But before she could reach to wipe them, she felt Eddie wipe them away with the pad of his thumb. She looked up at him and smiled. Zaire took her hand and kissed the back of her knuckles.

"She's right," said Nadine. "Seeing your new relationships gave me the courage to be so fearless and embrace happiness on my own terms. We owe so much of this to Franklin's love for you. That oath that he made his friends promise, it opened all of us up to a whole new world, Tate."

Tatum hiccuped as a cry lodged in her throat. She was speechless. Cassidy, Miles and Deacon joined her at her side, each giving her a kiss on the forehead. When Cassidy intertwined his fingers with hers, she finally let her tears break free. "It's ok, Mama," he said, his voice slightly above a whisper as he wiped her tears. "We've got you. Always."

"Well, if you all would join me, I'd like to propose a toast," directed Christophe, holding up his glass. "To a man I didn't know personally, but whose presence is still felt, appreciated, and honored by everyone in this room. May my son carry his name with pride. To Franklin."

Everyone raised their glasses, and in unison, said loudly and with love…

"To Franklin."

The End

Bonus

ONE YEAR LATER

"Welcome back to Secrets, Mr. and Mrs. Moody. Ms. Baxter. We have your premiere suite in The Dungeon ready per your instructions. Please follow me."

One of the well-dressed concierge led the trio down the hall, into the back rooms of Secrets. The sheer massiveness of Secrets never failed to impress Nadine. Each time she came, it was as if she unlocked a new world of sexual pleasure and satisfaction. Nadine, finally, wasn't afraid to ask for what she wanted, in and out of the bedroom.

The concierge handed Eddie the key card. "Only non-alcoholic beverages are allowed in the Dungeon. No drugs, legal or otherwise are permitted. Your personal bartender is there to attend to any refreshments you may need. Please, enjoy yourselves." As quickly as he led them to their suite, the concierge was gone.

"You ladies ready?" Eddie asked, a smile on his face.

Nadine and Zaire were already kissing. When they finally realized that Ed was looking, they broke away from their kiss and started laughing.

"I take that as a yes." He simply shook his head as he tapped the key card to the door. Inside, they were welcomed by the bartender, a cinnamon complexioned woman with braids who was topless except for black pasties. Given the circumstances with Alex, they specifically requested that Malcolm not be their bartender for the evening. Just in case. Carrying a tray, the bartender handed them their requested mocktails.

Eddie looked around the room as he sipped. "I think everything is here." He looked at the massive bed. "Man, I cannot wait to see you two right there."

Nadine nodded toward the very intimidating bondage chair facing the two-way mirrors. "Ed, are you sure you're down for this?"

He gave Nadine a quick peck on the cheek. "Of course I am. Stop worrying, Deanie, baby. Tonight is supposed to be about having fun. My team is heading to the tourney. Your first year of Deanie's Decadent Desserts was one for the record books. We could use the release."

"Yeah Cookie," Zaire added, kissing Nadine near the curve of her neck. "You're blowing up, mami."

Nadine's bakery was indeed flourishing. After one very popular food blogger's review, business skyrocketed. She'd baked cakes and pastries for local celebrities and even appeared on a few morning shows, with offers to pivot into television. She was opening a second location in her hometown of Waycross at the end of the year. She loved all the business and accolades, but the best feeling was still making treats for the people she loved. Making Tatum and Cassidy's telescope-shaped wedding cake had been one of her most cherished moments.

Nadine leaned into Zaire's kiss. "And we're celebrating you too. Passing your comprehensive exams on the first go-round isn't easy, love."

Zaire smiled against her neck, then nipped at the delicate skin. "Yeah, but don't want to think about that right now. I'm trying to think about us and how much fun we're about to have."

Nadine looked up at her husband "You ready, Ed?"

Eddie finished his drink, placing it on the bar. "Yeah. I am. Are you?"

Nadine kissed Eddie on the lips, breathing all of him in with a moan. "Absolutely."

Nadine and Zaire took off their matching Bottega leather coats, gifts from Eddie for tonight. Underneath, all they wore were Versace thongs. Nadine's was white, while Zaire's was green, of course.

Eddie's eyes roamed all over their bodies. His dick getting harder by the second. "You two look fucking amazing. Especially you, Deanie, with your new jewelry."

Nadine had recently gotten her nipples pierced. Barbells with diamonds on the ends and delicate gold chains adorned her sensitive, hardening nipples.

"I told you they'd look so fucking good, baby." Zaire stroked one then gently tugged. Eddie stroked the other nipple, eliciting a moan from Nadine. The electric pain was pleasurable, going straight to her gently throbbing clit.

"Z, don't get me worked up until we get Eddie handled."

Zaire chuckled. "Right. Can't start the show without him. Ready, Big E?"

Eddie chuckled at the newly acquired nickname. "I am." He pulled down his silk boxers, tossing them to the side. His dick was semi-hard as it bobbed freely. He moved to sit in the bondage chair. "Ready whenever you are, ladies."

Nadine picked up the ball gag that was on the corner table and walked over to Eddie. He looked up at her, a smile forming at the corner of his lips. Nadine moved close to him, putting her nipples in his face. He darted his tongue out, flicking it quickly before leaning back. He was being bad already, asking for punishment.

"Remember the safe responses. One snap if you want it tighter. Two snaps if you want the gag out, ok?"

Eddie nodded. "Yes, dear. I'll remember." He was being sarcastic. He knew she'd make him pay for that.

Nadine tightened the arm straps on the chair while Zaire tightened the leg straps. Eddie's dick was already leaking. Nadine reached down, swiping a bit from his leg and putting a finger in her mouth, savoring the taste. Eddie's eyes flickered with delight.

"Open up, baby." Nadine gently slid the bright red ball gag into Eddie's mouth, then secured it. With how excited he looked, you would have thought Nadine gave him a piece of Belgian chocolate. She loved how obedient he was.

Nadine and Zaire stepped back, admiring their handiwork. "Look at you, baby," Nadine said. "Wrapped up for us as a present. Doesn't he look good, Z?"

Zaire nodded. "Absolutely. Totally at our mercy." She took Nadine by the hand, leading her to the bed. "But I am ready for you to be at my mercy, Cookie."

As soon as they got on the bed Nadine and Zaire began to kiss, their pace turning from soft and tender to heated in a matter of minutes. On their knees, they reached inside the other's panties, stroking through the wet heat of their mutual arousal. When Nadine stroked Zaire's pierced hood, the moan that escaped her lips let her know she was getting her close.

Nadine held Zaire by the neck as she stroked. "Gonna come for me, gorgeous?"

"Fuck, yesss…"

"Not yet, baby." Nadine looked over towards Eddie, his hands clenched into fists as he watched. His moaning let her know that the anticipation was killing him, but he had incredible restraint. In all the times they'd played together, Eddie never once came quick. This would no doubt be one of those times.

Nadine and Zaire removed their fingers from the dampness, putting them in the other's mouths to savor the taste of their own arousal. Once they were done having their fill, they quickly removed their panties. Nadine couldn't wait any longer to touch Zaire fully, to devour her completely.

Playfully, she pushed her down onto the bed, eliciting a giggle from Zaire. Nadine straddled her, bending down to kiss her deeply. Her hands roamed all over the soft, plush curves of her deep, dark skin. Nadine tweaked her nipples and Zaire moaned. She loved that she could do that to her.

"Let's see who can make who come first," Nadine challenged as she kissed down Zaire's torso.

"You're gonna lose," teased Zaire as she watched Nadine move closer down to the center of her pleasure.

Nadine looked up, raising a brow. "We'll see, baby." She parted Zaire's wet, fat lips until her clit was exposed. Nadine had bought her a new diamond clit piercing, and it was gorgeous. She swiped the flat of her tongue up and sucked. Nadine felt Zaire's hands got into her hair, pulling her deeper into her pussy. She was drowning in her essence and didn't want to come up for air.

"Fucccck!" Zaire screamed as Nadine's tongue licked inside her walls. That was all it took for her legs to shake and for Zaire to come all over her face.

Nadine lifted up, face wet, and kissed Zaire nastily, letting her taste the fruits of her desire. Two snaps were heard across the room. Nadine stopped kissing Zaire momentarily. She walked over to Eddie, looking at the drool running down his chiseled chest. Slowly, she undid the gag.

"Kiss me," he begged. "Please Deanie."

Nadine kissed him deeply, sucking his lips. "You good? Need some water?"

Eddie nodded. She walked over to the bartender who gave her an Evian. She slowly poured the water into Eddie's mouth.

"Better?" Nadine asked

Eddie stretched his neck, the cracks of tension audible. "Yes. Put it back in. Please."

Nadine stroked Eddie's face before putting the gag back in. She made her way back to the bed, where Zaire now held a vibrator. Sitting back against the wall, she motioned for Nadine to come here.

"Sit between my legs, Cookie," she instructed. Nadine did so. Before she knew it, Zaire had wrapped her arm around her, pulling her in close.

"How many times can I make you come? We are gonna count. In Spanish." Zaire said as she licked the shell of Nadine's ear. Heat rushed down to her toes.

Zaire started the vibrator and placed it on Nadine's clit. She moved it around, letting it tease and torture Nadine with precision. Steadily, Zaire increased the pace, adding another speed.

Nadine felt an orgasm about to come on strong. "Oh, God..."

"Uno," Zaire responded as she increased the speed.

Nadine grabbed the plastic covering the bed. "Shiiiitt!!'

"Dos..."

Nadine felt heat running down her spice and to her toes. She tried to move, but it was useless. Zaire's grip on her was strong as hell.

"Don't close your eyes. Look at Eddie watching you," Zaire instructed.

Nadine's eyes fluttered open to see Eddie staring, his dick leaking down his thighs and onto the floor. Zaire placed the vibrator on the highest speed.

"Fuck!. Fuck! Fuuuck!" Nadine yelled. She was about to see colors and stars, she was coming so hard. She was sure the people on the other side of the mirror could hear her. They certainly could see her. The faint outline of bodies could be seen stopping to enjoy the show.

"Tres..." Zaire counted, smiling against Nadine's neck.

Within seconds, Nadine's essence shot out like a rocket, all over the bed and the toy. She tried catching her breath, but it was useless. Zaire was preparing to do it all over again.

"Zaire, baby, please," Nadine begged, resting against her shoulder.

"Nah, Cookie. You said I'm gonna lose. I'm trying to prove you wrong."

Zaire placed the vibrator against Nadine's throbbing clit. She came so hard that she may have blacked out. It wasn't until she felt Zaire kiss her temple that she came to.

"How many was that?" Nadine asked.

"Cookie, you didn't even make it past five."

Z went to the bar to grab a bottle of electrolyte water for both Nadine and Eddie. Nadine drank as she watched Zaire give Eddie sips of water before putting the gag back and kissing him on the cheek. It was sweet how all three of them took care of each other. It'd taken a while to get to that level of comfort but, eventually, they did.

Nadine was still wet and sensitive as she massaged herself. She could hear Eddie moan as she stroked.

"Poor thing," Zaire said as she came back to the bed. She placed a kiss above the landing strip of hair on Nadine's pussy. "Wanna tap out?"

Nadine smirked. "I won't concede, but I do want my revenge."

Zaire gave Nadine one last suck to her sensitive clit before easing back on the bed. "You know what I want...and what Ed wants to see."

Nadine turned to look at Eddie. Beads of sweat dotted his forehead, and his chest heaved. She knew he was so close. "Soon, I'll let you come, Eddie."

He nodded, his body rigid as he tried to control the urge to come. Nadine knew this was part of his fantasy, his desire to prolong the orgasm for as long as possible. She wouldn't deny him for too much longer, but she had to get her girl off too.

Nadine moved to the cabinet on the far wall. Inside, she found a harness and several dildos that she could attach to it. She chose one that was fat, black and with ridges. She knew Zaire would approve. Quickly, she pulled the harnesses over her thighs, securing them and attaching the dildo.

When Nadine turned around, Zaire was on the bed, fingers deep in her pussy. She paused, admiring the sight. She swore she'd never see anything as pretty as Zaire's pussy as long as she lived.

"You gonna fuck me or just stare, mami?"

Nadine reached for the lube on the table, slathering her dildo with it. Before Zaire could talk anymore shit, Nadine pulled her by the legs toward the edge of the bed. She pushed her thick thighs upward, knees nearly near her ears, and slowly entered her pussy. She teased her over and over with the ridged tip until Zaire was squirming.

"Please," Zaire begged. "Fuck me, Cookie."

Nadine increased her pace, thrusting harder into Zaire's pussy. Her nails dug into her thighs so hard she was sure Zaire would have bruises the next morning.

"Am I fucking you? Or just staring?" Nadine asked as she pumped inside Zaire. When she didn't answer, she released her legs and moved her hands to her nipples, pinching them hard.

"Yesssss, you're fucking me, Nadine. Fuck!"

Nadine watched as Zaire succumbed to her will, the noise of her pussy and Eddie's moans being the only soundtrack in the room. She looked over at her husband, his throbbing dick leaking, creating a puddle between his legs.

"You like watching me fuck her, don't you Eddie?" she asked.

He moaned, nodding his approval.

"You want me to make her come?"

Eddie nodded, his eyes rolling to the back of his head.

Nadine looked down at Zaire, her highlighted ringlets flopping in her face. "You want to come for me?"

"Yes, Deanie, Fuckkkk!" Zaire screamed, her greenish-black nails digging into Nadine's fleshy thighs.

Nadine reached between the two of them and stroked Zaire's clit, the hot slickness of her arousal providing the best friction. She'd learned Zaire's body so well, she'd gotten it down to a science how to make her come in a matter of minutes. Her expertise paid off when Zaire's body rocked against her hand and the dildo, and a slow, steady stream released from her body.

Nadine pulled out, then kissed Zaire deeply as she came down from her orgasms. "You did so well, pretty girl," she praised.

"You fuck me so well, mami." Zaire moaned. "But you aren't done yet."

"I know." Nadine unhooked herself from the harness and dildo and walked over to Eddie. Beads of sweat mixed with his saliva ran down his well-defined chest and abs. Tears were forming in the corners of his eyes and Nadine knew he needed to come soon.

"Did you like watching me fuck Z, baby?" Nadine asked as she stroked his low waves.

"Mmhmmm," Eddie moaned, the gag still in place.

"You want to come, baby?"

Eddie nodded yes. Then snapped his fingers twice. Slowly, Nadine unhooked the gag. She gave him more water until he was quenched. "Speak," she commanded.

"I need to drain this dick inside you, Deanie. Please let me, baby."

Nadine looked down at Eddie's dick. He'd made a mess of the floor in front of him, the sticky trail beginning at his thigh. She reached out and stroked his dick, savoring the way it pulsed in her hands. Eddie gritted his teeth and hissed like the release of pressure from a tire.

Nadine rubbed her hand across Eddie's cheek. "You've been such a good boy, Eddie. So obedient. So patient. Imma take care of you." She reached for the lube that was near the chair and poured some in her hand. Slowly, she stroked up and down his length, coating him from tip to balls. By the way his fingers flexed with each stroke, she knew he wanted to touch her, but she wasn't going to untie him. Not yet.

Once he was fully coated, Nadine slowly lowered herself onto her husband. They both moaned their satisfaction at his dick fully stretching. At this angle, she felt every inch of his dick. Nadine began to rock up and down, moving her hips to the pulsating rhythm of the house music blaring from outside their walls.

Nadine's nipples, taut and erect, throbbed from both being aroused and the weight of the piercings. As she rode, she felt Eddie's tongue dart out to lick them. She pushed her breasts together, giving him better access to please both her nipples at once. Eddie sucked greedily, his teeth grazing against the barbells with every movement.

"Don't stop," Nadine demanded as she drove her hips down harder onto his dick. The sticky wetness of lube and sweat against their skin amplifying the sound. Nadine looked over her shoulder to see Zaire playing with her pussy with another clit sucking toy. By the sound of her moans, she definitely enjoyed watching Nadine fuck her husband.

"Faster," Eddie begged. "Ride me faster, baby."

Nadine held on to Eddie, her nails digging into his shoulders as her ass slapped against his thighs. He tried to push up deeper into her, but his legs were still bound. Nadine grabbed Ed by the chin.

"I got this," Nadine said as she looked into Eddie's eyes. "Let me handle this dick."

Eddie gave her a smirk, turning to kiss her palm. "Say less, then."

Nadine held on to the back of the chair, planted her feet on the sides and dropped her pussy on Eddie's dick. Each time she dropped, she squeezed her pelvic muscles around him. The move had him squirming underneath him. *Guess the kegels were paying off.*

Eddie bit his bottom lip. "Ah fuck, Deanie. Shit…this pussy is so fucking good…"

"Come for me, then." Nadine licked Eddie's bottom lip, prying it away from his teeth. "Show me how good it is."

That was all it took for Eddie to roar underneath her body, coming deep inside her walls. At the same time, she heard Zaire come, yelling her satisfaction. Hearing them climax together was melodious. Nadine stilled, letting Eddie catch his breath before finally lifting off. As she did, cum dripped out of her and back onto his lap.

Nadine loosened his arms and bent down to loosen the leg straps of the bondage chair. Looking up, she asked, "You good?"

Eddie looked down at his lap. "You made a mess, baby."

Slowly, Nadine rose, her face eye level to Eddie's dick. Without a word, Nadine licked around Eddie's balls, then up his cum coated shaft. Nadine wiped the corners of her mouth and winked. "All clean."

"You're so nasty, baby." Eddie pulled Nadine up, pulling her onto his lap. He kissed her until she was breathless. "My good, nasty girl."

Zaire walked over to Nadine, giving her an equally satisfying kiss. "You mean *our* good, nasty girl."

Nadine looked between Eddie and Zaire, a satisfied smile on her face. "Yours. Forever."

Acknowledgments

It's so hard to say goodbye.

I hope you enjoyed the story of Nadine, Eddie and Zaire. It was different for me, but I hope that it made you both horny and happy.

As always, thank you to God from who all creativity flows. I couldn't have done this without you.

To my fellow Wordmaker, Karmen Lee, who inspired me to go in a different direction with this story. I was resistant but she told me to take a chance. It challenged me and made me think about the stories I wanted to tell, now and in the future. For that, I am eternally grateful.

To author Briyanna Michelle. Thank you for all of the help with the nanny stuff. Your kiddos are so lucky to have you. You are such an invaluable resource and I love being your sister in this writing game.

To my most faithful beta reader, Lourdes. You are family now, sis. I love you so much.

Thank you to the magnificent group of betas for this project: Jaime, Natalie (my sensitivity reader for this project), Crystal, Federica (all the way in Italy!!!), and Krishana. You all did it again! Your feedback was and is essential to my success. I love you so much.

To my bestest author friends: Ms. J, ML Eaden, Lily Flowers and Terri Ley. Thank you for keeping it in the group chat and talking me off the cliff. I appreciate you all so much..

To my friend of twenty-plus years and podcast partner, Dr. Yakini Etheridge. Thank you for being the consultant for all the therapy sessions. I learned a lot about what happens between client/patient and how to make these sessions sound authentic. I know readers will appreciate all the hard work you put into it to make sure I got this right.

Thank you to all of Black BookTok, Bookstagram, BookTwitter, (and now Black BookThreads) I know I took forever to write this but thanks for sticking with me. Thank you to all of my newfound readers and friends who discovered me from reading **The Oath** and **The Offer**. I hope you enjoyed the conclusion to the series as much as I enjoyed creating it.

To my writing groups, Wordmakers and Inclusive Romance Projects, thank you for always sending me positive energy. Even if I've been ghost these past few months, please know my heart carries you there forever.

Thank you to my muse. You shouldn't be so damned sexy, but you are. You make it easy to write the way that I do.

Finally, I know some of you couldn't stand Nadine in the earlier books of *The Secrets Series*. But I hope that learning her story, you get a better understanding of why she was the way she was. Many women are conflicted about themselves. Including married ones. Sometimes that inner turmoil manifests itself as judgement and ridicule of others, especially those who are living the life that we wish we could. It is not an unusual scenario.

There were times I had to stop and cry. Because I've been Nadine: ashamed, confused, and misunderstood. Given the current temperature of the nation, Black women don't have time to feel this way. You deserve joy. *Unspeakable joy*. Whatever that looks like.

As Alisa said, "We can do whatever we want because we are happy, free Black women." I hope that this book touched some of you. I hope it brought you joy. And I hoped it helped you to get free.

Is *The Secrets Series* over? For now. But I'll always give myself room to bring back characters here and there. You never know! :)

Sign up for my newsletter and keep in touch just in case I change my mind!

Love and Lust,

T.M.
Richardson

Also by T.M. Richardson

The Oath: A WhyChoose Novel

(Book 1 in The Secrets Series)

The Offer: A Polyromance

(Book 2 in The Secrets Series)

Real Girls Get Down: A Novelette

Learn more about T.M. Richardson (and Tati Richardson) by clicking the QR Code